S0-ACS-940

LETHAL INTENT

Center Point
Large Print

Also by Cara Putman and available from
Center Point Large Print:

Beyond Justice
Imperfect Justice
Delayed Justice
Flight Risk

**This Large Print Book carries the
Seal of Approval of N.A.V.H.**

LETHAL INTENT

CARA PUTMAN

CENTER POINT LARGE PRINT
THORNDIKE, MAINE

This Center Point Large Print edition
is published in the year 2021 by arrangement with
Thomas Nelson.

The text of this Large Print edition is unabridged.
In other aspects, this book may vary
from the original edition.
Printed in the United States of America
on permanent paper.
Set in 16-point Times New Roman type.

ISBN: 978-1-64358-905-3

The Library of Congress has cataloged this record
under Library of Congress Control Number: 2021930426

To Becca, my fighter. As I wrote this, you were eleven like Bethany. You courageously faced blood draws, weekly injections, and more as we sought a diagnosis and fix for inflammation in your body. While I praise God it wasn't cancer, the search for answers was exhausting. There were tears, more from me than from you. You have so much grit and resilience, have from your earliest days. I love to watch you worship God with passion. I cannot wait to see how God writes your story.

To Heather and Dr. Jodi. These women allowed me into their stories, Heather as the mother of a son who has battled leukemia multiple times through multiple transplants and CAR T-cell therapies, and Dr. Jodi as the one who explained the science to me, and in the process showed me her passion and calling to treat these very hard cases. I'm grateful and indebted to both of you.

LETHAL INTENT

PROLOGUE
NORTHERN VIRGINIA
SATURDAY, JANUARY 23

The phone felt warm against her cheek. Caroline Bragg ran a hand along the edge of the clothes hanging in her closet and inhaled, then slowly released her breath.

"What should I wear?"

"Other than a little black dress?" On the other end of the line, Jaime Nichols shushed her mewing cat. "Rhett misses you and says send tuna."

Caroline's nose wrinkled as if she could smell the foul fish. She'd fed the cat during her weeks of crashing on Jaime's couch. "I miss him too. Seriously though, what do I do?"

"Brandon's been your friend for years. Pick something comfortable yet feminine." Jaime's tone was no-nonsense. "You're the southern belle. Anything you pick will be perfect."

It should have been that easy, but it wasn't. Not this time. "Easier said than done. My closet is filled with work clothes." And a few frothy dresses that were better for garden parties than for January. She sighed. "This is important, Jaime. I don't want to blow this chance."

Caroline had thought close friendship was all

she and Brandon Lancaster would share, but now he was asking her to be something more. Tonight they'd define that "something" over dinner.

"Grab that dress you wore to Emilie's bridal shower. The cream one with wine-colored swirls."

Caroline nodded even though Jaime couldn't see. "That's perfect. Thanks." She ended the call, and her hand trembled as she pulled out the flowing dress that had a cream background splashed with large cranberry paisley and flowers. Paired with boots and a leather jacket it would hit the right note of fun and flirty. Had she really just thought those words related to a dinner with Brandon? And when had Jaime become her fashion guru? Two unexpected but welcome evolutions in her life.

Brandon was a big teddy bear of a man, unless you'd faced him on the football field in his days as a defensive linebacker for the Colts. When Caroline first met him, he was a rookie who'd just bought acres outside of DC for his off-season retreat. She'd watched as women threw themselves at him, but as the evening wore on he ended up next to her sharing sweet tea and jokes. As the kid from the wrong side of town fighting her way through the first year of law school, she hadn't expected to see him again. Then their paths intersected a few months later. The intersections became more frequent in the off-seasons, when he asked her advice on his postfootball dreams, which involved creating a foster home for hard-to-place sibling groups.

His teddy bear side emerged when he interacted with the kids who lived at Almost Home, the group foster home he'd founded to keep sibling groups together until they found permanent placements. But tonight was for Brandon and Caroline, just the two of them. No friends serving as buffers. No kids seeking his attention or a hug from her, though she cherished those moments when little arms wrapped around her waist or sticky cheeks pressed against hers.

Tonight she wanted to help Brandon forget all the challenges that came with serving an at-risk population and help him imagine what could be.

And maybe she'd let herself believe this was real. That her quiet, long-held dream really could come true: a man like Brandon could love her.

A soft smile tipped her lips as she slipped on the dress and touched up her makeup. She glanced at her watch then pressed a hand against her stomach to settle the butterflies. Where was he?

As if in answer the doorbell rang. She hurried across her small living area to the door and after she opened it took a minute to appreciate the sight of his navy suit softened by a forest-green hoodie poking out the top of the jacket.

He tugged the jacket down and quirked his head to the side. "What?"

"You look good, Lancaster."

His eyes began to smolder. "So do you, Caroline." He offered her his arm. His smile edged on tentative before becoming one that could melt knees across America. "Let's grab some food."

An hour later, after a pleasant drive to Ashburn, a small community outside the DC metro area, they sat across from each other in a red-velvet booth at Clyde's of Willow Creek Farm. Caroline's eyes darted around the space as she tried to take in every detail. It was DC-staple Old Ebbitt's meets rural horse ranch. Some of the dining rooms were designed with heavy beams that made her think of a barn, while others had heavy leather chairs pulled against four-top tables, and large paintings of birds lined the walls. Dimmed lights made the varied spaces intimate, and Persian rugs dotting the hardwood floors muted the sounds of the chairs.

"Do you like it?"

"It's nice." She smiled at him. "Quite the place for dinner." Her gaze traveled to the old horseless carriages suspended from the ceiling. "Do you think they'll crash onto us?"

"If they do, I'll protect you." He waggled his eyebrows as he made a small flexing gesture—not quite small enough, as one of the waitstaff sidestepped to avoid getting knocked by the movement.

The woman smiled at him as she slipped past, somehow managing to keep the steaming plates from sliding off her tray.

Caroline reached across the table and took his hand. "Relax, big guy. It's just me." She fought a grin as he stared at her.

"Did you just call me the Hulk?"

Leave it to Brandon to notice the oblique Marvel reference. While not a typical romance, the interactions between Black Widow and Bruce Banner had always tugged at her. The Hulk might be scary and angry, but Bruce was soft and sweet. Much like the man sitting across the table from her. She shrugged lightly. "Maybe."

His Adam's apple bobbed as he swallowed. "Caroline, there's nothing normal about this, and I'm glad." His grip tightened on her hand. "You've meant a lot to me for years, but I want to take this deeper. I'm not one to play around." He paused, and she nodded. "I waited until I was sure this"—he gestured between them—"is what I want for the rest of my life."

Her heart skipped a beat as she let his words sink into her heart. She'd had a front-row seat to his life for years. He was a reliable man who didn't play the field. Instead, he opted to go solo rather than give any woman false hope he was interested in her. It was one reason Caroline's stomach had been tied in knots of anticipation and trepidation all day. She didn't want to get this wrong. Not when so much rested on what happened next.

No, she wanted to build forever with this man she'd loved from a distance for years.

Now was their time.

CHAPTER 1
TUESDAY, APRIL 20

Caroline shifted in the high-backed chair. The massive conference room table made her feel more petite than usual. Quentin Jackson, the man propelling Praecursoria through its rapid growth, vibrated with energy as he studied her.

"We are on the cusp of amazing developments and a transition from the lab to trials. We have a few CAR T-cell therapies in early stages now with more in our pipeline."

She racked her mind for the importance of T cells, and he gave a hearty laugh.

"Don't worry if the science overwhelms you. We'll have you up to speed in no time. All you need to know right now is that T cells are one of the two cells that make up white blood cells. The treatments we're working on could be the difference between life and death for young cancer patients. We need your legal expertise and quick mind to synthesize the science with the map to market."

"I've overseen several court trials related to patents, which should help with that process." It had been an unforeseen aspect of her days clerking for Judge Loren. She swallowed against the lump in her throat that still welled up when she thought about his untimely death from pneumonia. A month ago she couldn't imagine interviewing for a job somewhere else, even if a part of her knew that she should stretch her wings.

"When can you start? Today?"

She felt rooted to the chair. Everything was moving so fast. Could she really transition her experience managing clerks for a judge into managing patents and contracts for a start-up? While Praecursoria had been around for a decade as a cancer research lab, about eighteen months ago Quentin sold off its lucrative genetic testing branch to focus exclusively on the development of cutting-edge CAR T-cell therapies. Starting over that way was a bold if risky move.

She lifted her chin and forced a smile that didn't waver. "If that's what you need. First we have a few details to work out."

He laughed. "I like the way you tackle issues head-on. That will be key in this role. I know how to steer the ship, and my chief scientist can navigate the research, but you'll keep us on the legal straight and narrow." He tapped his pen against the legal pad in front of him. Then he picked up her résumé and named a salary that pressed her against the chair. "There will be performance bonuses tied to the successful conclusion of trials. We want to look into stock options as well. That will be one of your assignments in conjunction with HR." He slapped his hands on the table and she jumped. "My enthusiasm gets away from me sometimes." He shrugged but never wavered as he examined her. "Let's start with a field trip. The best way for you to understand why we're doing this work and research is to show you."

Thirty minutes later, after a drive from Tysons Corner to Falls Church, she was chasing Quentin down the halls of Inova Children's Hospital. If they could figure out how to bottle his energy, the company would be a huge success.

"Follow me." Quentin swiped a card in the reader next to the door to the pediatric oncology wing. He held it open for her and she brushed past him, then waited for him to lead the way. He glanced over his shoulder as he strode down the vibrant purple and teal hall. "I want you to meet someone who brings the importance of our work into focus."

"How do you have a keycard?" It seemed like a huge liability for the hospital, but maybe she needed to remove her risk-management hat. She didn't work for the hospital but for Praecursoria.

He didn't slow as he approached the nurses' station. "It gives me limited access when I'm meeting with the trial team. I called ahead while you took a break."

Disinfectant couldn't hide the scents of fear

and desperation that hung in the air like a heavy perfume. She felt like a voyeur as they walked past rooms where people and machines gathered around small beds. "What did you want to show me?"

"The doctor I want you to meet is a pioneer. She had a research fellowship at the old Praecursoria during her summer between undergrad and medical school." Quentin's steps quickened as if he couldn't wait to see what would happen in the next minutes. "Word is she's having success with our trial therapies, but I like to check for myself." He slowed as he glanced at the room numbers. "I like to be hands-on. If she's having the success I've heard, she can help us expand testing to additional research facilities. And that gets us closer to the next stage of FDA approval."

"What are you hoping I'll learn?"

The man turned his charismatic grin on her. There was a reason he was on the city's top-ten list of eligible bachelors, but she wasn't interested. "To be an effective part of my leadership team, you need to understand the impact of the work we're doing. That'll light the passion you need for the long hours and fiscal uncertainty. Also, at times you'll need to answer questions related to the process."

An average-sized woman with stylish spiky blonde hair exited a room, and he threw his arms wide. "There she is. Anna."

The woman turned, a hand on her pregnant

stomach and a flit of a smile on her face, but a weary slump bowed her shoulders. "Quentin." She accepted his hug, then moved her hands into her lab coat's pockets. "Did I know you were coming today?"

"I set it up with your assistant."

The woman nodded. "That would explain it. Haven't connected with her yet because of an emergent patient."

Caroline sensed a tension in the woman and turned on the southern charm she was known for. "We can come back." Quentin started to speak, but Caroline placed a hand on his arm. "We've all had times where plans change. Nothing is life-or-death about why we are here."

The woman studied her with a hazel gaze, then her posture relaxed. "I like you. I'm Dr. Anna Johnson." She pulled her hand from her pocket and extended it to Caroline.

She shook the woman's hand. "Caroline Bragg, the new counsel for Praecursoria as of two hours ago, give or take."

Now the woman grinned. "If the trials continue the way they are now, you'll be very busy. We should do lunch so I can answer any questions you have about the protocol." She focused on Quentin. "What do you need today?"

"I want to give Caroline a quick introduction to the real work." He glanced up and down the hallway.

Dr. Johnson started down the hall. "You can come along."

The wing was typically wide, allowing for gurneys and wheelchairs to pass, but the walls were painted brilliant colors rather than the standard sterile white. Rooms hopscotched down each side past the central station that housed several nurses and a bank of monitors.

As she walked, Dr. Johnson turned to Caroline. "You know Praecursoria is developing CAR T-cell therapies."

"Yes, but I don't understand what that means yet."

"The short answer is we're engineering a patient's own cells to be ninja fighters that take out specific cancer-carrying cells like leukemia. They become little superhero cells. I'd like to introduce you to a young lady who may be a candidate for the trial. But first I need something to drink." Dr. Johnson led them down another corridor to a break room. The woman stepped in front of a vending machine loaded with various waters and sodas. "Can I get you anything?"

"I'm fine." Caroline held up the bottle of water she carried.

Quentin pulled out a credit card. "I'll get yours."

"No, you won't. You know the rules." She batted his hand to the side, then swiped her badge in front of the reader. A moment later a bottle of water clunked to the bottom of the machine, and she crouched to pull it out.

"How are the trial participants doing?" Quentin asked.

"As well as can be expected." She uncapped the lid and took a long drink. "You won't have results overnight. This is going to be a process—and a long one—but everything I'm seeing from the first patient is positive. We should start looking for additional participants."

"Give me something concrete. A story I can take to funders." Quentin's smile barely wavered, but Caroline sensed an edge of desperation in his tone. "It's not inexpensive."

"It never is." Anna headed to the door. "Let me show you something."

Brandon hovered over the bed, longing to do something. Bethany Anderson was eleven and leukemia was ravaging her body. She'd already had two failed bone marrow transplants, and he hoped she would qualify for a new treatment option that was in its earliest stages of development. It was Bethany's last resort.

Her eyelids fluttered, and suddenly he was pinned in place by large blue eyes.

"Hey, Bethany."

She licked her lips and tried to sit up a little. "You came back."

"Yep. I promise I'll keep coming back too."

Not because it was his job, though the state of Virginia had entrusted the care of her and her little brother, Gabriel, to Almost Home while the caseworker looked for a permanent placement. No, he'd do it because he was the kids' protector. Normally he felt up to the task, but here on the pediatric oncology floor, he doubted his ability to make a difference for this little girl.

The idea of subjecting her to a treatment that hadn't been proven yet felt wrong to Brandon, but the doctors said there was nothing more they could do without a Hail Mary pass. They just needed the state to agree. He might be Bethany's guardian, but the state would control her medical treatment until she was placed with a family.

"Why are you frowning?" Her words snapped him from his thoughts.

He forced a grin as he sank into the chair next to her hospital bed. "Sorry about that."

"You don't need to worry about me." She straightened the sheet under her arms. "I'll be fine. I always am." She jutted her chin as if that made the words truer. "How's Gabriel?"

"He misses you. I told him I'll bring him to see you as soon as he's cleared."

"He won't be." She spoke with the life experience of someone who knew. "It's too dangerous." She didn't clarify whom it was more dangerous for.

Today she was a shadow of the girl she'd

been six weeks earlier when the siblings arrived at Almost Home. They'd settled into a cabin with his best house parents, but soon after the leukemia reappeared, and her body lacked the reserves to fight. She was running out of time.

"That might be true, but I get to be here when I want to." As long as he submitted to frequent blood tests to ensure he didn't expose her compromised system to anything. The vinyl squeaked as he leaned back in the chair. "I can't think of anywhere else I'd rather be right now."

"I can." She said the words so deadpan, he laughed.

"I bet you can." He might feel helpless and inept as he tried to watch the various monitors and interpret the displays, but he could help her dream. "What's the first thing you want to do when you get out of this place?"

"Go to the beach and feel the sun on my face."

"That sounds good." He made a mental note to take her. "You keep doing what the doctors ask, and I'll see about getting you some sunshine."

She studied him as if not sure whether to believe him. "Really?"

"Scout's honor." The smile she gave him signaled he'd have to make this happen somehow. He didn't want to set her up for fresh disappointments, because he was out of his element. Almost Home didn't host medically complicated kids. He would need skilled staff to deal with the unique needs of that population, something he couldn't contemplate right now. Worrying about how Virginia might interpret the new federal Family First law consumed all of his attention. Depending on what the state decided, Almost Home might have to close.

A machine started beeping. Loudly. He glanced around but didn't know what to do, so he stood and hurried to the hallway, where he collided with a soft mass.

CHAPTER 2

Oomph.

The air burst from Caroline's lungs as she crashed into someone.

Quentin steadied her. "Watch where you're going, mountain man."

Caroline glanced up. "Brandon?"

His gaze barely took her in before he latched onto the doctor. "Anna, the alarms are screaming in Bethany's room."

Weariness fled the woman's posture as she stepped into the room Brandon had exited. "Let me see what's going on."

Brandon followed her with Caroline a step behind.

Quentin tightened his hold on her arm. "You can't go in."

"Yes, I can. Brandon's my friend." And he'd been worried about Bethany for weeks. She tugged free and stepped through the doorway, then stood aside as a woman in scrubs rushed in.

The doctor glanced at her. "Please stay against the wall and away from the patient." She masked up then held a quiet consultation with the nurse as she watched the various screens and monitors.

Then she murmured soft words to the little girl who lay pale against the pillows.

Brandon slumped against the wall next to Caroline, his gaze fixed on the bed.

"You okay, big guy?"

"I can't make this go away." He whispered the words into her ear.

Caroline took in the small form on the bed. "I'm glad to see her." She squeezed his hand. "I'm so sorry."

"She's a fighter, but she's not getting better." He sighed and then rubbed his face with his hands. He barely glanced at Caroline before returning his attention to the bed. "I don't know how to help her."

"You're here." Caroline leaned into his arm. This man was such a rock for everyone, including her. He was the kind of support she'd never had as a kid struggling to survive an alcoholic single mom. She would have given anything to have someone like Brandon in her life as a preteen. The least Caroline could do was let him know he wasn't alone. "How can I help?"

He shook his head. "I don't know."

"You're doing the right thing, being here. She isn't alone."

"It's not the same as family."

"Is there any way you can bring her brother?" Gabriel was one of those kids who vibrated with energy and would bring a smile to the girl.

"It's not safe for either of them. It seems like such a small thing I should make happen, but can't."

"You can't, but you're here. That's something."

His chin lifted a bit, and his shoulders shifted back to their usual squared-off position. Her rock was back.

"Thanks."

"That's what girlfriends are for. You're always there for everyone else. It's nice to do that for you."

He roused to look at her, curiosity filling his eyes. "Why are you here? I thought you were interviewing."

She tilted her head toward the hall. "Come meet my new boss."

He grinned. "Of course they hired you on the spot."

"Dr. Johnson is working with one of our trials. Quentin wanted me to see what the company's work is."

The men greeted each other in the doorway, and Brandon stiffened before relaxing. "This is your new boss?" he whispered out the side of his mouth.

"Yes. You know him?"

"Not really."

"If it isn't Brandon Lancaster. I didn't recognize you at first. How's my newest investor?"

Brandon hesitated before extending his hand. He kept his voice down. "Good to see you."

Investor? Caroline let the word bounce around her mind. She'd need to remember that.

Quentin cocked his head. "What brings you here?" He glanced into the room at Bethany. "Is she yours?"

"Yes and no. I run a group foster home. In that sense, she's mine."

"I hope she'll be all right." Quentin studied her as if checking for symptoms.

"Me too."

Caroline looked between the two. "You didn't mention investing in this company."

"Didn't think it mattered. Didn't know it's where you were interviewing." Brandon shrugged, then returned his focus to Bethany while Dr. Johnson made notes in the computer.

Dr. Johnson leaned down to speak a few more words to the girl, sentences that coaxed a smile from her, then the doctor stepped away from the monitors and approached Brandon. "She's fine. It looks like a malfunction on one of the machines, but we will keep a close eye on it and change it out if needed." She studied Brandon carefully. "You should go home and get some rest. We'll call you or the caseworker if anything changes."

"She shouldn't be alone."

"She's lucky to have you in her corner, but if you get sick worrying about her, you won't get to advocate for her here. Her immune system is compromised, and I won't allow anyone near her who is sick. Anyone." The emphasis on the last word seemed to register as Brandon stepped back.

His transformation was instantaneous. He held up his hands and quirked the small grin that tipped the corner of his mouth and made Caroline's heart skip every time. "All right, Doc. You're the expert and I trust you."

"Just keep doing that, and we'll be good. I'm serious, cuz. Get some rest."

"Cuz?" Caroline's gaze bounced between the two.

Brandon glanced down at Caroline. "This intelligent woman is related to me. Can you believe it?"

"Is this the child you want to add to the study?" Quentin's words jarred the space.

Dr. Johnson nodded. She motioned everyone to step farther down the hall and lowered her voice so Bethany couldn't hear. "I'm waiting on test results to confirm she qualifies." A sad knowing filled her expression. "I'm going to do all I can to push her into this trial."

Quentin's expression sobered. "Can we start harvesting and preparing her cells while you wait on the results?"

"Possibly. I'll call Samson about it right away."

Brandon lifted a hand. "Wait. Harvesting her cells? Help me understand."

Dr. Johnson's compassionate gaze shifted to

Caroline and Brandon. "I know it's a lot to take in. The treatment I want to try from Praecursoria is autologous, which means the patient both provides and then receives her own stem cells. We would harvest Bethany's cells, then send them to Praecursoria to be adapted to fight the cancer before returning them to her."

"Isn't leukemia usually treated with a bone marrow transplant?" Caroline felt her neck flush. "Sorry to interrupt, but I want to understand."

"No need to apologize. Bone marrow transplants are usually the first type of immunotherapy we try. They've been used since 1956, but they're not perfect. Unfortunately, this has failed twice for Bethany. Here's what happens."

Anna pulled a small notebook and pen from her lab coat and started sketching. She drew a large circle and labeled it *stem cell*. "You hear a lot of talk about stem cells. Stem cells found in bone marrow can make red and white blood cells as well as platelets." She drew three more circles connected to the stem cell and labeled these *red, white,* and *platelet*. She pointed to the white cell. "In bone marrow transplants we take healthy white blood cells from a donor and give them to the patient. In a successful transplant those healthy white blood cells can strengthen the patient's immune system, but it doesn't always work. Sometimes the cells aren't available in a format the patient can accept."

Caroline nodded as she studied the sketch. "You mean there isn't a match between donor and recipient?"

Anna smiled. "Exactly. That can lead to complications, especially with blood-borne cancers. For example, graft-versus-host disease happens when the patient's body attacks donor cells."

"So you want to treat Bethany's cancer with her own white blood cells?"

"That's right. But specifically, we want her T cells, which is something the white blood cells make." She drew two more offshoots from the white cell and labeled one of them with a T.

"How can you do that if the cells aren't healthy in the first place?"

"That's where CAR T-cell therapy comes in. We genetically modify the patient's T cells to recognize and fight cancer cells—turn them into those superhero ninjas—then reintroduce them to the body. The results have been exciting, but it's all still early. In the beginning, CAR T-cell therapies used mouse cells to modify the patients' T cells, and some bodies rejected them."

"So what is Praecursoria's therapy, specifically?"

Quentin spoke up. "We've found a way to hide the mouse cells inside the patient's own cells."

Dr. Johnson nodded. "If it works, Praecursoria will be on the cutting edge of what we in oncology are calling the fifth pillar of cancer treatment. But bone marrow transplants will remain the first-line standard of care until we get more therapies and better longitudinal studies. We need data and time to support that CAR T-cell therapy can be used as an alternative to bone marrow transplants rather than a last-ditch option."

Caroline looked into Bethany's room. "This trial is her only option?"

"Her Hail Mary. I hate to be so blunt, but yes." Dr. Johnson's shoulders lifted and fell. "If Samson—Dr. Kleme—agrees, we could start harvesting her T cells tomorrow in anticipation of the test results coming back positive."

"And the state approving her treatment," Brandon added.

"That too." Dr. Johnson sighed. "Every day matters for her."

So this was what Praecursoria did. Offered terrible hope to those who had none.

CHAPTER 3
WEDNESDAY, APRIL 21

The next morning Caroline sat in her Mustang on I-495 and realized she'd need two things for her new commute to Praecursoria: more time to battle traffic and audiobooks. Or a route other than 495, one that involved back roads that moved. By the time she rushed through the doors at Praecursoria's generic building, she felt behind. She got turned around twice trying to find her office, and her phone rang the moment she walked in.

Over the phone Quentin's assistant informed her she was late for a meeting. When Caroline finally found a pen and the right room, she stood outside the closed office door and exhaled, then turned the knob and entered.

"Good morning, everyone." She tried for a breezy tone, but no one smiled. *Alrighty then.*

Quentin gestured to the empty chair next to him. "Join us here. Everyone, this is Caroline Bragg, Praecursoria's new general counsel. She comes to us from the courts, where she clerked for a judge and managed a caseload. Now she'll help us navigate the legal land mines of getting our trials approved and therapies on the market."

She sank into the chair and looked around the table. "I'm excited to join the team."

After quick introductions, everyone resumed their discussion of the status of trial applications with the FDA. She took furious notes as she listened. She felt like a blank slate when it came to the technology, but when Chief Science Officer Samson Kleme talked, Caroline kept seeing Bethany dwarfed in the hospital bed. Even in the child's version, she looked small.

"I've heard of three other companies working on similar therapies." Samson tapped the legal pad in front of him. "We've got to push fast or we'll lose the market."

"Do whatever you need to make that happen." Quentin's hair flopped in his face as he jotted something down. "I can't emphasize strongly enough that even with the latest round of funding, we've got months at most to get this off the ground."

Caroline swallowed hard at the thought she'd started a job with an unstable company. What had she done? She set her pen down as her fingers trembled.

Quentin caught her expression. "Do you have something to add?" He shifted toward her as he pushed back from the mahogany table.

Was this what it felt like to be called on at King Arthur's Round Table? Her stomach dropped to her toes and she waited for the words "Off with her head!" Wait, she'd mixed her children's stories. When she'd taken the job with

Praecursoria, she'd hoped to land in a safe place, not a fire.

"We can't shortcut the approval process."

Everyone at the table inhaled. Their faces swam in front of Caroline as she searched for the words to explain how terrible the CEO's idea was. The fact her new colleagues had just consumed all the oxygen didn't help her rattled nerves.

Samson whatever-his-name-was steepled his manicured fingers. "You've been here how long?"

"A couple of hours." She would not be intimidated by him.

"You've attended how many meetings?"

"This is the first."

"And that makes you the expert?"

She tipped her chin. The arrogant man had asked the wrong question. He might be a scientist, but she was the one with the legal experience. "Actually, yes. I'm here because none of you are lawyers." She glanced around the table and tried to make eye contact with each person there. "My job is to make sure you stay within the guardrails of the law and regulations. The work you're doing is too important to have the FDA halt it because we didn't follow the right process."

The scientist leaned back and smirked. "Even if it means saving the life of a child who will be dead within a week if we do nothing?"

His words sliced into her heart. She knew

what he expected her to say. Quentin had taken her to see Bethany, after all. She had a face and name to put with the company's work, but that didn't mean she could ignore what she was hearing, even if he currently knew the FDA trial process better. What the team at the table didn't understand yet was that she'd managed several cases for Judge Loren that involved disputes related to FDA trials. Smug Samson could look at her like she was some dumb young thing, but she'd prove to him she knew the legal process better than he did.

She glanced around the table and confirmed no one else seemed to understand the issues she'd spotted. "I'm not saying do nothing. Exactly the opposite. The research y'all are conducting is too important to get sloppy. If we shortcut any of the FDA's processes, you could lose your license and the ability to test this or any future drugs and therapies."

Quentin doodled on his legal pad as his attention switched to the science officer. "Kleme, she has a point."

The man's jowls sank into heavy lines of sadness. "We exist to ensure other children don't die needlessly like my son. I've invested my life in developing the science so that today we could prevent his death." He focused on Quentin. "What's the name of the girl that Anna wants us to add to the trial?"

Quentin hit a button and a picture of Bethany, happy and healthy, projected on the wall behind him. "Bethany Anderson. She's eleven and in her third bout with leukemia. Two failed transplants and she relapsed four weeks ago." He shook his head as he studied the image. "She's the same age Jordan was."

Samson pushed to his feet. He was taller than Caroline expected. "That's exactly why we have to get her in the trial now. I don't want to wait until she's beyond hope, not if we can give her a real chance."

"Of course." Quentin moved his hands in a placating gesture before he directed his attention back to Caroline. "But if we do this in the wrong way, we jeopardize everything the company exists to achieve."

A man with a shock of red hair and heavy dark-framed glasses raised his hand. Quentin nodded toward him, and the man turned to face Caroline. "I'm Dr. Brian Silver and work with Dr. Kleme." Then he focused on Quentin. "Has the testing been completed to see if her body is strong enough?"

"Dr. Johnson is waiting on results."

"Good." The man, who was maybe ten years older than Caroline's thirty, swiveled toward Dr. Kleme. "Then we have time to do this the right way. There's no reason to rush before the patient qualifies for the study."

"I don't like to wait." Dr. Kleme crossed his arms. "My son's death is why I'm here. If we aren't working to prevent other children dying from acute lymphoblastic leukemia, then I'm done. That's why our mission statement is posted in every room of this building. After our efforts to narrow the focus on these CAR T therapies, we need to push hard or lose it all. Bethany Anderson will die if we don't give this a shot. We need to start therapy as soon as we can harvest her cells."

His words fell with the heaviness of a gauntlet thrown down.

Caroline glanced around the table again, but no one met her gaze. They all seemed inordinately interested in Bethany's image, the healthier version of the girl. "You can't rush ahead of the FDA process without breaking the law." Bending it almost to breaking, at the bare minimum.

"Think of it as giving a little push while saving a life." The man shrugged, his can-do attitude sounding forced. "And we all know we'll be in official Stage 2 trials in weeks."

Or months. That was the thing about trials. Even when everyone was racing to find a common cure, as when COVID-19 had ravaged the world, the FDA approval process took time, and this situation was not as globally dire. If the FDA got wind of this? The company's application for Stage 2 trials could be placed on hold. Indefinitely.

She hoped no one noticed how her breathing shuddered. Was this the company's version of hazing the new girl, seeing how far she could be pushed? "I can't urge you strongly enough. While this might be the right thing to do, it is the wrong way. Again, the long-term consequences with the FDA could be catastrophic."

Even when the child they wanted to bend the process for was one of Brandon's.

Dr. Kleme leaned back. "I gave Dr. Johnson permission to harvest the girl's T cells this morning."

When Caroline walked out of the meeting thirty minutes later, she felt the weight of the law on her narrow shoulders. No one looked at her or said a word as they filed out and back to their jobs.

She'd never felt so alone. She wanted to tell her colleagues she'd received the message. Speaking up wasn't permitted, but if silence was what they expected, they'd learn they hired the wrong woman.

Her phone buzzed in her pocket, and she tugged it free as she walked down an empty hallway that she thought led to her office. Her heart lifted when she saw a text from Brandon.

everything okay?

How did he know she needed his balance right now? It will be. Just hard starting a new job.

what else were you going to do?

That question had paralyzed her in the days after Judge Loren died. He'd let her stay years after she could have moved to a major law firm and taken clients of her own. Instead, she'd remained in her clerkship and made the judge her sole client. While the work had been interesting, his death left her stranded.

I don't know. It'll be fine. Guess I'm just missing what I lost.

understandable. i'm sorry.

Thanks. Her fingers froze over the screen. You really invested here?

yeah. reid said it would be a good one.

Reid Billings was Brandon's financial adviser. He was also engaged to one of Caroline's best friends, Emilie Wesley.

Caroline bit her lower lip as she considered Brandon's words. She was now an insider and he was an investor who could benefit from anything she shared. Gotta find my office and get through onboarding.

sounds fun. He inserted a smirk emoji. you've got this. let them see the amazing intellect housed in the caroline bragg we all know and love.

I'm not all that special.

you are. all that and a bag of cool ranch doritos.

Thanks. She sent him a smiley face she wasn't really feeling, but if she didn't, he'd probe. He was good at that. Worming beneath the barricades she'd erected around her life and story. Right now she didn't have the bandwidth or stamina to banter him back to a safe distance. Not when her heart wondered how to handle the fact that he was an investor in her employer. Their relationship would be fine as long as she didn't talk about work.

I should be asking how you are.

Brandon shifted against the uncomfortable hospital chair as he studied his screen. How could he answer? Truthfully, it looked like Virginia wouldn't apply the new federal foster home law in his favor. Under Family First, group homes could be utilized only for a limited time for kids in crisis. To be compliant, Almost Home would have to become a "qualified residential treatment program" equipped to care for kids who'd experienced trauma—a designation that would exhaust his financial resources and overtake his simple vision for keeping hard-to-place sibling groups together. If he didn't comply, he'd lose state funds. The possibility that Almost Home might be shut down kept him up nights.

As for Bethany, he was over his head providing what the terribly sick girl needed. Gabriel begged to see her each time he saw Brandon, but seeing her like this couldn't be a good idea, even if he could sneak the boy into her room. Putting

Bethany in the trial felt overwhelming. Anna told him they had started harvesting Bethany's T cells that morning, but that was only the first step. Now the girl was wiped out and napping.

He didn't like feeling small and out of control.

Hated it.

Telling Caroline would only make it more real.

He glanced at the girl in the hospital bed and started typing words that maybe he'd come to believe if he said them often enough.

never better

She hated when he didn't use capital letters and punctuation. That little act of rebellion made him grin.

Brandon . . .

She thought she knew what he was going through, but he'd held back. Their relationship was young. She didn't know what it was like to watch someone die. Someone who was weak and needed a champion to fight for them. He'd done this before when his mom had wasted away, and then he'd been separated from his brother and lost in the cracks. He'd mentioned it to Caroline, but sympathizing wasn't the same as living it.

He was an adult now. He could make sure no one disappeared like he had.

That was his role for every child who lived at Almost Home. And especially this girl.

He hadn't looked for it, but it had come anyway. He'd barely been home in the last few days. It didn't matter that Tara, Bethany's caseworker, said it wasn't his job to spend hours at the hospital. He couldn't leave Bethany alone, not when there were house parents at Almost Home to manage the other kids' day-to-day needs. They had a schedule and a plan they followed.

How's Bethany?

alive. they started the harvest this morning, hope it's the right step

The words were terse, but it was all he could manage.

Praying for wisdom for her doctors and healing for her. Do you need anything?

wisdom of solomon

Then I'll pray for that too.

Brandon slid his phone into his pocket, then leaned forward and put his head in his hands. He should pray. It felt too small, even though he knew simple prayers could move big mountains. *God, would You do it this time?*

There was a knock on the door, and he looked up as Anna entered. In her white lab coat she was all experienced doctor, not the scrawny preteen cousin who'd yelled when he tugged her braids at family dinners before her dad's military career moved the family to Japan. Now she stood in front of him and studied him as if he were the patient.

"Your patient is there." He hitched a thumb over his shoulder toward Bethany's bed.

"I'm concerned about you right now." She stepped closer and brushed hair from his eyes as if she would read his mind. "I wish I knew what happened the years we were apart."

"I was fine."

"I almost believe you."

He glanced away. "Bethany's the one who needs your skill."

"Yes, but I'm concerned about you."

"You can stop talking about me." Bethany's voice pulled Brandon's attention to her. She swallowed. "Can I have the remote?"

He gave it to her, then returned his attention to Anna, who'd stepped to the computer in the corner of the room and started tapping on the keyboard. Then she gestured for him to follow her to the hallway. She eased the door shut behind them. When she spoke, she kept her words soft.

"The T-cell retrieval went well, and they're on the way to Praecursoria. I've got one more person at the state who has to authorize her for the study, and as soon as we have the approval, and her test results, we can start the process." Her shoulders slumped and she looked exhausted. "I've almost got the hospital committed to covering the costs of her care."

"Thank you, Anna. What can I do to help?"

"Stay well." She looked back at the room. "You're the closest thing she has to a caring, stable adult. If you get sick, she'll be alone."

"You'll be here." She couldn't place all of this on him.

"Yes, but I'm managing multiple patients. You have her."

And another thirty-five kids back at Almost Home, spread among the six cabins. "I'll do what she needs."

"I know you will." Sorrow filled her eyes as she watched him. "It's not good, Brandon. I'll fight hard for her, but there are no guarantees. Even if we can get her in, the therapy is experimental and risky."

"Tell me the name of it again?" He pulled out his phone to take a note, but she held up a hand.

"Don't, Brandon. Don't research it. Not until we know if that's the path we're taking."

"All right." He slid it back to his pocket. "But tell me—cart something?"

"CAR T-cell therapy."

She might think he was acquiescing, but he'd investigate as soon as she was gone.

Anna might be the doctor, but he was Bethany's foster parent.

He stared at the patent application.

His name wasn't on it.

He flashed hot then cold then back to hot. He'd been promised by his boss—and her boss—that he would reap the benefit of his labor. The long nights and never-ending hours in the lab babysitting the cells. Making sure they responded as expected. He'd done it for months, all on a handshake.

In the end, *he* was the one who'd identified the magic cells.

She'd promised he would be included. She said she'd taken care of it.

What a fool he'd been! He knew better. Had seen Jackson do this sort of thing since their fraternity days at Mississippi State. Brotherhood didn't matter to Jackson any more than his word. His mistake was expecting more out of his supervisor.

Now he'd right this wrong.

He could take what he knew to a competitor.

No. That wasn't a heavy enough penalty, not when Praecursoria could net millions on his technology anyway.

It was nice that Jackson was ready to use it on a dying kid or two. But this was about more than saving lives.

This was about integrity. And this was the breach that went too far. He'd given up too much to take it without a word. The challenge would be how to make it matter. Raise the stakes so he could get Jackson's attention and make sure he realized he was paying for broken promises.

Punishment without awareness was ineffective.

He was nothing if not effective.

And Jackson would experience that firsthand.

An idea came to him and he smiled. It would start now.

CHAPTER 4
THURSDAY, APRIL 22

Caroline stood outside the door to the large conference room at Praecursoria. Was her new job going to involve frequent all-call meetings? She'd spent an extra half hour in the building the prior night, learning to navigate the halls, but she needed to spend her time reviewing what the company had in the works, not getting lost on her way to more meetings. This morning she'd found herself in the lab wing before she made her way back to the public-facing areas.

About forty people had already congregated for the meeting, and the staff chatted like an excited group of high school friends who'd known each other forever and were reconnecting after summer break.

She hesitated in the hallway. No one noticed her as they brushed past to join the others inside. That was fine—she wasn't ready to meet the large group despite her usually extroverted nature. When she'd worked for the judge, he'd had a secretary and two other clerks. Serving as his permanent clerk had put her on a trajectory different from the others'. She was perennial, staying year after year, older than the one-year clerks. They hadn't cared that she graduated from law school only a few years before them. She was the ancient one who couldn't possibly understand their lives and struggles.

Now she felt her newness and the fact she wasn't a scientist.

The energy was heavy and intense. In the judge's chambers she could spend hours, head down, reading and analyzing cases and briefs. Here her door was to stay open unless a sensitive conversation required a closed door. At least she had a door. Many of her colleagues worked in open labs or pod-type spaces.

Snippets of conversation flowed around her.

A woman wearing a lab coat walked toward the conference room with a bald colleague. "Can you believe it, Justin?" she asked him. She swiped a tissue under her eyes.

He shook his head and stroked his goatee. "She was so excited Monday. Kept saying they'd found miracle cells."

"Like HeLa?" The woman snorted. "I heard that rumor. I don't think that's likely. Those were one-in-a-trillion kind of cells."

"Maybe you're right, Lori, but Sarah wouldn't have talked about it if she wasn't sure."

"Unless she told you something she didn't tell the rest of us, it was just talk. The kind that is optimistic but unfruitful in the end."

"Maybe." The man shrugged and moved on, ending the conversation.

"You coming in?"

The words startled Caroline. "Dr. Johnson?"

The woman's smile reached her eyes as she held out her hand. "It's good to see you again. Please, call me Anna. You don't want to be late to a meeting Quentin calls. He can be late, but you can't. Fortunately, I don't work for him anymore. At least not directly." She led the way through the door. "How do you like being the new attorney?"

"I thought I was the first."

"Quentin probably likes to forget about the first, since he only lasted a couple weeks."

Caroline frowned at the information. "Any idea why?"

"I heard he found different work." The woman shrugged as she rubbed her stomach. "Praecursoria isn't for everyone. It's basically a start-up, which can be too chaotic for some."

"I don't have that luxury." Caroline slapped her hand over her mouth. "I didn't mean to say that out loud."

Anna laughed, and the sound burbled from her soul. "You did, but it will be our secret. Let's grab lunch soon when I'm out this direction. You do get lunch, right?"

"I'd enjoy that. How's Bethany?"

Anna sighed as she slid between a couple of people. "Her case is a hard one. Sit with me during the meeting. Depending on how long it runs, we'll grab that first lunch today."

"Sounds good." Caroline followed Anna toward some vacant seats and smiled as the woman introduced Caroline to everyone they passed.

The fact Anna had worked for the company before medical school was evident in how well known she was by the staff. Anna was chatting with a researcher when the meeting kicked off with housekeeping details. Then Chief Scientist Samson Kleme stood. He ran through some jargon and Caroline took detailed notes. She had the ability to understand the science behind Praecursoria's research if she gave it her full mental engagement. If not, the words flowed over her like water on an otter's coat.

"First let me address a rumor. Sarah Hill died last night at Arlington Hospital." The tall man bowed his head as he shoved his hands into the pockets of the white lab coat he wore over khakis and a button-down. "She was an important part of our team and will be missed, but we will work to quickly replace her so the work continues.

"Sarah led cutting-edge work on adult stem cells that showed promise and progress while also overseeing the CAR T trials. Brian Silver worked closely with her and will ensure the work she began continues." Dr. Kleme gestured toward Anna. "Dr. Anna Johnson has agreed to serve as lead research physician on our latest CAR T-cell therapy trial. Please give her your full cooperation, as she is critical to the next step in this protocol."

There was applause, and Caroline used it to lean closer to Anna. "Congrats."

"Condolences would be better." A troubled furrow marred her expression.

"Why?"

"Sarah's death makes the process more difficult. She was a gifted scientist. In the best of times, these applications and trials can become quagmires it's impossible to escape. Now?" She forced a smile to her glossed lips. "I'm here today for the announcement. After this you'll find me at the hospital maintaining a professional distance."

Caroline sensed something was going on, but this wasn't the time to dig deeper.

Dr. Kleme continued. "The research we're doing in CAR T is why this company exists the way it does today. We've put all of our resources into this area and are close to a breakthrough. This is it." He swallowed hard. "I could tell you the future success of our company depends on CAR T cells, but you each know it's more than that. You understand how intensely personal this quest is for me. Ten years ago my son lay dying in the hospital, and I was desperate. My little boy couldn't die." He looked down and seemed to gather himself. "But he did, and I vowed to do everything to ensure that doesn't happen to other families." His pause stretched uncomfortable seconds.

Quentin stood and popped over next to Dr. Kleme. "This commitment is why we've invested so much to hire the team of scientists and researchers in this room. It's why I've circled the globe raising additional funding. It's why so many of you have attended conference after conference to share what we've learned and have our findings tested by experts." He spread his arms wide. "Our success is your success. It takes each of us, working together, to make the dream a reality. Very soon children will no longer fight for survival because of inadequate therapies."

He patted Dr. Kleme on the shoulder, and the older man moved to a vacant chair in the front row.

Caroline wiped a finger under each eye.

Anna leaned closer. "This is your first one, right?"

Caroline nodded.

Anna slipped a Kleenex to her. "It's why I always carry a packet of these in my pocket. Dr. Kleme and Mr. Jackson always tug on all the heartstrings."

At the end of the meeting Anna glanced at her watch. "I have to be at the hospital at two. Let me connect with Brian, and then we can grab lunch. That work for you?"

Caroline knew the rest of her day was free and clear. "Perfect." She pulled a card from a slot in her portfolio and jotted her cell number on it.

"Text or call when you're ready, and I can meet you at the front desk."

"Great." Anna gave her a quick smile, then slipped out of her chair and went up the aisle toward Samson Kleme and the man standing with him.

Caroline headed the opposite direction toward her office, Quentin's words reverberating in her mind. In her interview he'd said similar things about the mission, and it reminded her that it was a privilege to work for a company committed to curing others. It would get easier. She needed to give herself time to learn the job.

Back at her desk she pulled up her research on Praecursoria's history. For ten years it had been a combination research and public lab that provided genetic testing for a price. Science advanced so quickly that the results had to be tweaked all the time. Still, that part of the company had been at the forefront of the market, but when his son died Dr. Kleme convinced Quentin to focus on cancer research. When CAR T-cell therapies emerged as cutting-edge treatments, Quentin sold the genetic testing division to fund the move into this area.

Her phone dinged. Anna was ready, and they agreed to meet at a small sandwich shop a few blocks away. Caroline walked, letting the sun warm her face even as the cacophony of traffic formed the soundtrack.

When she reached the restaurant, Anna already

stood in line. Caroline joined her, and five minutes later they were seated at a small bistro table. The restaurant catered to the professional crowd with a limited breakfast and lunch menu of simple, hearty soups, sandwiches, and salads. Anna had a cup of tomato soup and a Greek salad while Caroline opted for a Fuji apple salad. Caroline didn't have time to worry about how to start the conversation because Anna dove right in. Soon they had covered how they picked their fields of study and careers.

Caroline slid her half-empty salad bowl to the side. "How did you get affiliated with Praecursoria?"

"I wanted a research experience that allowed me to test how much I liked medicine. One of my professors connected me with Samson. The company was much smaller and more unfocused then, when he was part of the genetic testing division. Working in that area confirmed I was passionate about preventive medicine. If testing could show us what might happen to a person in the future, I wanted to be part of curing identified problems. Otherwise, we were telling people their bodies were essentially ticking time bombs, and I don't want to know that about mine."

"And that led to hematology?"

"In a roundabout way. I started with oncology but became fascinated by the blood cancers and diseases during a rotation. The rest is history."

She pushed her empty soup bowl to the side. "Each year we discover more and more keys that unlock our understanding of disease. It's mind-boggling. When I was in medical school, these discoveries were more science fiction than real possibilities." She wiped her mouth with a napkin. "How quickly it changes." She told a couple of stories about patients who'd been saved by the different experimental treatments, then gave her head a small shake. "Tell me more about you."

"I wanted to be someone with a job that mattered, but I couldn't handle blood, which ruled out a swath of careers like yours."

"So you picked law."

"Or it chose me." Caroline gave a little shrug. "I was good in those sorts of classes and it looked like a field where I could use my skills to make a difference." Speaking of. "Do you know what HeLa cells are?"

"HeLa? Sure, every researcher does. Why?"

"I heard someone talking about them and the scientist who died."

"Sarah? Well, HeLa cells are named for Henrietta Lacks. He-La. They're her cervical cancer cells, harvested before she passed away in 1951. They're unique because human cells die, but hers continue to replicate. They've been involved in medical research breakthroughs ever since. I'm not sure how they would relate to Sarah though."

Caroline made a mental note to do some research.

Anna's phone vibrated, and she glanced at it. "Sorry, but this is a page from the hospital. Hate to cut our lunch short, but I'd better head that direction." Anna started packing up her Greek salad.

"Understand. Is there anything I can do to help with Bethany?" Caroline reached for the lid to take her salad with her.

"Have any friends in the Virginia Department of Social Services who can fast-track her approval to be in the trial?"

Caroline grimaced.

"If it were that simple, my life would be easy." Anna sighed. "I'll let you know if you can help me knock down barriers."

They stood and Caroline led the way to the door. "I'm still new, but can you tell me one thing about Samson and Quentin?"

"Maybe."

"Should I be concerned about the company having a culture of cutting corners?"

Anna stopped on the sidewalk. "What do you mean?"

"I'm not sure other than Samson seems inclined to push past the FDA limits as I understand them."

"He gets passionate about the work, thanks to losing his son." She swallowed hard. "I lost my husband in an accident six months ago. He never even knew I was pregnant."

"I'm so sorry." Caroline hated how tongue-tied others' grief made her.

Anna waved the words away. "It's a chapter in my story, but it helps me understand Samson in ways I didn't before. Even so, he knows the risks of pushing too hard and fast."

"I guess I'll keep reminding him."

"I would."

They went their separate ways, and Caroline had a sense Anna could become more than a work acquaintance. As she walked back to the office, she prayed for a way to be made for Bethany to participate in the trial and for the next stage to be approved quickly by the FDA—keeping everyone legal.

There were many more kids like Bethany who needed options. That meant Caroline had to do everything she could to propel the research through the FDA's process.

The better she understood the science, the better she could do her job. She'd start with a visit to the lab. When she reached the research wing, it was slowly coming to life after lunch.

All of the doors off the main hallway were heavy fire doors with small windows inserted at a level she could see through when she stood on tiptoe. In the first, Dr. Kleme looked through a microscope. Beside him, Brian Silver brushed his long red hair from his face and adjusted his glasses. She lightly tapped on the door, and a woman about her age glanced up, then came toward her.

"Can I help you?" The woman gave off a vibe of indifference, as if Caroline was an annoying disturbance.

"I'm Caroline Bragg, the new attorney."

"Yes, I know." The woman waited, but Caroline determined to wait longer. "Lori Clark. I run the day-to-day in this lab while those two think big thoughts."

"Nice to meet you, Lori." Caroline extended her hand, but Lori just stared at it. She pulled it back. "Is this a sterile lab?"

"Yes." The woman closed her eyes, then stepped into the hallway. "Look, we're busy, so can you just tell me why you're here?"

"I need to understand the process and the status of the research you're working on." She shrugged and smiled. Maybe she could appeal to her solidarity as a woman. "I'm the new girl and need all the help you'll give to get up to speed quickly."

"Really the guys are the ones you need to talk to." Lori looked back through the window in the door. "I've got to get back to work."

Before Caroline could respond, Lori swiped her keycard in the door and slipped back into the lab, shutting the door in Caroline's face.

What exactly was going on in there that they wouldn't tell her about?

CHAPTER 5
FRIDAY, APRIL 23

At the end of her first week, Caroline's accomplishments included finding the women's restroom and figuring out how to dial out. She'd also started understanding the science behind Praecursoria's research, but it had taken some intervention on Quentin's part. Before that, she'd encountered an element of secrecy, or at least intent to razz the new girl. Maybe it came from the scientists' race to reach the patent office ahead of other companies, but it had been difficult for Caroline to get actual access to the labs. She'd told Quentin that if she didn't comprehend the depth of what happened there, she could miss something important for the various trials and patent applications.

There would be layers to uncover for years to come. It was amazing to be part of a team that pushed the envelope of what was possible. She'd gotten chills a few times as she'd met with different researchers.

When Caroline entered the break room Friday morning, a group clustered around the overpriced cappuccino machine. She clutched her *Morning, Gorgeous* mug and considered elbowing her way in.

She recognized Brian Silver, the redhead who worked with Samson Kleme and the late Sarah. He acknowledged her with a brief nod as he moved toward the door. "There's a priority meeting at ten." He pushed his thick, dark frames up his nose, dislodging a shock of hair that flopped along his forehead. "You'll be there, right?"

Caroline mentally ran over her calendar. It was already nine thirty, and she hadn't heard or seen anything about a meeting. "Where?"

"The conference room, I think." His gaze darted away, and she stared at him so hard she felt her nose crinkle.

Great. That always made her look about fifteen, not the image she wanted to portray as she proved her value. "No problem. I'll check with Quentin's assistant. She'll know the details." She gave the man a smile then eased toward the coffeemaker. "But first, coffee." She paused. "Are you doing okay? I mean, after the death of your colleague?"

He glanced at her and then away as he cleared his throat. "She'll be hard to replace. She had that unique ability to take a crazy, science-extending idea and apply it in the lab. She and Samson were unstoppable."

"I'm sure you were in the mix."

His lips tipped slightly on the sides. "I thought we made a good team. Now I'll carry forward her research around CAR T therapies. She had exciting early results." He nodded toward the door. "Quentin has special guests today. It's another set of parents begging for access to our therapies."

"Does that happen often?"

"Often enough. Quentin's got a soft heart for the right sob story. The challenge is everyone who comes here has a heartbreaking photo of a kid." He shook his head. "Doesn't mean we can help. See you at the meeting."

After inserting a pod and waiting for the coffee to spew from the spout, she left the kitchenette and headed down the hall. The break room was close to the four labs, all of which were tucked behind the executive suite at the back of the building. The sterile labs required the researchers to wear what looked like space suits as they worked on turning adult stem cells into lifesaving therapies. What had been a maturing company had started over with new focus on CAR T and other experimental therapies.

Her role? Secure patents for the research and contracts for the therapies. Provide guidance on the regulatory processes. She'd barely wrapped her arms and mind around everything that was in the development stage, not to mention what Praecursoria already had in trials. With three research teams in FDA trials and two more ready to apply, she needed to attend the leadership meeting in case it had anything to do with those.

Maybe everyone was off because of the pall

that hung over the office. An email had arrived that morning announcing services for Sarah Hill. Though Caroline had never met the woman, her death had to cast a shadow over those who knew her, because she was only in her late forties. Too young to be gone.

Before returning to her office, she took a quick detour to Quentin's suite and his assistant's desk. The twentysomething's blonde hair was slicked back in a French twist. Her perfectly manicured nails, in a vibrant red that matched her lip stain, tapped away at her keyboard as Caroline approached. The door to Quentin's office stood open, and a murmur of voices flowed from it, the words indecipherable. Caroline took a step closer, but Lillian looked up and stopped her with a death stare.

"No one can go in there." The young woman's voice matched her gaze, firm and unyielding. Had she taken a class to perfect that?

"But the door's open."

"Doesn't matter." The woman stood and walked to it before pulling it shut. She settled back at her desk and returned to her typing.

Caroline waited a moment. "Do you have the agenda for the ten o'clock meeting?"

Lillian frowned and clicked the mouse a couple of times. "You aren't invited."

Caroline tried to hide her wince. No need to be so blunt. "Is it about the trial applications?"

"I'm not sure."

It was Caroline's turn to use her version of a death stare. "You can tell me or I'll ask Quentin."

The door opened, and Quentin swept them with a quick look. "Everything all right?"

"Caroline had a question but is leaving." Lillian smiled sweetly, the look as fake as saccharine.

Caroline forced a smile. "Getting info on this morning's meeting."

He nodded, then gestured toward his office. "Have a minute? There's a couple I'd like you to meet."

"Absolutely." She walked past Lillian and followed the CEO into his office.

A couple sat on the brown pleather loveseat beside his desk. A box of Kleenexes rested on the small wooden coffee table in front of them, a stack of Praecursoria brochures artfully arranged on its surface. The woman gripped the man's hand. She had the look of someone who hadn't slept well in months, maybe years. He held tight, their wedding bands flashing in the light, as if he could keep her from drowning in a storm. In her other hand, the woman clutched a sodden tissue that had mascara streaks across it. As she noticed Caroline, she leaned into her husband and seemed to shrink, while he seemed to grow larger and more protective.

Caroline swallowed as she imagined what had brought them here. She glanced at Quentin and murmured, "What have you promised them?"

"Nothing yet." He gave the couple a reassuring smile as he stopped Caroline with a light touch on her arm. "But we will help them." His jaw firmed, and a glint in his eye warned her this was nonnegotiable. Then his charisma bubbled to the surface as he motioned her forward.

She hesitated and he glanced at her. "Is this related to the trial Ms. Hill was working on?"

"Why would you ask that?"

"Because if it is, we might not be ready yet. Are we approved to begin trials? Let Brian Silver make the transition before we promise it to anyone." Surely that was reasonable, but as she looked at the couple, their demeanors indicated they might not have time to wait.

"It's not connected, nor would it matter if it was." He turned to the couple with a charismatic smile. "This is my right-hand gal, the one who makes sure everything stays on the legal up-and-up." Caroline cringed at his characterization but forced a smile anyway. "Caroline Bragg, I'd like to introduce you to Mary and Michael Robbins. Their son Patrick was here four months ago for testing. Other CAR T-cell therapies bought him time but have stopped being effective. So they're back to see if one of our new therapies will work better for him. I'm pleased we have one to suggest." The warning in his eyes dared her to challenge him, but she had to.

"It's a pleasure to meet you both, and I hope we can help your son."

Mr. Robbins straightened as he met her gaze. "We're grateful for the chance to pursue a miracle for our son." He edged his wife to the side, then pulled out his wallet. "Here's a photo of him a year ago in remission." He held the photo out to her, and she saw the gap-toothed grin of a young man in a baseball cap that was too big for his head with a bat slung over his shoulder. "He doesn't look like that today. Not since the cancer returned."

Mary Robbins reached out and caressed the boy's image. "We're willing to try anything to get our son back." She eased the photo from her husband's hand and held it out to Caroline. Then she pulled up an image on her phone. "This is what he looks like now. He's dying."

The words were stark. Yet the woman didn't flinch or blink them away.

Caroline took the photo and felt the image of the little boy sear into her memory. The two photos could have been of different boys. In the first he had a big toothy grin. In the other he sat on a couch with a blanket, his active leanness reduced to skin and bones. While he tried to smile, no energy radiated from him. Her heart crimped at the radical change.

"How old is he now?"

"He turns eleven next week."

"The same age as Bethany."

The woman frowned in confusion. "I don't know who that is."

"A patient I met earlier this week." She handed the photo back to Mrs. Robbins. "Thank you for showing me Patrick's picture. He's a handsome boy."

His mother sniffled. "We've spent days at the children's hospital having more tests run by your researchers. They must have taken quarts of blood."

Quentin cocked his head as if surprised by that fact. "Really?"

The woman glanced at her husband and then nodded. "Monday he was hooked up to the machine that takes his blood and then returns it to him. We joked he was lighter when he left."

"That's right." Quentin nodded. "We were getting a jump on it because of his status. He can't afford delays."

"You're right. He's a very sick boy." Mr. Robbins squeezed his wife's hand. "We will do anything you need to give Patrick this chance."

Caroline watched the interplay, then focused on Quentin. "Which therapy are you hoping will work for him?"

"Trial CAR T 463."

Her heart sank. They had barely completed the application for Phase 1 trials. Like the trial they were trying to get Bethany into, the CAR T 463 therapy contained mouse DNA, which might be harmful to human recipients' ability to accept the cells. Just yesterday the FDA had asked them for more information. They still had much to do.

"Hopefully we'll be ready soon. The research team is working round the clock to address the FDA requirements." She didn't mention it would take a miracle to get the packet back to the investigator by Monday.

"We'll make Patrick Patient 1."

The hope that flicked across Mrs. Robbins's face threatened to be Caroline's undoing. But she squared her shoulders and met Mr. Robbins's gaze. "We're still seeking approval for Phase 1 trials. Until we receive that, we can't offer the trial or sign up Patient 1. Not yet, but hopefully soon."

Quentin stiffened but didn't hesitate in his response. "That's fine because we'll have Patrick enter as part of the Phase 0 trial. He's dying without treatment, so he will play an important part in telling us whether the treatment works like we anticipate."

"I don't understand." Mrs. Robbins leaned forward, desperation edging every line of her stiff body. "What do you mean by Phase 0?"

"These are pre–Phase 1 small studies. Fewer than fifteen people, where we test whether the therapy has any intended benefits without negative toxicity."

She swallowed. "That sounds . . . bad."

"We would typically give Patrick and any other patients in Phase 0 a low dose of the treatment.

We've got the paperwork well under way for Phase 1, but this would allow us to start treatment, albeit on a smaller level, earlier." Quentin pointed at Patrick's photo on the coffee table. "He may not have time to wait for Phase 1."

Mr. Robbins rubbed his hand on the back of his neck, then looked at his wife. "Do we have another option?"

The desperation in her eyes pierced Caroline. "Please. We need hope."

Quentin leaned his elbows on his knees and clasped his hands under his chin. "I want to be very clear with you. This may sound callous, but Patrick will likely die without the therapy. The current standard of care is no better than what we can hope to accomplish. If it works, we'll buy time to get him on a higher treatment plan."

Mrs. Robbins flinched at his words, but he plowed on. "My team has fully informed you both of the risks. If you give consent, Patrick is the perfect candidate to be Patient 1." His calm smile seemed to reassure the couple. Mrs. Robbins relaxed and eased a bit away from her husband. "If necessary, I'll fly a team to Mexico to administer the therapy, if we can't get everything ready here in time. It will work because it has to and Patrick is out of options. This is his Hail Mary."

Caroline noted the phrase, the same one she'd heard Dr. Anna Johnson use in regard to Bethany.

At the time she'd thought it was because Brandon was her audience. What else could you do when you were out of options besides heave the ball as hard as you could and pray for a miracle?

CHAPTER 6

"Alaina and I have accepted a job in Arkansas."

Jeff Stone stood with Brandon at the split-rail fence that surrounded the playground at Almost Home. Three of the boys who lived in the cottage Jeff and Alaina managed chased each other around the equipment in some high-energy form of tag. Bethany's brother, Gabriel, seemed to be settling in as he tagged one of the others.

Brandon shook his head slightly as if his ears needed clearing. "I don't understand."

"We're moving to a home in Arkansas." Jeff turned to look at him, and Brandon saw the resolution in his gaze. "Especially since Ellie was born, we're more than two young college grads saving the world one kid at a time. We have to think of our future."

"I need you here, making this work alongside me."

"I'm sorry, but we've waited as long as we can." Jeff's expression tightened as Luke picked up a stick. "Luke, be careful with that." He returned his attention to Brandon. "Look, we believe in what you're doing here, but chances are good you'll lose state funds and have to shut down, and we can't wait for that to happen."

"We aren't going to close."

"You've fought to keep this model harder than anyone could ask."

Brandon exhaled then rubbed the back of his neck. Almost Home had been in tight spots before. There were times he'd been certain the rats had the right idea jumping overboard. Then Reid or someone would come alongside him with funding, and the organization would live for another year. The difference this time was that the organization's future rested in the hands of lawmakers and regulators who couldn't decide what they wanted.

It should be a simple process. Read the new rules and spit out a perfectly formed plan, but every time he did, the proposed regs changed.

"Look, Virginia is supposed to clarify the new regulations by the end of the summer. Then I can make some definitive plans."

Jeff sighed. "They've been telling you that for over a year."

Brandon felt the tension tighten his gut until the familiar surge of nausea welled up. So much rested on how Virginia interpreted and applied the federal law. He'd lived with the uncertainty, but it was plain he'd underestimated the effect on his employees.

Wait a minute.

"Is this place in Arkansas a group home?"

"It is."

"How are they working around the new

residential treatment requirements?" He'd been looking for a loophole—something that would allow him to keep sibling groups together while also providing the necessary trauma care. "I've thought about switching our model so my house parents like you and Alaina are the licensed foster parents. Then I'd 'place' the kids with you instead of Almost Home."

"That's what they're doing. Alaina and I will be licensed in Arkansas. But we'll live on their property and rent our cottage for a nominal fee from the group care facility. In theory, it will operate like we do here, only the kids will be assigned to us rather than the larger home."

Brandon's mind spun as he processed that information.

"Who gets paid by the state?"

"I'm guessing we do. Then it looks like we'll pay the facility for the group meals, use of the facilities, things like that."

"If I committed to doing that here, would you stay?"

"I don't know, Brandon. If we pass on this opportunity—"

"You and Alaina were the first couple to join me. It won't be Almost Home without you." He tried to do the math in his head but knew he'd have to dig deeper to see if he could actually make the numbers work. "Can you give me time?"

"I'd have to talk to Alaina, get her buy-in."

"Of course. Will you ask?"

The man sighed, then nodded. "I'll do that, but I'm not making any promises. Security is pretty important to her, even more so now that we have our own little girl."

Brandon clapped a hand on the smaller man's shoulder. "I'm sorry I haven't done a better job managing this. Give me at least a few weeks, okay?"

"I'll try, but we can't put off accepting the offer for long."

"Thanks." If needed Brandon would get down on his knees and beg. With thirty-six kids residing in the various cabins, he needed the Stones. He needed all the house parents. He felt a vibration and pulled out his phone.

The hospital was calling.

If you want to break the law, it's best to do it without an attorney looking over your shoulder.

That was what Caroline's professional responsibility professor had preached, but she didn't think anyone at Praecursoria would agree with her that they edged close to that line. That didn't stop fear and anger from coursing through her as she barely made it through the "priority" meeting—a departmental budget review she needn't have attended after all—and returned to her office upset to have wasted precious time.

They couldn't give the Robbins family what Quentin had promised. How could he ignore how much trouble the company would be in if the FDA found out? The look in his eyes as she left his office indicated his displeasure that she hadn't enthusiastically fallen in line, but that wasn't what he'd hired her to do. Maybe this was why Reid and his group of investors had insisted the CEO hire in-house counsel.

It would be a challenge, but she could stand firm.

In class, ethical issues were always clear-cut and easy.

You made the right choice, and the world kept spinning without a hiccup or bump. It sounded so much easier in a law school lecture.

In reality . . .

This felt like a moment in which her choices would set the course of who she was.

As she slipped into her office her phone rang, and she scooped it from the corner of her desk. "Hello?"

"Caroline?"

At the mellow voice, her shoulders relaxed and she sank onto her leather chair. "Brandon."

"You okay? You sound . . ."

"Flummoxed? Yeah, that's me."

"So it's a good thing I have lunch and am sitting in the parking lot?"

She glanced at her exercise tracker. "Is it really eleven thirty? Wait. Did we have plans?"

"I was in the area and thought I'd surprise you." He hesitated. "A bad idea?"

Her eyes teared up. "You have no idea how much I need a friendly face."

"You can explain why when you get out here. Grab your jacket and meet me at the picnic tables. The sun's shining, and it sounds like you need vitamin D therapy."

Her lips curved into a smile, and she glanced at her computer. Everything could wait until after she spent time with Brandon Lancaster, the one she let into her heart and thoughts. "I'll be out in a few minutes."

"Don't wait too long. Your tomato soup will get cold."

"You had me at tomato." Yep, her man had her grinning from ear to ear, all because he remembered that creamy tomato soup with Panera's fresh croutons was her favorite comfort food. Funny how he knew she needed that today. Maybe she could bounce her predicament off him. The former football player had a clear head when it came to right and wrong.

But this was about a company he'd invested in, so maybe she shouldn't.

As she pushed to her feet and swiveled to grab her leather jacket, there was a rap at her door. When she turned around, Quentin was already sitting in a chair in front of her desk. She eased back down. "Soup is waiting on me."

"I'll keep this short." He held his hands beneath his chin and studied her. "There's something you need to understand. Something I explained during the interview, but today puts it in context. The protocols are why we exist. Yes, the FDA is important, but when we can try to save a life, we will. Work your legal magic and draft a waiver of some sort." He waved his hand in the air as if she had one waiting on the computer. "You're here to ensure what we do is legal and on the up-and-up."

"I'm not sure what you want to do for the Robbinses fits that criteria."

"Every law has a gray area. Find it, or this"—he gestured between them—"may not be a good fit." He pushed to his feet. "The Robbinses will sign the release Monday morning. Put in plenty of language about them accepting the risk of treatment and that their son is terminal. Lillian has all the information you need."

Then he was gone.

Brandon cooled his heels at the picnic table for more than a few minutes. The steady hum of traffic on Virginia 123 robbed the setting of its pastoral effect. Little about Tysons Corner, the small area immediately outside the Beltway in Northern Virginia, felt planned. It was a crazy mix of government agencies, odd pockets of housing, and industry that had erupted over thirty years. Mix in the shopping center and strip malls and it was an odd conglomeration.

Maybe this hadn't been his best spontaneous idea. But after his conversation with Jeff, he'd needed to clear his head. Time in Caroline's stabilizing presence was a good way to do that. When his world was upended, she could right it. He hoped she didn't understand the power she wielded.

All he knew for sure was he needed her, and if she distracted him, all the better.

He hadn't been kidding about the soup growing cold. Panera might be the way to her heart, but it was a simple fact that soup was better hot. If she took much longer, they'd have to hunt down a microwave.

He glanced at his watch as a pair of Canada geese strutted past on their way to the retention pond. Where was she?

He sighed as his thoughts returned to that meeting.

He should know better than to believe he could share his burden with anyone else. Almost Home was his alone. A few of his guys tried to help, but if the Stones were ready to bail, he'd have to admit no one cared about it like he did. Maybe he should have listened to those who told him he was a fool to pour so much of his time and savings into Almost Home, but he knew better than most how critical the safe space was for kids in crisis.

A door closed. He stood from the picnic bench and shoved his hands in his back pockets.

Caroline looked frazzled and upset as she sprinted down the sidewalk in the ridiculous high heels she favored. One misstep and he'd be speared while she toppled on a busted ankle.

"I am so sorry." She emphasized each word in her southern accent. "What a day."

"Yeah." She had no idea how much of a day. "What a week. I can leave if you need the time."

"No, I need this time with you even more than when you suggested it." She gave him a quick side hug, and he tugged her around and closer even as he forced his thoughts to focus on what she said rather than the feel of her with him. She lingered in the circle of his arms a moment before she pushed back. He immediately felt the distance.

"You're here for a reason." She focused the full wattage of her attention on him. "What's up?"

Such a simple question, loaded with meaning. Should he answer fully or stay on the white horse and pretend everything was okay? He didn't know which he wanted more, but he hesitated before forging into the truth. "The Stones have an offer to leave Almost Home. They could be gone in weeks."

"Oh, Brandon." She took his hand and sank onto the bench. "What can I do?"

He plopped next to her. "Find the solution that

puts us on solid ground in a week." He pinched the bridge of his nose. "I can't imagine the place without them. They were the first house parents I hired."

She looked at him, round eyes quizzical. "So talk them into staying."

"I'm trying, but Alaina wants security and I can't promise that." That was putting it mildly.

She twirled a strand of hair around her finger, then released it and grabbed another one. "So we look for a solution. Where are they going?"

"Some place in Arkansas."

"Why there?"

"The home seems to have found a way around the trauma-informed care requirement."

"That's the part that says group homes have to be qualified treatment centers?"

He nodded.

"Adapt their model here."

"I'll try, but I'm not sure I can do it fast enough to keep the Stones. This is my problem. It wasn't fair to share it."

"Brandon, you have to accept we're in life together. We share burdens so they aren't as overwhelming."

"Hasn't worked for me yet." He groaned as her face blanched. "Sorry. That's not what I meant. This has me all upside down. If they go, how will I keep the other couples?"

She glanced at her hands as if collecting herself.

When she looked up, the steel was back. "You'll find a way. There has to be a solution. How is the Arkansas home doing it?"

"It's actually an idea I've been kicking around." Might as well tell her his crazy idea. It was likely to be his last. "What if the house parents were licensed foster parents who rent the homes from me? They could rent them for free or a dollar? Something very nominal. Then we're not technically a group home, but a place where independent foster parents happen to live together."

Caroline studied him for a minute, her face reflecting she was intrigued but thinking through his words. "Tell me more."

"I don't have much. It's only group homes that have to meet the residential treatment requirements. That prohibits me from focusing on the real needs of the kids at an individual level and requires me to give them all the same level of care." He shrugged and infused confidence in his words. "But I think my idea would be good for the kids and fit the law."

"It might work." Caroline looked past him in the way she had when cataloging and analyzing information.

He pulled food from the paper bags. Still . . . "How's my main investment?"

CHAPTER 7

Caroline's mouth gaped in an O, and she edged away from him. "We really can't talk about my work."

Brandon looked like he'd been sucker punched. "What do you mean?"

The wind rustled through the trees. "Let's say my boss decided we need to give an experimental treatment to a young man who's dying."

Brandon watched her as if waiting for the bad news. "That's good, right? It's what they're doing for Bethany."

"Not exactly. This therapy isn't approved for trials on human subjects yet, but there may be a way to make it a Phase 0 trial."

He stared at her as blankly as she'd probably looked on Monday.

"Phase 0 trials are for those who can't be helped by current treatment protocols. In theory, volunteering for an untested drug or treatment doesn't hurt them because they're already dying." She tugged her jacket closer. "Listen to me. Earlier this week I didn't know there was such an option, but for some who've run out of time it's the only way to get access to treatments."

She rubbed the knots developing in her shoulders. Then she felt his big, strong hands go to work and relaxed into his touch. He knew how to find the tension and use enough pressure to release it without making her squeal. There was something about being with Brandon that allowed her to exhale in a deep way. She felt safe by being there with him. Seen by the way he leaned in when she was stressed. Heard by the way he listened. Sheltered by the way he stepped into her problems. She knew if she went into more detail about that morning's events, Brandon would lend a sympathetic ear and troubleshoot options like she had with him. But she couldn't do that and risk giving him too much information.

"How is this therapy different from Bethany's?"

Caroline wished she knew. "We've got so many variations of research in process, and I don't understand all the nuances yet." She would have shrugged except his fingers were still working their magic on her tense muscles. "Enough about my work."

"Your shoulders are rock hard."

Brandon's methodic circles made her want to moan. She scrambled for a new topic. Usually they could talk nonstop for an hour, but now she felt stilted and returned to his news. "You successfully renewed the accreditation," she said, referring to one of the new law's requirements that Brandon already had in place.

"Yes, but it won't matter if the Stones leave." His hands stilled and she turned to look at him. "How can I bring in anyone new while everything is so unstable? This process has been a mess since the law was passed without a clear framework for what it means for places like Almost Home. Even the language used doesn't make sense. It dictates that group homes like mine aren't the best option. Never mind that for some kids it's the only option to keep a family together. I moved a sibling group of six into one of the homes on Tuesday. Six, Caroline. No one else could take them on for a transition to a permanent adoption placement." He rolled his neck. "How can I convince Alaina that their employment at Almost Home is stable when it's taking the state so long to decide what the federal law really means and when it all has to be in place?" The frustration in his voice was mirrored on his face.

"So what will you do?" She kept her voice calm and low.

His hands paused a moment before he started working on her knots again. "Play through. Pray for a miracle, but work until the path is clear."

She frowned, glad he couldn't see it, then mentally eased from his touch, feeling the separation instantly.

"What?"

Oops, maybe he'd sensed her withdrawal after all. "So build on your idea. Flesh it out and see what your state contact says."

84

"It won't matter. They'll just move the ball again." His words were edged with sarcasm.

She turned and his hands fell to his sides. "I did not deserve that little bit of personality, big guy."

His eyes widened and then he choked back a laugh. "That's what I like about you, Bragg. You call me out."

This time, though, calling him out was only a cover-up for the larger issue: she wasn't sure how to navigate the boundaries between her job and their relationship. She'd have to be careful, because as much as she loved Brandon Lancaster, if she couldn't open up to him the way he opened up to her, she'd only disappoint him.

After all, her mom had insisted that was all she knew how to do.

Just like that, Caroline backed away without moving an inch. The transformation was complete and instant. He knew it but didn't know why. He reviewed their conversation, and other than his quick flash of frustration, it all seemed good. He'd even taken her pushback with good humor because they were comfortable with each other in the way friends-turned-more could be. He could be real with her.

She glanced at her watch. "I'd better get back inside. Big decisions to make."

"But you didn't eat." His words sounded inane, but he wanted to keep her here. Something about her steady presence made it easier to exhale. It also pushed away the panic that had edged in after Jeff's announcement.

Caroline paused, seeing into him. "Brandon, you have everything you need to make this work. I don't know anyone more disciplined or focused than you. In this season focus on patience and doing whatever it takes to keep Almost Home going. Those kids need you."

The intensity and belief in her words radiated through him even as the gap that had opened between them remained. "Thanks."

"You know I don't say things I don't mean." She gave him a small smile. "I'll heat up the soup. Thank you for bringing it. This has been the best part of my day. I'm praying for you."

From other people those might be mere words, but from Caroline it was a promise. But how could he close the gap that had developed between them?

He grabbed her hand, felt a tremor flow through her fingers. "I . . . I need . . ." Why couldn't he spit the words out?

She nodded. "I know. Right now I need to figure out how to advise my boss in a way that allows him to help one boy without going too far." She froze as if capturing what she'd said. "That's exactly what I need to tell him." Now her smile was radiant, the woman he knew so well. "Thanks, Brandon. See you tomorrow night?"

"Sure."

She hurried to the door.

Her tomato soup remained in its cardboard bowl on the picnic table.

In the next minute the sky opened up, the gray clouds releasing a gully washer of rain that matched his mood.

Something like hope buoyed Caroline as she hurried toward her office. Her stomach grumbled, but she ignored it. She could have creamy tomato soup tomorrow, but today she had to guide her boss away from making a critical misstep.

Please, God, let me find the right words to push the lever that will slow Quentin down long enough to think.

She sank onto her leather chair and woke up her computer. Then she went to work searching for the sanctions the FDA could level against her employer if they failed to follow the rules.

The case of *Regenerative Services LLC v. United States of America* was instructive. If Prae-cursoria's treatment was deemed autologous, with the patient providing and then receiving the stem cells after a manipulation, then the therapy must follow a clinical trial process. Phase 0 was for use on a very small number of patients for low, infrequent doses. That did not sound like the plan for Patrick. The way Quentin had explained it to the Robbinses, he was proposing Phase 1 "light."

She punched the speaker button on her phone and tapped in Anna Johnson's number. It rang through to voicemail and she left a message.

Then she tapped her fingers against her desk while she thought. If Anna didn't return her call, who else could Caroline ask to help her chart a strategy to convince Quentin they needed to slow the train down? The potential trials being developed in this building were worth following every rule right now. They needed the FDA investigators to trust that the company's applications and processes were exemplary. Eventually that would build the goodwill to allow the company to push for leeway.

A deliberate, conservative approach was right and would pay off with what he wanted down the road. That's how the government game was played.

Her phone buzzed and she grabbed it. "Hey, Anna, thanks for calling me back."

"Sure. What can I help with?"

Caroline gave her a quick rundown. "Any ideas on how to get Quentin to follow the process?"

There was a moment of silence. "It's bigger than that."

"What do you mean?"

"It could get him blackballed by the FDA, and he could take some of the researchers with him." The woman sighed. "As brilliant as he is, this is his blind spot. You'll have to be careful, or you'll be shut out."

"Surely he knows breaking the law is hazardous to the future of Praecursoria?"

"Yes . . ."

"But . . ."

"Did you know he was the godfather for Samson Kleme's son, Jordan? That's why Quentin gets myopic about this particular illness. He is committed to saving as many as possible."

"A savior complex."

"Yes." Anna paused before rushing on. "But there are ways to shock him out of it. Unfortunately, Samson Kleme is even more focused on saving every child. He'll be a bigger problem. I'll get back to you with some ideas. Until then, you should talk to Brian Silver."

"They're planning to start Patrick in Phase 0 treatment Monday as soon as I draft the informed consent and get it signed."

"Has he informed the family that the therapy has only been tried on animals in a lab setting?"

"I think so. I'll make it clear in the consent."

"Yes. There always has to be a first human subject, but if the patient doesn't understand that's who they are, the company could face huge liability issues."

"That's the smaller of our issues. The FDA has to be our emphasis." She doodled on the pad of paper on her desk in front of her as her thoughts raced. "Okay. Thanks for getting back to me. Now to confront him."

"You've got this." Anna's voice sounded firm, and Caroline was grateful.

In the short time she'd worked for him, Quentin had proven to be a logical businessman who understood the importance of following the rules. As for Samson, she'd seen how losing his son was his Achilles' heel. Until this morning she hadn't seen how it also impacted Quentin.

She picked up her phone again and dialed his assistant. "Lillian, I need a few minutes with Quentin this afternoon."

"What's this about?"

"This morning's meeting."

"He doesn't have time for that. He gave you marching orders." The way Lillian was ordering her made Caroline's blood boil.

"This isn't negotiable. When can I see him?"

"You can't."

Caroline tilted her head to the side and felt the warrior rising inside her. It didn't happen often, but she did not appreciate being told she couldn't do something. It was the surest way to get her fight on. "I'll be right over."

CHAPTER 8

After the botched lunch with Caroline, Brandon headed to the hospital to spend an hour with Bethany. Anna scanned something on the computer monitor as she stood next to Bethany's bed in the darkened room. He made his steps audible as he entered so he wouldn't startle either one.

"Happy Friday."

Anna glanced at him briefly before looking back to the screen without a word. Hmm. That wasn't like her. He shifted his focus to Bethany and quirked a smile when he saw she was awake.

"How's Princess Bethany today?"

The girl shifted against her pillows, and he stepped forward and propped an extra pillow behind her. She looked pale but seemed in good spirits as the ghost of a smile tilted her lips. "Hello, Mr. Lancaster."

"Remember, you're supposed to call me Brandon. Don't make me feel ancient." He took the chair on the side of the bed opposite Anna. "Read anything good lately?"

She glanced at the pile of books he'd brought her on Wednesday. "I started *Heist Society*." She swallowed. He reached for her mug of water and held it so she could drink from the straw.

"Dr. Johnson said I can start the next part of the treatment tonight."

Brandon startled and met Anna's gaze. "That's good news." He left the *right?* unsaid.

"It is." Anna shoved her hands in her pockets as she watched Bethany. "I got approval from her caseworker yesterday, and Praecursoria did a speed run on the engineering, so we should be good to go later today." Then she glanced at the clock on the wall. "We'll start the infusion in a few hours. Chemotherapy has already suppressed her immune system, which is why you're the only person other than hospital staff allowed in here after last Tuesday."

"Well, that's good news." He turned to Bethany and tried to infuse as much hope as he could muster into his voice. "Are you ready to get better?"

"I'd like that."

"Then we need to get Mr. Brandon out the door so we can finish prepping you." Anna smiled at the girl, but he heard the order in her words.

"I'll check in on you tonight."

"Make it tomorrow. And call first."

He saluted Anna and then headed to his car. An hour later he turned onto the lane that led to Almost Home, his hands tight on the steering wheel. He hated leaving Bethany alone, but other people needed him too.

He shifted his focus to what lay in front of him.

Almost Home was an old property with a house and several buildings that his grandpa had left to him. Each of the fruit trees lining this path was one Brandon had planted. He hadn't realized at the time how the ten-foot saplings would prepare him for the kids he'd envisioned hiking all over the property. The trees had an inner resilience, but they required water, fertilizer, protection from bugs, and tenacious care. The kids needed the same level of care and more.

Kids placed in foster care bore scars. Some wore them on the outside, but all had the marks on their spirits. While he'd thought his social work degree had prepared him, it was his personal experience that connected him on a soul level with his charges.

As he drove toward the cottages that surrounded the larger lodge, he remembered the children who had come and gone, adopted into families. They were wins, kids who integrated with families who wanted to nurture and provide for them. It wasn't easy work, but the lives changed made every moment worth it.

Today, two boys were swinging on the elaborate playground Brandon and some buddies from the Colts had built his first off-season. The guys hadn't fully understood his vision but gave brawn and cash to his efforts. They'd been quick to say it's what teammates did, and he was grateful.

He parked the home's battered pickup in the

space that let him watch Zeke and Evan as they pumped higher and higher. He scanned the area, looking for Jeff.

There. He sat turned away from the picnic table, his elbows planted behind him on the tabletop. Alaina must be inside the cabin they oversaw with their newborn, Ellie. It wasn't unusual for couples to move on once they had a child of their own, but the Stones were committed to foster kids and the work. Brandon had just thought they'd stay committed to Almost Home.

The kind of security they needed was about more than money. It involved knowing the rules wouldn't change again, and that wasn't a promise Brandon could make. At least not the way the laws and regulations stood now.

He picked up his cell phone from the dash and dialed Reid Billings. In addition to being his financial manager, Reid was one of his best friends and had been a ferocious advocate for Brandon as he cleared one hurdle after another. The man had even helped raise funds when the state landed on him with a series of excessive upgrade demands. His gaze slid to the one cabin that still hadn't met the state inspector's exacting standards. Closing that cabin had reduced Almost Home's numbers by six.

Reid answered. "Brandon, what's up?"

"Nothing much."

"Sure." Reid's voice lacked humor. "That's why

you're calling me in the middle of the workday."

The boys had put their elbows in front of the swing chains, preparing to jump off midair. Brandon grimaced and held his breath until they both landed on their feet with laughter.

"Brandon?"

"Sorry about that." He climbed from his truck as he watched the boys approach Jeff for high fives then race back to the still moving swings. "The Stones have an offer from another home. They're inclined to take it." Jeff waved at him but didn't walk over. A bad sign.

There was silence. "They've been with you from the beginning."

"Yep, but the uncertainty with the regulations got to Alaina. The accreditation we just got helps, but the state keeps moving the bar. At the moment it looks like I'll need a full-time therapist—or an active plan to get these kids out of Almost Home into permanent placements if I can't figure out an alternative." He pulled the phone from his ear as Evan prepared to tackle the smaller Zeke. "Watch out, Zeke." He moved the phone back to his mouth. "Sorry about that."

"Did Zeke make it?"

"Based on the laughter as they roll in the grass, he's fine." He leaned back against the truck. "If I shifted the model from the state paying me and then I pay the house parents as my employees, would I have enough to make it?"

"Tell me more."

Brandon explained his basic idea. "So the house parents would have to be individually licensed foster parents. The state would place the kids directly with them, and then the house parents would rent the cottages from me for some negligible fee and pay to use the other facilities, for group meals, that sort of thing."

"I can run some numbers for you. Try to get a feel for how much you'd have to charge."

"It's not about making a profit. Just breaking even works. Especially if my investments keep churning out dividends."

"It's a good idea." The man asked a few more questions. "All right, let me work on some options and get back to you."

"Thanks." He ended the call and tucked the phone in his pocket. Looking into switching the funding model at Almost Home might not be enough to change the Stones' minds in time, but it was the next right step. He'd keep doing that over and over again until he ran out of steps. He was good at that, even when he couldn't pull a big breath like the time Jeff Saturday pile-drived him at a Pro Bowl practice. Man, that had hurt, and it had taken twenty minutes to get his lungs cooperating with his brain again.

"Mr. Brandon, will you catch the football?" Zeke's voice pulled Brandon's attention back to the playground area. Grass stained the boy's sweatshirt along the arm. Alaina would have fun getting that out.

Brandon clapped his hands. "Send it right here."

Zeke's pass wobbled like a lame duck, but Brandon chased throw after throw until his shirt was as grass-stained as Zeke's. Then he picked the boy up instead of the ball and ran to his cottage with the boy bouncing against his shoulder. Evan chased them, and each time he got close, Brandon would sprint ahead just enough.

These boys. They were worth every bit of struggle and creativity it took.

He'd make it work for them. And if he was lucky, he'd find a way to keep the Stones too. Somehow.

Caroline's toes felt pinched in her shoes as she stalked down the hallway. Being short had its hazards, and one for her was the high heels she shoved her feet into each day to get the extra four inches that put her closer to average height. Next to Brandon she still felt like a pixie, but right now she needed to be seen like an avenging Wonder Woman type. The one who demanded the truth and would fight for what was right.

Lillian stood in front of her desk, arms crossed, but if that young twentysomething thought she was going to stop Caroline, she had another thing coming.

"Excuse me, Lillian."

"You can't go in there."

She made a flicking motion with her hand, but Lillian didn't so much as flinch. "Move aside."

"It's your funeral."

Caroline knocked once before opening Quentin's door. She might be small, but she had learned to appear mighty even when she quaked on the inside. She'd ignore the tremors until they disappeared or she forgot about them, a skill she learned in junior high when home life got so bad. She stepped into Quentin's office. "Could we discuss Patrick Robbins?"

The man wasn't behind his desk. As she spun to take in his office, he wasn't sitting on the loveseat or staring out one of his massive windows. He wasn't anywhere.

She spun on her pointy heel and stalked back to Lillian. "Where is he?"

"Out." The girl's hot-pink lips tugged into a smirk that Caroline didn't understand. As far as she knew she hadn't done anything to earn the hostile vibe. She'd probe later, but right now she needed to find her boss. She glanced at the desk, snagging an upside-down look at the old-school paper calendar. Lillian had marked the man out for the rest of the afternoon but with a note about his off-site office.

Lillian stood in the doorway watching her.

"Where's his off-site location?"

"It's a coffee shop down the street." The girl watched her warily as she crossed her arms. "You haven't been here long enough to know how much he hates being bothered there."

"Thanks, but this is important."

"That's what everyone says until they pack their office."

"Which coffee shop?"

"The Sheepdog. He loves the dark roast. Says it powers him through the days."

Caroline had been there a couple of times. It had good coffee, but the real perk was the multitude of little nooks where one could hunker down and work with limited distractions. It was the perfect place for the CEO to slip out and focus.

"Thanks."

Lillian shrugged and Caroline wondered if it indicated a slight thaw. "Just be careful. This is his time to focus."

It took Caroline ten minutes to walk to the coffee shop, and when she entered the cute storefront tucked in a strip mall, she spotted Quentin at a table slid next to the window with a couple she couldn't identify, thanks to the glare. Caroline hesitated inside the front door. She should get something before she rushed his way.

The atmosphere of the small coffee shop was a vibe of books and jazz mixed with the aroma of rich coffee and warm pastries. The tables were dark wood, and the color and grain were mirrored in the exposed beams that crisscrossed the ceiling. It was the kind of spot perfect for spending a Saturday morning nestled at a corner table with a journal and book. An excuse to get out of the house while also spending a bit of time solely for her.

The barista had a bright smile, her hair curling in humid wisps around her face in a way that suggested a long day serving the caffeine-deprived. "What can I prepare for you?"

"A macchiato would be great." The price reflected how great it would be, but this new job gave Caroline more flexibility to enjoy the treat. She added a tip as she signed the receipt, then went to wait for her mug of coffee. Five minutes later she had her order but hesitated to approach Quentin's table. Lillian's warning came to mind. Maybe this wasn't the best idea she'd ever had.

"Ma'am, can I help you with anything?" The bright-faced barista was smiling, but her eyes and forehead crinkled as if she was worried. "The sugar and sweeteners are on the stand over there."

Caroline smiled apologetically as she picked up the mug and saucer. "Thanks."

After she collected a packet of raw sugar and a wooden stirring stick, she scanned the space for an open seat. Many of the tables were filled with one or two people hunched over laptops. It was the office-away-from-the-office for many, the place gig-economy workers went to be productive.

Unfortunately, she hadn't grabbed a file to work on, so she couldn't stall too long without it being obvious she was stalking her boss.

Her phone dinged, and she set the mug on the counter in front of a vacant stool. A glance at her screen showed an email from Justin Grant, a colleague in charge of one of the CAR T-cell trials.

> Heard from my contact at the FDA. Says we're about a week from approval pending answers to a new round of questions headed our way Monday. Something to look forward to.

She keyed a message back.

> Thanks for the heads-up. I'll be ready to hit it hard with you.

A shadow fell over her, and she glanced up to find Quentin standing next to her, a frown marring his face. "Please tell me you didn't follow me here." As she opened her mouth, he held up his hand, stopping her words. "Lillian texted me. Let. It. Go." Each word was a punch.

At that moment Caroline decided to change her approach from antagonist to ally.

"You're right. I know you are." Caroline watched as some of the defensiveness leached from his posture. "While you might not believe this, I'm very aware of how much I have to learn about Praecursoria and all the good you want to do in the world. But I'm also really good at what I do. I know the law and I know how to find answers. There's precedent, Quentin. The law is clear that the kind of therapies you're working on *must* follow protocols. Don't get so excited about helping one terminally sick child that you race ahead of a process that's designed to protect you and this company and all the other terminally sick kids who could benefit down the road." She edged the cup a quarter turn on the saucer, then glanced at him. "Please understand that's all I want. Keep me in the loop. I'll learn fast that way and be better positioned to do my job." The work the company did was important, but maybe she was there to help protect them from a reckless rush to save everyone they could.

After she finished, he waited as if convinced she'd start talking again. "That's it?"

"Yes, sir. It's your company, but I'm here to help you make it stronger if you'll let me."

He seemed to ponder her words before he nodded. "I will, but you need to understand this about me. I'm willing to take some risks to save a life. Someday when you're a parent, you'll understand." He leaned closer. "If you can accept that, we'll be good."

"Yes, sir."

"Good." He glanced back at the table where the couple had turned.

"Is that Mr. and Mrs. Robbins?"

"It is. They'll be by first thing in the morning to get their copy of the informed consent. That way they can have an attorney review it before they sign."

"I'll have it ready for them tonight."

He nodded. "I know how to protect my company too."

As he walked back to his guests, she waved to the barista. "Can I get this in a to-go cup?"

CHAPTER 9
SATURDAY, APRIL 24

Brandon slipped his hand into Caroline's and glanced down at the way their fingers intertwined. Her slim fingers were engulfed by his. He wanted to hold on tightly, amazed that she would choose to be here with him.

"You okay, big guy?" Her face tipped toward him but he couldn't read her eyes thanks to the Jackie O sunglasses she wore. She didn't really need them, not with the dappled sun that shone in spots through the trees lining each side of the trail. He couldn't have ordered better weather for a couple of hours hiking along Seneca Regional Park trails with his girl. She bumped her shoulder into his side. "Huh?"

"Yeah. I'm good." Couldn't be better actually, except . . . There was always a cloud on April 24, but it was a cloud he didn't share with many.

"I almost believe you."

Their arms swung in unison, he trying to keep the pace slow enough that she didn't have to two-step to keep up. If he wanted this relationship between them to develop to forever depths, he had to let Caroline in. But once he started, where could he stop? "Today is my brother's birthday."

Caroline stopped and he turned around on the

pivot of their connected hands. "Brandon, I'm so sorry." She pushed her sunglasses up, and the pity in her eyes . . .

It was why he kept this part of his life securely quarantined, especially from the good parts like Caroline. "I didn't say it so you'd be sorry for me."

Pain flashed through her eyes but didn't disappear. "Where is he? We could call and sing 'Happy Birthday' to him. I don't have the world's best voice, but I make up for it with enthusiasm." She grinned and started singing loudly enough to cause the couple coming toward them to start laughing. "See? Even they're entertained."

The couple clapped softly as they walked by, and Caroline executed a small bow.

His phone buzzed and he pulled it out to check the message. One thing about running Almost Home: he was never off the clock.

"What is it? Do we need to head back?" Caroline started to pivot. "I'm not as fast as you, but we can run, well, jog back to the car."

Thinking about you today, Brandon. We'll find Trevor. Someday he'll walk back into your life with a story you won't believe, and you won't care because he'll be back. Call if you need anything.

Brandon swallowed as he read Anna's text. She might not be his official sibling, but she did her best to keep pulling him into the family circle, especially when others ignored his existence. If they felt guilt for what happened after his mom died, they exhibited hostile indifference.

"Brandon?"

He shook his head then turned his phone so Caroline could read the screen. "It's from Anna."

"I like her."

"Me too. She's the closest thing to a sister I have."

"What happened to Trevor? You never talk about him." Caroline started tugging him toward a large boulder that sat next to the trail. "We can sit here and you can tell me about him."

"I'd rather keep walking if you don't mind." If he was going to share this part of his story, it would be easier if he couldn't see her expressions.

"When our mom died, Trevor was eight to my seventeen. We had different dads, but the state couldn't find either one." He shoved his free hand into his pocket as his shoulders hunched forward. "Somehow I got my caseworker convinced I had a good place to live. I did, too, until the family relocated a month later, but by then she wasn't checking on me. Other kids had more urgent needs. Why focus on me when I'd age out in a year?"

"Oh, Brandon. I'm so sorry."

"Don't be." The words were harsh, and he sighed. "I'm sorry, too, but I made it. I'd crash on couches, kind of like the kid in *The Blind Side*. Only I didn't get adopted."

"What about Anna's family? Why didn't they help you?"

"They were halfway around the world. It wasn't as easy to keep up internationally then as it is now. Amazing how barely a decade can change things." He swiped under his eyes, hoping Caroline missed it, but the tightening of her grip suggested she'd noticed.

"Trevor was initially taken in by some paternal aunt who wouldn't take me because I wasn't a blood relative." One more person who hadn't wanted Brandon. "We couldn't even get visitations scheduled. Then he disappeared."

"No wonder you give Almost Home everything you have."

"I don't want other kids to experience what I did."

His story was one of those tragedies that happened too often. Family too far flung to step in. Agency too overworked. And siblings split, a family destroyed by circumstances. The fact both boys had different fathers and essentially no contact with their paternal families made it easier to get lost.

"Where's Trevor now?"

"I don't know. As soon as I got my first paycheck from the Colts, I hired a private investigator." The first of several. "None of them found Trevor. Even as his brother I couldn't get his records from the state. He's gone." Brandon

107

stopped and Caroline turned toward him. "The crazy thing? I really thought that when I made it to the pros he'd show up. That's what everyone warns you about. The supposed relatives who crawl out of the woodwork looking for handouts. I would have gladly given him anything, only he never came."

The pain in Brandon's voice could be her undoing.

This big teddy bear of a man had experienced the worst of life, yet he still gave freely of himself to those who needed him. She hadn't thought she could love him more than she already did, but her heart was proving her wrong. He was a hero in the way he'd turned his point of greatest pain into a call to help others.

"I think I love you, Brandon Lancaster." Her free hand flew up to cover her mouth. "I didn't mean to say that."

His lips turned into a grin, the one with a bit of Jack Sparrow and Cary Grant mixed in. "Oh, I think you did." He tugged her closer. "Come here, fair lady."

She squealed and tried to tug free. "What are you doing?"

"A woman can't say she loves a man and then walk away."

"She can't? And I didn't." Was it getting hotter in the shade or what? She wanted to fan her face to ease the red that must be gushing into it. "Brandon Lancaster, let me go."

"Not until I get my tribute."

"What's that?" Her voice sounded breathy to her own ears.

"A kiss will do."

She reached up to peck him on the cheek. But he swiveled and their lips connected.

The world stopped, then turned into a kaleidoscope of colors that swirled around them. Two people. Standing on a trail. In a forest of tall trees. The sun shining above them. The hint of forever filling her heart.

Applause and whoops startled her, even as Brandon pressed her closer. He growled, actually growled, and she peeked around him to see a group of college-aged guys grinning at them.

"Way to go, dude."

Brandon stiffened even more. "Nothing to see here, boys."

"Then get a room."

Caroline giggled. "Let's get out of here."

Life felt good and rich right now. She wanted to take a camera and capture it. Why not?

"Hey. Would one of you snap our photo for me?" She pulled out her phone and handed it to the kid in the Georgetown sweatshirt. "Thanks."

She turned to Brandon and grinned at him. Then he surprised her and turned for a kiss that he deepened. The boys started whooping it up again, but she couldn't speak. Didn't want to. Then he eased back.

"Be careful what you ask for, Bragg."

The guy in the sweatshirt laughed as he handed the phone back to her. "Way to go, man."

Brandon's smile for this kid was more like baring his teeth. "Wait until you find a treasure like my girlfriend. She'll be worth it."

The guys chuckled then continued down the path.

Caroline pulled up the pictures and scrolled through several shots. She'd have a closer look later, but she liked what she saw: a man who looked at her with adoration. She could get used to it and wanted to bottle the moment so she could pull it out when she felt alone.

When the nights were dark and she couldn't sleep.

She wanted to remember what it felt like to have his hand covering hers.

Remember the feeling of security and lent strength.

Remember that he found her worth loving.

CHAPTER 10
MONDAY, APRIL 26

First thing Monday morning, Caroline read the informed-consent release form one more time, then printed three copies. The Robbinses would take one with them, but she wanted one for the patient's file and one for hers. A backup just in case.

At nine she walked the halls to Quentin's office.

The door was closed, but when she tapped on it, Quentin told her to enter.

Samson Kleme sat with Michael and Mary Robbins at the round table in the corner of the office. Quentin stood at the small refrigerator collecting bottles of water. "Have the forms?"

"I do." She approached the table and smiled at the Robbinses. "I'll walk through the form with you. I haven't made any changes from the draft you picked up this weekend. Did you review it with an attorney?"

Michael Robbins nodded. "He made time for us Saturday. Told us it looked good." He rubbed his hands down his pant legs as if his palms were slick with sweat. Then he looked at his wife and they seemed to communicate without saying a word. Then he nodded. "We're ready to sign."

Caroline looked at Mary. "Do you agree? You have to each agree that this is best for Patrick and that you are giving informed consent. If you have any concerns, don't sign."

The woman gave a couple of tiny nods like a miniature bobblehead. "I think I'm ready."

"You can't think you are." Caroline glanced at Quentin. "You have to know this is the right thing to do. Once you sign, the court will look only at this."

Samson cleared his throat and made a small "get on with it" motion with his finger.

Caroline licked her lips and forced a smile. She hadn't had butterflies like this since her first telephonic hearing at the court. "All right. Let's go through this paragraph by paragraph. Dr. Kleme is here to answer any medical or study questions you have. I'll try to explain the legal aspects, but if you have any concerns you'll want to consult your attorney again."

And then it was signed, and she prayed that this would be the answer that Patrick needed.

THURSDAY, APRIL 29

It made no sense. Bethany had been running a fever all week—not a good sign for a terminally ill girl with no functioning immune system.

As she stood beside Bethany's bed, watching the small girl sleep, Anna wished Sarah were here. Together they would get to the bottom of this crisis immediately, as they had with a half dozen earlier trials. The mix of lab and application had created a partnership she missed.

She felt the loss of her friend deeply.

The T cells Anna had returned to Bethany came from Bethany's body. If the process of converting her T cells to CAR T cells had been done properly, her body wouldn't reject them. The magic of CAR T-cell therapy was that rejection shouldn't happen. At the same time, a certain amount of rejection meant she had a functioning immune system. The challenge for Anna was detecting whether the balance was right.

The research from similar trials showed rejection *did* happen in a handful of cases. And it seemed to be what was happening in Bethany.

But there was also noise in the data. Numbers in Bethany's lab work that didn't compute.

Anna should set up a meeting with Brian Silver to sort out what she was seeing.

Anna's hand absently trailed to her stomach, where she rubbed the bump that protected the life growing inside.

Maybe Brad had been right. Her late husband had encouraged her to move away from over-seeing trials and focus on building a practice. He'd served in the National Guard and was killed in a training accident, upending her world—especially now that baby Jilly was on the way.

A shift to private practice might be essential if she wanted a more manageable life when Jilly arrived. Her baby was due in two months.

How was it possible her life had changed so much in such a short time?

She missed Brad. So much. The thought of raising their daughter without him was daunting. It wasn't the way this part of their life was supposed to happen. It should have been a partnership. But as with so much of life, the *should* bowed to reality. Their fairy tale had ended abruptly.

She wiped under her eyes and refocused on the monitors.

There was so much work.

Anna moved to the computer. Her fingers started clicking against the keys, forming a search string without conscious thought. There was an explanation for this nonsensical data, and she wanted a working theory before she talked to Brian. If she could figure out what it was, maybe Bethany still had a chance.

FRIDAY, APRIL 30

The tap at her door jolted Caroline from the patent application she'd been reading. Her head tilted and she smiled slightly at the sight of the woman in the doorway. "Anna. Can I help you?"

The doctor smiled as she shoved her hands in

114

her pockets. "I wondered if you had time to grab coffee. I met with Samson and Brian, and we got done early."

"Let me check." Caroline glanced at her calendar, which had a clear slot after a week of meetings. "Spontaneous works. Want me to drive?"

"I'll need to head back to the hospital for evening rounds." The woman smiled and stepped backward into the hall. "Does the Sheepdog work for you? It's a cute coffee shop not far from here."

"I love the coffee there." Caroline stood and collected her purse. "How much time do you have before rounds?"

"A couple hours. Plenty of time to grab a cup and then wind through traffic." She hitched her purse higher on her shoulder. "How's Brandon doing?"

"You've probably seen him since I have." Caroline closed her door firmly, then started down the hallway. They hadn't had more than a couple minutes to chat since the weekend. He was head down working on the new business structure, while she'd spent evenings reading files.

"Only because Bethany is my patient. Otherwise we go months between catching up."

"And you think I'd know?"

"I've noticed the way he looks at you." Her smile held a teasing edge.

Caroline laughed as they walked down the

hallway. "Is this an interrogation, because if it is, I can cut it off. We're still pretty new into our relationship."

The woman chuckled, and it was a pleasant sound, warm and tinged with good humor. "I know Brandon better than that."

"Don't jinx anything for goodness' sake. He's one of my best friends."

"He's good at that."

"What do you mean?"

"He holds people only so close and no closer. I can understand why, but I'm glad I've met the woman who crashed through his barriers."

Caroline swallowed hard as the words ricocheted inside. "I think I would like to be that for him, but we have some living to do first."

"Don't be so sure. My parents were friends through college. When they decided to date, it only took five months for my father to propose."

"Wow. I guess the friendship accelerated the courtship."

"Sure did, and it cemented their love. They've been married thirty-five years."

They sidestepped a clutch of researchers who were huddled around a tablet of some sort. Caroline gestured down a hallway. "I'm parked this way. Meet you there?"

"Sure."

As the doctor continued toward the lobby, Caroline pondered Anna's comments. In some ways it was hard to imagine things between her and Brandon could move that quickly. At the same time, they had the benefit of years of friendship.

When she reached the coffee shop, she placed an order for a basic Americano rather than another macchiato, then found a table tucked in a corner.

"You look serious."

Caroline startled as she looked up into Anna's face. "Sorry about that."

"Everything okay?"

"Yes." The barista called her name, so Caroline pushed to her feet. "Have you already ordered?"

"I did."

Soon they both had steaming mugs, and Caroline doctored her Americano with a packet of raw sugar and dollop of cream. Each mug was the creation of a local artist, giving them a unique and artistic flair.

Anna took a cautious sip of her tea, then set the mug back down on the table. "Thank you for meeting."

"Sure. I'm always up for coffee. You can give me a download on Brandon, right? Something to keep in reserve if I ever need ammunition?"

Anna grimaced and looked everywhere but at Caroline. "We didn't spend much time together as kids thanks to my dad's work with the military. He had us moving all over the world. Mom even lost track of Brandon's mom for a while before she died." She blinked away a flash of sadness. She toyed with the edge of the mug, running a finger along the top, then took another sip. "I've worked to reconnect with him. He's such a good guy, but life hasn't been easy for him." She cleared her throat. "How are you settling in at Praecursoria?"

Caroline accepted the change of topic. "Well, I think. I have to keep reminding myself this is only my second week."

"Is Quentin letting you do your job?"

"He's quick to share his opinions about what he thinks the law should be. Then I remind him what it actually is. We're hitting our stride."

"He needs someone like you."

"Why do you say that?"

The woman smiled as she raised and dropped a shoulder. "He's a force to be reckoned with, so many don't even try. I get the sense you have the backbone to take him on. He won't like it, but he needs you."

"Sounds like you know him well."

"I suppose I do." Her gaze drifted off as her hand went to her swollen stomach and rubbed in a slow circular motion.

"Is everything okay, Anna? I don't know you well, but if there's anything I can do or anything you need, please let me know."

"I'm fine. Just tired." She sighed. "I never imagined raising a child alone." She cleared her throat. "I'll just blame it on the hormones." The woman met Caroline's gaze with an earnest expression in her eyes. "The job'll get better as you make the transition. My meeting left me with more questions than answers. I guess you could say my mind is a jumbled mess right now."

Caroline took a sip of her coffee to create space for Anna to share more if she wanted.

Anna pushed her tea toward the middle of the table. "Did you know Sarah Hill and I worked together?" Anna continued without waiting for an answer. "We interned at Praecursoria, and when I went to medical school, she stayed. She had a brilliant mind. She could sit and imagine what might be possible. Science fiction–type things. When she died, medicine lost a beautiful mind. And I lost a longtime friend." She rubbed her thumbs under her eyes. "In addition to losing my husband, Brad, it's a lot to process."

Caroline reached across the table and touched Anna's arm. "I'm so sorry. You have so much to grieve. What happened to your husband?"

"Killed in a training accident. He was in the reserves, but I expected him to be safe here in the States. Sarah's death seems to have been my tipping point. That combined with this pregnancy is making me crazy emotionally. I'm sorry."

"Please don't apologize."

Anna took a gulp of her tea and grimaced. "Should have sipped. I'm also concerned about

Bethany. I've monitored her closely. I always do when a patient receives an infusion of T cells. I'm still investigating, but I think it means her body doesn't think the CAR T cells are hers. I think her body may be rejecting them."

Caroline pictured the girl and the way Brandon had interacted with her. "Is there anything I can do to help?"

"Listening helps because I don't have Sarah to talk it through. I'm going in circles in my mind." Anna leaned back and her shoulders slumped as if pressed down by a weight. "How is Patient 1?" Caroline's face must have been blank, because Anna's voice became more insistent. "Patrick Robbins."

"Oh, right." Caroline turned her mug another quarter. "I don't know. What y'all do is still far beyond my knowledge. You should ask Samson or Brian since they're overseeing his case." At least she thought that's who would be overseeing his care.

"Sarah was very excited about studying Patrick." Anna glanced away. "She said there was something very special about that boy and was upset that he wasn't added to a trial sooner."

"Added sooner? He felt rushed to me. I didn't realize she worked with him."

Anna shrugged and took a sip of her drink. "I don't know."

Caroline frowned and crossed her arms. "How

did she meet him? She passed away before the Robbins met with Quentin." She shook her head. "No, that's not right. Quentin mentioned he'd come in for preliminary testing a few months ago."

"Exactly."

"Sarah did that?"

"I think she's why Quentin was so confident the study would work for Patrick. She fell in love with him and wanted to help." She rubbed her forehead with one hand as if pushing back a headache. "She said he was the perfect candidate for many reasons."

"We got the approval to begin the trial this morning." It had taken hours, a meeting, and several phone calls over the week to make it happen.

"Good." Anna blew on her mug and took a sip of tea before she continued. "Sarah would be glad."

"Brian Silver seems to be doing a good job continuing her work."

"He's the lead on Trial CAR T 463." She pulled her lower lip between her teeth, worry etched in the sudden lines on her face.

"So what do you want to know, Anna?"

Caroline's question seemed to catch Anna by surprise as she glanced around the coffee shop. "How much do you know about the therapy we're testing?"

"More than what you told me. This treatment with the CAR T cells is the Hail Mary for kids like Bethany who've had failed bone marrow transplants. This is the last-chance treatment for patients because it's at the frontier of research."

"There aren't many studies like this, and they're limited to cancers like ALL."

"You'll have to spell that out for me."

"Acute lymphoblastic leukemia. Cancer of the blood." Anna sighed. "Cases like Bethany's push me to the limits of my knowledge and require us to explore the boundaries of current medicine." A shadow darkened her features as if she was remembering those she hadn't been able to save. "This first month is critical. If she survives that, then she'll have a chance, but this fever lowers her odds dramatically. Something is wrong, but I can't figure out what."

"So why talk to me about it? Why ask about Patrick Robbins?"

"Because you're in Praecursoria, but you're new. And because Patrick was all Sarah wanted to talk about the last time we got together. She said he was going to push the limits of science."

"What does that mean?"

"I don't know." She worried her lower lip between her teeth. "But I have a feeling it has something to do with Bethany fighting the CAR T cells."

The moon glimmered on the retention pond's surface as he walked toward it. His dog, Patches, tugged on the leash, wanting to sniff every blade of grass and squat at each tree, but he needed to keep moving. The gun weighed down his jacket pocket.

It had been easy, too easy really, to make it look like a suicide. He'd shown up unannounced to talk, and she'd foolishly let him in. While she had her back turned, he'd slipped a drug into her drink. Working for a pharmaceutical company had its advantages. Then it was a matter of waiting for the drug to take effect.

She'd tried to call the police, but the gun had stopped her cold.

He'd seen the moment she realized her fate.

Like the coward she was, she stopped fighting and waited.

He'd placed the gun to her head.

Watched the fear flare her nostrils and widen her eyes.

Then he'd laughed, forced her to finish the drugged drink, and waited until she was gone. Then he'd grabbed his gun and left.

No one was saying *suicide,* at least not yet, but one well-placed comment would get the rumor mill operating.

The whole mess could have been avoided.

Sarah could have ensured he was on the

patent application and didn't. Of course when he brought it to her attention and exposed her betrayal, she'd told him it was a mistake, one she'd refused to fix.

Patches pulled against the leash until they reached the edge of the water. A light breeze furled the surface, creating miniature waves that lapped at Patches' paws.

If it had been that easy to take care of one enemy, maybe he should consider the same for Quentin Jackson.

No, that man's death would come in the form of his precious company.

He pulled the gun from his pocket, felt its heft in his palm, then hurled it across the surface as if skipping a rock.

Praecursoria gave the CEO the illusion that he could be a savior to many. In reality Jackson was nothing without him. He was the brains of the operation. It was his mind that found novel solutions for every problem.

All his efforts were for nothing but turning him into a pansy for the rich boy one more time. Forcing him to do Jackson's homework through college hadn't been enough. Jackson kept the facade going even now, years after.

Shame on him for putting himself in a position to give Jackson this kind of power over his future.

Well, it ended now.

He turned and started the walk back to his house. Even if someone found the gun, they wouldn't connect it to him. Not when he lived three subdivisions over. Thanks to his hyperactive dog, he knew the area well enough to use the trails, but not well enough to be recognized.

He hadn't even had to fire the gun.

There was nothing to tie him to the gun or the suicide.

He took a deep breath.

Having control felt good.

By the time he moved a few more pieces on the chessboard, Jackson would be begging him for help. Only this time he would be the one with the influence. All Jackson's money wouldn't matter when he finished with Praecursoria.

Jackson would be blackballed and his company would be in ruins.

CHAPTER 11
FRIDAY, MAY 14

Three weeks passed in a blur as Caroline managed a half dozen patent applications and the legal side of FDA trials, and participated in leadership meetings with Quentin, Samson Kleme, and Hannah Newton, who oversaw HR and other company resources. Caroline was finding a rhythm to her days, as well as a better commute while slowly building friendships at work. When she arrived at her office Friday morning, she paused.

Something felt . . . off.

She slipped behind her desk, and it was too organized. She liked order but had left the prior night in a rush to get to a book club a neighbor had invited her to attend. She'd thrown her calendar and notebook on top of the other items before she grabbed her bag and dashed home.

Now everything was in ordered piles.

Her file with notes on Bethany's trial was stacked in that pile. It had been in her drawer last night.

Someone had been in her office, and it wasn't the cleaning crew. They always left her desk in whatever state of chaos she abandoned it.

She pulled out her phone and snapped a

photo before she sank to her chair. A quick shuffle didn't show anything missing that she remembered. How would she know if anyone had been on her computer? She placed a quick call to the IT guru. "Was there any sort of update that would require someone to be at my computer last night?"

The guy scoffed. "Nope. We push everything out over the server. Anything wrong with your computer?"

"I don't think so but will lct you know. Thanks." She hung up before he could ask more questions.

Maybe she'd left her desk more ordered than she thought. Why would someone dig through her files? She hadn't been at Praecursoria long enough to make enemies. From a corporate espionage perspective, the truly important information was stored in the labs or password-protected servers. She pivoted and scrambled to unlock the drawer where she stored the patent applications. Those draft documents were filled with proprietary scientific content competitors would love to steal. When she thumbed across the tops, they looked undisturbed and in order based on internal filing deadlines. However, that didn't mean someone hadn't been careful. Pulling a couple of files to spot check wouldn't reveal if someone had snapped photos of the scribbled pages. Most of the real work she did in the PDF forms, but she scanned a few files to make sure nothing was in them that could be harmful if stolen.

After confirming there was no obvious intrusion, she leaned back in her desk chair.

Her computer dinged and she woke up the monitor to find an email from Justin Grant. He'd taken to updating her about once a week on the trials involving Bethany Anderson and Patrick Robbins. Other children were also participating, but she'd met Bethany, talked with Patrick's parents, and seen his picture. They were the two who put a human face on the work, and Justin appreciated this. Both were in the critical first month, which had proven pivotal in other trials as to whether the transplant would be effective.

Caroline still struggled to understand how sometimes someone had to get sicker before their body could heal.

It was a truth that felt counterintuitive and wrong.

Yet the scientists insisted it was true. And Anna had backed them up.

She opened the email from Justin.

Patrick's doing AMAZING. The kid's a walking miracle. Looks like Sarah was right all along that his cells might be the new HeLa cells. I'm still skeptical. I mean we've only ever found one HeLa, and scientists have scoured the planet for another since the 1950s. Even tested Henrietta's family to see if it was a family trait or something. But Bethany needs a miracle. That week he's ahead of Bethany is showing. She's a trooper but still one very sick little girl. Her body's so weak. If you're a praying woman, now's a good time.

Caroline locked on to his words about HeLa. There was more to the story, and one way to get it. Take a field trip to the lab.

Ten minutes later Justin walked with her from the lab to the break room. He stretched, twisted, and turned, his lab coat wrapping around his body in a weird dance as if he'd sat trapped in a chair for hours. "Feels good to get out of there for a bit."

She rolled her eyes as she grabbed a mug emblazoned with the company's logo. "It can't be that bad. It's barely nine o'clock."

"For you the day might start at eight, but for those of us in the lab, our hours are controlled by our experiments and work. I've been here since four."

"Can I ask what you meant about Patrick having HeLa cells?"

He glanced around the break room then leaned

close. "His cells seem to have similar properties. They just keep dividing."

"And that makes them special?"

"HeLa double every twenty-four hours. It's this crazy rate of growth that has actually led to them taking over labs. The average red blood cell takes four months to be replaced."

He acted like there was a significance to this quality that she couldn't grasp. "I must be missing something."

"HeLa cells are . . ." Someone walked in and he closed his mouth. "Let's get our coffee."

After they'd each filled a mug, they sat at one of the room's four tables, Justin looking decidedly uncomfortable. "HeLa cells . . ." He shook his head.

Okay, it was time to change the topic. "Can you explain why Bethany isn't improving?"

Justin ran a hand over his bald head and glanced around before he leaned closer. "Remember that a patient has to reach a certain level of toxicity the first month for the therapy to have a chance of success?"

"Sure. But I can't say I understand why."

"Before a patient like Patrick or Bethany gets a CAR T-cell transplant, we use chemotherapy to kill their immune system."

"Yeah, Anna told me that."

"It's critical. The patient has to reach a certain level of crisis to have the chance for all to ultimately go right. We like to see a certain amount of chronic graft-versus-host disease in transplant patients because it means their bodies' immune systems are engaged and fighting back." Justin leaned even closer and tugged on his goatee. "Here's the thing. Bethany's body shouldn't be fighting so hard that she's in graft-versus-host. GVHD is a reaction unique to allogenic transplants."

"The ones where the donor isn't the patient?"

"Correct. Now I've seen case studies where one or two patients had GVHD when mouse cells are the carriers for the patient's T cells. But Bethany's trial is different. The mouse cells are actually hidden inside her cells. Her body *should* be happy with an immune system that's welcoming the CAR T cells with wide-open arms." He took a gulp of his steaming-hot green tea, and Caroline winced.

"So her body's fighting like it's not her cells?"

"Yes. That's what we can't figure out." He fidgeted in his chair like an anxious three-year-old. "I've rechecked the cells we sent over twice. They're hers."

"Maybe she wasn't a good candidate."

"It's possible but doubtful. Dr. Johnson runs her kids through an exhaustive battery of tests before she'll let us do anything." He tapped a finger against the table. "That girl should be sailing through this."

Her heart ached as she pictured the young girl in her hospital room. "There are no guarantees."

"Right, but she shouldn't be this sick with GVHD."

"So what do you do?"

"Keep digging. There's a reason. I'm a scientist, and I'm trained to make hypotheses."

"Do you need anything from me?" She could find a way to elegantly stand for what was right, and not just because Bethany was one of Brandon's kids. Her heart lurched a bit. It had been a good week since she'd seen him, and she missed him. When he'd reached out, she'd made excuses. It was easier that way on days when she worried about the potential effects of Quentin's risky behavior on Brandon's investments. Tonight they were going to watch a movie though. That would be good, just what she needed after the long week.

Justin glanced at a couple of folks who stood by the coffeemaker. "I gotta get back to work."

Caroline startled from her thoughts. "Sure. You okay?"

"Yeah. Just a busy day and there's not much more to say."

"Let me know if you need anything."

He stood and hurriedly left the room without putting his mug in the dishwasher. Caroline grabbed it and took the two mugs to the sink. One of the men watched her openly, so she pasted on a smile and extended her hand. "I'm Caroline Bragg and still relatively new here. Don't think we've met. You are . . ."

The man took her hand and smiled. "Here for the coffee. Then it's back to work."

He elbowed his companion, who chimed in with a "Right."

"Who was that guy you were talking to?" the man asked.

"You work in the labs. I bet you know him." Her fitness watch vibratcd, an alert to move, but the men wouldn't know that. She tugged her hand free and flicked her wrist to glance at the screen. "Gotta take a call." She didn't look back as she left the kitchen. How silly to get worked up because Justin had left abruptly.

She mulled Justin's comments as she walked back to her office. There was much she didn't understand about what they did and why it would work for one child and not for another.

When she reached the hallway near her office, Samson Kleme stood outside the door. He leaned against the wall, his arms crossed. "Morning."

She startled. "Samson. I'm sorry. Did I forget a meeting?"

"Nope." He pushed from the wall. "Do you have a minute?"

She glanced at her watch. "I have a couple minutes."

"This won't take long. I've heard you're asking

a lot of questions." He chuckled, but it wasn't a happy sound. "Anything I can answer for you? Everyone has important work to do, and if I can streamline this for you . . ." He let the sentence dangle at the end.

"I'm still wrapping my head around the science." She forced her posture to relax as she looked up at him. The man had to be six four. At least Brandon's height, but Brandon didn't intimidate her like Samson could. Why was he really here? "Brian and Anna have been a huge help to me, and Justin is helping me track what the studies mean for real kids. I'm starting to grasp the whys behind what we do. Y'all are crazy smart."

His stance relaxed a fraction. "Some, but in different ways."

"You could say that. I can write a mean brief and parse the meaning out of any law. But chemistry is still a mystery to me." She gave him a small shrug. "So what did you need to see me about?"

He studied her and then shook his head as if changing his mind about something. "Wanted to see how you're settling in. Sounds like you're talking to the right people."

She watched him head toward his office, unsure why he'd picked that moment to offer her extra help.

The day passed quickly, and when she left at

the end of the day, the offices were dark and unoccupied as if it were ten at night instead of five. It had been a good week, but it was time to disconnect for a couple of days. Brandon could help with that. Especially if he took her to the Disney movie they'd discussed. In those, everything worked out in the end even if there were hiccups and heartaches along the path to a happily ever after.

Brandon drove to Caroline's apartment building in his beat-up pickup. He'd considered pulling out his Porsche, but it hadn't started. Tonight they would finally get to connect after a long week. She wanted to see one of those Disney movies she could quote pretty much verbatim. Some kind of re-release event. He had agreed to the evening's agenda only because he really wanted the time with her and the chance to forget Bethany's pain and Almost Home's challenges.

Such times were increasingly rare.

Earlier that morning, Zeke had asked when the field trip to the horse farm would start Saturday. As Zeke's little sister, Lexi, had watched, Brandon had to tell him it had been moved again but didn't mention it was because the adult volunteers were suddenly busy. These volunteers were the key to giving the house parents a break, a few hours to run errands or grab a date lunch.

As Zeke's face fell, Brandon wished he could ask those volunteers what was more important than this boy, who'd already been disappointed by too many adults.

Instead, he'd agreed to reschedule. It was a no-win situation. Some kids like Zeke wouldn't believe an excursion was happening until vans pulled into the parking lot. But he also couldn't make it a surprise, because plenty of Almost Home kids only knew surprises to be terrible.

Caroline's Mustang was parked in its slot at her place. The complex looked a little worn down on the outside, with two-story buildings connected in a side step up an incline, but the interior had been updated right before she moved in.

Maybe he should suggest they take her car. She'd get a kick out of it and might even give the keys to him. The engine hummed with a roar that let those in the vicinity know it was ready to run hard and fast.

He climbed from the truck and took the exterior stairs to her second-floor unit. When she'd given up on her prior apartment, she'd insisted she wouldn't live in a ground-floor unit again. Being on second or higher was safer than being close to terra firma, even if that meant hiking up the stairs in her silly heels.

She must have heard his approach, because she stood in her open doorway wearing an adorable pair of black pants that hit around her ankles and a leopard-print blouse with matching shoes. Her dark brown hair hung loose around her shoulders, and she wore makeup but not as much as she wore to work. Everything looked natural except for her lips, which were a captivating shade of chocolate brown, a color he was tempted to taste with a kiss.

He gave himself a mental shake and forced his hands in his jeans pockets so he didn't reach out to tuck a strand of hair behind her ear.

"You okay, big guy?"

"Does that mean we're headed to a Marvel movie?"

She gave him a blank look. "Don't tell me I said something I didn't know I said." Then she grinned as she grabbed a sweater and small purse that matched her pants. "Of course not. We're going to see *Beauty and the Beast* and you will love every moment."

"The cartoon version or the one with the dude from *Downton Abbey*?"

She gave a startled chuckle that ended on a snort. "Seriously? I'm impressed you know there was a dude."

"There's always a dude, and he's typecast as the hideous beast only to reveal his true self in a resurrection from the dead."

She frowned at him and her pert nose wrinkled in that way he liked. "I'm not letting you dis my favorite princess movie. Even if the live action leaves a bit to be desired."

He almost didn't catch the last bit as she mumbled it.

"You're going to owe me after this, Bragg."

"Not a chance. This is payback for all the crazy things you make me do."

"Like what?"

"It'll come to me." She stopped next to his truck. "You going to be a gentleman and let me in?"

"Yes, ma'am, though we could take your Mustang."

"Not tonight. I'm looking forward to being driven around."

He hopped to her side and opened the door with a flourish. "After you. Wait." He reached in and moved the small stack of birthday cards. "I'll get these out of your way."

"Who are those for?"

"Some of my kids. I almost missed their birthdays."

"That's so sweet."

"Not really. I just always wished I had someone to remember mine."

"This is why I love you. Your heart is so big."

"I don't know about that, but tonight your wish is my command."

She rolled her eyes but grinned. "See, this is exactly what I needed."

An hour later as she leaned her head on his shoulder and he slipped his arm around her, he had to agree.

This was exactly what he needed too. For every day of the rest of his life, if he could convince her to let him.

CHAPTER 12
MONDAY, MAY 17

Monday morning Caroline parked her car in Praecursoria's employee lot. The weekend had been wonderful, and she wanted to extend it by enjoying the warmth of the sunshine on her face and the song of returning birds. No, she really wanted to go back to Friday night and being tucked into Brandon's side at the movie and listening to his chest rumble as he hummed along to one of the songs.

That memory put a smile on her lips as she walked the last few feet to the main door. The man wanted her to believe he only tolerated her Disney movies, but that hum revealed his heart. Whether it was watching movies with the kids at Almost Home or with her, he'd become a closet fan. She started humming the tune and had to keep from spinning at the edge of the sidewalk with her arms flung wide like Belle.

A middle-aged man wearing khakis and a button-down shirt held the door, shaking his head with slightly tipped lips.

She grinned at him. "Thanks."

There would be no apologizing or hiding the joy she felt in this moment. She slid through only to stop when she spotted the congregation of employees in the lobby. When everyone was in the building, there were probably a hundred employees, and they all had to be standing in this space.

She glanced at her watch. It was only eight, and she hadn't received any sort of email about an all-staff meeting. What was going on?

Quentin stood on a chair in front of the assembled group wearing a massive grin. He looked like he'd either won the lottery or become a grandparent. Neither was a viable option since you had to play the lottery to win, and older children were a prerequisite for grandchildren. Then he glanced down at someone, and Caroline strained to see around, over, or through, but couldn't. Short-leg syndrome.

She sidled her way around the crowd to the receptionist, who watched from her perch behind the front desk. "Who's he looking at?"

"That young boy who came for treatment a few weeks ago."

"Patrick?"

"Yes, Patrick Robbins."

Had the treatment failed and the release she'd drafted been insufficient? Had the Robbinses brought their young son here to demand something that wasn't possible? No, that couldn't be it, or Quentin wouldn't be holding court with a grin.

"There are whispers he's something of a

miracle child." The receptionist glanced toward the crowd as if she wished she could get closer.

"What do you mean?"

The woman shrugged. "Not certain. I'm left over here without all the details." A light on her phone lit up, and she tapped a button. "Praecursoria. How may I direct your call?"

Caroline wormed her way closer to Quentin. A small cheer rose from those in front, and Caroline stood as high on her tippy toes as she could without toppling forward. The glimpse she caught was stunning. The boy who had looked so close to death weeks earlier had a smile on his face. The transformation might not be complete, but an aura of health seemed to surround him. And his mother. The cautious joy on her face told the story of how far Patrick had come.

Quentin held up his arms. "This result is only because of the vital work you do here each day. Whether you're in the lab looking for new therapies and treatments or helping us navigate the process to get these treatments to the people who need them, you helped Patrick make this amazing turnaround." He glanced at the boy again, then stepped down from the chair. "Each of you is vital to this work. I want you to remember this on the hard days when you wonder if what you do matters. It does."

Everyone applauded again, and the young man shifted uneasily in his wheelchair. His look said he wasn't comfortable being the focus of all that attention. The poor kid probably wanted to be with a friend playing video games of some sort.

Quentin motioned for everyone to quiet down. "Now it's time to get back to work so we can help and find more Patricks."

Find more Patricks? That was an odd way to phrase it.

People seemed reluctant to leave, instead pressing closer to the front as if to see the miracle with their own eyes. Caroline held back. She didn't know what to think, other than to admit Patrick looked like a different young man, a child with a new lease on life.

She should be ecstatic, but instead she felt like Mary Robbins, who stood immediately behind her son with her hands secured to his wheelchair's handles. While she had a smile on her face that communicated hope, it contrasted with the shadows under her eyes. How long and arduous had her journey been to get to this moment? Had hope been beaten out of her each time it raised its head? Was it too scary to risk it again? Whatever the case, Caroline sensed the woman couldn't relax into the promise of the moment.

Caroline closed her eyes and imagined every emotion she'd feel in the same space.

She didn't want to know the pain and strain of caring for a terminally ill child, one who had made a turnaround.

Had Quentin been right? Did the ends justify the means?

Had saving this life been worth risking failure and pushing FDA regs?

As she looked at the young boy in the wheelchair, her heart screamed yes, but her rational mind warned no.

Caroline stayed a few minutes longer, then started toward her office.

Mary Robbins caught her eye. After leaning down to say something to Patrick and then her husband, she wound through the crowd of well-wishers to Caroline. "Thank you."

Caroline blinked. "For what? I'm not the one who dreamed up the treatment that's helping your son."

"But you are part of this." Mary pushed a lock of her bobbed hair behind her ear. "Quentin told me how hard you worked to get that consent form prepared. Crazy start to your first week."

"Just doing my job." And it felt silly in light of what everyone else at Praecursoria did. She gestured to the other employees. "The superheroes are around you."

"And in front of me." Mary's gaze was so intent, Caroline couldn't look away. "I am so grateful." Someone tapped on her arm, and after squeezing Caroline's hand, Mary turned away.

Caroline pondered the emotion the interaction had generated.

She'd been so certain Quentin was wrong and she was right. That the answer was clear-cut. Mary's words felt emblazoned on her heart and mind. She was a part of the magic done here. And it was something she could be proud of.

The preliminary numbers Reid had put together for Brandon swam on the screen. Brandon knew they would make sense to someone who understood accounting. He didn't and wanted to email Reid back that this was exactly why he had a financial manager and a CPA. Instead, he focused on column after column. Then he clicked on the document Reid had sent with the spreadsheet.

After another fifteen minutes spent trying to get it all to make sense, he picked up his phone. "Can you give me the bottom line?"

"Hey to you too." Reid didn't sound amused, and Brandon stiffened.

"You could have let me go to voicemail."

Reid chuckled. "Trying to make the numbers make sense?"

"Yeah."

"Is the spreadsheet open?"

"Yep."

"All right, go to the top row. It names what's in each column."

Brandon growled. "I don't need it that simple."

"Okay. So the first columns explain how much

you pay each set of house parents now, next to a column with how much the state pays on a monthly basis for the kids in each cabin."

"Makes sense."

"The numbers in row forty are the totals of those amounts. You'll see there's a positive balance of roughly $8,000 a month."

"That's what I use to pay for upkeep, group meals, and activities."

"And yourself."

"When there's any left over."

"Which there often isn't."

"That's why I have investment income."

"As long as the economy and those companies thrive, you're good." Reid paused a moment. "See the bottom of the screen? Click on Sheet 2. That's where I've tried to play out what would happen if the funding model flipped."

"Why not just take the $8,000 and divide it by the five cabins?"

"That won't capture everything you need it to. You need to create an emergency fund that's separate from your personal funds."

"Why?"

"You'll be a landlord."

"That's really not any different than now." He'd had to replace a water heater earlier in the week. "But I get your point." He ran a finger along the screen as he tried to find the bottom line. "So does this work? Is there a chance we could try this model and make a bit of money? Enough for a cushion?"

"Like I said, this is a starting point, but yeah, with a bit of creativity and a lot of frugality, it should work." A chime sounded in the background. "Gotta run, Brandon."

"Thanks for the time that went into this."

"My pleasure. I can't foster kids, but I can help with your mission. Those kids need what you're providing."

Brandon hung up and turned from the computer to stare out the window.

In the distance he saw three of the boys playing a game of kickball. They'd arrived in April after their mom OD'd on opioids. She'd be okay, but it would be a long road to get her kids back if she could manage it. The boys were struggling to adjust, and he monitored the game in case things got too intense. It hadn't reached the point that anyone needed to intervene, but he'd seen more than one kid with a bloody nose after a ball was kicked a little too hard and too high.

As he watched them scamper after the ball, Brandon felt the heaviness of the responsibility. He could review the spreadsheet again tonight. Right now he could be out there with the boys. Let them know he saw and valued them.

He wasn't powerless, not like he'd been when he watched his mom lying in that hospital bed, dying. So still and quiet, and there was nothing he could do other than stay out of trouble so she could heal.

But she hadn't.

Afterward he'd drifted from one couch to another while his brother disappeared from family care into foster care. He knew firsthand how important it was to keep siblings together, because he still hadn't found Trevor. At times Brandon wondered if he had died.

He grabbed his sweatshirt and tugged it over his head, then headed outside. As he walked across the field, he marveled he hadn't become a statistic, maybe a high school dropout who couldn't keep a job because he was addicted to substances and had a kid or two of his own.

He'd beaten the odds. He wanted the same for each of the kids entrusted to him.

Brandon thanked God again for saving and protecting him. He often added to it desperate pleas for wisdom and mercy.

"Mr. Brandon." Joey, one of the boys living with the Stones, raced toward Brandon and collided with his hip like a poor tackle. "You gonna play with us?"

"It's why he's got his Colts sweatshirt on." Parker was a couple of years older and liked to pretend he knew more, like all older brothers. "You gonna show us some moves?" He juked back and forth until Brandon picked him up around the waist and hiked him over his shoulder.

"You mean like this?"

The boy bounced on his shoulder, laughing, as Brandon chased the other boys, who kicked the ball back and forth. He let them stay in front of him, then pretended to be worn out and flopped on the grass and set Parker to the side. The boys piled on top of him in a giggling mass.

This moment. These boys. This was why staring at a spreadsheet for hours trying to find a way to make it work mattered.

That evening after dinner, he pulled up the accounting software on his computer again. Then he went to the banking software. His friends had helped him raise a lot of money to supplement what Virginia paid. They had good cash reserves, but not enough to bring in trauma counselors. Even that wouldn't solve the problem, because the kids he served didn't usually need trauma-informed care. Without knowing what the state would do with the final regs and how that would affect their funding going forward, any step was risky. Yet the more he considered it, the more he liked the idea of flipping Almost Home's model on its head.

Reid was right. If he was careful and creative, there'd be enough to keep his rainy-day fund in place. He reached for his phone and dialed Caroline's number because he wanted her take on it. He'd run Reid's numbers by her logical mind.

The call clicked over to voicemail, and he

sighed. He missed his girlfriend and best friend.

Her new job was taking more of her time and energy than when she worked for the judge, and she was more reluctant to talk about her work. He'd thought she was bored, but now he wished that was the case, because he needed her.

The thought made him stop cold.

He couldn't need her.

He needed to be self-sufficient. That was how he survived. On his own. Without relying on others. He wouldn't change now.

It was what his world demanded.

CHAPTER 13
WEDNESDAY, MAY 19

Caroline paused in the sunshine before she stepped into Praecursoria's lobby. On nice days at the courts, she'd throw on her tennis shoes and take lunchtime walks along the National Mall. It had emphasized what an amazing city she had the privilege of working in. These days she rarely felt the kiss of the sun on her skin, and she missed it.

As she walked through the lobby toward the hallway that led to her office, she remembered the space so packed she could hardly move. Ever since Patrick had reappeared Monday looking better, the company had pulsed with an energy that motivated everyone to do more, work longer, and find a way to speed his treatment through trials so that more people could access it and be saved.

The new energy showed even as she walked by the open workspaces. Several people had rearranged their desks into pods where collaboration was easier. Caroline smiled as she took in the activity. This was a dynamic she'd never experienced at the courts. She loved the energy, the sense of purpose, and the knowledge that what she did was a piece of this.

Everyone who worked at Praecursoria had

a role to play. She was realizing hers was as important as any. Without her legal knowledge and direction, the work the others did wouldn't make it through trials and to the marketplace. This was why she was here.

It felt good.

For once, the voices that told her she wasn't good for anything and was one great cosmic mistake disappeared in the light of purpose and challenge.

She was even sleeping better at night. That was a bit of a mystery, but maybe her new sense of purpose carried over to her dreams, silencing the fears that something awful would wake her. As a child, that foreshadowing had been too real. And as an adult it had been hard to shake.

After dropping her bag behind her desk, she settled down to work. When her cell phone vibrated across her desk, she noted Brandon's number and smiled. Before she could take his call, Justin walked in with his team, Lori and a guy she hadn't met, for a meeting regarding filing a patent for another experimental therapy. Timing was critical. Wait too long, and a competitor could beat you to the patent office. Then your only option was to sue and prove it was your idea first. Do it too soon, and time and money could be wasted on a worthless protocol.

The four crowded around the small round table in front of her desk, and Justin made quick introductions. "You've met Lori, and Tod is a colleague who works with us in the lab."

Tod's glasses slid down his nose, and he pushed them up with a finger. "Nice to meet you."

Caroline smiled and leaned forward to shake his hand. "You too." She glanced at Justin. "What do you have for me?"

Justin pulled a file from the bottom of his stack. "I'd like to discuss when we're ready for Phase 2 with Trial CAR T 463."

Caroline had anticipated this. "Not anywhere near close. You don't have results of Phase 1 for us to build the case for moving to a broader Phase 2."

"But we can start compiling the data so the process is faster when we are there."

"Okay." Caroline stood and grabbed a file from her desk drawer.

The next twenty minutes were filled with a technical discussion about supplemental questions that needed to be answered on the Phase 2 application.

She pushed back from the table as she tried to relax her neck. "I'll circulate these notes for input. The file will be thick when we're done."

Lori grimaced. "You should see some of the packets we've responded to in the past."

Justin nodded as he stroked his goatee. "Your attention to detail has helped close some of the more obvious holes." With a red pen he made marks on his copy of the latest iteration. Then he looked at her with steady intensity, the kind she imagined he applied to his research and analysis of data. "I think we should include the information about Patrick."

"What information is that? He's already part of the data pool."

"About what we're seeing with his cells."

"Does it impact this moving to Phase 2?"

"What do you mean?" Tod looked between them.

"Is what you're seeing a result of his participation in the trial? Receiving our therapy?"

"Well, his recovery, sure." Justin pinched the bridge of his nose. "What I meant was the possibility his cells have HeLa-like qualities."

Caroline shook her head. "If it's not related to the treatment Patrick has received from us as part of the trial, I don't want to include it. No need to distract the reviewer from the purpose and focus of the treatment."

"Understood." Justin slid the papers back into the pile then leaned into the table. "Do you understand what a game changer this therapy could be?"

"Yes. Seeing Patrick Monday was an exclamation point on that."

"We want this to give thousands of other very sick kids the same chance."

"Then we're all on the same page."

The trio left, and Caroline returned to her desk where she found a list of unopened emails. She started clicking through and deleting what she could, but she paused when she spotted one from Quentin.

Need you in my office.

When she clicked to open the email, the message was blank.

She hated not knowing why people wanted to see her. Wasn't it common courtesy to indicate the topic? She grabbed her phone and let Lillian know she was on the way. Then she collected her old-fashioned notebook and a pen before grabbing her blazer from the hook on the back of her door. As she stepped through the door, she shuffled her things from hand to hand as she slid her arms into the navy jacket. A moment later a cluster of employees in lab coats strode past her, jostling her into the wall. They didn't notice her as she rubbed her shoulder where it had hit.

She didn't enjoy feeling overlooked. It brought all the memories of growing up with an alcoholic mother racing to the forefront. This time she knew it wasn't personal, but she could still feel the accidental bruise forming.

Lillian wasn't sitting behind her small oak desk when Caroline reached Quentin's suite, so Caroline rapped on the door briskly. When she pushed the cracked door open, Quentin sat with his back to the door, his chair tipped against his desk, his feet propped on the credenza. He appeared deep in thought as he listened to someone on the phone. He mumbled something, then hung up and turned toward her.

"Good. You're here."

"Yes, sir. Had to wrap up a meeting." She tried to stop the apology for working when his email arrived.

"Have a seat."

She floated to the edge of the leather chair, just as her mother had taught her before all those pageants. A lady never plopped; she floated. The lesson was one more reason life had been so confusing. Her mother was all about appearances yet drank herself to sleep more nights than not. Caroline rubbed the thought away. Without the scholarship money pageants had provided, her life would look very different. Still, she tipped her chin and forced herself to wait with a small smile.

Quentin studied Caroline a minute. His white shirt looked like it had lost some of the starch in the heat of the day. Somehow it only added to his aura of intensity. She remained frozen beneath his scrutiny.

"Surely you didn't have me come here to stare at me." She'd hoped her words would surprise him, but they merely amused him.

He barely shifted as he watched her over his fingers. "I'm trying to decide what to do."

"About what?" She poised her pen to take notes, but he shook his head.

"This isn't a take-notes meeting."

She set her pen down and waited.

"Did you know Sarah Hill killed herself?"

"No, sir. I never had the chance to meet her."

"You would have liked her. She was smart, always pushing for more, but I just can't reconcile that she killed herself. Before she died, she came to me, excited about something she was seeing in a potential subject's pretrial workup." He shook his head. "I just don't see how someone that excited would turn around and end her own life."

"Police are certain it was suicide?"

"Seem to be, though it's hard to believe." He sighed and there was a slump to his shoulders that mirrored the echo of grief in his words. "Any chance you know an attorney or officer who can dig a bit?"

"Not really. I'm sorry, but we did civil law at the court."

"Understand." He sighed as his phone rang and he reached for it. "I needed to ask. One more thing." He pulled an envelope from a file. "We received this last week. I want you to handle it. Make it go away."

Caroline took the envelope that was

emblazoned with an attorney's letterhead. "What is it?"

"A demand letter of some sort." He waved a hand as if it was nothing. "It's related to something from Genetics for You."

"The old genetics testing arm?"

"Right. Do an investigation, but don't let it become a distraction."

"When does it need a response?"

"Sometime next month."

"All right."

He didn't seem concerned, so she'd follow his lead. His phone rang again, and he waved her from the room.

Caroline walked to her office and set the envelope in her top drawer before she collected her bag and purse. She'd read it first thing in the morning, but right now she had to scoot. Tonight was dinner with the girls, and she needed it. She glanced at her phone and grimaced as she read the text from Brandon.

Meet me for dinner?

Oh, Brandon. She leaned against her car and typed a quick reply.

Not tonight. Il Porto with gals.

She hit Send and then climbed into her car. The three dots waved on the message, letting her know he was responding. He had so much weighing on him, and she didn't know how to help.

guys meeting for basketball at nine. come watch?

She wrinkled her nose at the thought of spending a Wednesday night in a smelly gym watching guys chase each other up and down the court. Brandon moved with the grace of someone who'd spent years playing defensive back in the National Football League, making him kind of fun to watch.

Let me see when dinner ends.

I bet some of the gals will head this direction.

She smiled. Maybe. Try not to get hurt.

I won't if you're there.

Nice try.

I always try.

And I appreciate that about you, but if I don't quit texting I'll be late for dinner, and that definitely means no basketball.

i'll let you go. see you tonight. He included a thumbs-up emoji.

Crazy man had ignored everything she'd texted, but she couldn't help smiling as she pulled out of the parking lot.

CHAPTER 14

Since she'd made it her job to set up reservations, Caroline always wanted to be the first to arrive for the monthly dinner of her gal pals from law school. Then she could ensure everything was perfect before her friends arrived. It hadn't been too long ago that Hayden had announced her engagement by flashing a beautiful ring around. With the way her friends' lives were developing, she wouldn't be surprised if more announcements like that were on the way.

But for announcements to be made, she had to get there. Most weeks that wasn't a problem.

Tonight she wasn't going to make it there first since traffic from Tysons Corner headed toward the District was clogged. She should have hopped on 495 and skirted the Beltway but had opted for the more direct route. Someday she'd learn the ins and outs of her new commute.

Instead, she tried to be patient while listening to a podcast.

It wasn't working.

Her friends had grounded her through the highs and lows of law school. Now they supported each other through life's merry-go-round experiences. She couldn't imagine doing life without them. Her study group gals were overachievers in poured-out living. Hayden McCarthy used her legal skills to help an immigrant family whose son had been murdered while detained by the government. Then she'd turned that experience into volunteer work with her fiancé's nonprofit, which helped immigrant children adapt to the United States. Emilie Wesley had devoted years of her legal practice to working with domestic violence victims, while Jaime Nichols had tackled her dark past by confronting her abusive uncle in a public forum. Jaime continued to represent criminal defendants because she was committed to the ideal that everyone deserved an adequate defense. With Savannah Daniels, the woman who continued mentoring all four of them after their law school graduation, these women were Caroline's closest friends.

She sighed with relief when Il Porto's white-painted brick building with burgundy shutters finally came into view down King Street. It sat proudly on the corner of a busy intersection that Caroline circled a couple of times while she searched for street parking. Finally she gave up and found a spot in the underground lot near the city building. Once on foot she waited for a car to pass, tires spinning as if the driver had something to prove, before crossing the street.

Her stomach unknotted as she opened the door and the rich aroma of fresh Italian food enveloped her. Tonight she needed the comfort food as much as she needed the time with friends who knew her and loved her still.

A voice at the back of her mind asked how much they really knew, but she ignored it as she passed the hostess stand and her heels echoed against the red tile floor. She was more transparent with them than anyone else in her life, other than Brandon.

There was something about the atmosphere of the restaurant, with its heavy beamed ceiling and textured walls, that made her feel she'd stepped into old-world Italy, and she could take a full breath. It had become a visceral and immediate response after so many years of good, fellowship-filled meals within its walls.

As she crossed the room, Caroline spotted her friends around a cozy table in the corner. That would be their spot as long as they wanted to stay, the waitstaff used to their periodic binges on great Italian food and friendship. She worked her way toward it past tables covered in red-checked or green-checked tablecloths.

As she neared the table, Emilie Wesley smiled small, yet it conveyed her pleasure at seeing Caroline. Hayden Wesley, now related to Emilie through marriage to her cousin Andrew, stood and wrapped Caroline in a firm hug. It was the kind that didn't let go, as if Hayden took seriously the research that everyone needed more twenty-second hugs. Normally Caroline was the one giving the squeezes, but she let herself relax into it.

"Sorry I'm late, y'all. Traffic was, well, traffic."

Hayden laughed. "I think you're entitled to get caught in traffic once in a while." As Hayden pulled back, she eyed Caroline as only a big sister would. "You okay?"

"It's been a week already." She could amend that to *month,* but why muddy the waters of her life?

"Sounds like you have a story to tell." Emilie gestured to the seat across from her. "Sit and grab a piece of bread while we wait for the other two. Then you'll be fortified to explain what you mean."

"It's not quite that easy."

"But it can be." Emilie gestured again, and Caroline took off her trench coat and eased onto the chair. "What's going on?"

"It's probably just the strain of a new job. I like the work, but there's an urgency to it that's new."

Hayden nodded. "That's not unusual with entrepreneurs. It's all scramble to stay ahead of the curve, whether it's funding or product development. They have to have a certain amount of reckless drive or they won't survive."

A commotion at the front grabbed her attention, and she waited for Savannah Daniels and Jaime Nichols to join them. Savannah had been her mentor since the first day of law school orientation. Then Jaime had been the last to join their small study pod at the end of the first semester. They were a big reason Caroline had felt at home at George Mason. While the most private of the group, Jaime had somehow completed it. Thanks to these women, Caroline had thrived. Not bad for the gal who'd practically camped out in the dean's office and begged to be admitted. She'd known the only way she'd survive was to pick her friends carefully. She was grateful God had helped her collect these women.

She thrust off the burden of work to push to her feet and squeal as she welcomed Savannah and Jaime with hugs. She grinned at Jaime. "Do you miss me?" Caroline had camped on Jaime's futon for a few months while her former apartment was being renovated. When the renovations went on for months, she gave up and moved to a new complex.

"You kidding? My apartment is so much bigger without you, though I'm sure you're glad to have your own place again." Jaime grimaced as she eased from Caroline's hug. "Rhett misses you spoiling him. He'd welcome you back in an instant."

"Tell him I miss him too." The feline reflected his owner in so many ways that Caroline had counted it a win when he voluntarily climbed onto her lap one day.

After a round of hugs, the gals settled at the

table and placed crisp white linen napkins in their laps. Savannah smiled like a proud mama, even though she was barely ten years older than Caroline.

The waiter approached the table in his black pants and white shirt covered with a gold and black vest. A few minutes later he left with the standard orders. Capellini primavera for Jaime, lasagna for Hayden, and an uber-healthy salad for Emilie. Savannah ordered the gnocchi, and Caroline randomly selected the alfredo with shrimp. At least one of them had to keep the waiter on his toes.

The moment he walked away, Emilie turned the attention to Caroline. "Tell us what's going on. You're not usually on edge."

That observation testified to how deeply she was feeling the strain at work. "Work is good. Just trying to keep up." She inhaled. "Brandon is a heavy investor in Praecursoria."

Savannah dipped a piece of her bread in the olive oil. "Did you know that when you took the job?"

"No. I don't know if I would have taken the job knowing that."

Jaime smirked. "Of course you would have. You needed work, and this can be intellectually stimulating without the pressure of trials." Leave it to Jaime to see the world in such black-and-white terms.

"True, but it's not that simple now that I know Brandon's a stockholder."

"Yes, it is. There's a right and a wrong." Jaime pulled the bread basket closer. "Stay on the right side and it's easy."

"Says the defense attorney." Caroline blew out a breath. "Sorry. But what's the right side here? It's not like talking about Praecursoria is a violation of attorney-client privilege."

Emilie's words were quiet. "No, it's just insider trading." She'd understand, having an uncle who was a US senator.

"Textbook insider trading is clear. Don't say anything about what's happening inside the company to someone who could use that information to make a profit. But now that I'm in the middle of it, it's murkier."

Hayden swirled her straw through her glass. "It doesn't have to be complicated. You just can't talk about work."

"Which is why I'm dodging Brandon's calls. He's going to notice and get hurt."

"You don't have to stop communicating with him. He's your boyfriend."

Jaime leaned back and crossed her arms. "A boyfriend who's invested a pot of gold in her employer. Yep, you've got a pickle there."

"Definitely not making me feel better, Jaime."

Hayden swallowed a bite of bread. "What's the worst thing that happens?"

166

Caroline wrinkled her nose. "Brandon quits on me because I can't let him into my work."

Emilie shook her head. "That's not going to happen."

"How do you know?"

"Half of his calls with Reid are about you."

Hayden shrugged. "So, the next worst-case scenario?"

"Hayden, why are you pushing me on this?"

"Fears lose their weight when they're brought to the light, so let's get it all out there."

Caroline huffed. "Fine. I'll have to choose between Brandon and my job."

"You'll be out of a job."

The gals laughed but Caroline didn't see the humor. "Why's that funny?"

"Let's put it in context. You have an emergency fund, right?" Hayden arched a brow at her as if there was only one correct answer. "So you can leave in an instant if you had to?"

"Not anymore." When she'd moved to her new complex, the additional parking fees and moving expenses had seriously cut into her savings. Savannah had stayed quiet, but Caroline turned to her. "What should I do?"

"You stand firm and don't tell Brandon anything that could get him in trouble. Gloss over what you do at work. It's not like you told him details when you clerked. Stay vigilant. If you compromise once, it's easier to do it again in the future." Savannah's advice was sound, but Caroline knew it wouldn't be easy.

"I'll do my best." It was all she could do. "It doesn't help that one of our trial participants is one of his foster kids."

Savannah nodded. "That isn't easy, but you have to know who you are and who you want to be. These small decisions add up to who you'll be in the end."

"No pressure." Caroline tried to smile, but couldn't push it to the surface, as she pushed the plate filled with bread crumbs to the side. "I'll figure it out."

"Let's have dinner at your apartment soon." Jaime grinned as Caroline nodded. "It'll give us all a chance to see your new place."

"Sounds good."

"Next week?"

Hayden shook her head. "I'll be out for a conference until Memorial weekend."

"June then. First Friday?"

Everyone agreed and the conversation moved on, but Caroline's mind stayed put. How exactly could she not talk with Brandon about how she spent ten to twelve hours of every day?

When Brandon arrived at the YMCA, the basketball gym was mostly empty but carried the aroma of a million basketball games. On the far court a few men played a pickup game, shoes squeaking against waxed wood, the sound ricocheting off the walls and high ceilings.

Brandon tossed his duffel onto one of the bleachers and sat, then pulled his basketball shoes from the bag. Someone who hadn't lived and slid on the football field might not understand the importance of having the right shoes, but his trunk held shoes of all athletic types ready to be pulled out for the right moment and setting. A hand clapped on his back, and he jerked forward, almost eating his knees. He finished tying his shoe as he wrenched around to scowl at whoever had tried to knock his teeth out.

Reid Billings. Payback for all the times Brandon had done the same thing to his friend. He mock frowned as he finished double-knotting his right shoe, then stood to give his financial adviser a man-hug. "How's my fund looking?"

"It's good. It'll look better when Praecursoria gets product out of trials to market."

"How much longer? I really need the payday."

"That's above my pay grade. My understanding is this can take years."

Brandon rolled his eyes at the idea that the man who was second in command at a private investing firm even had a pay grade. "Can you check for me?"

"Sure. We've got an inside source now."

"Hey." Brandon held up his hands. "I don't want insider trading tips."

Reid frowned as he pulled off his battered GAP sweatshirt, one he must have had since his undergrad days, and then started a ridiculous combination of calisthenics that looked more like Pilates hocus-pocus than real stretches. "It's like I told you when I mentioned the company. These things are a gamble. If they take off, the return can be incredible. But getting to that point is always risky." He studied Brandon with a practiced air. "You seemed okay with the risk then."

"I was. I still am." He stood. "Thanks again for running the numbers for me. It gives me a good idea of what I can do."

"Glad to help. Do you think the house parents will agree to the switch?"

"I hope so." It would be a big switch though. "Right now they're my employees. If we make the move, they'll be the ones answering to the state's caseworkers." He did a few small stretching twists. "If I think the process is fluid, they might too. I just hope they hang in there for the kids. The ironic thing is, Family First increases requirements but doesn't require states to increase funding to cover the costs. That will affect the parents if we switch models." He rubbed his hands over his head quickly a couple times, then pulled his personalized basketball from his duffel. "I may not be the smartest guy here"—Reid had that title until David Evans showed up, if he did—"but I know talking won't change a thing."

"What's your next step?"

"A meeting with the house parents. See if they'll agree. Wish I had a huge slush fund so I could help them out more. No one warned me how fast my football pay could evaporate."

"Hey, I tried."

"Not that old song again. I also want to develop a better system for finding my kids permanent homes. The ultimate goal is still to find them forever homes where they'll be adopted." Brandon palmed the ball and stood as the emotional weight pressed against him. "Let's get some shots in while we wait for the others."

Reid joined him on the court, where Brandon schooled him on all things basketball.

They were in the middle of a game, his shirt covered in sweat, when Caroline arrived. She still wore pants and a jacket that indicated she hadn't made it home. She waved when he caught her eye, then sat on one of the bleachers, her back straight and attention focused on the court.

He jogged up to her at the break and plopped down with a grin. "You came."

"Sure." She wrinkled her nose in that adorable way she had. "And you smell."

He pulled his shirt out and made a show of sniffing. "Just the manly smell of an athlete."

"Eau de stinky."

"You love it."

"I love you. There's a difference."

"Difference without a distinction."

"Says the guy who smells."

"How'd your day end?"

"It was fine." She glanced away before returning her focus to him. What had snagged her attention? "But it's all boring law stuff. Nothing to bother you with."

"I've always enjoyed your stories." While he might not have the law degree, he appreciated the look into her world and days.

"Quit swooning, Lancaster, and get back on the court." Reid's words held a joking quality, but Brandon didn't appreciate the interruption.

"We good?"

She pasted on a smile and it almost reached her eyes. "Absolutely."

"Grab ice cream after?"

"Can't." She glanced at her watch. "In fact, I should go now." She brushed her hands along the outside of her jacket lapels. "I haven't made it home yet. Tomorrow's another early day."

As she pecked him on the cheek, then stood and left, he had the feeling something was off. No idea what, just a sense she was holding back.

CHAPTER 15

It was almost midnight when Brandon returned to Almost Home. The lights in the group homes were out except for one shining from the Stones' suite at the back of their cottage. Little Ellie must be keeping Jeff or Alaina up. He didn't envy them juggling her along with the six children who lived in their cottage. Those kids would someday appreciate the love Alaina liberally poured out on them and the firm hand Jeff kept while also giving them experiences their own parents hadn't.

It took a special heart to lavish a parent's care and concern on children who weren't biologically yours and were entrusted to you only for a season, but Brandon had seen over and over how it had a positive impact on the kids. The Almost Home house parents played a key role in the children's long-term success.

Usually the physical activity of a basketball game released the building pressure on Brandon to comply with the state's yet-to-be-settled requirements. Instead, the pressure had intensified rather than released in spite of almost two hours of shooting up and down the court. Moreover, his knees felt creaky. Proof he needed more nights like this to stay limber.

Brandon frowned as he scanned the parking lot in front of the lodge.

It was unusual that the lights were out.

They were on a timer and should have come on automatically. He pulled into the slot closest to his small apartment inside the lodge. The light over his parking spot had been lit last night. It was bright enough that he'd been grateful for the blackout blinds Caroline had helped him select. They'd spent an entertaining hour discussing why certain curtains would work (solid, plaid, manly) and others wouldn't (lace, frilly, pink). He was ready to live with sunlight streaming unhindered through his windows, but she'd kept it fun.

When he stepped from his car and came around to the front, he saw a pile of shattered glass at his feet.

He bit back a choice word at the idea of how much work it would take to clean that up so kids running around with bare feet didn't end up with shards in their toes. Then he turned on his cell phone's flashlight and pointed it at the lamp. Where the bulb should have been was a ragged edge of glass still attached to the base. Exactly what he needed. An excuse to climb a tall ladder and play with electricity. He'd add it to his list of things to take care of in the morning, along with figuring out which kid decided to throw a rock at the bulb and not tell anyone about the damage.

Right now he needed a shower and sleep.

Tomorrow he'd clean up the glass and then set up a time to meet with his house parents.

Caroline tossed and turned in her bed, the sheets tangling around her knees. Her friends were so sure they knew the right thing for her to do—so easy when you only spoke the words and didn't have to follow up with action. How many times had she done the same to them without realizing it?

Usually she spent the dinners laughing until her sides hurt and tears rolled down her cheeks. Tonight had been different. She didn't like having their attention focused on her. She didn't like being the recipient of advice.

She glanced at her alarm clock again and groaned. Only seven minutes since the last time she looked. The night would last forever at this rate, and she'd be exhausted in the morning. What a great way to go into a workday. She grabbed her phone from its charging pad and pulled up messages. Would Brandon still be awake?

Though she'd made it to the basketball game, she was still reeling from the dinner's pointed advice. She'd felt Brandon's gaze as she escaped their short conversation made awkward by the hangover of her friends' suggestions. For all she knew, he was still at the gym. The games could go until the facility closed.

With a few clicks she texted Brandon.

You up?

She waited, wishing it wasn't so late. She wanted to hear his voice. Have him tell her she was right and okay. That they didn't have to talk about her job to be right and okay. She wanted to share the good the company was doing and talk through what was in the pipeline. Sharing any of that could put him in a difficult position though.

She watched for the little winking balls to let her know he was responding.

Midnight wasn't usually too late, but he'd been as distracted as she was.

She sighed and started texting another message.

Sorry I've been a distracted girlfriend lately. And when you need one. Forgive me?

She set the phone back on the pad. He'd respond when he could, but maybe he was getting the sleep she needed. At least one of them should.

After another fifteen minutes alternating between squeezing her eyes shut and grabbing her phone to check for a response, Caroline thrust her duvet from her body and climbed out of bed. She turned on the hallway light and took the few steps to her kitchen. Then she filled her electric teakettle and with a flick of the switch turned it on. She pulled her tea caddy across the counter and sifted through several tea bags before deciding on a lavender lemon combination. Hopefully it would help soothe her mind into sleep. She needed the rest more than her body

176

acknowledged. She pushed the caddy back in place and then straightened the trivet she'd decorated at a paint-your-own-pottery place.

She grabbed her *Smile, y'all* mug, which Jaime had given her as something of a gag gift while they'd been roommates, and filled it with the boiling water. Caroline had never really excelled at bouncing out of bed with a wide smile. It took a cup of coffee to get her going. Tonight it looked like it would take a mug of tea to calm her thoughts. She carried it to her couch and sank onto the cushions while holding the cup's warmth and inhaling the soothing aroma. While she loved the speed of the kettle, it heated the water too hot to sip.

As she waited, Caroline tried to center her thoughts. She needed to settle in her heart and mind what she was going to do about work. She considered that Savannah was right—she could not continue to live in this tension between who she wanted to be with Brandon and how she was acting right now. She shifted a throw pillow until it fit the small of her back and tucked her feet under her. She wanted to share the excitement and questions about what had happened with Patrick Robbins but couldn't. She needed to do what she was hired to do—provide legal guardrails for the company. The fact that she even had to ask what was right unnerved her.

She knew better.

She did.

Her phone buzzed, and Caroline settled her mug on the edge of the square coffee table before grabbing the device.

The screen was lit with an incoming text, but she sighed when she realized it wasn't from Brandon.

Have something I'd like to discuss. I may be crazy, but you're the best person to evaluate.

The message from Anna didn't make sense.

??? I'm up now if you need to talk. I'm also happy to come to you tomorrow.

Sorry, I didn't expect you to be up. I wouldn't have texted if I'd thought. Can I blame Jilly brain? Now get some sleep.

Seems you need it more.

Tell that to my peanut. There was a pause, then Anna continued. Seriously, get some sleep. You'll have to get some for me too. The girl is tap-dancing inside me.

Some of us wonder if we'll ever experience that sensation, you know.

You will. In the right time with the right man . . .

A minute later the blinking dots reappeared.

On second thought can you meet for lunch tomorrow? I have a window at eleven.

Sure.

After they set the time and place, Caroline opened her Bible app to the Psalms. Reading a few of them might calm her mind enough to rest. She needed that even more now that her thoughts buzzed with what was keeping Anna awake and reaching out.

THURSDAY, MAY 20

Brandon stared at his phone as morning sun streamed through his window. Frodo hopped on the bed and walked from the foot of it up his legs to his chest. Then the cat plopped down and began purring, effectively covering the phone with his furry body. Brandon chuckled as he began rubbing under the cat's chin. "Guess you wanted some attention, huh, boy?"

The cat's eyes closed to slits as he amped up his rumbling purr, then arched his neck to give Brandon better access.

After a minute Frodo stood and stretched each of his legs, one at a time. Then he meowed before jumping off the bed. "All right. I'll get your breakfast in a minute."

He needed to get outside and spend some time with the younger boys who weren't in school, because Thursday was the day he freed the house moms to do whatever they needed or wanted. He'd heard Caroline call it self-care. It was a perfect day to put the boys to work outside, help them learn the value of hard labor and how it made you feel about yourself. He'd begin exploring who'd knocked out the light. Wouldn't be the first time an errant ball had shattered something.

He grabbed his phone and sat on the edge of his double bed reading the text from last night.

Forgive me?

Reading the words burdened his heart. Caroline had done nothing to forgive. Instead, he was the one who made her feel like she'd done something. The text symbolized what felt like a growing distance between them, and he wasn't sure what had started it.

He should reply and say all was good, yet the words would mean little. She already believed something about what was going on, and it wouldn't be easy dislodging that and replacing it with the truth.

This would take some thought. He shoved the phone in his pocket.

He needed to feel strong in one area of his life. Relationship. Work. Somewhere. He hadn't even won the basketball game last night. Sure, it was only a pickup game with friends, but the way they pounded up and down the court until his shirt was soaked with sweat, it always felt like more.

His head dropped back against his headboard with a *thud*. Ouch. He rubbed the back of his head. Maybe he should have bought the fabric-covered one rather than a basic wood frame.

God?

It was the only word he could squeeze out. He hoped God could interpret everything that was packed into that three-letter word.

His thoughts jumbled, so it was time to move. To do something he could control. If only for a minute.

Frodo strutted back to the bed. "Mwrrr."

"Time to feed you." After he took Frodo to the kitchenette area of his apartment and filled the food bowl, he fixed a cup of coffee and sat at the bar.

Then he sent a text to the five sets of house parents, asking for a quick meeting in the early afternoon. When he walked down the stairs from his apartment, carrying his protein shake filled with kale and other green things, Alaina Stone stood in the foyer, her infant daughter strapped to her chest somehow. Four little boys ran in circles around her.

"Hey, Alaina. Hope you didn't wait long."

"Nope." She didn't meet his gaze as she continued to marshal the boys. "I'm not sure why, but these kids have hummingbird energy this morning."

"At least it's a great day to get them outside. Fresh air for a couple hours will wear them out."

"One can hope." She saluted him. "They are yours. And Lexi's having a tea party with Roselyn and her girls. Lexi declared this morning she's had enough of smelly boys and doesn't want to come back until the other girl returns."

Brandon chuckled as he imagined the little girl placing her hands on her hips and stomping her foot. "Tell her I hope Bethany is back soon too."

"I will." She paused at the door. "Jeff and I should be at the meeting." She finally met his gaze. "We never wanted to leave."

"I know. I may have found a way so you won't have to."

Her lips tipped up on one side. "I hope so."

Brandon turned his attention to the boys as the door closed behind her. "Who's ready to have some fun?"

"Me!" The boys yelled over each other at a decibel level that left him wincing.

"All right, you rascally young men. Outside." He opened the door and then let them troop out in front of him.

Ranging in age from a tall five to a chubby eight, the foursome looked like they belonged with Peter Pan's lost boys. Evan's tennis shoes had a hole in the toe. Hadn't Brandon recently replaced them? And Luke's sweatshirt sleeves were an inch too short. Good thing summer was on the way. Brandon ruffled the top of Zeke's tight black curls as he walked out the door.

"To the shed."

Zeke and Luke turned it into a race, which

worked great until Evan stumbled and fell hard on a knee and his lower lip began to tremble. Brandon picked him up, dusted off his knee, then patted him on the back. "You okay?"

The little boy sniffled before nodding. Gabriel watched from a distance. Slightly older than Zeke and Luke at eight, he hadn't joined in the race, instead choosing to lag a couple of steps behind Brandon. "You all right, Gabriel?"

"Sure." The boy didn't meet his gaze, as if his shoelaces were super interesting.

"All right."

A minute later Brandon handed out child-sized rakes and gloves to the boys. Zeke, Evan, and Luke took them and immediately started using the rakes as swords, while Gabriel just looked at his. Then his big blue eyes looked up at Brandon. "Is she coming home, Mr. Brandon?"

"She?" Brandon swallowed hard. "You mean Bethany?"

The boy nodded as he worried his lower lip between his teeth.

"I'm praying she will." He put an arm around the young man. "Do you understand why you can't see her?"

"This isn't the first time." Those few words contained a fountain of knowledge that no eight-year-old boy should carry.

"Youch!" Luke rammed into Zeke and the boys went tumbling. "Say you're sorry."

"For what?" Zeke grappled on top of Luke.

"For hitting Evan."

"It's what swords do." The seven-year-old spoke as if he had years of experience in swordplay.

Brandon separated the two. "All right. Let's get to work." He met Gabriel's gaze. "All right?"

The boy nodded and soon they all called out to each other and vied for his attention as he set them to work along a sidewalk between the playground and two of the cabins. As the time slid by with the sun warming his face, Brandon felt the tightness in his gut loosen even as his shoulders and legs felt the strain of the physical activity. As he helped the boys, he worked on a mental outline of what he wanted to say to his employees.

"Mr. Brandon?" Evan stood in front of him, a pout on his pale face.

"Yep."

"Zeke won't let me pull the weeds."

Zeke, crouching near the pansies and petunias, huffed with seven-year-old wisdom. "Only 'cause he already pulled out two of the tulips." The boy pointed to the evidence along the sidewalk. "I've got to protect Miss Caroline's flowers."

"I didn't mean nothing." Evan's lower lip pushed out even farther.

Brandon crouched in front of him. "When we're done, you and I can cut a bouquet for her."

"Okay." The boy traipsed back to his rake, and Brandon smiled.

It was a brilliant idea because it gave him an excuse to drive into town and see her. He shouldn't need an excuse, but the boys soon had a handful of flowers picked.

"Nice work, men."

They puffed their little chests out.

Evan reluctantly surrendered his crumpled pansies. "Can I come?"

This was a solo assignment. "Not this time, soldier."

"Take a picture?"

"Sure." Brandon ruffled his hair.

Yes, his day was looking up, and it had everything to do with seeing the woman he loved.

CHAPTER 16

Even as she kept an eye on the clock, anticipating her lunch with Anna, Caroline spent the morning working on a patent application. Her gaze would dart to her phone, and when she didn't see a text from Brandon, she would force herself to return to work even as she hoped he wasn't mad. The details required for the patent were enough to make her wish she'd paid more attention in her science classes. Fortunately, Praecursoria kept an expert IP attorney on retainer to complete the nitty-gritty aspects of the application. Her task was to compile the information in as perfect a format as she could to give him a head start, which lowered Praecursoria's overall cost.

At the appointed time, Caroline walked into Dixie's, a new-to-her restaurant several miles from the office. It was located in a strip mall that hid its charming character: a southern barbecue joint with gallons of sweet tea, trays of corn bread, and tubs of coleslaw. An assortment of board games hung on the back wall, and military patches decorated the pillars. This place had a unique personality. After taking in the ambience, she snagged a menu to peruse while waiting for Anna. If the amazing aromas coming from the kitchen were any indication, this would be a great meal. She'd intentionally worn a red blouse since barbecue was on the menu.

As soon as Anna stepped inside, a waiter led them to a table in the corner. After taking their sweet tea orders, he disappeared and Caroline settled against the booth. "How's Bethany doing?"

"She's fighting hard, but her body seems to be fully in graft-versus-host disease. I don't understand why, but when we test her blood, it's showing a different DNA."

"So she got the wrong infusion?"

"Samson and Brian both insist the right cells left Praecursoria." She rubbed her forehead as she frowned. "And Justin verified it too. I know our process at the hospital. A mix-up did not occur there. I'm having the lab run another test to see if their results are off. But her symptoms are classic. You shouldn't have GVHD when you're getting your own cells."

"Why do I sense that's not all that's going on?"

The woman swatted at her spiky blonde hair, but that didn't hide the purple shadows under her eyes. "I think there's something else, but I'm still trying to figure out what." She leaned her elbows on the table and lowered her voice. "Can I hire you as my attorney?"

"Does this involve Praecursoria?"

"Yes."

"Then I'd have a conflict of interest." Concern

pulsed through Caroline. "You should talk to one of my friends from law school. I had dinner with them last night, and they cover the gamut of legal fields. Plaintiff's work, criminal defense, family law."

Anna shook her head. "I don't know if I need an attorney. I really don't know what I need. Maybe nothing." She huffed. "I'm probably imagining things."

"I doubt that." At Anna's raised eyebrows, Caroline hurried on. "You are a smart, professional woman. You wouldn't be doing the kind of work you are if that wasn't true. Something's bothering you, and I'd like to help if I can."

Anna's fingers twisted together on top of the Formica table. "I think the data Praecursoria is working with on the new protocol is wrong. At a minimum it's insufficient."

"What do you mean?" That didn't sound like a legal problem.

The waiter returned with their teas, and Caroline could tell without tasting it this was the kind of sweet tea that could hold a straw upright. The good kind that southern-bred women adored . . . in moderation. She was going to enjoy every sip and then drink nothing but water for the rest of the week while her blood sugar recovered.

After he took their orders and left, Anna twirled her straw between her fingers, not making eye contact. "I'm trying to identify exactly what's wrong, but for lack of a better way to state it, the data looks too perfect." She rubbed her left shoulder as if wanting to release tension. "Something is off."

"How can data be too perfect? Collecting data is the purpose of the trials."

"Yes, but each of our bodies metabolizes substances differently. No two of us are exactly alike. Instead, there will be slight variations. Especially in the early stages of a trial, it's not unusual to find varied responses to the dose and medication. That's why we have Phase 2 trials to dial in what the correct dosage should be for the average patient." She sighed as she traced the edge of the menu.

"Phase 1 only started a month ago. Prior to that, the treatment was only tested on animals. For starters, there's too much human data for such a new trial." She rubbed her forehead as if pushing against a crash of thoughts. "Look, on its own, this is an anomaly and something I'd investigate. But when I add it to what's happened to Bethany, I can't shake the feeling someone is interfering with this study. What I can't figure out is who or why."

"You're still convinced she was given the wrong infusion?"

"It's the only thing that explains how her body is reacting. None of the other patients have GVHD. None of them should. The whole point is that the mouse cells were embedded so recipients' bodies won't realize they're there. With that, there should be no rejection, no part of the patient's body attacking the infused cells."

Caroline didn't know how to help Anna as a scientist, so she slipped into counselor mode. She'd heard Hayden and Emilie talk about the importance of walking clients through what they knew and helping them differentiate that from what they feared. "What got you thinking this direction?"

"Like I said, there are too many data strings. At this stage, there should be fifteen, twenty, at the most thirty people being considered for the study. But I've got a data set of forty-three who've already received the drug. And some of the data looks identical."

Caroline frowned as the significance of the words settled over her. "That can't be right. We had to push to get it approved for Patrick. That was only in April."

"Exactly. So it might be data for a different drug that is further along in the process. I've got a call in to one of my contacts in the research department but haven't heard back. It wouldn't be the first time files got swapped by mistake." Anna paused as she caught sight of the waiter returning with their platters. "He's doing some checking for me, but it still feels like something more is going on."

The waiter set down their meals and the spicy scent of her barbecue beef sandwich elicited a growl from Caroline's stomach. She stabbed her fork into the coleslaw and added a bit of it to the sandwich before setting the top bun back in place. This was going to be a mess. She took a bite to buy a little time as she considered how she could respond. As the meat began to fall off the back of her sandwich, she set it down and took off the top bun. She'd make this an open-faced sandwich to make sure it ended up in her stomach rather than all over her clothes.

After chewing, she focused on Anna. "What do you need from me?"

Anna looked away then squared her shoulders. "Can you see what you can learn about the CAR T 463 study? Confirm there aren't other trials in place? Maybe happening outside the country?"

"There aren't. I was reviewing the trial yesterday to prep for Phase 2." She ran back through the details in her mind. "As far as I could tell, everything is right."

"But that's the problem. You're too new to know what's normal. And I'm on the outside. I have ideas of what's wrong but can't prove it."

Caroline rubbed her temples, confusion pressing in as she tried to determine Anna's core fear. "You're going to have to spell it out for me; otherwise I could look at something and not see what you're seeing. Why does it matter?"

"When this therapy gets through the trial to market, if Phase 2 results are based on bad data, the standard of care that doctors use to treat patients will be wrong. If it's wrong, it could harm or kill our patients."

"So the stakes couldn't be higher."

He swore softly, holding still so the women at the table wouldn't notice him.

Dixie's had been a last-minute choice for lunch, an inspired one it turned out.

How had Johnson figured out what he was doing with the data? She wasn't supposed to have access to it, let alone interpret the data. When she'd interned for the company, she was terrible at data analysis. How had that changed with medical school?

He stayed quiet as he eavesdropped on their conversation. The fact Johnson was talking to the attorney made his gut tighten. Of all people to confide in, why that pipsqueak? She hadn't shown any affinity for the work they were doing with her constant questions and prodding. Instead, she was as prepared to work at the high-tech pharmaceutical company as a third grader, the one who always asked why. She was so out of her league it made him want to laugh.

How did Johnson think the attorney could add anything of value to her concern?

No, the bigger concern was what Johnson thought she'd found. It sounded like a guess.

An intuition.

Some sort of feeling.

What a waste! But as he continued to listen, his contempt turned to concern. He'd forgotten how determined Johnson was. The fact that she'd made it through medical school was one illustration of that nature.

He'd just have to muddy the waters more.

So she was onto the fake data that reflected patients who didn't exist, at least not officially. You wouldn't find a record of them in the Praecursoria files. As long as she didn't figure out what he was doing in Mexico, he'd be fine. It wasn't really illegal. It just hadn't been authorized by the big guy. But especially with the new attorney and her dogmatic insistence they follow the rules, he'd needed a way to get data about dosage and efficacy more quickly. Then he could file his own patent and jump to market in front of Praecursoria. He'd laugh all the way to the bank while Jackson wondered what had happened.

Fortunately, it sounded like Johnson hadn't made the connection to the Robbinses' son. His cells could be a gold mine if they continued to replicate and worked the way he anticipated. The test of those cells in Bethany Anderson would let him know. He'd need to stay close to Johnson.

If she threatened his ability to take down Jackson, she might have to join Sarah.

CHAPTER 17

At one o'clock, Frodo followed Brandon down the stairs from his apartment to the main floor of the lodge. Brandon stopped at the base of the stairs, taking in the wide-open yet homey space. Four of his five sets of house parents were seated on the couches that surrounded the fireplace.

Tables lined one half of the room, with seating capacity for all the children. A couple of times a week he served community meals, partly to give the house parents a break and partly to keep sibling groups connected. Though it wasn't his first choice, sometimes larger family groups had to be split between cabins. Several multicolored couches were arranged around a large fireplace. Stacks of games filled a bookshelf on one side of the fireplace, and on the other were books appropriate for young kids through tweens. A selection of YA books was on another, higher shelf.

Brandon glanced at his watch, then at Jeff. "Do you know where the Lances are?"

"Tom had to run into town but thought he'd be back by now."

Alaina nodded. "Tina has to stay with the kids while they nap. She's got them very much on a schedule."

"Want me to text Tom?" Jeff had his phone pulled out and ready.

"Sure."

Ten minutes later, Tom hurried in. "Sorry about that. The line at the pharmacy took a while."

"No problem." Brandon looked around the small group. "I really appreciate you making time on short notice. As you know, I've been working hard to figure out how Almost Home will navigate the new regulations the state is putting in place thanks to the federal law." His employees nodded.

"It's been a tough time." Jeff glanced around the loose circle. "But we appreciate your leadership."

"Thank you." Brandon looked down at the floor as he gathered his thoughts. He'd wanted to be smooth and polished, but now his outline had fled. "I've been looking at the numbers and I have an idea that should work. It'll take some creativity and flexibility, but in the long run should work well for all of us."

He took the next fifteen minutes to flesh out the idea of the house parents becoming individually licensed foster providers. "That would allow the state to place the kids directly with you and remove a group home from the equation. If we're no longer classified as a group home, we can do a better job of our main mission, which is keeping these sibling groups together."

Jeff studied him. "And what would you do?"

"I would take care of the property, manage group activities, and build community partnerships. The goal would still be to have this be a place for children to come while they're waiting for a permanent placement."

"But we could change that dynamic. If we're foster parents." Tom looked up from his phone where he was typing notes. "If we wanted to, Tina and I could switch to foster-to-adopt."

"I suppose, but you'd pay me rent and for the activities and group functions. If you're fostering to adopt, those things may not matter to you anymore."

"And we'd provide support to each other?"

"Correct. We could work as a team on what that looks like. It could be providing a certain number of group meals a week. Maybe planned time off on rotation. You need to take care of your relationships as couples."

Roselyn had crossed her arms and leaned away from him. The thirtysomething woman glanced at her husband before raising her hand. "Why would we take on the added risk when I can go work somewhere else as an employee?"

Her husband, Scott, nodded. "This upends the system we've had. And we'll be on the clock even more than we are now."

"It does, but I think it will actually allow us to be stronger as a group moving forward. I haven't been able to do as much for you as I'd like when it comes to time off. This could give us the chance to rethink all of that. Traditional foster parents don't get many breaks, but they also don't have as many kids. I think it's something we can find a solution to, but it will take creativity." Brandon glanced at each of the couples. Roselyn and Scott seemed the most resistant, but he couldn't read their minds. "I'd like to have each of you continue with me, but I understand it'll take time to think and pray about it."

The questions and brainstorming flowed for another half hour. When everyone left, he wasn't sure who was on board, but nobody seemed turned off to the idea. "If you could let me know your thoughts in the next two weeks, that would help me out."

Jeff waited until everyone else had left and then approached him. "Alaina and I will definitely be praying, but I wanted you to know that the Arkansas home has come back and asked what it would take to get us there by June 15."

"That's fast."

"It is, but I told you they'd need an answer."

"True." Brandon shoved his hands in his back pockets. "Look, I can't imagine doing this without you."

"We haven't made a decision, but I didn't want you to be surprised later."

"Thanks." What more could he say as he watched his friend walk out the door?

• • •

Later that evening, Caroline pulled into her parking spot a half hour after Brandon expected her home. It had seemed like such a great idea to surprise her with the bouquet the boys picked for her, but now the pansies had wilted despite the wet paper towel he'd wrapped around the stems at Alaina's insistence. It had felt dumb, but she'd insisted it would keep them fresh. Not so much. Would Caroline even want them or toss them straight in the trash? He rubbed the back of his neck as he considered them. Some romantic gesture this was.

Her steps stopped when she spotted his truck, and Brandon sighed. No slinking away now. Maybe he could leave the flowers on the seat, but he'd brought them this far. Might as well offer them to her. She'd appreciate the thought. Right? And the boys would want to see the photo he'd promised.

He stepped down from the pickup and then reached for the pitiful offering.

A smile creased her face and then grew bigger when she noticed the flowers. "Are those for me?"

He nodded as he felt a flush of heat climb his neck. "The boys and I were weeding this morning, and we picked these for you." He thrust them at her and felt like some blushing teenager instead of the tough, strong man he wanted to be.

How did she do that? Pull out the insecurities he'd buried under layers of confidence? And then sweep them away with a smile?

"Was Evan part of this?"

"His pulling tulips instead of weeds might have had something to do with launching the idea." He let a grin grow on his face to match hers as he rubbed the back of his neck and she took the flowers. "It held off a war."

"And I love flowers."

"That's why we planted them." His feet shifted and he forced himself to stand in place. "I gave the boys chores, and the next thing I know Evan's pulling tulips like they're weeds."

"Sounds like a teaching opportunity." She grinned. "Don't forget he's five."

And she remembered the detail. "Yep. When he realized that wasn't how flowers should be picked, he was duly chastised." Brandon nodded at the flowers with a quirky grin. "Those are for you with all the love and admiration of the boys of Almost Home."

"What about the men?" A whisper of pink slipped up her neck.

"Well, Jeff's taken."

"How could I forget that?" She tapped her palm against her forehead. "Thanks for clearing that up for me. I miss those boys." Her gaze met his and sent a pleasant shock through him. "And you."

Brandon glanced up and down the sidewalk.

"Any chance I can come up so we can pretend your neighbors aren't listening to every word?" He chuckled and watched color slowly climb Caroline's neck. She caught him watching and swallowed . . . hard. He wanted to tug her closer, explore what it would be like to touch that place along her jawline, the one teased by a strand of her hair that wouldn't remain stuck behind her ear. His heart took off at the thought.

A harrumph came from somewhere, and his gaze scanned the windows on the ground floor. Yep, there she was. "Hello, Mrs. Haney." He gave a big wave.

The woman waved back but then yelled, "She deserves better flowers than that. Why, my friend Doris's grandson would bring roses. Red ones. The kind that smell good for weeks."

"I'll remember that."

"See that you do. Competition. That's what you need. Men don't treat women like princesses anymore. That's what Caroline is. A princess."

Brandon glanced at Caroline and saw that her shoulders were shaking. "You okay? Choking on something?"

She sputtered. "Is she gone?"

"Not looking out anymore."

"Oh, good." Caroline snorted, then started laughing. "My friend Doris . . ."

"Has a grandson." He chuckled. "I can get you roses."

"I don't want roses. These mean so much more because you and the boys picked these for me." She held them up to her nose and inhaled, never taking her eyes from his. "They might not smell for days, but this is what I want. You're what I want."

"Then why are you pushing me away?"

"I'm not." Caroline swallowed again and looked away, breaking the spell. "I'm not the one who didn't answer a simple text."

"Caroline." He wanted to pull out his phone and show her a text but couldn't. "I dropped the ball. I didn't know what to say. I'm sorry. Forgive me?"

She studied him a moment, then nodded. "Come on up." The flowers flopped in her grip as if the stems were made of bendy straws. "How long can you stay?"

Her soft southern accent drew him closer. Time might as well stop when he was with her, because there was nowhere else he wanted to be. No matter how much he needed to do, he wasn't leaving. "Order takeout?"

"Not yet."

"Then let's get Indian. The more curry the better."

Her nose scrunched up in that adorable way it did when she didn't want to say yes but would to keep the peace.

"Just kidding. Let's make it Chinese."

"Sold."

That old country song his mom liked popped into his head. The one about the county auctioneer and someone's heart. Because in that moment it felt like his heart had opened and been sold all in one moment.

She looked unchanged even as he felt his world shift.

CHAPTER 18
SATURDAY, MAY 29

Another week evaporated and it was the weekend again. Saturdays by design should be a day to relax. A day Caroline could sleep in and then wander without agenda through the moments until a peaceful evening was complete.

Too bad real life often didn't match that ideal.

But maybe she could change that. Midmorning Caroline grabbed a book she'd been meaning to read and pulled a can of sparkling water from the fridge. Then she pulled on a light jacket and headed out for a quick walk to the neighborhood park. The temperature might edge up to the high seventies before the day ended, but in the shade it could still feel cool.

When she reached the park, she noticed a high-energy cluster of adults and kids around a pop-up canopy tent. A man stood to the side of the tent manning a grill while other adults set up tables with chairs under the covering. On the side opposite the grill, someone had set out some yard games and a bucket of chalk. One little girl sat on the sidewalk, decorating it with the chalk, making rainbow splashes of powdered color with an intensity that might have rivaled Michelangelo working on the Sistine Chapel.

Caroline watched the activity for a few minutes. Several adults were actively engaged with the kids, and it looked like some sort of mentoring event. Could it be tied to Big Brothers Big Sisters? She ambled closer and smiled as she saw a banner flapping from the edge of the canvas cover. *All God's Children.*

One of the adults noticed Caroline and stepped closer. "Can I help you?"

"I was curious about all the fun happening here." A little boy dashed by, laughter lighting his face as he was chased by a girl of similar age. "The joy is contagious."

"It is. My name is Nicole Walker."

"Caroline Bragg."

"Nice to meet you, Caroline." The woman smiled as she gestured to the gathering. "We're a ministry of a local church. Since the weather's so nice we abandoned the building and brought the kids here, rather than sequester them inside. These kiddos need sunshine, exercise, and love."

Caroline studied the mishmash of kids. "Are they at-risk?"

"Only in the sense they're part of the foster care system. We give their foster families a four-hour break every other weekend. It's a chance to get shopping or appointments completed that can't be done otherwise."

A game of tag erupted around the slide and swings on the small playground. Caroline froze as she noted all the ways someone could get hurt and launch a lawsuit. "Are they okay?"

The woman nodded sagely. "I'm guessing you don't have kids yet."

"Or a husband." Caroline gave a little shrug but continued to watch the kids racing around. "What you're doing here is beautiful."

"Just being the hands and feet of Jesus in a small way."

"But it's a big way to them." Caroline gestured to the little girl who was still coloring, now with her tongue between her teeth. "My friend runs a group home, and he's trying to ensure that his house parents get the time off they need to fill up before they pour into the kids."

The woman studied her with a curious expression. "Who is your friend?"

"Brandon Lancaster. He runs Almost Home."

"The football player?"

"Well, he was."

"He'll always be one to the folks who remember his playing. That boy could run."

Something about the way the woman said it made Caroline giggle. "He's not exactly a boy. In fact, he's pretty massive, in a really fit teddy-bear sort of way."

The woman shook her head. "I can imagine. Excuse me a moment." The woman stepped under the tent and squatted next to a little boy whose lower lip was stuck out so far a bird could have perched on it. She said something to him and then tickled his tummy, and a moment later he ran over to one of the balls and started throwing it to an older man who wore a Crocodile Dundee–style hat to shade the sun. Nicole returned to her side. "Davon is having one of his hard days. Needs a bit more attention." She turned back to Caroline. "Wonder if your friend would like us to come alongside his home?"

"I bet he would." Caroline could feel hope burbling inside her. "The encouragement would be so wonderful for him."

Nicole pulled her phone from her pocket and slid a business card from its case. "Have him call me if he's interested in learning more."

Caroline took the card, smiling so big her cheeks stretched. "Thank you. I'll give him your information." Forgetting her book, Caroline turned back the way she'd come. On the walk back to her apartment, she pulled out her phone and called Brandon.

"Hey."

"You won't believe who I just met."

He laughed. "Whoever it was, sounds like they were interesting."

"So I walked to the neighborhood park where a church was providing activities for kids in foster care. I was talking with a woman who helps who was interested in learning more about Almost

Home." Caroline didn't mention the woman was a fan. "I got her card."

"Great. Can you text it to me?"

"Sure."

"Depending on what they do, this could be a help here. I'll call her later."

A minute later she slid her phone back in her pocket and climbed the stairs to her apartment. She went inside and was putting her jacket on its hook when a series of vibrations from her fitness tracker alerted her to multiple text messages. She frowned. Her phone was usually silent as a graveyard unless Brandon or one of the girls texted or called. When she glanced at it, she sighed. It was a series of calendar alerts reminding her she was supposed to take a snack to her Sunday school class tomorrow. She looked in her small pantry, which was bare other than a box of brownie mix. She usually loved cooking, but it seemed pointless when her hours at work were longer, so she'd let her stores diminish. What could she do to spice up the sweet treat?

This last weekend of May was a holiday for most folks. He'd come to town to get items for Almost Home's annual cookout celebration. Many would abandon the city for Memorial Day, but Brandon preferred to stay with the kids. Often his buddies and their gals helped with games, food, and even fireworks. It made the day special while allowing the house parents to slip away.

This year Reid and his fiancée, Emilie Wesley, were handling food. David and Ciara Evans were organizing outdoor games, since that was something they could manage with an active toddler. Caroline would be around too.

He found himself pulling into the hospital parking lot rather than beelining for home. He had a book for Bethany and wanted an update from Anna.

When he reached her room, Bethany was watching some Disney Channel show. She smiled when she saw him. "Mr. Brandon."

"Hey, princess. How are you doing today?"

"I'm okay." She glanced around the small room. "Did you bring Gabriel?"

"No, he won't be able to visit while you're here, but I know he misses you. He looks a little lost without you."

"Tell him I miss him too." She sighed, then forced a small smile. "The nurse said I could go to the playroom later if I feel up to it."

"Want me to take you?"

"That's okay. I think there's stuff they have to do first." She glanced at the table next to her bed. "I finished the books you brought me."

"Then it's a good thing I have another one for you." He pulled the slim bookstore bag from the oversized pocket of his cargo pants. "The saleswoman told me you'd love it."

She smiled at the cover, where a girl rode a Pegasus. "That would be fun."

"Yeah. It would." To be able to get on a big winged horse and take off sounded amazing, but definitely fiction.

They chatted for a while until her eyelids got heavy.

"I'll come back tomorrow."

"Okay." The word was quiet, and then she was out.

As he stepped from the room, Anna walked down the hallway.

"Good, you're still here." She hurried to a stop in front of him. "Follow me." After she led him to an alcove, she shoved her hands in her lab jacket pockets. "How long were you with her?"

"Not more than twenty minutes. She seemed worn out."

"Her body is fighting so hard, but it's fighting itself. We're getting ready to try a new round of treatment to see if we can get the fever down."

"She mentioned going to a playroom."

Anna's smile was sad. "That won't happen today. She needs to be fever-free first."

"Anything I can do?"

"Just keep checking on her."

"Should I start preparing to bring her home?"

"Not yet. We could still be weeks away from that. We'll have to see if her body rallies."

"And you're sure I can't bring her brother by, even to wave from the doorway?"

"Her system is too compromised right now." She rubbed her stomach. "I know it would do her good to see him, but it's too dangerous."

Brandon kneaded the back of his neck. "I know you're right, but it's hard to see Gabriel like this. Poor kid doesn't know what's going on, other than he misses his sister and has been down this road before."

"Cancer is hard on the siblings in a different way." Anna glanced toward Bethany's room. "We're doing our best."

"I know." Brandon gave her a side hug and was surprised when she leaned closer. "It's going to be okay, Anna."

"There are no guarantees."

"That's called life." He gave her another squeeze and stepped back. "You coming to the cookout Monday?"

She shook her head. "I think I'll stay close to home. The time off my feet will be good."

He nodded. "All right. Let me know if anything changes or she needs me."

As he left the hospital, he had to acknowledge that despite all of Anna's efforts, the girl was slipping away and he couldn't protect her.

He needed Caroline.

On a whim, he stopped and picked up bagels and coffee, then drove to her place.

Caroline Bragg drew out the best in him and made him feel complete. When she wasn't around, it was like the best part of him was absent. He wanted to protect her, but it was different from the protectiveness he felt toward anyone else. With Caroline it was because she was a part of him. He felt empty without her, like something was missing.

It had snuck up on him. Then they'd decided to date. Everything was going great. Then her job changed, and their equilibrium did too.

He turned off the Fairfax County Parkway from Centreville and onto Telegraph Road. Traffic was cooperating, and he made good time as he steered along familiar roads until he finally arrived at her complex.

Now that he was here, he was frozen in his seat.

This wasn't like him. He was the defensive back who blew by people toward his goal.

But Caroline was the prize he couldn't figure out how to attain.

His phone buzzed, and he glanced at the screen. You stalking me? ☺

The smiley face at the end of the sentence softened the words and brought an answering smile to his face. This was why they could be such good friends. She got him enough to poke at him when he needed it. Like this moment when he needed the prodding to man up, climb from his pickup, and get up the stairs to her apartment.

Got time for me to come up for a bit?

Sure. It's a quiet day.

He grabbed the bagels and coffee and left his truck, hitting the lock button after he slammed the door.

Here went nothing . . . and everything.

CHAPTER 19

Caroline glanced out the window through a slit in her cream and gray curtains and watched Brandon slap a ball cap on his head. Looked like it was time for a haircut as dark hair curled beneath it. What would it feel like to run her fingers through it?

She tried to clear the thought.

Her attention was captured by the way he moved up the sidewalk with an easy gait that hinted at his athletic past. Despite his size, he didn't plod, but almost danced on the balls of his feet. What would it be like to go dancing and be held within the circle of his arms?

She had to smile as she noted the bag of bagels that dangled from his grip. What had prompted him to come by with those? The tulips and pansies he'd brought Thursday wouldn't last much longer but reminded her of his thoughtfulness. Had he ever brought his mom gifts like flowers? He didn't talk about her, but watching him approach her stairs with a slight hesitance made her want to know. What parts of him did he barricade to protect himself?

The scent of freshly baked brownies lingered in the air as Brandon mounted the stairs. She stepped back from the window and glanced around her apartment. One of the pillows on her poppy-covered loveseat was out of place, so she quickly righted it and straightened the magazine and her Bible on the coffee table. The sleek glass top resting on the metal legs made the small room seem larger while providing a place to set her coffee mug when reading or watching something on TV. When was the last time she'd turned it on?

After Brandon's quick rap, she opened the door. Her heart clenched when she noted the shadows under his eyes and slumped shoulders. "I didn't expect to see you today."

He shrugged then held up the bagels and coffee. "I checked on Bethany." He exhaled.

She nodded and pulled the door wider. "Come in. How is she?"

"Not good." He tried to smile, but it didn't work. She knew him too well. "Anna seems really concerned. Said I wouldn't be taking her to Almost Home for weeks." His shoulders sagged further. "I thought this trial would help, but it isn't. She seems to be sicker. And her little brother keeps looking for her. He's a smart kid. He knows enough to be worried she won't come back. Then who will he have?"

"How can I help?"

"There's nothing we can do other than pray. And share a bagel with me." He handed the bag to her. "Tell me everything will be okay."

"Oh, Brandon." She studied his face, looking

for the right words to bring him peace. She reached up and brushed one of those curls that teased the back of his neck. "I wish I could."

"I know." He closed his eyes as he leaned toward her touch. When he opened them, she could feel a shift. "What's that I smell? Brownies?" His grin was that of a little boy wheedling a treat.

"You guessed it. They're still hot."

He gave a contented groan and rubbed his belly. "That's why I'm here. Your brownies called to me."

"From the hospital?" She pulled a knife from the block next to the stove and sliced a large section for him and a sliver for herself. She could always make another batch for her Sunday school class, after a trip to the store. She set the large brownie on a napkin and handed it to him. You'll have to tell me if you like them."

He set the bagels and coffee on the counter and then eyed the brownie she handed him. "What did you add this time?"

"Andes mint pieces."

"Sounds okay." He took a nibble, which looked ridiculous for a guy who could usually consume a corner in three bites. Then his eyes widened, followed by a Brandon-sized bite. "Wow. These are delicious."

"Thank you." She wagged a finger at him. "Don't tell anyone. It's my new secret ingredient."

"Mum's the word." He licked his fingers, then eyed the pan. "I don't suppose I could have another."

"Only if you give me your secret for not blowing up like a blimp." Her gaze landed on the bag. "What about those?"

"We can eat bagels anytime. Hot brownies are rare." He patted his muscular stomach. "My secret is simple. Hours of exercise. That's why I keep all those kids around. Chasing them and keeping them busy is good for my manly figure." He waggled his eyebrows at her wolfishly. "Glad you like it."

She nodded to the fridge. "Want to grab the milk? Brownies are so much better with it."

They worked side by side, and even in the tight confines of her kitchen, it was easy. She liked having him there. She wished she could bottle the security of his presence for all the times he was away. Especially those middle-of-the night times when she struggled to sleep as she heard creaks and moans around the apartment. "I was thinking."

He paused in the act of returning the milk to the refrigerator. "About?"

"The woman at the park. All God's Children."

"I'll call her next week. First thing Tuesday after the long weekend."

"Why not invite her to the cookout?" She pulled the woman's card from her back pocket and handed it to Brandon. "She could be a great resource for you. Maybe do something similar at Almost Home."

"Pushing, Bragg." Still, he tapped the card against his other hand. "But it has merit." He pulled out his phone. "As we move to change the way Almost Home operates, the house parents will need time to relax so they can give their best to the kids. It would be great to have a church come alongside us."

Caroline picked up the plate of brownies. "Shall we pick a movie?"

Brandon nodded but tapped away on his phone for a minute. "Just sent her a message. We'll see if she's free Monday."

Ten minutes later, after agreeing on a movie, they settled on the couch with the brownies resting on the coffee table. She was relieved to have the movie to fill the space between them. It was hard not to talk freely about what was happening at work. And that change made their relationship feel tenuous in a way it hadn't just a few months ago. Could she settle into this relationship, or would he disappear the moment she did?

Caroline had been a little distant, and Brandon wasn't sure what to make of that. They were always on the same page. Well, other than the time he'd insisted they wear matching ugly

Christmas sweaters to a party. He'd even bought hers, and she still showed up looking like an elegant yet petite sophisticate with a penguin sweater and black skinny jeans and boots. He'd looked like a doofus, which would have been okay if they'd looked ridiculous together.

Almost Home gave them a shared purpose, though, and was one of the reasons he'd taken the risk of asking her to be more than friends. He hadn't thought it would be all smooth sailing. Relationships didn't work that way, but it seemed unnecessarily rocky at the moment.

She turned toward him on the couch, and he paused the movie as the credits prepared to roll.

"Why'd you stop it?"

"Caroline, is there a reason you don't tell me about your work anymore? Since you started at Praecursoria, there's this growing gulf between us."

"No, there isn't." The words were right, but she didn't meet his gaze. Instead, she snuggled into his side.

"What's changed?"

"Nothing. I'm as committed to us as ever."

"But that means sharing our lives. All of it. The good and the bad."

"I just have to be careful, Brandon." She sighed but still wouldn't look at him. "You're an investor."

"You keep saying that like it's a problem."

"It doesn't need to be, but it does mean I need to be careful about what I say." *And don't say* was left unsaid.

"So you're shutting me out of your life to protect me?" That was crazy talk.

"Yes."

He shook his head. "That doesn't make sense."

"But it's true. I want to make sure I don't do anything that puts either of us on the wrong side of the law."

"You wouldn't." He'd never been surer of anything.

"I wouldn't intentionally. But it's too risky. Insider trading is real."

"Okay." He drew out the word, and then his phone vibrated, and he glanced at his watch. A text from Nicole Walker. She'd be delighted to stop by Almost Home for the Memorial Day festivities. What could she bring other than a few more people?

Caroline glanced at him. "Good news?"

"What?"

"The message?" She gestured toward his wrist.

"Looks like your new friend is around this weekend and will join us Monday."

Caroline's grin was immediate and joy-filled. "That's wonderful!"

"It is. One of the house parents raised a concern about getting any respite care if the model switches. I really need help in that area because

I can't do it for everyone each week." For the new structure to work at Almost Home in a way that stayed child focused, he needed to find the right sort of relief and future homes for the kids. Maybe Nicole's group could help provide that support.

He'd find out Monday.

Brandon settled against the loveseat and stretched his arm across the top of the cushions, letting his fingers trail over her shoulder, and felt her shiver. He couldn't hide the grin that tugged his mouth. She might want to act like she was unaffected by him, but her body wasn't playing along.

While that was gratifying, he wanted her heart.

He wanted to know they were on the same page and pursuing the same thing. Forever sounded about right, though she would be crazy to consider it with a man who spent his time trying to keep a nonprofit foster home afloat.

She deserved someone who could give her the moon.

CHAPTER 20

Saturday night after Brandon had gone home and she'd run to the grocery store, Caroline settled at her laptop while the new batch of brownies baked. Anna's concerns about the CAR T 463 data nagged at Caroline. The silence in her apartment pressed against her, so she might as well work.

Remotely logging in to Praecursoria would allow her to review Anna's data. If she waited until Tuesday, the day could slip away without the chance to poke around.

A little time tonight would enable her to determine if there was a way she could dig deeper from home. It only took a couple of minutes to log in remotely, but then she hit a roadblock. The CAR T 463 folders were password protected. Her password should get her into any section of the company's site, but she was locked out. She frowned and tried again.

Still nothing.

Her cell phone rang and she picked it up. "Caroline."

"Miss Bragg, this is James Reynolds with IT. Can you tell me why you're trying to log in to the CAR T 463 trial data files?" The voice was deep and gruff.

"I'm sorry, who are you again?" And why

would he call so quickly on a holiday weekend?

"James Reynolds with IT."

"And you're calling me on a holiday weekend because I logged in remotely?"

"No, ma'am. Access to those files is limited per company protocol."

"I'm the corporate attorney. I should have access to everything."

"I'm sorry, ma'am, but you don't have access to those."

"Why not?"

"Because the CEO and chief science officer haven't authorized you."

That would need to change. "I need the access now."

"I can't help you with that. You'll need to take it up with one of them on Tuesday. Until then, if you try to log in again, your access to the site will be blocked."

"To that part of the website."

"No, ma'am. To the whole site."

"The whole site? You have to be kidding. I need to do other work from here."

"No, ma'am, I am not kidding. Log in again and you'll be blocked."

"If you ma'am me again, I might scream. I'm going to take a crazy guess we're the same age." She blew out slowly as she tried to keep from losing her temper. "Do you call everyone who accesses the servers remotely?"

"No, ma'am." He cleared his throat. "Sorry, ma'am. Only those who access unauthorized areas. Good night."

He hung up, and she stared at her phone. What company put such tight controls on their data that even high-level employees couldn't access it? It seemed like overkill, but what could she do on a long weekend? Work on something else.

First she drafted an email to Quentin and Samson asking why she didn't have access. Then she turned to the letter Quentin had tossed her way a week ago.

She checked the attorney logo on the envelope. Baird & Associates. Not a firm she was familiar with from her days clerking, but that wasn't unusual. The DC area was overrun with people pursuing legal careers.

Her quick scan came to an abrupt stop after the first paragraph.

I represent two generations of women whose health was irreversibly damaged by the test results and recommendations received from Praecursoria beginning with a letter dated December 3, 2015, to Helen Noreen Smith and followed by a letter dated February 5, 2016, to her daughter Avery Smith Blake. Lauren Smith Hahn received her test results and recommendations in a letter dated

March 16, 2016. Copies of the letters are attached.

Caroline quickly flipped to the back and found each letter, essentially a Praecursoria boilerplate stating that each woman's genetic test had shown she carried the breast cancer gene and an 84 to 90 percent probability that each would have aggressive breast cancer at some point in her life. It further recommended that each woman consult with her doctor and consider a course of treatment, including double mastectomies, to avoid cancer.

She didn't need to read further to know that was the course the women had chosen. What she didn't know is why that had led to a letter to the company a little over five years later.

The letter continued for a couple of pages. After she finished, she picked up the phone. The thrust of the letter was that the women had suffered complications and everything that a mastectomy, and in Lauren's case a hysterectomy, entailed. Then they had received letters in December of last year informing them that based on new research their risk of cancer was indeterminate. The news had devastated the women, especially Lauren, who had hoped to have more children prior to her surgery.

In their letter they claimed that Praecursoria and its employees had been negligent if not guilty of malpractice while also inflicting intentional emotional distress on the family. The attorney closed with a settlement demand of $500,000 per woman. Steep, but not outlandish. It at least gave her a starting point to negotiate down if their claims were validated. The last thing the company needed was a class-action lawsuit that could threaten its existence. Before she could decide best strategies, though, there was still much to learn about the background of the claims.

Her heart hurt for the women, but her mind knew she needed to dig deeper. Likely these weren't the only women who had been impacted by letters like this. She picked up her phone and left a message for Quentin.

"Quentin, I just read the letter you gave me earlier this week. The allegations could represent massive liability. I need your full attention on this so we can accurately assess the risk and harm to the company. Call me any time of the weekend. Oh, and I need access to the CAR T 463 data. Actually, I need the ability to log in remotely. Your overzealous security guys have shut me out."

As she ended the call, her heart felt burdened for the women and what they'd endured.

What would those women do next?

A shadow waited on a bench as Brandon pulled into his spot near the lodge at Almost Home. He parked the truck and climbed from it, keeping his eyes on the form.

"Jeff, that you?"

The man stepped into the halo of light Brandon had replaced last week. "Hey, you have a minute?"

Brandon didn't like the heaviness in Jeff's words. "Honestly? It's been a hard day, so if it's good news, sure. But I'm not sure I can take a whole lot more heavy news."

"Did you stop and see Bethany?"

"Yeah. It's not good, and I feel more than helpless. Not my favorite position."

"It never is." Jeff waved his arm toward the lodge. "Can I come in? I'd like a drink while we talk."

Brandon pushed his shoulders back. If Jeff had bad news, better to hear it now and know where he stood. "Sure. I've got some sparkling water and Dr Pepper." He opened the door and waited for Jeff to enter, then pulled it shut and led the way to the commercial kitchen. Once he'd grabbed a soda for each of them, he leaned against the large island. "What's up?"

"So I told you the home in Arkansas is pressing Alaina and me for an answer. Today they upped their offer."

Brandon closed his eyes, the words landing like a punch to his gut. "What do you want me to do?"

"I don't know." Jeff took a swig of the Dr Pepper and then set the can down. "I didn't think they'd offer more, especially when we hadn't turned them down. But they did, and we have to consider it."

He was always fighting with one hand tied behind his back. "I don't know what to tell you. Your income in this new model would come from the state. Probably like it would in Arkansas. Either seems like a gamble. Here you gamble with me, there you gamble with strangers."

"Strangers who have a solid plan, and one that's been approved there. He's also planning to pay something for our help with planning and activities and family meals. Maybe you could hire me to do some of the planning here?" Jeff leaned against the island next to Brandon. "Look, I need to tell Alaina that it makes sense financially to stay."

"My hiring you part-time wouldn't change that this is an experiment. I believe it will work, but I can't promise anything, not until I see how this works in practice. I'd have to charge you rent, then turn around and pay you. That doesn't make sense."

"Can't you give me something to take back to her?"

"What do you want? Where do you want to invest your life?" Brandon crossed his arms over his chest, not caring how his body language was perceived. "If you believe in Almost Home and what we're doing, stay. If it's a job, then go where the money is better."

"Look. We're for you. Alaina and I both believe in what you've done and are trying. You've kept Almost Home afloat during all kinds of challenges. You're doing it again."

"Will you be with me this time?"

Jeff rubbed his hands along the sides of his scruffy beard. "I'd like to be, but there are two of us in this marriage. We both know Alaina's the one who makes it work. I can hang with the kids and give them stability, but she's the magic ingredient of unending love and patience."

"I need you both." Brandon shifted slightly so he could watch Jeff from the corner of his eye. The reality was this wasn't just about him and what he needed. He'd known the Stones too long to want anything but what was right for them. "I also want what's best for your family. You have Ellie to think about now. If that changes things, I understand. I may not like it, but I'll get over it."

"Maybe I can get a raise with my IT job."

"Is that what you want to do?"

Jeff took another drink, then pushed away from the island. "I have to give an answer to the Arkansas home in a week. Guess you'll know by then."

"Have you heard anything from any of the

house parents?" They'd all been silent about their thinking with him.

"Not really. It's their decision to make and share with you." Jeff headed to the door, then turned back. "We are for you, Brandon."

The words seemed to echo in the emptiness after Jeff left, the lodge door closing, leaving Brandon alone.

The emptiness overwhelmed him.

Would anyone choose him?

He shut off lights as he made his way upstairs to his apartment and then collapsed on the leather couch. Frodo stood and pranced toward him, leaping on his chest before standing nose-to-nose with him, his paws on Brandon's chest.

"Glad to know you're still here."

The cat stared at him, green eyes fixed on his. They'd hosted a *Frozen 2* showing in the lodge for his kids, and this felt like an interaction between Sven and Kristoff. "I refuse to speak dialogue for you, Frodo."

The cat didn't flinch.

Maybe that was the reminder he needed. That there were people in his life who didn't flinch away when he got a little gruff and prickly.

God loved him in spite of himself.

Caroline kept choosing him.

And he had good friends like Reid Billings and David Evans, who showed up for pickup basketball games and lent him their strength when he needed it. Even Jeff had done that for the five years Almost Home had existed. He needed to remember that he was surrounded by people who saw him. He was no longer that teenager on a couch. Even then, he'd had couches to crash on. If he'd asked for help, maybe he would have had more.

Frodo settled against his chest and rumbled a purr.

He'd get through this. And so would his kids.

SUNDAY, MAY 30

Anna's rounds started at the hospital in twenty minutes, and as things stood, she'd be late. Between the holiday traffic and heavy rain, she'd underestimated her commute time. At the moment, she was stuck at another red light.

She was many things but never late.

Not when families and their very sick kids relied on her. Bethany's case weighed on Anna as she waited. Her complications and prognosis made the girl's case particularly challenging, but Anna wouldn't give up. She loved the way oncology pushed her, but it was heartbreaking to watch the kids she fought so hard for slip away a little bit each day as treatments failed.

Her light turned green.

Nothing was turning Bethany's prognosis around. She had to figure out why. By now the

231

cytokine release should have ended, and she should be planning the first of six monthly boosts of CAR T cells for the girl.

Instead, Bethany was still in crisis. Anna couldn't proceed without stabilizing her. The data was too thin to know the best course of treatment. That was a risk of Bethany being part of Phase 1. They were all learning in real time how patients reacted to the therapy.

Friday she'd had a thought in the dead of night about the cause. She'd slipped the data on a flash drive along with her questions and put it in Saturday's mail for Caroline. Everyone deserved a holiday weekend, and this way it would arrive on Tuesday and she could call Caroline about it then. This morning she worried the holiday would hold up delivery and prepared an email, then closed her laptop. Together they could review the data.

Maybe it wasn't fair to get Caroline involved, but she wasn't sure who else to trust.

A dog dashed across the road twenty feet in front of her, and she slammed her foot on the brakes.

The car's tires slipped and skidded on the rain-drenched road.

As Anna pumped the brakes, it continued to slide.

Adrenaline surged through her as she tried to keep the car on the road.

The tires finally gripped the road, and she rolled her shoulders to force them to relax as the dog scampered into the grass on the other side of the street. When had her tires gotten this bad? If Brad were still alive, she'd ask him to get them changed the next time he had a day off. Instead, it was one more task for her overcrowded planner.

The baby kicked, a lunge that brought a smile.

She'd never tire of the sensation of life growing in her even as she wearied of the restless nights and uncomfortable days. She rubbed where she'd been kicked. "Soon, little one."

Anna glanced in her rearview mirror.

The car behind edged closer than she was comfortable with. Closer than the weather would recommend. Hadn't he seen her fishtail?

She eased on the brake.

She'd adjust her speed to compensate for Mr. Aggressive behind her.

After glancing in the rearview mirror to note his reaction, she grimaced. He edged closer rather than backing off.

The light at the end of the block turned red, and she slammed on her brakes to stop before entering the intersection.

Again, her car didn't stop. Then the fool behind her didn't stop either. He collided with her. The impact reverberated through her.

She gasped.

Clutched the steering wheel harder.

Stomped on the brake.

Didn't notice the truck bearing down on her from the left until it was too late.

Barely heard the blare of the horn before the crunch of metal.

Shattered glass.

Pain.

Darkness.

CHAPTER 21

MONDAY, MAY 31

Brandon woke with a start.

He groped for his phone. "Yep?"

"Is this Brandon Lancaster?" The woman's voice wasn't familiar.

"It is." He leaned onto his side and rubbed his eyes, then pulled back the phone to read the number. Nicole Walker? "Can I help you?"

"I wondered if my husband and I could come out to Almost Home an hour earlier than we'd discussed. The others from our ministry will arrive at noon or a bit later, but Eric has explored your website and wants to see how we can intentionally come alongside what you're doing. Those kinds of conversations happen best without a large audience."

His sleepy brain struggled to catch up with what she was asking. "There's a lot to do before the kids can enjoy the day."

"We can help. I assure you both of us love stepping in and filling needs."

"If that's what you're looking for, we have a few."

"I thought that might be the case." Her words had warmth as if she was smiling.

What could he do? Not that much other than

welcome them and delegate even more. "I can make that work."

"Great. We'll arrive at ten and be prepared to pitch in as soon as you give us the tour and heart behind your work."

Heart?

She knew he was a dude, right? He didn't lead with his heart. Then a pair of chocolate eyes filled his mind. Okay, unless it involved a certain woman who made his heart want to leap from his chest. "I'll be glad to share the mission."

There was so much to do before everyone arrived for the festivities. Okay, the *cookout* with outdoor games they held each year as long as it didn't rain. He was grateful Nicole Walker was bringing a team out, but he didn't know what she expected. Would she find it here? Would trying to guess be a waste of his time?

He didn't really want to think about it that way, but she could be an answer to his prayers or a drain. In a couple of hours he'd know.

Time to kick into overdrive.

When the Walkers arrived a few hours later, Brandon was ready in an Almost Home polo and khaki shorts.

The man stepped from the SUV and then hurried to the passenger side. A sixtysomething woman stepped from the car and took a moment to look around before her gaze met his.

Eric was about six feet tall, good-sized for

a man, but Brandon would be taller by a few inches. Eric's gray hair was cut short, not a buzz cut, but still no-nonsense. It was easy to tell the two were a couple because they both wore red T-shirts with blue shorts and comfortable shoes. Nicole was a good six inches shorter than her husband, and there was an intelligence to the way she took in what she could see of Almost Home that made Brandon curious. What was she seeing?

"Welcome to Almost Home." Brandon extended his hand to Eric.

They shook hands as the man spoke. "Eric Walker, and this is my wife, Nicole."

She took his hand with a smile. "It is a pleasure to meet you officially and be here. You may be an answer to prayer."

"How do you figure?" He didn't want the pressure that last sentence carried.

"Ever since our youngest left the nest a few years ago, I've been looking for the place where kids needed us." She gestured to the grounds. "I haven't seen much yet, but this could be it."

Eric took her hand. "Now, Nicole, not everyone gets your instant ability to see things as they could be. Mr. Lancaster also doesn't know how you're a modern Pied Piper of sorts." The man laughed as he gave Brandon a conspiratorial wink. "Kids adore her almost as much as she adores them."

She swatted her husband's arm. "I don't know about that. Young man, why don't you give us the twenty-minute tour and tell us about what you're trying to do."

"Sure. First, it'd be great to know what you do so I can tailor what I talk about to what will interest you."

"I'm a bored housewife who no longer has kids of her own at home." Nicole shrugged. "I'm looking for a place to volunteer that can benefit from my help." She slipped under Eric's arm. "Eric is a state senator."

Brandon frowned before recovering a neutral expression. Was it a good thing to have a legislator here seeing what he was doing?

As if reading his mind, Eric spoke. "Today I'm here as a concerned citizen who wants to help. Is this a group home subject to Family First?"

"It is."

"How's that going?"

"If you want an honest answer . . ."

"I do."

"Not well. The requirements under the law are still evolving. That's made it hard to figure out how to comply."

"Have you found a way?"

"I believe so." Brandon led the way to the lodge's doors. "First let me show you our main family space. Then if you're interested, I'll tell you about the model I believe will work for homes like mine that are sibling group–focused."

The tour went well, with both State Senator Walker and his wife asking thoughtful questions. After a quick walk of the grounds, the senator stopped and studied one of the cottages. "You don't have trauma-informed care."

"No."

"Then how are you going to continue your work after the regs go into effect?"

"My house parents are considering becoming fully licensed foster parents, independent of my license. If they agree, instead of working for me, they will be foster parents who rent the cabins from me for a nominal rate. I'll work with the state as a liaison as needed, but the children would be placed directly with the house parents." He wished he knew how to read the senator's thoughts. "I'll focus on the long-term placement of the kids and providing the services they need while here."

Nicole glanced around the space. "This is a wonderful setting for kids."

"Yes, and the goal is to get them into forever homes, generally through foster-to-adopt. But this becomes a place where siblings can stay together while termination is occurring or a permanent placement is located."

Eric glanced toward the firepit, where Jeff Stone was tending a large grill with two of his sibling group in tow. "I can see where that is a good plan. Does anyone else do it that way?"

"Some were doing a version of it before Family First went into effect. I've talked to an executive director of a home in Arkansas who's adopting the same model, but I don't know anyone here." He inhaled as he tried to gauge the senator's mood. "Someone has to be first. Why not me?"

Memorial Day had dawned warm and muggy, the promise of rain hovering in the air.

Caroline dressed in a pair of denim capris and a navy tank with an off-the-shoulder red T-shirt thrown over it, trying to hit the right holiday note. As she glanced in the full-length mirror hanging on the back of her closet door, she wasn't sure she'd succeeded. But one glance at her watch had her pulling her hair into a high ponytail and grabbing a sun visor as well as a rain jacket, just in case.

Then she grabbed her picnic basket, which was filled with carefully decorated cupcakes. The kids would annihilate them, but for a few minutes the treats would look amazing. She just hoped Annelise saw that Caroline had made two in her favorite color. The purple didn't match the Memorial Day color scheme of the others, but she hoped it would make the seven-year-old feel remembered. When Emilie texted that she and Reid had arrived, she hurried out the door and down the stairs to their car. Emilie was wearing a cute white sundress splashed with large yellow sunflowers and had a floppy-brimmed yellow hat with white ribbon around the band that highlighted her blonde hair.

Emilie rolled down the passenger window as Reid pulled to a stop. "Need any help?"

Caroline shook her head as she hefted the basket. "I'm good. Want this in the trunk?"

Reid hopped out and took it from her. "I'll set it next to you. Less likely to slide around."

"Thanks." After he opened the door, she slid into the back seat and strapped in as he took care of the basket.

The miles passed as Reid and Emilie had a quiet conversation about some event they'd gone to over the weekend. Sounded like one of Reid's financial clients had hosted people on his yacht. The two were so cozy and connected, their hands intertwined on the console between them. Comfortable in a way that made her heart yearn for the same. Most of her friends were paired with amazing men, the kind you could count on in life, the ones who would stick around through the ups and downs and roller-coaster speeds of life. She could have that with Brandon if she could let herself relax into what he offered.

"You okay?" Emilie's quiet words pulled her from her thoughts.

"Why do you ask?"

"You sighed. Heavily." Emilie twisted in her

seat to look at Caroline while Reid flipped on his blinker, signaling the turn onto the road leading to Almost Home. "I've known you long enough to know when you're the kind of quiet that needs to talk."

"Conserving energy before we arrive." Emilie had been to Almost Home often enough to know how intense the time could get. The kids loved the extra attention that new adults brought, and it took focus to match their stamina.

Emilie eyed her but didn't press as the car slowed. "We'll talk later."

Caroline nodded, but knew she'd do her best to postpone that. What could she say? That she was jealous of her friends? That wasn't really true, she hoped.

She just wanted to replicate what they had in her own unique way—and feared she was doing a terrible job of it.

CHAPTER 22

The moment they parked, kids swarmed them. Caroline couldn't hold back a grin as she started hugging the girls and boys. Somehow Evan wormed his way through the crowd until he stood hugging her legs. "Hey, buddy." She swiveled his baseball hat until the brim pointed down his back.

"Miss Cawee." He pouted, then tugged it back in place.

She grinned at him. "Guess what I brought?"

"Cookies?" His eyes got big with eager hope.

"Close. Cupcakes with lots of icing and sprinkles."

"It's not the same." He crossed his arms then stuck his tongue out at her.

"Evan McDonald." Alaina stepped forward and grabbed his elbow. "That's not how we talk to people, let alone our friends. Say you're sorry."

"But I'm not." His little chin jutted out.

Alaina shook her head and closed her eyes a moment before giving Caroline an apologetic grimace. "We're still working on manners."

"It's okay. Where's little Ellie?"

"Jeff took her for a while." Alaina brushed a strand of hair behind her ear. The wind teased it back out.

The women started walking toward the lodge, a group of kids clustering around them. "I heard you and Jeff have a job offer out of state. Are you planning to take it?"

Alaina looked toward the playground and field, where a small canopy had been set up for shade. Several adults were moving picnic tables into place. "I thought for sure we were leaving, but now I don't know. It doesn't feel like we've got a good answer." She sighed. "It's so hard when you know you answered a call and you're where God wants you, then everything changes. How long do you stay? Or do you adapt? How do you know when God releases you to move on?" She glanced at Caroline and her eyebrows were knit together as her palms came up. "I'd give anything for a clear answer."

"I guess I've always operated by 'stay where you are until you *have* to move.' "

"Sometimes that works. Other times it's just stubbornness. Refusing to follow when God says go. That's what makes moments like this hard. How do you know if you're being stubborn?" She adjusted the strap of her sundress and rolled her shoulders. "It feels good not to wear the baby carrier for a few minutes."

Caroline didn't rush to answer Alaina's question. This felt important, like one of those moments when God had strategically placed her in the conversation. "What if the fact you're concerned about these issues is enough? That all you need to do is decide? Sometimes there really isn't a right or wrong answer. We get to choose. Maybe He wants to use you wherever you decide to invest your lives."

Alaina nodded. "Maybe. I'll think about what you've said. Right now I need to rescue Ellie before Jeff forgets he's carrying his daughter and not a football. Thanks for talking." The woman wandered toward the grill and her family.

Caroline watched the kids running around as if they were already on a sugar high. These kids were so resilient. She knew what it took to plaster a smile on, let alone have one that glowed from the inside after experiencing some of the situations these kids had survived.

To land in foster care meant something had gone wrong, usually tragically wrong. Yet she'd watched kids come back to life under the care of Brandon and his team of home parents. It was a calling worthy of respect.

A few of the kids were new. She'd make the effort to spend at least a few moments with each. One little girl ran full tilt into her, and Caroline reached down to steady her. Her gaze lifted above the little girl who hugged her knees and connected with Brandon's. He watched her with an odd expression, one she couldn't decipher but wanted to understand.

All she knew was that if he kept looking at

her like that, she was one perfect moment from falling hopelessly in love with this man who fit her heart.

Alaina walked toward the grill where Jeff was stationed, and Brandon wondered what they'd decide. He shifted to watch Caroline pull different kids close for hug after hug. Was anything more beautiful than a woman who gave love freely to those around her?

As he watched, she intentionally sought one of the children who'd arrived this week and knelt in front of her. She was amazing.

His aunt Jody, Anna's mother, had called earlier while he was giving the Walkers their tour, so it had gone to voicemail. How long had it been since he'd talked to her? He let Anna keep him up to date, but considering he hadn't seen her often before Bethany, he was doing a lousy job being part of his family. It had nothing to do with his aunt and uncle's failure to find him or his brother when they got lost in the system. His mind knew Jody and Clint were stationed overseas, too far away to be aware of what happened, but his heart argued that Aunt Jody had known Mom had died. Maybe she'd assumed Brandon's dad would step back into the picture, but that showed how out of touch she'd been.

There were other family members who could have stepped forward, too, but hadn't. He'd managed, but it was hard to want to spend time with people who hadn't wanted him.

His aunt had relocated to the area six months earlier when Anna announced she was pregnant. Aunt Jody had left Uncle Clint in whatever foreign city they lived in, thanks to his job, and moved to be closer to Anna after her husband's death.

He blinked and chose to focus on this moment. Brandon gave Reid a quick backslap hug before giving Emilie a side squeeze. Reid had met his match in the quiet yet firm Emilie. "Did you bring Kinley with you?"

Reid's niece lived with him since tragedy had befallen her family two years ago and often came with Reid to enjoy the other kids and the outdoors.

Reid shook his head. "Not this time. She was at some sort of sleepover that will continue for most of the day."

Emilie gave Brandon a wink. "He's having a hard time embracing the fact that Kinley's a teenager now and can have a bit more independence."

"A bit is fine. I like knowing where she is." *And that she's safe* was left unsaid. Understandable after her dad had almost succeeded in killing Kinley the day he killed her mom and sister.

Emilie moved on, and Brandon put a hand on Reid's shoulder to keep him from following her. "Quick question."

"Sure."

"Do you think I could sell the Porsche?"

Reid cocked his head and studied Brandon. "Why?"

"I might need to get creative to keep a couple of my house parents around. You know my funds are tied up. Thought liquidating it might get me some quick cash. It's just sitting in the garage."

"You love that car."

"But I love these kids more. If selling it will help me keep a key couple here, then it's worth exploring."

"I can do some checking this week."

"Thanks." One of the boys lobbed a ball at Brandon's head, but he grabbed it easily. "Excuse me." He waggled his eyebrows at Zeke. "I'm coming for you."

The passel of boys squealed and scattered.

Soon he was sweaty from romping with the boys, and Brandon called a time-out. The others had arrived to help. David Evans set up several yard games while his wife, Ciara, held toddler Amber and suggested how to set them up. Brandon could easily imagine Caroline doing the same someday. It was an image he liked. A lot.

As his gaze drifted to Caroline, he clearly saw her holding a child.

Their child.

He blinked away the image, and Caroline smiled at him.

"Did the Walkers come?"

"Yep. Gave them a tour and now they're helping get the food prepped in the kitchen."

"I hope that means Nicole will help you find people who can volunteer here."

"It sounds like she and her husband have a real interest in our work."

"That's great." Caroline held up her hand for a high five, when he wanted to pull her in for a kiss. "There was something special about meeting her Saturday. Like I was in the right place at the right time."

"Maybe." Brandon lowered his hand. "Did she tell you her husband's a state legislator?"

"No." Wrinkles appeared across her forehead as she considered his question. "That's good. Now he can tell others how important the work is that you and other group homes do."

"That's one way of looking at it."

"What's the other?"

"That he'll decide there's need for a new, more restrictive law before we've figured out the last one."

"That's certainly looking at the silver lining." Caroline handed him a large picnic hamper. "We need to deposit the cupcakes before they melt out here." Then she took his free hand and led him toward the lodge.

He could read her mind as if she'd spoken the words out loud.

• • •

Caroline had wanted a longer conversation with the Walkers, but before she could talk with them at length, a couple of the boys found her and grabbed her hands to tug her back outside. With an apologetic glance over her shoulder, she laughingly let the boys take her toward one of the games. She quickly proved how terrible she was at cornhole. Brock laughed as one of his beanbags knocked hers off the board before his slid into the hole.

His fist pump was worth the reality she would lose another game.

It was worth it to watch the kids abandon themselves to a good time.

Then Brandon was calling everyone together, and kids and adults meandered to the grill and shelter. After a quick prayer of thanks for the food, Brandon released the littlest kids first. Caroline jumped in to help fill plates for a couple of girls who would have filled their plates with cookies and chips if she hadn't guided them to hot dogs and fruit. While hot dogs weren't health food, they were better than sugar-loaded carbs. Once the girls were settled on a blanket on the ground, she returned to the back of the line to get a plate of food for herself.

Ciara was balancing Amber on her hip. The two-year-old's blonde hair curled around her face, making her look angelic even as she rubbed her eyes.

"Would you like me to take her so you can get food?" Caroline held out her hands to the little girl, who burrowed more deeply into Ciara's shoulder.

"That would be great, but she's decided she's a one-adult toddler today, aren't you, sweetheart?" Ciara brushed a fly from her daughter's cheek. "How are you enjoying your job?"

Caroline glanced around, but Brandon was talking with Jeff at the grill. "It's good. I love the challenge of the legal work, and the mission of the company is pretty amazing. If half of our products and therapies make it to drugstores and hospitals, I'll be proud to know I was part."

"But?"

"There's no but."

Ciara picked up a plate with her free hand. "You forget I've known you almost eight years. There's always a but."

"Brandon's an investor in the company. It makes me nervous to talk about work with him. It's making our conversations stilted." She scooped homemade mac and cheese out of a large pan onto Ciara's plate.

"If your conversations revolve around work, his or yours, then you have a problem. There's so much more to talk about. The fact you feel cautious about bringing up Praecursoria is good. It'll force you to talk about the things that really matter."

"But I work sixty hours a week."

"So does he, if not more." Ciara gave her the big-sister look she'd perfected ages ago. "But that's not who you are. Focus on everything else, not your job."

Caroline picked up an extra set of silverware and napkins for Ciara and then entered the line. "I guess you're right."

"You know I am." Ciara glanced down the line. "Now go get your man a glass of lemonade and find something to talk about. Like these amazing kids. Or his dreams."

The car was crushed like an accordion.

He should stop.

He didn't want to see.

Not when he knew the woman trapped inside the vehicle. He'd counted her a friend once upon a time. Now as he looked at the car, he knew there was no way she'd survive.

The smell of smoke was heavy. Would the vehicle explode? He needed to leave. Escape before people asked questions. Before anyone placed him at the scene.

Something touched his hand. He flinched.

Where was he?

He reached down, felt fur. Felt himself relax as he jolted fully awake.

He was on his couch, the TV illuminating the wall. That's right—he fell asleep in the middle of a show, his dog at his feet.

The accident was yesterday. A nightmare whether he was awake or asleep.

He hadn't meant for things to escalate like this.

Two women were dead or dying because of the research he protected. But the Robbins boy's cells were worth any cost, especially if they had a HeLa-like component. His only choice was to hold the course.

That was the easy part.

He needed more time for the experiments he was running in Mexico to succeed. Then he'd be ready to take Praecursoria out at the knees.

He should have resisted involving another child so soon, but he couldn't. When he saw the cells multiplying without end under the microscope, he'd gotten too excited to wait.

Imagine. Him replicating the work of George Gey, the man who had uncovered the unique aspects of Henrietta Lacks's cells. The cervical cancer cells were foundational to so many scientific advances, such as the polio vaccine. Those cells had changed the course of medical history and scientific research. Now he had the opportunity to spearhead similarly illustrious achievements.

He hadn't done anything to Anna Johnson. She'd driven into that intersection on her own. Hadn't she? He'd only bumped her, not hard enough to cause that accident.

He steeled himself. There was no time for regrets.

Scientific advances required sacrifices. Anna was simply one of them. If he told himself that often enough, he'd believe it. He was too vested to back off now. Whatever it took, he would see this through.

And if his gut was correct, he'd rewrite history

and advance science in dynamic new ways that mattered for the good of humanity.

Any cost was worth that.

Even Anna.

CHAPTER 23
TUESDAY, JUNE 1

Brandon's morning derailed the moment his phone rang. He scrabbled to find it on the nightstand, then glanced at the screen. It was barely seven o'clock, and his aunt Jody was calling.

"Hello?"

"Brandon, you'd better get here. Anna's been in a terrible accident." His aunt's voice shuddered to a stop.

He wiped his face. "Is she all right?"

"No. She's still in critical condition and the doctors aren't optimistic. I tried to call yesterday . . ."

"We had a big event at Almost Home. The day got away from me."

"Please come. My house is where we are gathered for now. The hospital still isn't letting people in who aren't close relatives. Do you know where my house is?"

He assured her he did and then got ready as fast as he could.

Anna in a critical accident?

Why hadn't he been told sooner? No, that wasn't right. The real question was why he hadn't returned the call. It didn't matter that he'd been so exhausted by the time everyone left that the last thing he'd wanted to do was call Aunt Jody.

Now, his aunt's words ricocheted through his mind like a ball let loose in a pinball machine.

Anna was critical.

What would happen to Anna's daughter?

No matter what had happened in the past, he wanted to be with Anna's family and tell them to get a good attorney who would make sure that mom and baby were protected.

It took almost an hour of navigating the congested roads to reach Aunt Jody's home. The brick exterior was neat with the flower beds exploding with a riot of colorful pansies and other flowers along the sidewalk. A few cars were in the driveway and more lined the road in front of the home. He parked a block away and walked back to the house, dread weighing down his steps.

A pair of cardinals chittered at each other from adjacent trees, the female blending in with the small leaves. The birdsong should have heralded hope, but it couldn't cut through his burden.

When he arrived, he paused at the door, bracing for whatever awaited inside. He knocked, then waited with his hands shoved in his pockets.

A moment later the door opened, revealing a woman of about sixty. Her face was lightly lined, but shadows purpled the skin under her eyes. "Brandon?"

"Hi, Jeannette."

Aunt Jody's stepsister had never warmed to him for reasons he didn't understand. The woman glanced around as if expecting someone to be with him. Then she refocused on him. "Why are you here?"

"Is Aunt Jody here? She called an hour ago about Anna and said to come."

"No, she got called back to the hospital." The woman stepped onto the small porch and closed the door behind her. "Something about the baby." There was a weary droop to her shoulders as if she hadn't been sleeping well.

"Is there anything I can do?" He hated being in situations like this. Where he carried the fog of helplessness just like when his mom died.

"No." The woman swallowed. "I'll tell Jody you came by."

"Can I come in?"

She sighed and looked down. "You could, but there's no one here that you know."

He didn't bother to respond. It shouldn't matter who was there. "What did I do to make you hate me?" He clenched his jaw to prevent saying anything more. Whining never helped.

"Who said you did anything?" She barely met his gaze before looking away again. "Some things are too complicated and long-standing to change."

"Not in my book. As long as we're both breathing, there's hope."

She inhaled sharply and then shook her head. "This is not the time."

He tried to extend grace, but it was hard. "This is like when Mom died."

"No, Anna wasn't sick. She was in a tragic accident." There was a slight softening around Jeannette's eyes, as if she was reliving Mom's slow decline, thanks to cancer. "I'll let Jody know you were here." She swallowed as her eyes turned glassy. "Someone will be in touch when we know more."

No words of comfort came, so he turned and walked back down the sidewalk and block to his car. He had expected more. Well, not really. But part of him had hoped. He was supposed to be strong. The one who took care of others because someone had to. The world was an incredibly unsafe place, and he was the only one he could count on. Aunt Jody insisted he would understand if he'd just let her explain, but nothing justified leaving a seventeen-year-old to fend for himself, nor letting his eight-year-old brother disappear. Maybe if Trevor showed up, the past and its pain would sink into the background.

Instead, he lived with the permanent limp of an orphan who struggled to let anyone other than Caroline close.

Wasn't his fault, but it was his problem.

He blinked as he turned the key in the ignition. He needed to get away, but his vision was blurred. A mess. Just like him.

• • •

Quentin never returned her call or email.

Yes, it had been a holiday weekend, but she'd conveyed how much she needed to talk to him about the letter and the high-handed IT move to shut her out of the company's files.

Even without the letter, it didn't take a high level of brilliance to know she faced another pressure-packed week filled with projects like pushing the CAR T-cell therapies through, getting the informed consents right, and triple-checking that the internal procedures minimized risk.

Caroline had enjoyed the Memorial Day cook-out, and she pondered Ciara's words during her commute. She could do better with Brandon and would.

By the time she reached the office, she was ready to slay the day. She'd try to head off the potential lawsuit as soon as possible. First order of business: to figure out where the liability lay.

She bypassed her desk and headed straight to Quentin's suite. Lillian sat at her desk, headset on and fingers clacking on the keys. Her nose was redder than normal as were her cheeks, likely the result of a Memorial Day weekend spent outside. The younger gal was also wearing all black with heavy black eyeliner as if she were giving the goth look a try for the day. Was that even a thing anymore?

She barely glanced at Caroline before her gaze returned to her monitor.

"Quentin in?"

The younger woman shook her head. "No. He took the morning off."

"I need an appointment with him as quickly as possible."

"That'll be next week."

"This is about potential litigation."

"It's a short week, so Monday's the best I can do." The woman paused and looked at her. "He's got meetings in the city today and flying up to New York Wednesday."

It might be the best Lillian could do, but it wasn't good enough. "Is he answering email?"

"When I send it through." Her tone communicated she could also hold it up.

That was all right since Quentin had given her an alternate private email her first day. It was for emergencies, and this qualified. She'd email each separately and see if she could land on his priority list. "I'll shoot him an email and would appreciate it if you could forward it to him. I'm trying to prevent a family from suing us but need more information about the sale of Genetics for You."

Lillian frowned. "Is that the part we sold about a year and a half ago?"

"Yes. Do you have any idea who I should talk to?"

Lillian rolled her eyes as if Caroline was asking

a ridiculous question. "Try Samson. If he's out for an extended weekend, try Brian Silver. He's been here even longer than Samson." She said it as if both were old enough to have seen dinosaurs roam the earth.

"Thanks."

Caroline returned to her office and drafted the email to Quentin. Among her most pressing questions: *Did Praecursoria ask the Genetics for You buyer to assume liability?* She addressed it to both of Quentin's accounts and had just hit Send when her phone rang.

Reid Billings? Why would he be calling her? She hoped Emilie was okay.

"Reid, hi."

"Hi, Caroline."

"Thanks for your help at the barbecue. The kids enjoyed it."

"I think I had more fun than they did." Reid's voice turned solemn. "Listen, David just let me know Brandon's cousin is in critical condition at a local hospital. He asked me to pass the word along to you."

"What?" Her heart plummeted. It couldn't be Anna—surely Brandon had lots of cousins. Many families did. "What happened?"

"Car accident over the weekend. It's been touch and go for her and the baby."

"Oh no." It had to be Anna. "Is the baby okay right now?"

"Sounds like they've been able to save her baby so far."

Caroline's shoulders collapsed as air whooshed from her. "I'll call him."

"Thanks." A phone rang in the background. "Sorry, I've got to take this call."

A minute later Caroline sat staring at nothing as her heart felt bruised for Brandon. How would the accident impact Anna's patients? The woman clearly saw medicine as so much more than a job.

She called Brandon but got no answer, so she sent a text. You okay? Just heard about Anna.

When he didn't respond, she went in search of Brian and Samson. Kleme was out as Lillian had guessed.

She looked for Brian in the lab. Looking through the window in the door, she saw several people moving about the room, doing sciency stuff, but Caroline didn't see Brian. She rapped on the door and Lori Clark, Brian's assistant, looked up with an arched eyebrow. She motioned for Lori to come her way, which she reluctantly did. Lori cracked the door. "What do you need?"

"Have you seen Brian?"

"Check the break room."

"Thanks."

When she reached the break room, Brian was seated at a table with a paper and cup of coffee. She made a beeline for him. "Brian, have a minute?"

He glanced at his watch, then nodded. "A few. How can I help?"

"Working on a project and need to know more about Genetics for You."

He studied her through his dark glasses. "Really?"

"What do you know about the sale?"

"Not much. It was sold to a group of investors." Brian shrugged. "At the time I thought Quentin was crazy. Genetic testing was our cash cow. But he knows best. Always does." There was an edge to those last words.

"Were you part of the sale?"

He studied her with furrowed brows. "No."

"When did you start working here?"

"Must have been within the first year." He frowned as he stroked his chin and looked into the distance. "I wasn't the first scientist hired but came right after my postdoc at Hopkins. I'll be paying off that debt for years."

"Were you part of the genetic testing when it was run here?"

"On the fringes. Once the program was up and running, it didn't require PhDs to maintain. Technicians received the tests, analyzed the results, and managed the process unless there were anomalies that required input from someone with more knowledge. The goal was to streamline the process from intake to results sent to customer as much as possible." He shrugged.

"It was profitable, but when CAR T-cell therapy came along, Quentin argued the genetic testing distracted us from the real reason Praecursoria exists. That's why Quentin and the others decided to sell that part of the company. The sale also helped fund new research that ultimately became what we're doing with CAR T cells."

"Who was it sold to?"

Brian considered the question for a minute. "I think Samson was one of the members of the consortium, but like I said, I wasn't involved. What's all this about?"

"I need to know who has liability for the tests performed before the sale."

"I'd say the buyer assumes all risk, wouldn't you?"

"Not necessarily. Do you know where I can find a copy of the buy-sell agreement?"

He shook his head. "Why?"

"Quentin received a letter threatening to sue for genetic testing letters Praecursoria mailed."

He rubbed his jaw. "We're a research company. Someone's always suing. That's why Quentin hired you. So handle it." He stood and tipped an imaginary hat her direction. "If you want to know more, talk to Samson. He was part of the group that bought that part of the business."

CHAPTER 24

The day was colored with grief and concern as Caroline kept trying to reach Brandon. Her mind spun out an endless variety of what-ifs and worst-case scenarios as she tried to learn how Anna was. Caroline tried to settle into work, but every ten minutes or so, her gaze trailed to her phone.

After an hour, she'd had enough.

She had to focus and get work done. Everybody had a point where a thing became too much. The tipping point where what had been precariously managed tumbled in shattered dreams and hopes. Brandon had edged closer to that with each roadblock that Almost Home had faced. Then he'd had the giddy wash of hope that he'd found a solution for the group home, and now Anna.

Caroline wasn't sure how to help, but if he didn't return her call or text, she'd go to him.

No hiding allowed, even if she had to wait until her workday ended.

Many items filled her to-do list, but her thoughts flitted among the letter and corporate research, the trials and internal controls, and Brandon and Anna.

Who would advocate medically for Bethany now? Who would ensure the trials were run properly from the medical side?

Caroline stood and grabbed her keys and cell phone. She needed to clear her head before she spent the day ineffectively. As she neared the side door, Lillian stepped out of the break room and ran into Caroline.

Lillian steadied herself. "Sorry about that."

"No worries. I was pretty focused." Caroline studied the younger woman. Mascara had flaked under her eyes and her eyeliner had smeared. "Are you all right?"

The woman nodded then shook her head. "But it's not your concern. I'll handle it."

"Are you sure? I'm headed outside for a quick walk. Want to join me?" Caroline gestured to the door. "Sometimes a change of scenery, even for a minute, helps."

"Okay." Lillian sighed. "A bit of distance would be good."

The moment she hit the side door, humidity slapped Caroline in the face. Walking out here wasn't like being in DC and near the Mall. Instead, the rumble of cars overwhelmed any nature sounds. Still, she took a moment to just be. Then she focused on Lillian. "Want to tell me what's going on? You don't have to, but I've been told I'm a good listener."

Lillian's hand fluttered to her ridiculously flat stomach. The girl must plank for hours. "I'm pregnant."

Caroline blinked. "Oh."

"Yeah. Aren't you glad you asked?" Bitterness crept into Lillian's voice. "This wasn't supposed to happen. Not some terrible romance novel gone wrong, yet that's exactly my life right now."

"Do you need help?" Her mind scrambled to pull up the name of the crisis pregnancy center her church supported.

"No, I'll just make the dad pay. He's got the money, but he's not going to like it." She sighed and closed her eyes as if the sunlight blinded her, but then a tear trickled down her cheek. "I promised myself I wouldn't make my mom's mistake, and yet that's exactly what I've done."

"Will the father want to be involved?"

"No, and I wouldn't let him." She shivered even in the heat. "I'd better get back to work. Promise you won't tell anyone."

"Attorney-client privilege." It was a weak joke, but she held up three fingers in the Girl Scout salute. "Why did you tell me?"

"You seem to really care about people, even when people like me aren't always welcoming." Her shoulders pulled in, and she looked away. "I hope I didn't read you wrong."

"You didn't. I'm humbled you've trusted me." The news was a treasure. "I'll pray for you and this baby, and if I can help let me know."

Lillian nodded and turned toward the building, away from Caroline, but didn't leave. Another tear slowly slid down her cheek. "I don't know how long I can stay."

"What do you mean?"

"I can't see him every day and pretend everything's okay."

"The father?"

Her nod was so small Caroline almost missed it.

"Oh."

"Yeah. Oh." The woman lifted her chin. "This is the only job I have right now, so I'd better get back to it." She marched toward the building as if it housed a firing squad.

What dreams had been decimated by someone who worked in there?

Caroline waited ten minutes and prayed for Lillian. This would not be an easy road for her, but Caroline would do what she could to be a friend in the process.

When she returned to her office, she forced her thoughts to turn from Lillian's revelation to digging through the company's server hunting for the corporate minutes. As she clicked, part of her expected to get a call from IT, but it never came. When she finally located the minutes, she combed through the prior years' reports until she found a record of Praecursoria's board vote to spin off Genetics for You, Inc., the genetic testing service. The vote occurred at one of the annual business meetings, but it didn't look like the sale was finalized until the following year. She tried to trace Genetics for You through the Virginia Secretary of State's online database, but the buyer hadn't filed paperwork for the last eighteen months. It might not be viable anymore, since an annual report had to be filed each year for a company to stay in good standing with the state. While it looked like a dead end, she'd call the number on record and drive by the address if necessary. One address was out in Chantilly, roughly twenty-three miles west of Tysons, while an older one was closer.

Where was the buy-sell agreement?

She backtracked through the records and printed off the list of officers. The officers for Praecursoria were the same then as now, but she paused when she spotted a familiar name on the Genetics for You list.

Brian Silver.

He had been the vice president of Genetics for You at the time it bought the testing arm from Praecursoria.

Why had he told her Samson was part of the consortium of buyers but failed to mention his own involvement? In fact, he'd denied any involvement. What did he have to hide?

Someone knocked on her door, and an intern from George Mason University stuck her head in the office. "I've got a small package for you."

"Go ahead and bring it in."

The young woman slipped into the office and handed a padded envelope to Caroline. "Sign here."

Caroline complied, then the intern slipped from the room, closing the door behind her.

There was no return address on the envelope, so Caroline examined it for a postmark. Falls Church. That didn't mean much without a return address. She flipped over the padded envelope and pulled the string that opened it. The small Post-it note simply said *for Caroline*. She didn't recognize the feminine handwriting. She tipped the package and a flash drive slid free.

She flipped the drive in her hand, looking for anything distinguishing. It was a small black drive with a silver cap with no markings. Caroline frowned as she looked at it. Should she insert it in her computer, or would that compromise the computer network?

It was overkill to think like that.

She'd listened to too many Gabriel Allon thrillers on her commute. Time to try a different genre that didn't have her seeing danger with each delivery.

After a quick call, an IT staffer strolled into her office and validated the flash drive as being free of malware or bugs.

As soon as the woman left, Caroline opened the drive and scrolled through the file directory. They looked like a random assortment of documents and Excel spreadsheets, until she reached the final item on the list. It was titled "ZforCB." Could that mean Caroline Bragg? She clicked on the document and waited for it to load, then she slowly scrolled through it.

It read like a memo draft with a bullet list of points that didn't make sense. There was a discussion of stem cells but with words she didn't know. Then there was a list of numbers that she thought referenced different research projects Praecursoria was running. She hit Print, then grabbed the pages from the printer on her hutch. She turned so her back was to the door and got out a highlighter and pen.

Somewhere on the company server was a list of the reference numbers matched up to their projects. One of the technicians, maybe Justin Grant, had shown it to her during her first week when she was getting the whirlwind orientation. She flipped over to the network to see if she could locate it. When she couldn't immediately put her hands on it, she jotted a note on her to-do list and turned back to the memo. As she read it, the contents confirmed this had to be from Anna.

It devolved at the end into a list of disjointed thoughts that barely qualified as sentences.

The list of projects is key.

We're missing something.

It's related to the cells.

Somehow we got them, but there's no clear chain of custody.

Whose are they? Do we have the requisite consent?

And what if someone else got the wrong cells? Is anyone else compromised?

The list continued, a sequence of disjointed thoughts. She picked up her phone to call Anna, then let it drop to her desk. She'd need to find other experts to help her until Anna was out of critical care.

Could there be a clue about the problem in the list of numbers Anna had included? There had to be a reason Anna included that list.

Caroline clicked on the Praecursoria files and continued hunting for the matching numbers but couldn't find them.

Then her computer started flashing that it would shut down in sixty seconds for a software update. She frowned at it and started closing all the open files, then ejected the drive as the computer started the shutdown sequence.

After she slipped the drive into her desk drawer, she reviewed the conversations she'd had with Anna. The early conversations hadn't indicated that anything bothered her about the work Praecursoria was doing. Instead, she'd seemed excited by the potential represented in the research. Then her perspective had changed. Why? Was it related to Bethany's decline? Had she dropped a clue that Caroline had overlooked during their lunch Thursday?

Anna had mentioned a concern, but Caroline had thought it was just related to Bethany's response to the trial. Caroline reviewed the conversation in her mind, but nothing came to her. Anna had been oblique, wanting to do more research.

This flash drive probably contained everything she'd found.

But Caroline didn't know how to connect these files to Anna's concerns.

She needed Anna's version of a Rosetta Stone to decipher the contents.

She went back to the memo.

Does it tie to the testing?

Silver might.

What did she mean by *Silver might?* As far as Caroline knew, silver wasn't used in anything, and what testing did she mean? All of the studies involved elaborate tests to determine efficacy of the proposed drugs.

She picked up her phone and dialed the lab.

"Silver."

"Do you have a few minutes? I had a couple more questions, and it's probably easier to ask in person."

"I don't know anything more than I told you about the sale."

"This isn't about that."

He seemed to weigh this. "Do you want to come to the lab?"

There'd be fewer people to overhear if he came to her. "Would my office work?"

He hesitated a moment. "I can do that but not for long."

CHAPTER 25

"The treatment's not working." Tara Descane, Bethany's caseworker, studied the girl where she languished in the hospital bed. She turned to Brandon. "I'm not sure we should keep her in the study."

"You can't give up on her." He motioned to the hallway. This was not a conversation they should have next to Bethany's bed. He lowered his voice but not his will to fight for his charge. "She hasn't given up."

"Look at her, Brandon." Tara pointed back at the ghostly girl. "She's disappearing."

He wanted to argue with Tara, but he couldn't force his attention to stay on Bethany.

Over the weeks Bethany had been in the hospital, Brandon had brought a few things to make the room feel homier, but right now she lay there without energy or animation. The books were unread, the movies unwatched.

He'd come to the hospital from his aunt Jody's home and now felt even more out of control.

Bethany shifted against the sheets. "Mr. Brandon."

He glanced at Tara and she waved him in. "I'll wait."

He settled on the edge of the chair and leaned close to Bethany. "How you doing, kiddo?"

Bethany swallowed, and he grabbed the cup of water and held the straw to her lips. "I'm so tired. When will Dr. Anna come? I didn't see her yesterday."

He ran his hands over his head and frowned. How should he play this? The truth. "I don't know when she'll be back. She was hurt in a car accident."

Bethany's eyes closed for a minute, and when she reopened them, they were glassy. "Will you fight for me?"

"Absolutely." A soft throat cleared in the hallway. "Would you like to see Tara? She's here."

Bethany glanced at the door but shook her head the smallest bit. "Not now."

"That's fine. I need to go talk to her."

"Okay. Will you tell Gabriel I miss him and love him?" Bethany closed her eyes again, and a tear leaked out.

"Yes." He reached out and wiped her tear. "I'll be back."

When Brandon reentered the hallway, Tara was standing with a man who looked like he should be a doctor in some sitcom.

"Brandon, this is Dr. Taylor Hamilton. He's taking on Bethany's care while Anna's recovering."

"I hear you're her foster placement." The man extended his hand. "I look forward to working with you as we try to get her to health."

"I won't give up on her." He leaned against the wall outside of Bethany's room.

"That's what she needs right now. We're treating her GVHD with heavy doses of steroids, but I'm not seeing a response yet. It can take a few days to a week to start a turnaround."

Tara shifted her messenger bag. "Brandon, you need to prepare yourself. She may not survive, no matter how hard she's fighting."

"Don't give up hope." Dr. Hamilton glanced at the door. "She's a fighter from what I can tell."

"So is Brandon." Tara cleared her throat. "That's why I placed the kids with you, Brandon. I knew you would keep believing and fighting for her as long as she needed."

"I will." He needed to be strong as one more boulder-sized weight landed on his shoulders. He tried to inhale but couldn't with the heavy antiseptic smell locked in his lungs. "Anna expressed concern Saturday. Thought something was wrong with the trial."

At his words Tara blanched. "I learned of her accident when I arrived."

Dr. Hamilton glanced at the tablet he carried. "Dr. Johnson didn't mention anything in any of our team meetings. She's a committed collaborator who brings problems to the greater team. I'll recheck her patient notes for anything that might be bothering her."

"Thank you, Doctor." He seemed committed,

but Brandon doubted anyone would pour their heart into Bethany's care like Anna had.

Tara lowered her voice as if to shield Bethany from whatever she planned to say next. "Bethany won't survive a month without a miracle. Praecursoria absorbs the cost of the trial, and the hospital has waived the costs of her continued care, but that's not enough to save her life. We need her body to fight too."

"It's easy to fight for her." With everything in him, he wanted to see her healthy. When he adopted the new structure, she and Gabriel would be the only children he personally fostered, and he couldn't lose her. Could not.

A classic chicken-and-egg situation. That's what Caroline faced. She needed help deciphering the files on Anna's flash drive, but she wasn't sure who to ask when she still didn't understand the foundation of Anna's concern. Yet she couldn't understand what she had without someone to interpret the files. She couldn't get one without the other unless she could find someone who could help.

Was Brian Silver the right person to trust? He hadn't told her the whole story about Genetics for You. But Anna had mentioned him.

Maybe Justin. She might ask him as well.

Asking either man felt like a long shot but was better than flailing in the dark on her own.

She shifted to the small round table set in a corner of her office. Meeting here would feel more collaborative than him sitting in a chair in front of her desk. Caroline moved her monitor so they could sit at the small table and examine the flash drive's content side by side.

Brian rapped at her door. His long red hair was pulled back, and he adjusted his glasses as he came in. With his starched white lab coat he looked like he was playing a role on *Grey's Anatomy* rather than using his PhD in biochemistry to fill a scientific research role of importance.

"What do you need, Caroline?" He settled in the chair next to hers. "I have five minutes."

"Anna Johnson sent me a flash drive that looks to have information on it related to Praecursoria and specific trials."

"Why would she have that?"

"She's the doctor overseeing part of the trial. Why wouldn't she have it? She mentions you in her notes, and I need help deciphering what's on the drive. It might as well be gibberish." She cringed inside as she said that.

"That's understandable. We're working on cutting-edge therapies that involve layers of innovation that can intimidate those of us who've been here from the beginning." His smile was kind even as he leaned toward the monitor and pointed at the screen. "Is this one of the files?"

She shook her head as she used the mouse to navigate to the directory. "How much time do you have?"

"Right now? About one more minute."

She clicked open a spreadsheet, and he scanned it.

"This is going to take more than a quick glance to interpret."

"I expected you to say that."

"Can I take the drive with me?"

She hesitated. "How about I email the files to you? I haven't made a copy yet."

"Sure." He stood. "Time's up."

After Brian left, Caroline called Justin and sent the files to him as well.

WEDNESDAY, JUNE 2

When Brandon left his apartment Wednesday morning, the school-age kids had met the school buses that transported them to the appropriate Centreville schools. The preschool kids were at their activities. Since it was Wednesday, a traveling gymnastics bus would come to them in about an hour. It was worth the expense to wear the kids' little legs out until they had lunch and naps in their respective cottages. Then Alaina and Roselyn, another one of the house moms, would hold a story time in the lodge. His team had quickly learned routine was the key to a smoothly running home. The kids knew what to expect, while the adults made the schedule flexible enough to innovate and experiment.

He ran a quick few miles, then hustled back to his apartment.

He needed to be ready for the follow-up meeting with the house parents when the gymnastics bus arrived. That was their window to meet as a team, and for him to learn the couples' final verdicts. He'd been surprised that no one had given him a firm answer one way or the other, but today he'd finally learn each couple's status.

After cleaning up he headed to the main part of the lodge and paused in the main room near a table covered in puzzle pieces. It would be a good idea to get some new games and puzzles. He pulled out his phone and made a note to order a few from an online store.

He grabbed a fresh mug of black coffee in the kitchen, then walked into his smallish office and settled in the secondhand leather chair behind his desk, which consisted of a door placed on top of two battered, locked cabinets. He shifted aside the stack of birthday cards ready to go to his former foster kids who had June birthdays. His chair was better than the two folding chairs in front of his desk, but not by much. It barely fit his frame. It was a spartan setting, but he'd chosen to spend money on the spaces the kids utilized. He'd had it all during his pro career and didn't need that now, not when the kids needed things more than he did.

Fifteen minutes.

That was all the time he had to pray and then outline any last arguments.

As he prayed, a peace settled on him. He'd said all he could. Now was the time to let the house parents speak. His proposal would upend the business model and change their worlds even more than his. He still owned the land. He could still foster kids, just on a smaller scale, if they decided to take different paths.

When he left his office a few minutes before ten, four of the couples were seated on couches and chairs around the lodge's fireplace. Alaina had brought cookies, and Roselyn was filling the Keurig with water. When Tina and Tom walked in, Brandon called the meeting to order, then prayed for them.

"Lord, guide our conversation and give us wisdom as we seek what's best for these kids. Almost Home is Yours, and so are we."

There was a chorus of amens, and he looked at the people who served with him. "Regardless of what you have decided, I want you each to know how much I value you and the time you have invested in my vision and these kids. Do you have any questions for me?"

Tim kicked it off. "How quickly would the transition occur?"

Brandon liked the direction that question indicated. "A few of you are already licensed. Those who aren't will be restricted by getting that taken care of. The leases and contracts shouldn't take long. I've got the outline ready for an operating agreement."

"So end of summer?"

"Probably. Since that's when the latest version of regulations is supposed to be finalized, we should be ready in plenty of time."

Roselyn raised her hand, then blushed when Alaina teasingly elbowed her. "You mentioned we would have responsibilities at Almost Home. How will that work when we're no longer working for you?"

"Part of the rent would include helping with activities and rotating time off. I'm cautiously optimistic we'll get some help from the church that was here on Monday, but we've heard that before without great follow-through. I don't want to rely on external help when our best help might continue to be from each other. If we plan right, we might be able to get each couple a weekend off every five weeks."

Roselyn looked from her husband to Brandon. "So we'd be responsible for our own respite care?"

"My goal would be to provide that for you. Part of the package to help you succeed."

Tom frowned. "A goal is great, but you're

saying we could lose even the support that we have now? It's not much, and we frankly need more for fostering to be sustainable. Several of us already work second jobs."

"I'm working on a solution."

"We can't commit until it's more than a goal."

A murmur of agreement followed Roselyn's words, and Brandon felt the weight shift back onto his shoulders.

Jeff sighed. "Look, we want to stay, but Roselyn and Tom make good points. We have to have the respite in place first."

CHAPTER 26

A stack of files waited on Caroline's office chair when she arrived at work Wednesday. She was exhausted from a night of tossing and turning without deep sleep. Her dreams had been restless, filled with images of Anna being hit, her body battered into critical condition inside her car.

She woke braced to hear the worst about Anna, but nothing so far.

Then her thoughts had turned to the flash drive. She needed help getting everything she could off the drive and making sure it was backed up. Asking too many at Praecursoria for help seemed ill advised, so maybe she should involve a professor who'd served as a forensic expert for one of Emilie's trials. Dr. Elizabeth Ivy had explained the most complicated computer-science technical jargon and processes in a way that made sense to a layperson. Maybe she could tell Caroline what the numbers correlating with each file meant. It might be a vain hope, but it was the best Caroline had at the moment.

She inserted the drive into her work computer, then stared in horror at the file list.

Where yesterday there had been multiple folders, today the flash drive was empty.

Caroline ejected and reinserted the drive.

There had to be a mistake.

When she'd left the office the previous night, the drive had overflowed with data and bits and bytes, 1s and 0s. She might not have understood them, but they were there teasing her to unlock their meaning.

She went to the cloud where she'd copied the files. She tipped her head and propped her chin on one hand while she scrolled down the lists of files and folders. While someone might have gotten to the flash drive— somehow—there was no way they should have gotten to her cloud drive. It was private and password protected.

Then she groaned and collapsed against the chair back when the files didn't appear there either.

She'd accessed it from her work computer. That meant the company could have done anything with it because she'd used its equipment and network to access her files.

She knew better.

She was an attorney.

She knew privacy was dead. That anything she did at work on work equipment was essentially accessible. She'd told friends not to fall for the belief that their privacy was protected at their jobs, and she'd done exactly what she counseled against.

Nothing else was gone from her cloud drive, not even moved. It was all where it should be except that set of backed-up files. She called and left a message for Dr. Ivy. Maybe the woman could work a miracle and recover what had been on the flash drive. Hadn't she heard that data never really disappeared?

Wait, she had a copy in her email. The message she'd sent to Brian with the spreadsheet would be in her sent mail folder. Only when she opened it, the folder was clean. Completely wiped.

She groaned and set her head on her forearms on the surface of her desk.

A knock on her door had her jumping out of her skin. She cleared her throat and straightened. "Yes?"

The door opened, and Justin Grant stepped inside. "Have a quick minute?"

At her nod, he eased the door closed. "You know that thing you asked me to check on?"

"Yes." How could she forget asking him to look at a couple of the files? "Yes! Do you still have those?"

"I do. Well, I did." He glanced over his shoulder even though the door was shut. "Last night my desk was rifled through. The only thing taken was my paper copies of the files."

"You're sure?" It was an open-concept lab after all.

"I have a precise way I leave it at the end of the day." He ran a hand over his smooth head. "Someone was looking for something."

"You think it was the files."

"They're all that was missing." He looked flummoxed as his hands now slid into the pockets of his lab coat and he shifted his weight. "I've never had this happen before."

"Ever?" She raised an eyebrow as she watched him carefully. "You work in an open space with others."

"Sure, but we respect each other's space. That's the only way to make it work."

"What about the email? Do you still have it? We can just reprint the data."

"It's gone. Like you never sent it."

Caroline leaned back. "The same thing happened to me. There must be something important about the files."

He paused, opened his mouth, shut it, then reached for the door. "You need coffee? I need coffee."

Then he walked into the hall, and Caroline launched to her feet and grabbed her phone and keys before following him. She locked the door, though it was unlikely that would do anything to prevent another invasion of her office or computer. As an afterthought, she grabbed the flash drive just in case Dr. Ivy returned her call.

He marched to the back door and then outside.

Caroline double-timed as she followed him. "Where are we going?"

"Somewhere we can talk without being overheard."

She stopped at the edge of the parking lot. "This is crazy."

"Not based on what I saw before the files disappeared."

"What is it?"

"I'm not telling you while we're here." He glanced around and then took a step closer before lowering his voice. "I've got what I learned safely stored, but you need me to decipher it."

"That's why I gave you the files."

"Without any idea what's on them, or you would have gone to someone bigger."

"What does that even mean?" She didn't bother mentioning she'd also emailed them to Brian Silver.

"Not now." He lowered his head and started walking toward an older-model Buick sedan. She two-stepped to keep up. Something in her stomach knotted as she tried to decipher his cryptic words. She wanted to tell him he was acting delusional, but she knew what had happened to the flash drive and her private cloud storage files.

She tugged her keys from her pocket before following him. "I'll drive myself."

"Meet me at the Starbucks in the mall."

"Sure." That seemed farther than they needed to go, especially with the Sheepdog within walking distance, but she'd play along. "Can you be gone that long?"

"Early lunch." Then he slid his key into the driver's side door. His Buick was nothing snazzy, but it suited him. "I have a quick stop but will meet you there."

"All right." That would give her time to swing by the closer Genetics for You address since it was near the mall and she hadn't done it last night. "See you in a few minutes."

Justin nodded and closed his door.

Her phone rang as she climbed in her car. She took the call as she noted Brian Silver leaving the building.

"Caroline, this is Dr. Elizabeth Ivy returning your call."

"Thanks. I have a flash drive that's been wiped clean. Can you pull the data back up?"

"Sure. That's usually pretty simple. Is this for a case?"

"I'm not sure, since it got wiped before I could analyze what's on it. I could bring it to you later this morning or early afternoon."

"Early afternoon is best. I'm headed into a class." She rattled off her office number at the Fairfax campus. "Text when you're headed my way."

"Thank you so much." Caroline ended the call then double-checked that the flash drive was in her purse. In a few minutes she merged with traffic onto Highway 123 and headed east toward the mall. The mall was past the Leesburg Pike overpass, but she detoured onto Highway 7 to drive by the address for Genetics for You. A few minutes later when she pulled up, she saw it was an abandoned strip mall. She sat in her car and stared, then parked and climbed out. The slot that should have been Genetics for You had faded signage for a Burrito Don's restaurant. Based on the notices taped to the door, it had been closed for at least a year.

Had Genetics for You ever rented space here?

Staring at the building wouldn't answer that question. She backtracked to 123 and to the mall until she turned onto International Drive and then Tysons One Place. From there it was just a minute to reach the parking garage by Macy's. She'd double-time it through the store to the Starbucks. Afterward she'd slip into Disney and see about a stuffed animal of some sort for Ellie, Jeff and Alaina Stone's baby girl. As much time as she spent at Almost Home, it would be a good excuse to walk through the Disney things.

She was pulling into a slot on the third level when she heard and felt a horrible impact. She glanced in her rearview mirror to make sure she hadn't been rammed, but her car hadn't moved. Instead, it felt like the garage had shifted.

She took a deep breath.

Should she stay in her car or get out of the garage?

If it was an impact or accident, someone might need help, and that meant she should get her phone ready to dial 911. She wouldn't sit in her car if she could help.

She locked her car and hurried to the edge of the garage and looked over the side. A small sedan sat crushed against a pillar on the sidewalk while a larger white SUV backed up. She fumbled with her phone trying to get it turned on. She flipped to the camera and took a few photos as the vehicle roared away. From what she could see it looked like the license was covered with mud or dirt. It was unreadable, and her fingers trembled as she switched to place the 911 call.

She kept her gaze fixed on the car as she told the operator where she was and what she'd seen. Then the phone slipped from her grasp as she recognized the vehicle.

CHAPTER 27

Justin didn't move.

Caroline wheezed as she looked at his broken body splayed across the sidewalk. The car had tossed him as if he'd unhooked his seat belt to get a ticket for the garage. She ran her hands along his wrists looking for a pulse but wasn't sure how to do it. Her fingers brushed against something hard.

A phone lay on the ground.

She slipped it in her pocket as a man hurried to her, phone pressed to his ear. "I called 911. Can I help?"

She shook her head. "I don't know what to do."

The humidity pressed against her. So heavy. Yet she couldn't get warm.

She turned again, but the man had disappeared into the crowd. Her free hand reached into her pocket for her phone. Only it wasn't. This was Justin's, so where was hers? She found it in her other pocket and looked at both. She couldn't turn over his phone, not when it might have something that would explain why he wanted to meet her off-site. She tried to open Justin's, but it was face recognition enabled. No way for her to open it. She felt faint as she slipped hers back into her pocket.

Next thing she knew several police cars raced to the parking garage. The area began to swarm with activity, and one of the officers pulled her aside.

"I need to stay with him."

The man's eyes were kind and sad. "There's nothing you can do, ma'am."

"Please. He's my coworker. We were meeting here."

"You need to make way for the paramedics." He guided her off the road and across the street from the garage to a green space next to Macy's, where she collapsed on the grass. Her body trembled. Was it from adrenaline? She shook her head to clear her thoughts, but it didn't work.

The officer asked about what happened, and she told him. He took notes as she spoke. "I felt the impact. Then hurried to the edge. Saw a white SUV pulling away." She sighed as she rubbed her chilled arms. "That's all." She shuddered at how close she'd been to learning whatever Justin saw in the files.

The officer asked her a few more questions, then put away the notebook and pen. "Did he have a phone with him?"

It blazed hot in her pocket and she tugged it free. "Here. It was on the ground when I found him."

"Why did you pick it up?"

"I didn't want anyone else to walk off with it."

He studied her a moment, then seemed to accept her words. "I'll come check on you in a few minutes. Don't go anywhere."

"I won't." She felt too weak to try.

A minute later a paramedic draped a blanket around her shoulders, but it didn't begin to cut through the cold that pierced her bones.

The kind where she couldn't feel her toes.

A detective approached with a to-go cup of Starbucks, then veered off to talk to a uniformed officer.

Caroline shuddered and clutched the blanket closer. Justin had brought her here because her office wasn't safe. Praecursoria wasn't safe.

Well, now she wasn't safe.

Was whoever had crashed into Justin here now? Watching? Gauging whether she was a threat?

What if she'd driven with Justin? Would she be lying on the ground next to him?

Had that one small decision saved her life?

The trembling intensified as the thought took hold. Simple choices could have terrible ramifications.

All she'd wanted to do was find out why Anna sent her the flash drive. Decipher the files that made no sense to her. Files that someone else wanted hidden. With Anna in intensive care, Caroline had to turn to others. Now as she watched the paramedics pull a blanket over Justin's body, she wondered. Was this her fault?

The detective approached, and Caroline wasn't sure whether he was friend or foe. The white SUV had looked like the security vehicle that patrolled the parking lot at work. People associated with Praecursoria were dying violent deaths. What was the name of the woman who had died right before Caroline started? Sarah? Was her death tied to the company? Before this moment, that thought would have been crazy. Now? It felt irresponsible not to consider the possibility. Caroline needed to be careful and extricate herself from the scene so she could get what she needed from her office tonight and then slip away. She had a tiny bit of personal leave accrued. It would have to be enough while she tried to sort things out.

She shook her head at the craziness of the thought. She wasn't in the middle of some suspense movie or book. She didn't need to leave . . . did she?

Maybe.

But she needed the truth.

That's why she had snagged Justin's phone when she saw it lying next to his body. She'd turned it over, but what if that was why the detective was walking her way now? She'd already told another one what she'd seen . . . nothing helpful. What more did they want?

She couldn't fabricate details.

Her shoulders hitched toward her ears as the

paramedics brought a gurney over, then stood next to it, in no hurry.

She couldn't let Justin's death be in vain. And she couldn't explain why that mattered to the police, when she wasn't even sure what could have led to this violent death. But she knew beyond a reasonable doubt that her request was linked to what had happened here today.

The question she couldn't unravel to an answer was why.

Why had her questions led here?

She clutched the blanket tighter. She was cold.

So very cold.

"Isn't that your girlfriend?"

Brandon glanced up with a start. He'd had his back to the door and the lodge's big-screen TV as he made a cup of coffee in the kitchen. Jeff had come over to talk through the weekend activities and had turned on the TV in the background. Now he stood, stance wide, in front of the TV, arms crossed as an accident scene filled the screen.

"Caroline?" What was she doing on TV?

"As far as I know she's your only special lady."

Brandon rolled his eyes. "Funny guy."

"You know it, but seriously, isn't that her?"

He studied the flashing emergency lights and uniformed men and women moving like loosely synchronized players in a drama. A woman sat on the ground near an ambulance, looking shell-shocked and frozen as she clutched a dark blanket like a cape. He frowned.

"Wait. That looks like Caroline."

Jeff rolled his eyes. "Isn't that what I just said?"

Brandon didn't bother to respond as he stood and snagged his keys and phone from the corner of the table. "Does that look like Tysons Corner?"

"Yep, the Center. That's also what the words at the bottom say."

"Thanks." Hc hurried from the lodge and to his truck.

The drive into Tysons seemed to drag. At this rate it was a fool's errand. He should have stayed put and called. At a stoplight, he dialed her number but it went to voicemail. He tried not to speed as he prayed she was okay. If the ambulance took her somewhere, he might not connect with her for hours. Or she could be released and on her way home before he ever worked his way through traffic to her. However, the glimpse he'd caught indicated she was cold and scared, not injured. IIe'd havc to trust that was the case.

Then it hit him.

Why was she at the mall in the middle of the day?

While Caroline knew how to have a good time and could be the life of a gathering, she also worked with single-minded focus and determination. She wasn't the type to step out for an extended break in the middle of the day. Not even for shopping.

When he was almost to the mall, he called Jeff. "Any thoughts on which parking garage?"

"Looks like the one closest to Macy's. Have you reached her?"

"She's not answering her phone. Have to go." He hung up and headed that direction.

Yellow crime-scene tape flapped in the wind, and a patrol officer blocked the road with his vehicle. He waved Brandon to the parking lot on the right. Brandon rolled down his window and pointed to the left. "I'm here to pick up my friend."

The officer put his hand on his utility belt and frowned. "The garage is closed."

"She was waiting at one of the ambulances." It hadn't registered in the blip of an image on the TV that multiple emergency vehicles were on-site.

"You still need to park over there. I'd recommend calling her to see if she's ready to leave."

"Thanks."

The man nodded, then Brandon started winding through the ground lot. He picked a slot with a view of the scene and quickly spotted Caroline. As soon as he parked, he pulled out his phone and called again. She glanced around as if in a

300

fog, then slowly pulled out her phone. "I saw you might need a ride."

"Brandon?" He watched her stand from the ambulance and look around. "Are you here?"

"A few rows over. Can I come get you?"

Her shoulders slumped beneath the blanket she still clutched with one hand. "Please."

So much meaning was infused in that word. He sat straighter in the truck's cab and turned off the vehicle. "Be there in a minute."

He tried not to strut . . . too much . . . as he made his way across the parking lot and past the officer who still blocked the road. Caroline needed him, a fact he knew before she'd thought to ask.

When she saw him she hurried toward him and fell against his chest. His arms circled her, pulling her closer. He needed this too, to know she was okay. She was so little, tucked into him in a way that made him think she wasn't wearing her going-to-war, spiky-heeled shoes. There were twelve-year-olds at Almost Home who were taller, but none had the fight and passion that Caroline did.

If he was fortunate, he and the house parents would help a few of the younger girls develop into her style of woman. The world would be better because of it.

"You okay?"

She shuddered at his words. "I don't know."

It didn't look like she was physically hurt, but the blanket acted like a cape to hide what was underneath. "Are you hurt anywhere?"

"Only my heart."

He held her slightly away from him as he scanned her. "Then why are you still here? They need to get you to the hospital."

"Not physically." She leaned back into him and wrapped her arms around him, the blanket loosening across her shoulders. "The victim was my colleague."

He blanched. "What happened?"

"Last night I asked Justin to look at something for me, and today he wanted to meet me at Starbucks because he didn't want to risk being overheard at work. He was hit and killed entering the garage. I heard and felt the impact." She shuddered and squeezed even closer. Nothing separated them now, and he wanted it to be like this forever.

"That must have been terrible."

"I was one of the first next to him. I tried to take a photo of the vehicle that hit him, but it's too grainy. It won't help anyone."

"The technology they use is amazing."

"On *CSI*, maybe. That's not all real."

"But it's cool."

She snort-laughed and pulled back, wiping the blanket over her face to dry her tears. "I suppose it is." Her posture slumped and she shrank again.

"You said his name was Justin?"

"Yes. Justin Grant." She glanced around. "Can you take me home?"

"Sure. Do you need to check with anyone?"

"I don't think so. An officer took down my information."

"What about your car? Where is it?"

Her gaze traveled to the parking garage. "It's up a couple levels. I'll get a lift here later to reclaim it. I want my home, comfy clothes, and some time." Her phone rang from somewhere under the blanket, but she ignored it.

"Do you need to get that?"

"I'm not ready to tell anyone at work what happened to Justin. It will raise questions like why he was here and why I witnessed it. We both should have been at work."

He wanted to ask more questions, but he'd wait until he got her home, to a safe place where she could relax. He tugged at the blanket. "Should you give this back?"

Caroline's nose wrinkled as she released it. "I don't want it." Then she stopped. "I have to get my purse from my car."

"I'll grab it for you."

"No way am I staying here." She shuddered, and he wanted to wrap her back up in his arms.

"Wait in my truck. You'll be safe there."

"Okay." Her voice was hesitant but her chin lifted.

There was the strong woman he was used to seeing. He held out his hand, and hers slipped into his grasp where it belonged. "Let's get you settled."

She pulled a small key ring from her pocket. "Here are the keys to the 'stang."

Nothing electronic or modern about the simple key that went with her hot rod. A smile slipped out at the thought of this slip of a woman driving a muscle car.

After returning the blanket to a paramedic who was packing up in the back of the ambulance, Brandon led Caroline across the street to his truck. Once she was settled in it, he hightailed it to the other garage, approaching from the opposite side so he didn't get stopped.

It took a couple of laps to reach her distinctive Mustang. But when he searched the car, her purse was gone. He pulled out his phone and dialed her. "Caroline, it's not here."

"What?" Her voice had the worn-out sound of someone who couldn't handle much more on an overloaded plate.

"Your purse. I checked everywhere. I can't find it." He stood and looked around the car. Still nothing. "Any chance you had it with you?"

"No." There was a moment of silence. "Maybe I left the car unlocked in those early moments. But I was sure . . ."

"I had to unlock it. And you didn't come back to it?"

"No, I hurried down to see if Justin could be saved."

"That was the right decision. Look, I'll bring the car over to the truck so you can look for yourself."

Nothing else seemed to be missing, but she'd know for sure.

CHAPTER 28

Caroline tried to steady her heartbeat with slow, steady breaths. She was safe in Brandon's truck. No one would bother her here.

But Justin had probably thought the same thing as he approached the parking garage.

When she heard the rumble of her Mustang's engine, she turned to find Brandon parking it next to the truck. She climbed out and gave the vehicle a cursory look to confirm it hadn't been dinged.

Then she climbed into the front seat and started feeling around for her purse. After a minute, she stood. "It's not here."

A pulse of panic flashed through her.

What was going on? Without the purse she didn't have the flash drive. There was nothing to give to Dr. Ivy. And without Justin, she'd need to get those files from Brian.

She felt the wave of panic building. Inhaling became more difficult with each moment.

She couldn't go home. Not with everything that was happening. Two suspicious deaths. And she was almost certain the driver of the white SUV had looked up and noted her presence at the garage. The thought was unsettling, especially when all she'd seen was a flash of a face under a navy ball cap. With her driver's license, it wouldn't take two minutes to figure out what the keys unlocked.

Where was a paper bag? She was on the border of hyperventilating if she couldn't calm her nerves, and she didn't want Brandon to see her like that. As far as he was concerned, her deepest fears involved cupcakes collapsing rather than being in her home alone at night. He didn't know about the way she kept every light on and then turned off those in the living areas only on the rare nights she felt settled.

Those nights were too few. She glanced at the man next to her. "Can you take me somewhere to get a new lock for my apartment?"

He understood right away. "Sure. I can even change it for you." He waggled his eyebrows at her, giving him a Groucho Marx air. "I've got skills."

Oh yes, he did. He had enough confidence for a football team's full defensive line, but she loved the way he tempered that with a deep care for those around him. "The way I'm trembling I shouldn't drive."

"I've got you."

And she knew he did in so many ways beyond this moment.

It took an hour to get a lock kit and reach her apartment. Her steps faltered as she tried to remember what condition it was in. She hadn't planned to bring anyone home, so she hadn't taken the five minutes to sweep the house for clutter before walking out the door.

She hesitated before getting out of the car. "How do I get in?"

"Call the super?"

"Right." The office would have a master key. In fact, they probably would have rekeyed the door for her. Her brain was a muddled mess. She dialed and then explained what had happened to the woman who answered. She promised to send someone over, and Caroline leaned her head against the headrest.

"You okay?" Brandon's voice penetrated her fog.

"I will be. I just wish I could figure out the reason behind what happened to Justin."

"That's for the police to determine. It could be an accident." She opened her eyes in time to catch Brandon's shrug. "Life is hard and unfair sometimes. Tragic accidents happen with no reason or explanation. This could be one of those."

She shook her head. "I don't think so, at least not this time. There was something about his demeanor when he was in my office. Someone had been in my office and wiped a flash drive and the backup files on the cloud. Then Justin said someone searched his desk and took his paper printouts. He refused to say anything else inside Praecursoria." She closed her eyes and imagined the scene again. "He was adamant he had something to tell me, but not there."

"Any way to figure out what he'd learned?"

"I don't know. It was related to the flash drive." What had Anna uncovered, and was it somehow tied to Justin's death? "I wish Judge Loren hadn't died."

"What would that change?"

"I would still be his clerk and wouldn't be at Praecursoria. I wouldn't have met Justin. Maybe he'd still be alive."

"That's taking a lot of responsibility on your shoulders."

"What I do best."

He wanted to tell her that wasn't what he'd witnessed. What she did better than so many was bring people together. She connected them because she saw them. She had empathy that let her see to the heart of who they were, and in a way that showed her care.

It was a rare trait.

"So how do we figure out if there's something that connects Anna's and Justin's accidents? Because I don't think police will see them as anything more than coincidence."

She looked away. "Right now all I can think is that the files Anna gave me have something to do with it." She paused. "Someone else at

Praecursoria died right before I started. At the time it sounded like a tragedy, but I find two deaths in a couple of months suspect."

"Maybe." He drummed his fingers on the steering wheel. Before he could continue, a man in jeans and a gray jacket walked toward the building.

Caroline straightened and then opened the truck door. "That's one of the maintenance staff." She stepped down and waved at the man. "Hey, Charlie. How's Meredith?"

The man turned toward her, a grin on his face. "Hey, Miss Carrie. She's good. Real good. The doctor released her to go back to work this week."

"Awesome." Caroline—er, Carrie—raised a hand for a high five the man willingly gave. "Someone stole my purse today, and it had my house keys in it."

"Need me to rekey it?"

"Can you believe we stopped and bought a new lock on the way here?"

"You let me install it. Save you some money and get it done today."

"That would be great. Thank you." She turned back to the truck and made a little "come here" motion with her hand. Brandon obliged and she waited for him to join her. "Charlie, this is my good friend Brandon."

The man gave him a solid looking over, like he

was trying to penetrate to the core of his being. Then he gave a slight nod as if pleased with what he saw. He stuck out his hand. "Nice to meet you. Name's Charlie Harris."

"Brandon Lancaster." There it was. The little widening of the eyes. Nothing over the top, but enough to let Brandon know his name had landed.

"It truly is a pleasure, sir." Charlie opened his mouth as if he wanted to comment on the Super Bowl or some other favorite moment, then shook his head as if clearing the thought. "You have that lock? If so, give it on over, and I'll get this changed out for you."

Brandon retrieved the bag from the truck, then Charlie unlocked the door and got to work as Brandon and Caroline stepped inside.

He glanced around the living room. "Carrie?"

"That's what you want to focus on?"

"I've never heard anyone call you anything but Caroline." He grinned. "Well, other than the kids."

Now it was her turn to roll her eyes, as if she could get a gold medal in the sport. "There's a first time for everything."

"Carrie." He let the name roll off his tongue, and she turned away with a harrumph.

"Have your fun, but you don't get to call me that."

"How does Charlie rate giving you a nickname?"

"He's a nice guy."

"I'm a nice guy."

"Maybe." She turned and evaluated him with a thoroughness that left him feeling a bit exposed. "But you haven't unclogged a drain or changed my lock."

"I was willing to. On the lock."

Charlie whistled from his post by the door. "I'll leave the new keys with you, Miss Carrie. Just take the one for the super."

"Thanks, Charlie. I'm here long enough to get a few things. Then I'm off for a couple days."

This was news to Brandon. "I thought you'd stay here."

She shook her head. "Not tonight. I wouldn't feel safe knowing someone has my address—even with the lock changed." Caroline lowered her voice. "What if someone saw me at the mall? Knows I was there with Justin? Am I safe?"

Brandon hated the question. He considered offering to sleep on her couch, but she turned away before he could say anything.

"Can you wait here while I throw a few things in an overnight bag?" She walked down the small hallway to the back half of her apartment.

The space was cozy and reflected her personality with bright throw pillows with clever sayings on them. One about coffee, another about books, and still one more about travel. Personally he thought such pillows were a waste since he was always putting them on the floor so he could get comfortable, but they did mirror Caroline's personality, though she didn't travel. Did that mean she might like to?

There were no photos on display. Nothing personal enough to stop her rooms from looking like they could fill the pages of some farmhouse design magazine. Had she found an example and replicated it, or was this really what she liked?

It felt a bit like a warm den with its deep beige tones. As he settled on the couch to wait, he wondered what she would do with his apartment, if given the chance. Would she come in and add black-and-white prints to the walls while taking down his football paraphernalia? Would she understand why those things mattered to him, or find them old? Relics of his past?

Based on this room, Caroline didn't have a past.

That wasn't possible, but as he took another glance around, he realized it matched what he knew. It was almost as if she showed up for law school without a background. She'd been a blank slate, and her friends had made her who she was.

While it was a package that was easy to love, who would she be if she took full control of her destiny?

He wasn't sure she knew.

The realization brought heaviness. The sort of heaviness that wouldn't dislodge with a roll of his shoulders and a mental heave-ho.

No, it demanded a response.

The challenge was determining what kind.

It was a puzzle he could work on. A goal to achieve.

When she stepped from her room pulling a rolling suitcase and work bag, he realized there was a lot more that needed tending. Tears were tracing down her cheeks as she approached.

The new key felt heavy in her hand as she handed it to Brandon. Stupid tears. She wanted to stop crying, but even more she wanted to be strong enough that tears weren't an issue.

"After everything that has happened, I need to know someone has a way to get into my apartment if anything happens." The act highlighted how alone she was in the world. "You're the closest thing I have to family."

"You have the girls."

She sniffled and gasped against the pain. "I suppose, but it feels pretty lonely right now. Besides, you're my boyfriend; just don't abuse the privilege of the key."

His eyebrows shot up. "Are you serious? The privilege of the key?"

She choked on a laugh and then leaned into his side, desperate for the warmth of his protection. "You know what I mean."

She was about to disappear.

He could feel it to his core.

He couldn't let that happen. "Come back to Almost Home tonight. Or I'll drive you to Jaime's." The words didn't seem to ping behind the wall she'd erected. "You're not alone, Caroline."

She sucked in a sob.

It did him in, and he tugged her into a hug.

She fell against him, feeling small and frail. His arms tightened, but she didn't relax. He rubbed her back, wanting to infuse her with the knowledge she was safe. He had her, and he had no plans of letting go.

"Caroline, you will not be alone unless you want to be. I'm here and won't leave."

"Don't say that." She stiffened and tried to pull back, but he didn't let her.

He held firm and prayed for insight. "What are you afraid of?"

"You can't promise you'll never leave. That's the one thing I can guarantee will happen."

"Impossible."

"Not in my experience." She sagged a bit. "If I didn't insist on being included, I'd be overlooked and forgotten. My mom forgot my sister and me every night. The alcohol was more important. Then in college everyone else was more fun or popular. I was the pity invite."

"You think that's still true?"

She buried her face in his shirt and gave a quick jerk.

"Caroline, I wish you could see what your friends and I see. You are an amazing woman, full of empathy and the vision that really sees people. Your heart is soft and you feel others' pain. You are strong and compassionate." He tipped her chin up so she had to look at him. "And you are the most beautiful woman I know."

Then he leaned down and lightly touched her lips with his. Slowly he deepened the kiss, trying to convey the depth of his emotion in this small act.

Her heart froze at the lightest of touches. His lips on hers.

Then she let herself lean into the moment. Forget her fears. Trust this man.

She deepened the kiss and his arms tightened around her waist.

The image of Justin's twisted body at the parking garage vanished. Her entire focus settled on the man holding her. And she didn't want to move or break the spell. She didn't want to risk waking up from the dream where the man she loved was kissing her.

She felt the weight of it.

He was offering himself.

And she didn't want anything more than the knowledge that he would be here, holding her as carefully as if she were spun glass.

This . . . inside his arms . . . was home.

Her chest caught and she felt the lightest touch on her cheeks as he brushed away the lingering tears. She shuddered and leaned into his touch.

He pulled back and set his forehead on hers. "Will you let me help you? I don't want you to be alone tonight."

"I don't want to be alone either."

He let go of her long enough to grab her suitcase. "That settles it. We're headed to Almost Home. It's remote and yet there are others if I need backup."

"I don't want to put anyone in danger."

He wanted to promise she wouldn't be, but right now that felt like a promise he couldn't keep. "Then we'll lay low."

She shook her head. "I'm not going to be dependent on you."

He stepped back so he could meet her gaze. "If you can't trust me, who will you trust?"

She swallowed and then leaned back in, hiding her face under a veil of her hair. "I choose to trust you."

He felt the significance of her words. The force of the choice behind them.

He wouldn't let her down.

CHAPTER 29
THURSDAY, JUNE 3

As soon as she woke Thursday morning in the unused cabin at Almost Home, Caroline called Brian. "Have you had a chance to look at the files I emailed you Tuesday?"

"Now's really not a good time."

"It's been a pretty rough week for me too." She didn't want to tell him she'd been with Justin, not unless she had to. "Did you get the email?"

He huffed and she heard something that sounded like pages flipping. Then clicking as on a keyboard. "Nope. I thought maybe you forgot."

"I sent it right after we talked Tuesday. Are you sure it's not in your spam or trash?"

There was a moment of silence. "Yep, it's not here. I'd be glad to look at it, but Justin was in an accident, and my workload just doubled again."

The silence became awkward, and she forced the words. "An accident?"

"He was at Tysons Corner of all places. During the workday. Got hit entering the parking garage." The man made a hissing sound. "Can you imagine? Random, and whoever hit him didn't stop."

She could imagine. In living color. Could feel the vibration. She shuddered and closed her eyes. "Awful."

After that call, all she wanted was to stay cocooned in the cabin. Instead, she got a call telling her she was needed for a meeting. She asked Brandon if she could borrow his truck and he agreed, though he made it clear he would have preferred to drive her himself.

On her way in, she circled the parking lot looking for the security vehicle, but when she found it, it was clean. No dents. No indication it had been in a hit-and-run the prior day. She wanted to laugh and cry at the same time. How would she even know what she was looking for?

As she moved to her office, she couldn't shake the image of Justin's broken body, or the idea that someone connected to Praecursoria had been behind the "accident." She'd tried, how she'd tried, but the thoughts kept pressing in.

She found a moment of peace as she relived the sweetness of Brandon's kiss.

She wanted to let herself lean in and trust what that moment represented.

Her thoughts shifted yet again. What had Anna been so determined to understand? What had she uncovered? And had Justin been killed for helping Caroline try to decipher it? She wanted to see if he had talked to anyone else in the lab but didn't want to put a bull's-eye on someone. And how did it tie to Sarah's death, if at all?

An hour after the meeting, Caroline knew she needed to leave. She wasn't getting anything accomplished within her office's four walls. But while packing her bag, she got a call to report to Quentin's office. How was he back already?

She sighed but set down her bag and grabbed her notebook, pen, and keys.

She wanted to retreat to Brandon's place. She wouldn't sleep, but she'd be home. She froze. Home? She couldn't let herself hope for that. Or maybe she could. Brandon had proven himself to be nothing but steadfast.

After a brisk rap against Quentin's door, she entered his office. Instead of sitting behind his desk, he was sitting on his loveseat, a stack of files in front of him and one open in his hand. He glanced up and pushed his reading glasses on top of his head. "Have a seat."

She edged to one of the wing chairs across the coffee table. "How was your trip?"

He looked at her with a tip of his chin. "What trip?"

"Lillian mentioned you were out of town."

"Nope. Too much to do here. Can I get you anything to drink?" He waved at the cup of coffee next to the files. "Lillian is out today, but the Keurig is still on."

"I'm fine." She didn't want to prolong her time at the office. "I hope she's okay."

"Lillian?" He waved a hand in the air. "She's fine. Just wanted some personal time." He set the files to the side. "Has she said anything to you? I'm concerned someone here is harassing her."

"She hasn't said anything specific, but I would ask her." Caroline considered how much to say. Without Lillian giving her a name, she didn't have anything to report to HR. "As her boss, it's always good to confirm everything's okay with her. She seems to do a good job."

"A great job. My schedule was a disaster until she arrived. I know she can be overly zealous at protecting me, but it's helped." He watched her carefully a moment. "You all right?"

"It's been a long week." Although the day would improve with Brandon and the kids.

He rubbed his eyes and then slid the glasses back in place. "It has. We've got a key employee to replace." He watched her a moment, but Caroline didn't flinch. "Are you doing all right? I heard you were there."

She swallowed hard. "I've never seen anyone that battered before. It'll be a while before I lose that image."

"That must have been hard. Is there anything I can do?" He put his hand over his chest. "We take care of our own."

There was something about the way he said it that made her cock her head as if that would help her understand. "I'm fine. Thanks." And she had friends who would help if she needed anything. "If that's all." She pushed to her feet.

"Actually, I need you to move the process along."

"What process?"

"Patrick Robbins's trial. With the FDA. We can't afford to miss this opportunity. It's time to go to the next level of trials."

She inhaled. "The FDA isn't the holdup. Our scientists and doctors are jumping through hoops as fast as they can."

"That may be, but as a shareholder I want to ensure everything moves as swiftly as possible."

"You aren't the sole shareholder. I'm sure you don't want anyone's investment to be at risk." She'd reviewed the list earlier in the week as she prepared annual filings to be filed with the Virginia Secretary of State. "You have a fiduciary duty to each of them." Including Brandon.

"And that means getting these therapies into people's hands." He growled. "I could move the operation to Mexico tomorrow and make this available to whoever wants to pay. But I don't want to. It's better if we do everything here."

She opened her mouth and then closed it. "What if Patrick's body is unique in the way it metabolizes and mobilizes the CAR T-cell therapy?" She straightened her shoulders and maintained eye contact with him. "Bethany isn't doing well on the same protocol."

"Who's that?"

"The little girl we met the day I interviewed."

"Oh, right."

"Her body is in full rejection of the therapy. What if we ramp up too fast for Phase 2 trials and learn her experience is not unique?"

"We'll never know if we don't get more people on it."

"I advise strongly against that." Then she stood but paused before leaving. "While I'm here, I need to know who has liability for the genetic testing done while Genetics for You was part of this company."

"Caroline, this is ridiculous. Of course Genetics for You has liability. That's why their letter shouldn't be a big deal."

"But Brian Silver and Samson Kleme were part of the consortium of buyers, and—"

"And that has nothing to do with anything. Send a letter and make it go away."

"Take this seriously, please. One lawsuit, if validated, leads to more. You could lose Praecursoria over this. Handling the complaint correctly must be a top priority."

"That's your job."

"Exactly. And I'm doing it. What are you afraid of?"

"Nothing. We're finished." He stood as red mottled his neck.

"You can't avoid this issue. This company's past and current actions can't be avoided by looking away and crossing your fingers." She sighed. "Look, they've made a reasonable offer."

"Is *that* what you think I'm doing? Think about it, Caroline: Genetics for You is defunct. That's the only reason those women are coming after us, because they can't go after the real target."

"Where is the buy-sell agreement?"

"It should be in *your* files."

"It's not."

"Then I'll have Lillian email a copy to you."

The community dinner had the lodge echoing with decibels that had to be higher than any auditory specialist would recommend. Tonight Brandon didn't care. The kids were excited and enjoying their hot dogs and homemade macaroni and cheese. They didn't know s'mores were coming, though he still questioned his sanity tackling a project involving sticks and fire without more adult supervision. Thirty-some sugared-up kids running around a fire with sharp sticks might not be his best idea, but he knew they'd love it.

He should be fully present, but his thoughts kept drifting to Caroline.

Was she okay? He'd been surprised when she asked to take his truck but had handed over the keys. That was hours ago. The noise level rose and he glanced around. The kids looked to be done with their food, so he stood and clapped his hands in three quick beats.

The kids' heads snapped his direction. As he glanced over the tables, his heart swelled. These were his Lost Boys, with a few Wendys sprinkled in for good measure and some calm in the chaos.

Now he just needed *his* Wendy to arrive. The only thing that would make the moment better was Caroline standing next to him.

The level of hyperactivity had him changing his mind. Instead of s'mores, they'd go with cups of ice cream. The fire could wait for a night when he had backup. The last thing he needed was for even one child to get hurt.

"All right, gang. It's time to pray for your families. Then we'll have dessert." The ice-cream cups might still be a mistake, but the kids would expect something sweet to end the meal. They were also easy to distribute. Only two choices: vanilla or chocolate.

"What is it, Mr. Brandon?" Eli's lisp made *Brandon* sound more like *Bwandon*. Made him want to tickle the kid until his laughter filled the lodge.

"Something everyone likes." At least they seemed to. Ice cream usually disappeared as fast as he pulled it out of the freezer. "Now let's spend a few minutes praying."

The older kids at each table took the lead. Brandon felt grateful as he watched even the youngest clasp their hands in front of them. He wandered from table to table, taking a few minutes at each to ask about the kids and see what their needs were. They wouldn't all tell him what was in their hearts and minds, but he found these weekly connections made a difference in his ability to assess which kids might need more help than they were currently getting.

He'd made it to the farthest table when he heard the front door of the lodge opening. He slowly turned toward it and felt warmth surge into his belly as he watched Miss Caroline Bragg walk in.

The tension eased from her as she walked through the door.

This was where she belonged.

Brandon's grin grew slowly, like a sunrise one had to wait for. But when it came? Lands, it stole her breath.

Lands? She stifled a giggle at the way she'd echoed her maternal grandmother. She hadn't thought like that since she'd spent time with the very southern woman at Christmas. Caroline waved to a couple of the kids as a swell of hellos echoed off the ceiling and walls.

"Hey, y'all. Can I join you?"

Chloe Johnson nodded until her blonde braids danced around her shoulders. "Mr. Brandon hasn't told us what we're having for dessert yet, but it's always good." She leaned closer to Caroline until she looked like she'd topple from her chair, then stage-whispered, "The macaroni was overcooked, so hopefully dessert is something he bought made."

Caroline bit her lower lip to keep from giggling as her gaze strayed to Brandon. "I'm sure it will be good either way."

He just shook his head. "Everyone's a critic." He leaned near to kiss her cheek, and she ordered her heart to keep its rhythm as she inhaled his unique blend of aftershave. "I'll even let you help me grab it." He tugged on one of Chloe's braids. "You, too, kiddo. You get to carry the spoons."

The waif of a girl grinned at him, completely uncowed in his massive presence. The girl might be nine years old, but she looked like a pixie next to Brandon. Ten minutes later the initial chaos of distributing the ice-cream cups had quieted. But the calm wouldn't last once the sugar hit the kids' bloodstreams. Brandon was as bad as a grandparent who sugared up their grandkids before returning them to their parents. The house parents would have to get some serious activity going if they wanted sleep tonight.

Brandon took her hand, his still damp from washing off ice cream. "I'm glad you're back safe."

"Where else would I be? I missed my best friend. And the kids." Being here with him tugging her closer made her heart want to melt faster than the ice cream. "I missed you, too, but I didn't drive all the way to see you." She paused dramatically.

"Wait. That's right. You have my truck. You had to come back."

"Really?"

He turned a slow circle, his arms wide. He winked at the kids, in his element. "Who else would bring you this far?"

She rolled her eyes dramatically, and a couple of the girls giggled. "It's Thursday night after all. And that means . . ." She waved her arms like she was conducting an orchestra, and the kids didn't disappoint.

"Family dinner!"

The eruption hurt her ears but was worth it.

He glanced around the lodge as if surprised to see it filled with kids. "So it is. That must be why all of them are in here." His grin slowly faded as he studied her. "You okay?"

She nodded, her words stopped by the sudden lump in her throat. She tilted her chin toward the table. "Your ice cream is melting."

She froze as she noticed the way he watched her lips. Everything in her stilled. Did she want him to kiss her? Oh yes, even in front of all these kids. Everything in her wanted to lean into him, initiate what her soul had imagined time after time. She let herself lean toward him.

A body barreled into her, bouncing her into Brandon's solid chest. Ouch, the man had solid muscles. He grunted as she landed against him, his arms tightening as he steadied her.

"Luke, how many times have I told you not to run in here?" Brandon's voice was firm with an edge of smile to it.

Caroline twisted to look at the imp who grinned up with a gap where his two front teeth should be. "Miss Carrie looked like she needed a hug. I helped."

Imp.

The boy couldn't be older than seven, and that grin melted her heart. Maybe someday she'd have a boy of her own with a gap-toothed grin.

The main door of the lodge opened and Jeff and Alaina walked in, Ellie strapped in a carrier across Alaina's chest. Brandon tugged Caroline close and she let herself relax into the moment. He hovered just a moment over her lips, and she would have tugged him closer to narrow the distance if they hadn't been surrounded by all the kids. That didn't stop him as his lips touched hers. The world exploded in sparkles around her and she leaned closer. When the kiss ended a moment later, she took a half step back, her balance having abandoned her, and he grinned with little-boy delight.

Was it wrong that he liked the effect he had on her? Nope, not in the least. Not when she enjoyed it too.

Jeff started chuckling. "It's about time."

CHAPTER 30

Brandon swung Evan up on his shoulders. "You here to collect your cabin?" At Jeff's nod, he grinned. "Good. I sugared them up with ice cream for you."

Alaina rolled her eyes. "You boys are all the same. All the sugar all the time."

"It's what's for dinner."

"At least when you're cooking." Jeff called roll for his kids. Caroline was glad she wasn't responsible for four boys and two girls ranging in age from about four to ten or eleven. She'd never had brothers, and other than classmates didn't have much experience being around boys. "All right, men, follow Alaina."

Alaina waved and then glanced at Caroline with apology in her eyes. "Guess we're headed out posthaste." She marched toward the door, and it was adorable to watch the boys fall in line behind her, their own version of *Make Way for Ducklings*.

"I feel like I should call them Jack, Lack, Mack, and Quack."

Brandon looked at her quizzically.

"Those are the names of the ducklings in a children's book." She waved a hand as if to clear the thought from the air. "Silly of me." She squared her shoulders and looked at the rest of the kids. "When do they get collected?"

"Anytime." Brandon shook his watch. "Maybe this thing is broken."

"Let's play a game until the other parents arrive."

He scanned her up and down, and she felt the warmth of his appraisal. "In those heels? Why do you do that to yourself? Go change. You can always come back." He waggled his eyebrows, and one of the kids laughed.

"I'm trying to add stature." She rolled her eyes. "Why else would someone wear stilts all day? I'll go change, then we can play something like Uno or War with whoever's still here." Slippers sounded really good, while tennis shoes sounded better. Her feet were weary and the comfort padding in her heels wore thinner with each passing half hour.

When she returned ten minutes later, she was more comfortable but several of the kids were spinning wildly in circles. "Think we can get them settled down?"

Brandon glanced around. "If they can sit still."

"The house parents will appreciate your not winding them up more than the sugar already has."

"Hey, you were an equal partner in distributing the ice cream."

She grinned at him. "But I get to leave while you're stuck here with them."

Her throat caught as she tried to swallow. She

331

didn't really mean it, not like it sounded. There was something so wonderful and homelike about being here with these kids. They were secure in a way she hadn't been growing up. Was it wrong to be jealous of them? Despite everything they'd lost or experienced, they'd landed here in a place of safety, rest, and love. All they had to do was embrace it.

While Caroline made an attempt, she wasn't quite present with the kids. She'd spark to life when flirting with him, then her light would fade. While she matched wits with kids in a game of train dominoes, her gaze would settle in the distance only to jerk back to the present when someone snagged her arm or said her name.

Even though she was distracted, she was at her most beautiful interacting with the kids. She'd always been that way, and it was hard to imagine any of the women who'd pursued him having the same attitude. Caroline genuinely enjoyed his kids without pretense or fakeness.

She was a jewel.

It was almost ten when the final group of kids staggered after their guardians.

He'd need to have a word with Darren and Michelle about the late hour, but not tonight. Right now he needed to learn how Caroline really was. The tension she couldn't quite mask made it clear something was bothering her.

He walked to the counter that separated the kitchen from the larger room. An electric kettle sat next to a Keurig with an assortment of mugs and boxes of tea next to it. "Coffee or tea?"

Caroline glanced at her phone and winced. "Better make it herbal tea. I'll need to pretend to sleep sometime."

"One mug coming up." He filled the kettle and hit the button, then slid a small basket filled with tea bags toward her. "I should know your favorite is . . ."

"If we were in London, I'd say English breakfast, but tonight I'll take mint." She selected a bag and had the small package open when he placed a red mug in front of her. It looked tiny in his mitt but large in hers.

London? He'd have to remember that. Could come in handy for a honeymoon. He sank onto the bench across from her and waited as she dunked the tea bag in the hot water repeatedly, watching it as if her sanity depended on doing it just right. Finally he reached across the table and stilled her motions.

"What's going on, Caroline?" As she just looked at the table, he reached across and tapped her forehead. "Where's your head?"

Her gaze bounced up to his, her chocolate eyes startling in their intensity, before her gaze slipped back to the mug. "I can't just come to spend time with you?"

"No. If you planned to spend the night again, you could have gone straight to the cabin."

"You're my boyfriend."

"Who you haven't spent a lot of time with the last two months." She started to sputter, but he put a finger against her lips, then lost his train of thought. He cleared his throat. "That doesn't matter, because you're here now. How are you doing right now?"

She blinked at him, then glanced down at the mug of tea. "I'm kind of a mess."

"Want to tell me why?" She swallowed, but he reached for her hand and held on. He couldn't let her disappear physically. Not when he could feel her trying to withdraw. "We're good together, Caroline. You love these kids as much as I do. And they love you back." He tried to ease his grasp. What was that saying about letting something go? "I want to understand how this week is impacting you."

She tightened her hold on his hand as if it were a lifeline. "What if I'd ridden with Justin instead of driving separately?"

"Wow."

"Yeah. I keep thinking about that and my mind freezes. I could be dead or in the hospital. One more casualty." Her eyes filled with tears. "All night I kept thinking that I was one decision from not being here tonight. With you. With these precious kids."

"It affects perspective."

"So much. I try not to live in fear, but it's a real struggle some nights. You should probably know I can't sleep in the dark."

"Because I'm not there."

She chuckled, but it was a strangled sound as she pulled her hand free. "Maybe, but last night every time I closed my eyes and tried to sleep, I saw Justin's body."

"That's understandable."

Caroline rubbed her forehead to press back the tension. "But I don't like it. What if it's my fault that he died?"

"That seems like a leap."

"Not when I know he died within twenty-four hours of me asking him for help with something at work." She bit her lower lip, then looked down at her hands. "I never should have done that."

"Isn't that part of having colleagues? Relying on them to help with projects?"

"Yes. But he's the second person at Praecursoria to die since I started."

His eyes widened at her words. "You think they're connected?"

"You're right. I'm being crazy."

"That's not what I said." Brandon studied her with an inscrutable look. "We can talk it through. Maybe you're onto something."

And put him at risk? Not a chance. "Let's chalk

it up to a rough day." She hoped he'd go with that, because she didn't want to edge closer to telling him anything that could get him in trouble.

"Don't back away now." Brandon reached for her hand again, and she let him take it. "Forget I'm an investor and let's talk this through."

"I can't. It's complicated." She forced herself to meet and hold his gaze. "How much did you sink into the company?"

"Enough to fully fund Almost Home if the company's portfolio takes off like Reid anticipates."

"But you know it's risky, right?"

He shrugged. "Life's risky. It was a calculated risk, and I leave the details to Reid."

"How much do you need the money?"

"It's a chunk of what I have left."

She stared at him as her heart sank. "A big chunk?"

"Is there an echo?" He rubbed the back of his neck and then leaned back until his chair teetered on two legs. "Reid made sure when I got out of the pros that my portfolio was diversified, but at this point little is liquid."

What if she got it wrong and he lost his savings?

"I'll be okay. Really." It was scary how he seemed to read her mind. "You do what you need to." Then he leaned back into the table as the chair clomped onto all four legs. "What's going on? Really?"

How could she explain in a way that protected the company but expressed what had her mind and soul churning? "Have you ever had a moment where right versus wrong lost its black-and-white contrast?"

"Everybody does or they aren't really living."

"In law school the professional-responsibility professors made it simple. All we had to do was put our clients first. As long as they weren't doing anything *too* illegal, they could proceed and we could advise." She nibbled at the edge of her thumb before his hand slipped across the table and eased her hand down. "Sorry, I only do that when I'm nervous."

"I know. I'm not letting you push me away, Caroline." He gestured toward the stairs that led to his apartment. "I could go up there anytime and be alone, but I choose to be here. With you. You need me right now, and you'd do the same for me."

"I don't need you." Caroline let the words slam between them.

"This is what couples do. Depend on each other."

Caroline wanted to fight back. "I'm here, aren't I?"

"I want more than your physical presence." He shoved to his feet and took a step back. "I want to know what's going on in your head." He pointed to his stubborn noggin, then to his heart. "And here. The woman I fell in love with is brilliant and kind. She sees other people more deeply than many. She sees me." He exhaled, his hands hanging at his sides.

And she saw him.

She really did.

She saw the young man who'd been overlooked and forgotten by the system. The one who'd been left to fend for himself when the hardest thing he should have been deciding was whether to take Calculus 1 or AP Econ. Instead, he'd had to figure out where to sleep and how to survive.

It was the source of his strength and superpower protectiveness. But it was also his kryptonite.

It was too easy for him to believe he was invisible and unimportant. Her heart broke at the realization she'd let him believe that's what was happening.

She stood, mirroring his posture and hating the table that stood between them. All she wanted to do was pull him toward her and let him know in any way that would reach his heart that she did see him. All of him. Instead, she was left with words.

"There's much of my days I can't share with you. Not because I don't want to or I'm hiding." She stepped toward the edge of the table as he stood still as a statue, arms hanging stiffly at his sides. "But without work, what do I have to share? That takes up so much of my time. I'm not trying to go silent. I'm trying to protect you."

His chin pulled to his chest like a turtle slipping into its shell. "I don't need protecting."

"Legally, you do. I can't tell you about what Praecursoria is doing or what I'm managing. Too much information could lead to you breaking the law."

"I don't do that."

"Not knowingly. But what if I said something that caused you to sell your stock? Or buy more? Now we'd be testing the insider trading laws. Then what happens to Almost Home? What happens to us?" She gestured between them as she came around the table, closing the gap. "I'm doing this for you."

"Keep telling yourself that. You have to trust me."

"No, this time you have to trust me."

"We can't be together if I can't have all of you. I don't want slices of your life that you get to pick and choose."

"So 'need to know' isn't a thing with you?"

He shook his head as he crossed his arms over his chest. "No. You're not a CIA officer." He quirked an eyebrow. "That I know of. Is there something you need to tell me?" He studied her. "What do you want me to do? Sell?" She stared at him, but stayed silent. That was not something she could ask of him.

She appreciated his attempt at humor but felt

a tension headache rumbling for release. "You know what? I think I'll head to the cabin after all."

"You walking away?"

"I think you already did." She turned and left, narrowly avoiding stepping on Frodo on her way to the lodge's door. "Sorry, bud."

"Maybe we need to take a break."

Brandon's words stopped her at the door. She slowly turned back to him. "What do you mean?"

"What I said."

The world shifted beneath her feet, and she clung to the doorknob. "Are you breaking up with me, Brandon Lancaster? You'd better be extremely clear and sure."

"I am." He scooped up his cat and headed for the stairs to his apartment, while she tried to breathe.

She hurried to the cabin for her things and five minutes later called Jaime. Before her friend could say hi, Caroline was sobbing. "Brandon just ended things."

CHAPTER 31

FRIDAY, JUNE 4

The call in the middle of the night rocked Brandon from a restless sleep. Could it be Caroline?

He'd watched from the windows of his apartment as Jaime picked her up and drove away. He'd called, but she hadn't responded. He'd wanted to break through her walls but had blasted through with all the grace of a defensive lineman. All brute strength thrust forward into the opposition, demolishing the one he loved in the process.

Caroline wasn't the opposing team, but he'd treated her that way.

The phone rang again, and he reached for it.

Nothing good came with midnight calls, but he fought through the fog to answer.

"Hello?" He cleared his throat.

"Is this Brandon?" The voice sounded familiar, but in his barely awake state, he couldn't place it.

"Yes, who is this?"

There was a sound like a sniffle. "This is your aunt Jody."

Brandon pushed up against the headboard. "Everything okay?"

The woman exhaled. "Anna died about an hour

ago. Her body gave out." She sniffled and then hiccuped. "It looked like she would make it, and now she's gone."

He rubbed his face, trying to wake up his brain to process what he'd heard. It couldn't be right. "Anna?"

"She'd started to wake up. She threw a clot or something, and the doctors performed an emergency C-section. Now she's gone and never got to see Jilly." A sob echoed across the phone. "I'm sorry. I thought I could do this."

There was a long pause, and Brandon unplugged the phone and stood. "What do you need?"

"My baby." Her shuddering sigh vibrated in his ear. "At least the doctors saved her little girl."

Anna gone? The reality was a shock. He couldn't help her, but could he help her mom and daughter? "How is the baby?"

"She's tiny but a fighter. I can't lose them both, so I'm grateful she's proving to be a strong newborn." The woman wept. "What are we going to do?"

It was an unanswerable question. "Can I help?"

"Come to the hospital? The staff are asking questions I can't answer."

Brandon looked at his alarm clock. Two thirty. "I can leave in ten minutes. Which hospital?" He jotted down the answer. "Give me time to dress and brush my teeth."

"Be safe." The words had extra meaning after what had happened. "And thank you." His aunt's whisper cracked his stoicism as the call ended.

Anna was gone.

It wasn't right or fair.

Her little girl would be an orphan, both parents already gone like his, though his parents had left in different ways of their choosing. He'd be sensitive to what his aunt needed since, after he was separated from Trevor, Anna was the closest thing he'd had to a sibling.

He threw on a pair of navy sweatpants, a gray T-shirt, and an oversized Colts sweatshirt, then headed to his truck. He'd alert his house parents closer to a reasonable hour but didn't want to risk waking them as he backed his pickup from its slot and drove to the highway.

Jilly was alone.

He knew what that was like.

He'd slipped one direction while his eight-year-old brother disappeared another.

His thoughts were in full riot mode by the time he reached Inova Fairfax Hospital. If he turned right, he'd be at Inova Children's Hospital. Instead, he parked and headed straight ahead as he texted Aunt Jody to let her know he'd arrived.

Come to the critical care floor. I'm in a small conference room off the waiting room.

Brandon straightened his shoulders and accepted his role as the support his aunt needed. He would be her rock, standing in for Uncle Clint, who would be here if not deployed halfway around the world. The man would let Aunt Jody lean into his side and take the weight of responsibility. Somehow Brandon would make the decisions she needed him to make while protecting her from the painful parts.

Somehow.

He only wished Caroline was at his side with her sweet blend of empathy and strength.

The memory of their argument speared him. He couldn't fix that right now, but he could be there for Aunt Jody.

After a late night with Jaime collecting her car and then Ben & Jerry's pints, Caroline woke early, trying to process everything that had gone so wrong with Brandon. Her thoughts were muddled as she replayed his affirmation he was breaking up with her. She couldn't begin to reimagine her future without him in it.

Productive. She needed to be productive and deal with Brandon in the light of day. She'd start by dealing with the threatened lawsuit.

She pulled out her laptop to draft the basics of a response to the women's attorney but paused when she saw an email from Lillian. Attached was a copy of the buy-sell agreement. She frowned when she read that Praecursoria had sold Genetics for You for fifty thousand dollars.

That seemed low, especially because—and there it was, in black and white—the consortium that purchased it had not assumed liability for any business conducted before the sale. Why would Quentin think otherwise? She'd bring it up at today's leadership meeting.

She glanced at her watch and rushed through taking a shower and getting ready for work. When she grabbed her phone, she froze as she read the notifications about missed calls from Brandon. There were no voicemails, so she returned his call but was sent to voicemail. She hung up and climbed into her car. After grabbing a cup of overpriced coffee to combat her fatigue, she joined the stream of cars flowing in fits along people's commutes. Today's listen was *Essentialism* and how to focus on what she did best. Her challenge was determining exactly what that was. Her phone buzzed, interrupting the book. She hit the button on her steering wheel to accept the call. "Hello?"

"Caroline, it's Brandon." He sounded terrible.

"Hey." Last night had ended . . . badly, but she wasn't sure where they stood today. Wasn't even sure where she wanted them to stand. Everything felt wrong and she didn't know how to fix it. "I'm sorry I missed your call last night. Everything okay?" During a pause, her gut clenched.

"No." He cleared his throat as if to push words out. "Anna died early this morning."

"Oh, Brandon." Her heart sank and she fought the tears that wanted to come.

"They saved the baby. I'm here at the hospital with Aunt Jody. She's overwhelmed between baby Jilly and Anna's death."

"I'm so sorry." She thought a moment. She knew Brandon well enough to know he had responded to his aunt's need without a thought, but who was thinking about his? "What do you need?"

"Nothing." The word was gravel crunched against her ear. "Can you inform whoever at Praecursoria should know?"

"Absolutely." She blinked rapidly as a car honked and pulled around her. She couldn't afford to fall apart here on the road. "I'll call later, but let me know if you need anything, okay?"

"Sure." He sighed. "Bye."

"Bye." The word whispered from her throat before the call ended. She immediately began praying.

Her heart was heavy as she pulled into a parking space and walked to the building. After clearing security, she detoured to Samson Kleme's office. As the chief science officer, he'd know who should be informed. He looked up from his computer with a frown when she knocked.

"What do you need, Caroline?"

"Anna Johnson died overnight. I'm not sure

who needs to know, but the family asked me to pass the news along."

He leaned back in his chair and his body seemed to collapse. "I'm sorry to hear that. I'd hoped she'd make a full recovery." His shoulders slumped. "She'll be hard to replace."

"If you or anyone else needs information, you can contact Brandon Lancaster. He's her cousin and is helping Anna's mother."

"The football player?"

Caroline nodded then rattled off his number.

Samson jotted it down. "All right. Thanks for letting me know." He shook his head. "I can't believe she's gone."

"Me either." Caroline hurried from his office and collided with someone. The ricochet had the woman dropping a stack of files that exploded in a paper wave across the hall. Caroline bent to help collect them, then noticed it was Lori Clark from Justin's lab.

"You need to watch where you're going."

"Sorry. How are you doing?" Caroline scooped up a stack of paper that had escaped a folder.

"Great. I've lost two people in my lab in less than two months." Lori scrambled to pick up other folders.

"It has to be hard."

"I'm just the technician. They're the ones who directed the research." She grabbed another set of folders and tapped them on the ground to get the papers back inside. Her tapping picked up intensity as a few papers refused to slide into place.

"Are you sure you're okay?" Caroline glanced at the papers she'd collected.

Status of Patient 1's cells as implanted in Trial CAR T 463 Phase 1 participants.

"I'm fine." Lori ripped the pile from her hands. "I've got it."

Caroline held up her hands. "Sorry."

Lori stood and walked away without a backward glance or apology.

What did what she'd read mean? When Caroline reached her desk, she sank onto her chair and quickly jotted down what she'd seen.

Bethany was one of the thirty patients in Phase 1. So was Patrick Robbins—Patient 1—whose turnaround was near miraculous. But Bethany's body was still in the throes of rejection, which shouldn't be an issue if the T cells were hers. As far as Caroline knew, none of the other patients had experienced similar issues.

A possibility rocketed through Caroline's thoughts. What if the cells weren't hers? What if the protocol had been ignored, and they were using Patrick's cells instead of the trial patient's? Even if it was a simple mix-up, it could have devastating consequences for Bethany.

Then she remembered that Anna had said the cells tested as hers and then hadn't later at the hospital. That testing was done at Praecursoria, which meant someone here would have had to mess with the tests. She didn't want to believe it.

Could similar questions be what had disturbed Anna and started her digging?

Before she could investigate further, she had to attend a leadership meeting. She grabbed a few files and walked down the hall to the executive suite. She didn't know the full agenda but needed to be sure they discussed the liability issue.

Quentin sat at the side of the small conference table closest to his desk, with Samson Kleme next to him on his right side. To his left was Hannah Newton, the chief resource officer, leaving the spot across the table for Caroline. She gave everyone a slight smile and settled into her seat.

"Everyone's here, so let's get started." Quentin set his hands on the table and turned to Samson. "Where are we on the CAR T 463 trial? Samson has updated us on Anna's unfortunate death. Can the trial still proceed, or do we need to call a halt to it until we replace Sarah and Justin and find another doctor to work with? I can't believe we've lost three people involved in one trial."

Samson raised his hands in front of him, palms up. "We can't stop, not while patients are actively receiving the infusions." He looked at Hannah. "I'll work with HR to speed up hiring. It's been a bad week, but that shouldn't derail our work. I'll fill in for Justin as needed. It would be good to be active in the research again."

"That works from my end." Hannah was tapping on her phone. "We always have a backlog of applicants who want a chance to work here. I've got a couple folks whose backgrounds mirror Justin's that we could bring in next week. Replacing Dr. Johnson will be harder."

"All right, you two work together on that. Samson, you should also check on who Inova has taking Anna's place in the interim. Maybe we should consider adding him or her to the team." Quentin looked around the table. "What other issues do we need to address today?"

Before anyone else could take the stage, Caroline held up her hand then dropped it, since she shouldn't have to ask permission to speak. She lifted her chin and pulled a file to the top of her pile. "We need to review the draft response to the women who were impacted by the genetic tests performed here in 2014 and 2015. I have one right here that I've worked on this week."

Quentin looked at her with a fierceness in his expression that made her very glad there were other people in the room.

Hannah glanced back and forth between them, then addressed Quentin. "What is she talking about?"

CHAPTER 32

Caroline slid copies of the letter across the table. "Quentin received a letter from women who allege they were harmed based on genetic recommendations from Praecursoria."

"Genetic information?" Hannah wrinkled her nose and looked at Samson. "Is this about the testing arm we used to run?"

"It's not relevant." Quentin waved her concerns away. "We sold that part of the business, so any liability isn't ours."

Caroline pulled a file from under her iPad. "Actually, that's not what happened." She slid a copy of the relevant page to each of the executives at the table. "Check the highlighted paragraph. The buy-sell agreement contains clear language that Praecursoria retained liability for any harm that occurred as a result of tests and information that was provided by Praecursoria prior to the sale. It's a standard clause, but one you could have negotiated out. You didn't, so when Genetics for You bought the testing division, it accepted liability only for anything that happened after purchase."

Quentin paled as he swallowed, then he rallied. "I'm not convinced there was actual harm."

Hannah raised her manicured hand. "What are

you talking about?" There was an edge to her southern tone. "This sounds serious, and I'm just hearing about it?"

"It's a letter we got from a tort-happy attorney who's representing a family that claims they were irrevocably harmed by tests they voluntarily took," Quentin replied.

"Not quite." Caroline turned to Hannah, hoping she could enlist the support of the only other woman in the room. "They were told that they carried the BRCA genetic marker and that they had an 84 percent or higher likelihood of getting advanced breast cancer. We recommended they consult with their health-care provider about a double mastectomy and other aggressive treatments to minimize that risk."

"That was the standard recommendation at the time." Samson waved the page from the buy-sell agreement. "This piece of paper doesn't change that."

"It might because the women followed our advice. They experienced complications and then received a letter from Genetics for You in November. It said oops, the results are inconclusive based on what we know now."

Hannah flinched. "You mean the new owners told them they didn't need to worry about BRCA anymore."

"Essentially, yes. But for these women, it's too late. One of them can't have children after the hysterectomy she had to limit her chance of reproductive cancer."

"I'm tabling this for now." Quentin's words were almost as tight as his jaw.

"You can't. We have to develop a response if we want to forestall a lawsuit."

Hannah looked at the paragraph again. "You're sure we have some liability?"

"Here's the best way to think about it. Corporations exist to protect their individual owners and employees from liability for things going wrong. When I work for a company, I'm responsible for any bad advice I give, but so is the company I work for. Selling or spinning off a company doesn't erase liability for past actions, but you can negotiate who is responsible for those past actions. Unfortunately for us, that remained here." Caroline studied Quentin. "With thirty focused minutes, we could draft a well-thought-out settlement offer that might cause the threat of a lawsuit to disappear. Then we can focus on the important work we're doing today."

"I will not settle when we did nothing wrong."

"According to these women, that's not true. And Praecursoria's advice hit them at the heart of their womanhood. That is not something they'll easily walk away from." Caroline glanced at the draft again. "We may be able to shift part of the liability to Genetics for You, because they sent the notification letter, but I drove by its registered office this week, and nothing is there." She turned to Samson. "You're listed as part of the group that bought the company. Who's running it now? Maybe we can negotiate with them to bear part of the responsibility."

The man paled as he stared at the copied letter. "Why would they have sent out that letter?"

"I don't know, but they did. And that's what kicked off the letter we have to respond to." She waited until he looked up. "This could turn into a class action. I won't know until I learn how many people received similar letters. Until then, defusing this situation is important. If any of you know anything, now's a good time to let me know."

Samson stuttered, "There's nothing here."

Hannah cleared her throat. "If what they say is true, Caroline's right—we have to deal with it fast."

Quentin's expression hardened. "Next topic. Trial CAR T 463 in Mexico."

Caroline froze. "What do you mean, Mexico?"

Quentin looked to Hannah and Samson. "Where do we stand?"

Caroline felt like she was racing to catch up. "Stand on what?"

"Launching more trials in Mexico."

"We can't do that." She looked among the three at the table and realized this decision had been made long before and without her. "Wait,

Quentin. You said that was always a last resort."

Samson graced her with an expansive smile. "You're such a smart woman it's easy to forget you don't understand our world." He placed his hands on top of the table, and a ring on his pinky flashed in the light.

She felt a ripple of unease at the way he said *understand our world*. "What do you mean?"

"We'd conducted baseline animal studies before you started working here. That's why we could move to Phase 1 with humans so quickly." Samson's light accent made the words musical, even as she sensed a willingness to push the process. "What happened with Patrick is almost miraculous, and we can't wait to clear all the red tape before we have this therapy tested in other kids. Waiting for them to find us won't be enough. We have to find them."

"But there is a trial. Bethany Anderson is part of it. And almost thirty others."

Hannah frowned. "The sick girl at Inova?"

"Yes. It's not working. She was getting much worse the last time I talked to Anna."

"That was a week ago." Samson's voice was modulated like he hoped it would calm her, but it didn't.

"How can you be so passive about her life? You're the one who lost a child to this terrible disease."

"And that's exactly why I'm pushing to expand

the study so we can get better results faster. There are good facilities south of the border where we can accelerate our data collection. Unfortunately, in our line of work, we can't save everyone, but if we do our job right, we'll be able to save many through what we learn from kids like Bethany and Patrick."

Quentin rubbed his hands together. "All right. Samson, get the next round of negotiations started with your contact in Mexico. A lot will depend on what he needs from us. Let's not lose sight of what we're trying to do here. Learn from those who are participating now and keep communicating about what's not working and what could or should be changed."

Caroline shook her head. "You can't have conversations like this without me unless you want more potential lawsuits like the one we were just discussing." She tried to understand what she'd heard, a conversation at least some in the room didn't want her to be part of. "You will need a completely different consent form to test kids not governed by US laws."

"Don't worry," Quentin said. "We have a good boilerplate."

"So now you're drafting legal documents without my input?"

Samson shrugged. "These parents are desperate enough to agree to anything, but we walk them through all the possibilities."

Quentin turned to Samson. "How quickly can we get a facility up and running in Mexico?"

"To test the process?" The man waited for Quentin's nod. "To do it right, two months."

"Why so long?"

"To get good results that support what we're doing here, everything must be perfect."

Hannah's smile looked forced. "We've got the facility. The same one we used before. You handle the science. I've got the rest. We can have it up and staffed in three weeks."

Quentin nodded and leaned back with his hands across his stomach. "I like the sound of that. We need a place people can go while waiting for the FDA to give us the nod for Phase 2." Quentin unbuttoned and rolled up his right sleeve, then his left. "Don't forget, we can press hard if we prove that our therapy and treatment won't do more harm that what is currently on the market." He said the words with a quiet authority as he met Caroline's gaze.

She rose to his challenge. "Then why rush to a clinic in Mexico?"

Hannah shook her head. "This is exactly why bringing in an outsider at this time was a terrible idea. I tried to warn you."

Quentin held up a hand. "We need her to make sure we do this right."

She shook her head before focusing on Caroline. "This isn't rushed. In fact, it's been in the works since we got the first hint that this new CAR T-cell therapy could work. Patrick's recovery just put an exclamation mark on its importance."

"Why are you willing to put so much on Patrick? The fantastic recovery of one patient doesn't justify anything." Caroline considered the papers she had seen Lori spill in the hallway. What was the connection? She tried to take enough mental notes that the others wouldn't realize she was absorbing every word. "How are we going to manage the hiring from here?"

"We won't. I'll send a list of what we're looking for in the clinical staff to an employment agency there and let them do the work."

"Will the key staff come here to be trained?"

"It's complicated with the immigration laws, so we'll send a few of our best there for that."

"That sounds risky."

"We aren't the first to do it that way."

She knew it was true, because she'd read the citations on the FDA's website warning consumers against using unregulated stem-cell therapies and clinics. "So we can learn from their mistakes."

"What would those be?" Samson's voice had an oh-you-sweet-thing tone to it.

"Not having a sterile environment. Over-promising what we can achieve."

Samson's grin didn't waver, but his eyes hardened. "We're following the law."

She took a moment to meet each of their gazes. "I'm here as a line of defense. Think of it as finding and maintaining the guardrails." She'd keep using that analogy until it finally stuck. She held up her hand as Hannah opened her mouth. "Let me finish. It is indisputable you know the science. Each of you understands it better than I do. But I know the law and regulations better. That's my trained expertise. So I'll ask questions. And I'll expect answers because that's what you pay me to do. Otherwise I wouldn't be doing my job."

When she left Quentin's office a few minutes later, her legs felt like jelly.

Samson followed her into the hall and caught up with her in a couple of steps. She kept walking until he reached out and grabbed her upper arm. She looked at his hand and then at his face. "What are you doing?"

"Watch your step." There was a mix of concern and hardness in his gaze. "You are on the edge of something you don't understand."

"Is that what happened to Sarah?"

Confusion flashed across his face. "What do you mean?"

"Did she land in something she didn't understand?"

Someone opened a door down the hallway, and he dropped her arm. "I have no idea what happened to her other than what the police have said. I like you, but you need to be careful. No one is irreplaceable, including you."

"Is that a threat?" She planted her feet and met him head-on.

"Take it as friendly advice. We don't make threats here." He pulled his shirt cuffs from under his blazer. "We don't need to."

The words thudded between them.

He took a step away before pausing and looking back at her. "I'd consider that carefully if I were you."

She stayed frozen in place after he continued down the hall.

The words reverberated through her with truth and heft.

Who else had he threatened?

CHAPTER 33

After leaving the hospital, Brandon headed into Arlington for lunch with Reid. He needed the encouragement and comfort of down-home southern cooking after an excruciating week made even harder by Anna's death. When Brandon arrived at the small restaurant, Reid was already seated at a small table with a Coke in front of him. "I ordered you a tea."

Brandon wrinkled his nose. "I'm still trying to like those."

"Without sugar."

"That's better." He eased into the chair, hoping it could support his size. Some restaurants favored furniture built for hobbits. Then he yawned and leaned back, wishing he still drank caffeine-infused energy drinks. He needed something after the too-short night.

"You okay, Brandon?" Reid eyed him carefully.

"Got woken up this morning. My cousin died, so I helped my aunt through some of the early decisions. Then I went to check on Bethany. She doesn't look good. I'm concerned about how she'll pull through without Anna fighting for her."

"Man, I'm sorry. That's a lot."

"Yeah." Brandon cleared his throat, and Reid

shifted them to small talk until they ordered. Then Brandon leaned forward, ready to change the subject. "Caroline and I were talking last night, and she said something curious." He'd skip over the part where he was an idiot and broke things off.

"What's that?"

"She asked how much I invested in Praecursoria."

"Did you tell her nearly everything you had left?"

"Maybe."

Reid carefully placed his napkin across his lap. "Why did she ask?"

"I'm not sure." He sighed as he balled up his own napkin. "She was upset about the fact I had invested."

"You invested a year before she started."

"You and I know that, but I don't think the timing makes a difference to Caroline. I asked if I should sell, and she didn't say a word. If anything that made her even more jumpy. To the point we broke up last night." Okay, so he would mention it.

"Wow. I didn't see that coming."

"Me either. It's been a heck of a twenty-four hours."

"What can I do?"

"Help me diversify. I figure if I sell my Praecursoria shares, I'll remove that barrier between us."

"It's going to cost you. I don't know what kind of buyer I'll find."

"It's okay. She's more important than any possible payoff in the future. None of it matters without her. And with the new direction Almost Home is taking, I need something lower risk." He huffed. "I shouldn't have gone that direction in the first place. I let fear play in my mind." He unballed his napkin. "Think you can sell it, even at a loss?"

"Yes. Between my boss and me, we're always talking to people who are looking for tech ventures. It won't happen today though."

"It's okay. I'll know it's in process and that's what matters. You'd do this for Emilie, wouldn't you?"

"Absolutely. When you find the right person, she's worth the cost. By the way, I might have someone interested in the Porsche."

"Yeah?" Brandon considered it a moment. He didn't need the car. Rarely drove it anyway. It was time to let it go. "They can have it."

"Are you sure? I still remember when you bought it."

"It's only a thing. Besides, it sits unused most days." Brandon tried to ignore the pinch in his gut. "It might have been my dream car, but it's ridiculous to pay all that insurance and maintenance on a car I don't even drive. I'll replace it with something more practical."

"If you're sure."

"I am."

The waiter returned to their table with two steaming plates. Reid's held some sort of seared scallops, while Brandon's was heaped with ribs. The waiter set the plates down, then pulled a stack of wet wipes from his apron. "You'll need these."

He grabbed Brandon's tea glass and took off for a refill before Brandon could say thanks. Still, Brandon was grateful for the reprieve. After a few bites from the ribs, he tore open a wipe and cleaned his hands. "How bad is it for us if something happens to that company?"

Reid shrugged. "I can review the company's financials and let you know if I see anything concerning. We can sell since she hasn't said anything specific, but it could look coincidental."

"Understood." Brandon took another bite of the spicy ribs that set his mouth on fire.

Reid pulled out his phone and made a few notes. "I'll double-check your portfolio when I get back to the office and make recommendations. Start-ups are high risk and high reward." He stopped tapping and looked at Brandon. "I haven't seen anything in the press that makes me nervous, but that doesn't mean it isn't there."

"Don't dig. I don't want to get anywhere near the insider trading line. My goal is to remove this barrier between Caroline and me." He licked his fingers, then sighed. "The rent agreements with my house parents will work, but a cushion would help keep Almost Home solvent if I'm wrong." The waiter returned with his drink, and he guzzled half of it. "It's supposed to be easier than this."

"What is?"

"Providing a home for my kids. It's a good thing, so why one hardship after another?"

"That's the way it often is for the things worth doing."

Brandon shook his head. "Sorry, man. I didn't mean to be a downer."

"This is real life. It's what friends do. We weren't made to walk life alone."

"You're right." But it was still a lesson Brandon was embracing. "How's Kinley?"

"Better all the time. She's really bonded to Emilie."

"That's a good thing."

"Being a family—it's already better than I expected. You ought to try it sometime."

Brandon pointedly picked up another rib and started gnawing on it.

Reid laughed as he waved down the waiter for the bill. "All you need to do is decide what you want from life."

When Caroline reached the small cafeteria, Lori and her colleague Tod were already there.

Neither seemed curious about why she'd asked to meet with them. Lori had the look of someone who spent her days in an office, with the slight plumpness of someone who occupied a desk. Tod was her opposite, looking more like a scarecrow than a lion, with thick owlish glasses and a bit of absentminded professor thrown in for good measure.

"Did y'all know Justin well?"

Lori paused and wiped her mouth with a napkin. "As well as anyone who worked with him. Why?"

"I was sorry to hear about his accident Wednesday."

Lori paled and inhaled sharply. "I told him to stop asking questions."

"Why?"

"Because he was poking at Samson's special project. That's never a good idea."

Tod nodded. "When he has a scientific insight, no one better get in his way." Tod glanced around, then leaned closer. "The man thinks he's a genius."

Lori took another spoonful of her soup. "Too bad his ideas don't work half the time. But I guess Einstein's didn't either. The two of them are working on something intense."

"Two of who?" Caroline tried to piece together what they were saying with what they weren't.

Tod put his napkin on top of his plate and

stood. "Samson and Silver. The two S's. We"— he gestured between himself and Lori—"have learned to steer clear, but Justin decided to get in the middle of it." He leaned close. "Hope that didn't cause the accident, if you know what I mean." He glanced around as if to make sure no one was listening. "It's all connected. It has to be. Sarah runs a trial and then dies as she's getting good results? Now Justin? How was he helping you?"

"What?" Caroline straightened.

"We all knew he was working with you."

"No, he was helping me understand the science."

"Sure." He gave her a small salute. "I'm out of here for the day. Let things simmer down over the weekend. Stay safe."

"What does he mean?" Caroline tried to still her hands that were clenching and unclenching in her lap. "Stay safe?"

Lori watched him leave, then turned to Caroline. "Be careful. Sarah was working on the research, and then she died."

"Her death was an accident." Wasn't it? Or were the rumors right that it was suicide?

"Is that what you've been told? If you ask me, there've been a lot of *accidents* surrounding my lab." Lori rolled her napkin into a straw shape. "Sarah was as determined as any other scientist to find the world's next HeLa cells."

"But the world already has HeLa cells. We've had them for sixty years. Why would a new discovery matter?"

"Because it's a billion-dollar industry. Every medical research facility in the world relies on those cells, even though they're so small they easily contaminate other experiments. That hasn't changed our reliance on them." Lori looked around and then leaned closer. "Imagine grabbing even a fragment of the market. It would fund everything else Praecursoria wants to do. Initially Quentin and Samson thought genetic testing would be the cash cow, but that didn't work out. So now the hunt is on for the next HeLa cells."

"But those were an anomaly."

"Yes, yet Sarah was convinced she'd found that next anomaly. She submitted a patent application a week before her death, just in case." Lori sighed. "I would have liked to be listed on it, but she only put herself and Quentin."

Lori's words echoed in Caroline's mind as she returned to her office. Tod had looked nervous as he left the table, and Lori had seemed to hold back as she talked. Why? Were they concerned that what had happened to Sarah and Justin could happen to them?

It was a string of tragic accidents.

Or was it?

She sat at her computer and pulled up Sarah's

obituary. From the obituary she found Sarah's mother's name and then located the woman's phone number on the white pages site. Her call was answered on the second ring. "Is this Mrs. Whitten?"

"It is." Hesitancy laced the woman's words and Caroline rushed in before she hung up.

"My name is Caroline Bragg, and I'm an attorney at Praecursoria."

"Oh, good. I've left so many messages I was beginning to think my answering machine didn't work. When can I come get Sarah's things?"

Caroline froze. "What things?"

"Her private things. It's been months, and I'd think you'd want to be rid of them."

"I'll be happy to check on that for you, ma'am." She started typing a message to Hannah as she continued. "I never met your daughter, but I'm sorry for your loss. Did you know one of her colleagues died Wednesday?"

"I'm sorry, but what does that have to do with me?"

"Did she ever mention Justin Grant? Or Dr. Anna Johnson?"

"She and Anna had been friends since undergrad. Justin? She mentioned several men she worked with, but I don't believe I met a Justin."

"Okay. Thank you. I'll check on Sarah's things for you. Would you like me to bring them to you?"

"That would be nice." The woman rattled off her address. "Or you can let me know when they're ready, and I'll drive over." She cleared her throat. "There was a Grant Sarah talked about." Maybe she'd called Justin by his last name? "They were working on some big project before Sarah died. She talked about how she was the brains and he was the brawn and how much Brian liked to sneak into their experiments."

Brian? "Do you mean Brian Silver?"

"I think that was his last name. They'd worked together for a few years, but I'd say he felt threatened by her. My Sarah was brilliant, and at least the way she described him, Brian wasn't at her level even if he had a postgraduate placement of some sort."

That had to be Brian Silver. "Thanks. Again, I am so sorry for your loss."

Caroline hung up and finished the email to Hannah. Almost as soon as she hit Send, her phone was ringing.

"Why are you asking about Sarah's personal things?" Hannah didn't sound happy about the interruption.

"Her mother asked when she would get them."

"And she was talking to you because?"

Caroline kept her voice calm and steady. "Do you know where they are so I can take them to her?"

"I'll have my assistant put them in the mail."

"I don't mind."

"You have other things to do." A crinkling noise like a necklace clanking against the receiver hurt Caroline's ear. "What's the address?"

Caroline rattled it off, then hung up.

A few minutes later she strolled by Lillian's desk. "Did Hannah bring a box to you?"

"Yes." The young woman grimaced. "I'm not her assistant, but she likes to act like I am."

Caroline eyed the banker's box at the side of her desk. "I'd be happy to handle that on my way home today. Then you don't need to mess with it."

"That would be great." Lillian gestured at a stack of files on the corner of her desk. "I'm supposed to read and condense all these articles for Quentin. The man is committed to keeping up on the research, but he thinks I need to help him. Have you ever tried to make sense of a medical study? It isn't easy."

Caroline picked up the box. "I'll take care of this for you, since I wouldn't be much help with those articles." She paused. "How are you doing, really?"

"I'm not as sick in the morning. That's good."

"Quentin mentioned you were out. Everything okay?"

Lillian dropped her voice. "It will be. I was interviewing and got an offer earlier today. I'll tell him Monday I'm taking it."

"That's good."

"Thanks. It'll make things less weird with the father." The way she said *father* was only slightly caustic.

"If you need anything, let me know. I can connect you with good attorneys."

The younger woman grimaced. "I didn't want to be in this position, but I'll take you up on that. I don't want him in my life anymore, but he will support his child."

"Anyone I know?"

"I hope not. He's in manufacturing. Let's just say I lost my head and good sense to a handsome face. If only there'd been more to him than that." She absently rubbed her stomach. "Guess I had to learn the hard way."

"I'll email you a couple names."

After taking the box back to her office, Caroline called Mrs. Whitten back. "I have Sarah's things and can bring them by tonight."

"I'm headed out now and will come by the office."

"Okay, just call when you arrive and I'll bring them to you. Was there anything in particular you were hoping to find?"

"Her calendar. She kept meticulous records, and I'd like to have it to remember her life this last year."

Caroline pulled off the lid and looked inside. "There are some magazines, pens, a photo, oh, and here's the calendar. Do you mind if I look at it?"

"That's fine. I'll be there within the hour."

Caroline took out the slim, spiral-bound booklet and flipped through it. There was a series of meetings with SK and others with JG, LC, and TT. None with a BS, aka Brian Silver.

That seemed odd since they all worked in the same lab. Maybe his presence was just assumed, but before she walked the box out to Mrs. Whitten forty-five minutes later, she snapped photos of several pages preceding Sarah's death just in case there was anything else she could glean.

Back at her desk, her email dinged.

An email from Anna?

That wasn't possible.

Was it?

CHAPTER 34

Was this someone's idea of a cruel joke? She didn't want to open it, not if it could unleash some type of malware on her computer and the Praecursoria server. But how would anyone know that sending an email with Anna's name and address would tempt her to open it?

She picked up her phone and dialed the IT office, where the call was quickly picked up.

"Reynolds."

"James, I received an email from someone who died overnight. Should I open it?"

"Forward it and I'll scan it."

Caroline bit her lower lip. "Is there a way you can come here? It makes me nervous to forward something that could be malware."

The man sighed. "I'll head your way. Confirm your office number."

After she did and the call ended, Caroline stared at her computer screen as she nibbled at the corner of her fingernail. The email's appearance didn't feel right. There was no reason for Anna to delay an email message a week. It couldn't be from Anna. It couldn't.

But if it was?

She didn't want to delete something that could be important.

Maybe Anna's computer had been off with the email waiting in the outbox, and now someone had turned it on. It might be a stretch, but it was possible.

When James walked in, his hair was pulled back in a ponytail and his soul patch made him look all millennial and her feel eighty years old. He gestured toward her chair. "May I?"

"Oh." She scrambled to her feet. "Sure."

He sat and clicked the mouse a couple of times. "This the email?"

"Yes."

He punched a few keys. "Looks clean. But let me check one more thing." He pulled up a program from somewhere in the bowels of her computer. Then he dragged the email to it and it started scanning. A moment later he pushed back from the desk and stood. "Good to go."

"So I can open it?"

"Sure."

"Quick question: how would an email arrive a week after it was sent?"

"Could have been scheduled, or maybe the computer was turned off. There are other possibilities, but those are most likely. Need anything else?"

So Anna really had sent it. Maybe in case the mail didn't reach her quickly.

"No. I'm good."

He tipped an imaginary hat and left.

Caroline returned to her chair. Her hand hovered over the mouse before she leaned in and clicked on the email.

There was no content except for an attachment.

She frowned. That couldn't be right. Anna wouldn't send her a blank email. James had scanned it, so she clicked on the attachment. A folder like the one that had been on the flash drive opened. It was like getting the flash drive data back.

She scanned through the documents as she printed each. To be safe, she would take the paper home with her. It was the same columns of numbers and page of random thoughts.

"What did you want me to see, Anna?"

Caroline stared at the numbers, wishing she understood. Numbers could tell any story you wanted. They could be tinged with all kinds of bias and perspective. Essentially all the data from experiments was just that: statistical data. Something about t-values and p-values, things she hadn't considered since her statistics course in undergrad. That was a long time ago.

She needed coffee, something to warm her hands, because her heart felt iced. The break room was empty, so she slid a cup beneath the spigot and inserted a new K-Cup. She waited as the machine whirred and bubbled, her thoughts spinning.

Her phone dinged. Brandon. anna's funeral is monday. can you come?

She should go. For him. It would be hard for him to walk into the den of relatives. She'd slip in the back and sit with him, then slip out at the end. No matter where their relationship stood, he needed her.

Yes. I'll be there.

After doctoring her coffee with a splash of whole milk and a tiny sprinkle of raw sugar, Caroline returned to her office and her work. Waiting in her inbox were several new contracts for review.

Her phone dinged again.

sorry for last night, can we talk?

Could they? It was foolish, but she felt drawn to Almost Home like a moth to a flame. She needed time with those kids . . . and with Brandon . . . like a fish needed water. Enough of the bad similes. She allowed herself to feel hopeful as she replied.

I don't have any answers. But we can talk. I'll come after work.

A few minutes later she received his reply.

thx

Lights were on in each cabin when Caroline arrived a few hours later, and she saw a couple of the family groups sitting at tables sharing food.

Some of the knots eased from her shoulders when she pulled into the parking lot and noted Brandon's truck in its usual slot. When she stepped into the lodge, the large fireplace stood empty, swept clean for summer. The kids would use it as a hiding place until Brandon put the large decorative screen across it again.

A clank came from the industrial kitchen, so Caroline headed that direction. Used to prepare the community meals, it looked like a standard church kitchen with a pass-through to the larger space. Industrial ovens stood next to a stove. Across from them was a large butcher-block table with a supersized refrigerator and freezer next to it. The sink was used only occasionally, because the large dishwashing machine was where the fun happened.

Brandon worked the lever that brought the guard down so the water and dishes could be superheated. He wore large headphones and was singing along to some song. His voice sounded a bit like a screeching cat, so she leaned a hip against the doorframe and watched, a smile teasing the edge of her lips while an ache pressed against her heart.

This man was something else with his enthusiasm for everything, even washing mounds of someone else's dishes. He raised the guard and steam swooshed around him. He turned to grab a large plastic bowl from the workspace and froze at the sight of her.

He slid the headphones from his ears. "How long you been standing there?"

"Long enough."

There was a heartbreaking vulnerability in the way his shoulders slumped. "I wasn't sure you'd come after last night."

"I'll always be your friend. Hopefully we can figure us out too." She felt shyness steal over her.

Brandon watched as color flamed up Caroline's cheeks. He might not know exactly where they stood right now, but he knew Caroline.

Her days were long too, and he wanted to chase the shadows from her eyes.

He cleared his throat. "I'm sorry about what I said last night."

She picked up a dish towel and started to dry a plate. "What part? We said a lot of things, Brandon."

"The part about your work. The part where I implied I don't respect your work boundaries." He took the plate and towel out of her hands, then stood in front of her. When she didn't look up, he tipped her chin up. "The part about breaking up. Caroline, I didn't mean it. You coming here? This is the best part of my days. You're the sunshine that makes life worth living."

"Don't say things you don't mean."

"I won't. I mean it so much I asked Reid to sell my stock in Praecursoria today so that it won't be a barrier between us."

Her eyebrows arched. "You can't do that."

"Why not?"

"What if the company ends up making tons of

money in a year or two? When it goes public, that could happen."

"It'll happen without me. I'd trade every what-if for a future with you, Caroline."

Her gaze darted everywhere but at him. "I can't let you do that."

"I've already done it. You are more important." He'd stamp those words on her heart if he could. Help her understand how much he meant them. "You are what matters."

"Wow." Before he knew what was happening, she reached up on tippy toes and pulled his head down. "You're going to make me cry."

"Not allowed when I'm around." He lowered his head the rest of the distance until his lips found hers. They tasted like peppermint. Fresh. Perfect. Intoxicating. Her fingers wove into the hair at his neck, and he picked her up. She squealed and kicked, and one of her stilettos fell off.

He eased her back down, and she hid her face in his chest. "We've got some things to figure out, big guy."

He nodded, but she couldn't see. "We will."

"We didn't last night."

"Today's a new day. It's a fresh start."

"Only if you want it to be."

"I do." With everything in him.

He returned the towel to her, snagged one for himself, and together they started drying dishes side by side.

"How are you, Brandon? With what happened to Anna?"

He'd wanted to keep things light, far away from the edge of grief. "Dreading the funeral. Grateful you'll be there."

She nudged his arm with her shoulder. He put a plate on the stack. He cleared his throat. "Do you have plans for tomorrow night?"

She looked at him with curiosity and something else, maybe hope, in her eyes. "Why do you ask?"

"Because I thought we could go out. Maybe a double date with Reid and Emilie."

"Did you just say date? That's the D-word, you know."

"I did." He swallowed as he waited for her response.

The slow smile let him know before she said a word. "I'd like that." Then she stood on tiptoe and brushed his cheek with a soft kiss.

He didn't move, willing himself to stay still. Instead, he did a mental fist pump and matched her grin. "It's a date."

She laughed. "Then I'm going to leave now so we can enjoy our time tomorrow night."

Without another word she turned and sashayed away, and it took everything in him not to drag her back into his arms. No, he'd focus on making tomorrow night an evening of promise. If he was lucky, it might become a foundation on which to build their future.

CHAPTER 35

When she reached her apartment that evening, it was extra dark.

Caroline frowned as she climbed the stairs to her second-floor apartment.

The lightbulb in the entryway must have gone out, but it was crazy no one had called maintenance. She pulled her keys from her bag and her fingers brushed against the folder filled with Anna's files. The weight of uncertainty and responsibility pressed against her. She was glad things were moving back to solid ground with Brandon but felt burdened with what was happening at Praecursoria. There were answers; she just wasn't sure how to find them.

Once this day was behind her, it would make sense. In comfy clothes, with a mug of warm tea and a cozy blanket across her lap, she'd parse the truth and figure out some things.

She had a feeling the answers were in those pages.

Like what was so special about Patrick's recovery.

And what Anna had theorized about Bethany's rejection.

And whether the flash drive's contents were enough to cause . . . what? Two deaths? Three?

She slid her key into the doorknob but hesitated as the door eased open.

That wasn't right. She always closed the door tightly. Made sure it was locked.

She glanced at the floor but didn't see a light shining. That wasn't right either. She always left a light on, the first moments in a dark space unnerving and unsettling, threatening a flashback to too many dark, fear-filled nights as a child.

Caroline tugged her keys from the door and stepped away. Her hand grappled in her pocket for her phone, and she pressed Call. Her most recent call had been to whom? Brandon?

"Caroline?"

She startled and pressed a hand to her chest as she clutched her phone to her ear. Then the door opened, and Jaime looked out. "You okay?"

"What? What are you doing here?"

"The maintenance guy let us in. He remembered me from when you moved in. Did you forget it's Friday night? We'd talked about meeting here for dinner last time we met at Il Porto."

"I'm going to have to talk to Charlie." Caroline forced a smile. "It's Friday night already? How long have you been waiting?"

"Long enough to be concerned." Jaime crossed her arms.

Hayden stepped around Jaime. "We're here like we promised."

"After you gave me a heart attack." Caroline

ended the call, then stepped up for a hug. She forced her pulse to slow down. "Y'all know how to scare a girl to death."

Hayden winced but tightened her hold. "Sorry about that, but it wasn't on purpose."

"I know." She glanced up at the light that wasn't shining. "Was that out when you arrived?"

Jaime nodded. "It was. Emilie will be here shortly. She's grabbing the food."

Caroline stepped inside and felt the chill of the air-conditioned room. It was welcome after the night's humidity. She gave the living space a quick glance, relieved it wasn't bad. Her thoughts had been so jumbled, she couldn't remember straightening it in her sprint out the door.

The pillows on the couch weren't precisely placed, the *Travel Dream Work Repeat* one looking like it had been tossed on as an afterthought. Caroline frowned as she walked by and adjusted it. Then she moved a glass from the counter to the sink on her way through the galley kitchen to her bedroom. After she pulled on a pair of yoga capris and a loose T-shirt, she lifted her hair off her neck and tied it in a messy bun, then headed back to the living room. Emilie was walking through the door Jaime held open, carrying two bags from a local Chinese restaurant.

When the food was divvied up, each getting

their favorite, Hayden and Emilie sat on the loveseat, while Jaime and Caroline huddled around the small table.

"Okay, Caroline. Time to come clean." Emilie maneuvered the chopsticks expertly into her little box of Kung Pao chicken. "What's going on?"

"I practically watched a coworker die Wednesday. I'm still rattled."

"Of course you'd be." Jaime tossed that statement out as if it were common knowledge.

"Who told you?" A jolt of adrenaline surged through Caroline. If her friends knew, who else was aware she'd been there?

"I noticed you in the TV footage." Hayden shrugged like it was no big deal, but Caroline didn't buy it.

"You just happened to see it?"

"Reid might have said something." Emilie looked concerned, the expression she wore when working with her domestic violence clients.

"Why would he?"

"Maybe Brandon mentioned something." Emilie set her box to the side. "It doesn't matter how we found out, only that you're okay."

Caroline knew she should sink into their concern. Allow herself to be embraced by their care. Instead, she felt something stiffen inside her, a wall pushing up. She inhaled deeply. These women had earned the right to check on her after a harrowing day she hadn't shared.

"Things are so weird right now. I don't even know where to start."

Hayden smiled. "I've always heard the beginning was a good place."

"Well, I was born thirty years ago."

Hayden tossed one of the throw pillows at her. "You can jump ahead twenty-nine and a half years."

Caroline moved the chopsticks through the rice and sautéed veggies as she collected her thoughts. "This will sound crazy." She walked them through the highlights and bullet points. "Anna mailed me this flash drive of data. Now she's gone, as is the person I asked to help. Someone erased the flash drive, then stole it with my purse. Oh, then Brandon broke up with me, but we're back together. I think."

Her friends blinked at her.

"Come on. Say something. Tell me I'm crazy and need to get a life."

Emily looked at her with eyes full of compassion. "That's a lot."

"This is where you say I'm out of my mind."

Jaime pushed to her feet and collected empty takeout boxes. "Can't do that. Sounds like you should be very careful."

"So what do I do? Stop going to work?"

Hayden shook her head as she brushed her fingertips on a napkin. "Not if that's where you have a connection to the answers."

"Anna was a doctor working on one of our trials. Justin worked at Praecursoria."

"Both were killed in car accidents." Emilie looked at Caroline. "Is that their only connection?"

"Both were involved in the same CAR T-cell trial. Another woman died the week I started. She worked in the lab with Justin."

Jaime deposited the boxes in the trash. "Yes, but that doesn't mean it's relevant. Coincidences like that happen all the time and are simply unfortunate tragedies." Jaime turned to Caroline. "So what is relevant?"

"The flash drive, but I can't decipher what was on it. Today I got a duplicate copy of the files in an email from Anna. Days after her accident."

"Who can help you interpret the data?"

Caroline thought a moment. "Brian Silver. Maybe. I emailed the original to him, but he said he never got it."

"Can he be trusted?"

"I think so." She didn't know who else to take it to, especially after the leadership meeting with Quentin's push on Mexico.

Hayden finished eating and put down her takeout box. "Who has access to the server? If it was sent on your work computer, then the email went through the server. If it did, there's a record."

"I should have thought of that." Caroline pulled

out her phone and typed herself a note. "You must work on large-scale litigation."

"You know it. Targeted at big companies." Hayden grinned. "Ask someone in IT to check for you. Then you'll know if this Brian is telling the truth." She stood and carried her fork and glass to the sink. "I need to head back home, but call if we can help."

The other two followed Hayden to the door. After a round of hugs, Caroline stood at the door and waved goodbye as her friends headed down the stairs.

Then she closed the door, slid the chain into its slot, and turned the deadbolt.

She flipped more lights on as she walked through the living room to the kitchen and brewed a cup of tea. She kept turning them on as she entered her bedroom. Then she sat down on her bed and composed an email to James Reynolds. If anyone could tell her whether her email to Brian Silver had actually reached him, she hoped he could.

Brandon sank onto the chair next to Bethany's bed. She smiled wanly at him.

"Hi, Mr. Brandon."

"Hey, yourself. I brought a couple movies if you want to watch something."

She smiled and then pressed the button to raise the head of her bed. "I'd like that. What did you bring?"

"*Up* and the new *Little Women*." Caroline had bought both movies for his kids. "My friend says they're the perfect way to spend a couple hours."

"I'd like your friend." She read the back of both movies. The girl looked worse somehow, a feat he would have sworn wasn't possible, but she'd become a ghost of the girl he first met. "This one."

He took *Little Women* from her and after getting it started settled in the chair next to her bed. He leaned his head back against the chair and tried to get comfortable without making too much noise as he shifted against the vinyl. It had to make cleanup easier in the institutional setting, but it didn't make for comfort. Something about being able to wipe a surface with industrial-strength bleach didn't create a homey setting.

His phone rang, and he glanced at the screen. Nicole Walker?

"I need to take this. I'll be in the hall." He pushed to his feet and toggled to the call. "This is Brandon."

"Hey, Brandon, this is Eric Walker. Nicole and I are at a late dinner. Is it okay if I put you on speaker so she can hear too?"

"Sure."

There was a click, and then he heard ambient noise. "Nicole and I wondered if you had a few minutes to discuss how we can work with you."

Brandon must have been exhausted, because

he felt pressure build behind his eyes and nose. "What did you have in mind?"

"We were impressed by what we saw at Almost Home Monday, but we were more impressed with you and your heart for the population you serve. Our church is really trying to take on the posture of leaving the building and being involved in our community. We've talked to a few folks and have a core to support your need for house parents' nights out. The hope is that as families volunteer, they may catch a vision for foster-to-adopt. If that doesn't happen, we can still provide respite care. Maybe get couples licensed to do that and even live there at Almost Home." The man paused, but Brandon was speechless. "How's that sound?"

Brandon cleared his throat as he tried to find words. "That's an answer to prayer and would be a great help. I need to provide support like this to my house parents as we flip the model."

"Just part of the body coming alongside." Nicole's voice held a smile. "You're doing impressive but draining work."

"Thank you." The conversation continued for a few minutes with them setting a time to get together in a couple of weeks to flesh out a plan.

Eric sounded exuberant, as if he were the one getting the support. "We should have a few families committed by then and can discuss next steps."

"The first one will be background checks on anyone who wants to volunteer."

"We can ask the children's church administrator to help with that process for anyone who hasn't already done it."

When they hung up a few minutes later, Brandon leaned his head against the wall. The time off would help prevent burnout for his house parents. It also might help him find people who would step into the vision when the Stones or another family moved on to new things.

He went back into the room, set the phone on the side table, and closed his eyes.

You still up?

He smiled at Caroline's text. yep. you?

An eye-roll emoji came next. Of course. No, wait. It's my subconscious texting you as I sleep. The efficiency. Imagine if I could teach others this skill. I'd be rich!

no need to snark.

Is that even a word? There was a pause. Sorry. The gals just left.

There was something about the way she worded it.

you okay?

I should be.

but you aren't.

No, I guess I'm not.

Anna? Justin?

Unsettled by life.

you don't unsettle easily.

If you only knew. She paused again, then the

dots that indicated she was continuing appeared. I don't want to be a burden, but sometimes even when I want to reach out . . . I can't.

guess I should be honored.

Huh?

you're reaching out now.

You're different.

why?

Not sure. Guess I don't have to prove myself to you.

He thought of all the times he'd seen that gang of four together. They had each other's backs in a rich and meaningful way. those women would walk across broken glass for you . . . just like you would for them.

Thanks. I don't know why I struggle to believe that.

if i was a therapist i'd ask what happened in your childhood.

No way, big guy. Not going there via text.

i'm cheaper than a counselor.

Maybe, but no. She paused again. Maybe her thumbs had gotten tired. Where are you?

the hospital.

How is she?

not good.

I'm sorry. That has to be so hard.

it is. guess what—all gods children is all in with us

That's wonderful!

A nurse walked into the room and startled when she saw him. gotta run. someone's here.

Congratulations. Hang in there.

you too.

He turned to the nurse as she erased the prior nurse's name from the whiteboard and scribbled something in its place. He didn't recognize her, but that wasn't terribly surprising. The hospital was huge and even on a wing like this had an immense staff. "Good evening."

She smiled at him as she capped the marker and slid it back in the drawer. "Hello. How's our patient?"

"Not great from what I can tell."

Bethany frowned at him. "I can talk."

"You sure can. Sorry about that, princess."

"I'm okay. Not as itchy as I was."

"Glad the steroids have helped. Dr. Hamilton is trying to dial in the right amount to give you relief while helping your body adjust to the new cells." The woman smiled at Bethany.

"I thought I was supposed to have ninja cells. They're asleep."

The woman's expression softened. "We're looking for a way to wake them up."

"Moving faster would be good. I'm tired of laying here."

"I bet you are."

"Dr. Johnson thought this was best." The woman's throat convulsed over his cousin's name. "Dr. Hamilton hasn't changed the plan."

Brandon nodded but couldn't force a single word out. Not when he had a lump the size of a boulder lodged in this throat.

"Can we get back to the movie?"

He had to smile at Bethany's question. The nurse nodded, and he raised the remote and hit Play. "Here we go, princess."

Bethany fell asleep before the first movie finished. He left both there for her to watch when she had more energy. It was a long drive back to Almost Home. When he arrived, he wasn't exactly sure how he'd done it, the drive to and from the hospital automatic.

Fatigue threatened to take over as soon as he walked in the door, but when he sat down to write an email telling his house parents about the good news from All God's Children, new hope swept his exhaustion away.

CHAPTER 36

SATURDAY, JUNE 5

There's a double feature at a drive-in near stephens city. couple marvel movies. game?

She had to laugh as she read Brandon's text. She was pretty sure she was the only person alive who called *Spider-Man: Homecoming* a rom-com because Pepper and Tony Stark get back together.

Sounds fun. Just promise to feed me, 'kay?

He sent a thumbs-up reply, and she inhaled as she rolled her shoulders. A night out enjoying a couple of her favorite superhero movies with her friends should be the perfect distraction.

She hadn't heard back from James even after a second email. Interesting considering how quickly he'd jumped on her using the server over a holiday weekend.

She and Brandon were finding their way back to each other, but how should she act? Play it cool? Or allow him to catch a glimpse of her high regard for him? If she kept thinking in those terms, she'd sound like a Regency novel come to life. She groaned and set her phone aside. She needed to quit overthinking and be herself.

She needed to relax. Go with the flow.

She stared at her closet, which overflowed with not a single thing to wear.

She rifled through the carefully hung blazers that felt too businesslike, blouses in all sorts of prints and bright colors, and pants that helped her legs look a little longer when paired with heels. She tended toward bright so she couldn't be missed in a crowd. The jewel tones made her feel like royalty. All of those options felt too workday. Tonight was a chance to forget about work and loss. It could be special if she let it.

When the door finally opened, Brandon fought to keep his mouth from gaping like he was a hooked fish.

This was his Caroline.

He'd made a profession of studying his opponents. While she wasn't that, she mattered to him very much, so he'd been careful to consider how to approach her.

He could see the tension in her, even though she was perfectly put together.

She wore a cute floral sundress that reached just below her knee and a filmy navy cardigan that emphasized her dark hair and chocolate eyes. Her face looked natural except for a brush of something berry-colored on her lips. Did she taste like strawberries or was it just an illusion? He'd have to find out before the night ended. She'd even opted for some kind of wedge sandal rather than her usual ridiculous heels. He let out a low whistle and then gestured for her to turn.

She pulled a cute grimace, but he spun his finger again and she obliged. Her skirt flared, and she smiled.

"You look great, Caroline."

A soft rose colored her cheeks as she glanced down. "Thank you." She dipped a small curtsy. "Should I grab anything?"

He blinked as he took one more look at the perfection in front of him. "Like what?"

"Anything I'll need for the date?" She giggled and the heaviness he'd noted in her disappeared.

"Nope."

They both needed a night off. A chance to forget the grief and pressure. While this might not be a Disney princess movie night, Caroline seemed to love the strong female leads who were showing up in superhero movies.

Maybe he could convince her she already was one in his story. That Thursday night had been a brief moment of him losing his mind, but now it was back. She had courage that had nothing to do with the size of her stature and everything to do with her heart.

"Ready to head out?"

"Sure." She grabbed her purse. "Where'd you find a drive-in theater?"

"A website. It'll take a little over an hour to get to. We'll grab a bite on the way."

"Aren't Emilie and Reid coming?" She had that

cute little wrinkle across the top of her nose as she considered him.

"They plan to join us at the theater." He held out his hand. "Ready to start our adventure?"

"Yes." Her hand felt soft as it settled against his rough one.

When they exited the building she jerked to a stop, then started laughing. "You brought it."

He grinned as he clicked a button and opened the passenger door for her. "It's just a Porsche for my princess."

"Just." She snorted. "I've never even looked at one of these, let alone ridden in one."

"Tonight it's your steed." He didn't mention that this was probably the last time he'd drive it.

"Here I thought it was a myth you liked to spin."

The light banter continued as he drove to 66. The miles spun by as they talked and let the silence fall in turns. The amazing thing was it never felt awkward. Just two friends who really enjoyed each other's company and wanted more.

Caroline leaned her elbow on the window ledge and then her head against her hand as she released a sigh. "This is nice."

"The car?"

"No." He caught the faintest smile on her face when he glanced over. "The drive. It's so easy to get caught in the pressure cooker inside the Beltway. To forget that just a few miles outside of 495 the roads open up, and we can be in the country."

"Hungry?"

"Sure."

"Great. There's a small place coming up that looked like a good option. One of those inns for fancy weddings and events, but it also has a restaurant anyone can enjoy."

"Sounds fun."

A minute later he glanced in the rearview mirror before turning on his blinker. He frowned. Hadn't that car been behind them for miles? Well, it was a country road. After waiting for oncoming traffic to pass, he turned into the gravel parking lot next to an old brick farmhouse that had an updated colonial feel. The long, wide porch would be a great place to wait if the reservation wasn't ready. He slid into an open slot and then waited with his gaze locked on the rearview mirror. When the car he'd noticed passed the driveway, he felt all kinds of ridiculous.

"You okay?" Caroline's soft words drew his attention back to what mattered.

"Of course. We're here." He flashed her his trademark grin that made ladies swoon, but she didn't bite.

"What's wrong?"

"Overreacting. Thought a car was following us. Being hypervigilant I guess." He gave a slight shrug then opened his door. "It's been a weird week for both of us. Ready for a good meal?"

Her stomach rumbled as if to answer, and she giggled. "Guess I can't deny it."

The interior had a rustic yet elegant feel, indicating the owner had worked hard to hit the right tone to draw diners from DC. The menu was modeled off of what the Founding Fathers would have eaten, on the gamey side. He had to grin as Caroline opted for a salad with shrimp.

"Sticking with what you know?"

She looked past him with a frown, then refocused on him. "Sorry?"

He gestured to the salad the waiter had set in front of her. "A salad?"

"It sounded good. I'm not much for squirrel stew." She shuddered then picked up her fork, but her gaze drifted back over his shoulder.

"You all right?"

"I guess it's my turn to be paranoid. What are the odds that someone from Praecursoria would be here tonight?"

"The restaurant was featured on the Virginia Is for Lovers website." He felt heat rush to his face.

Caroline grinned. "Isn't that what we're testing, big guy?" She gestured to the room with her fork. "This is a great place to do it. I'm sure that's why they're here."

"Do you know who it is?"

"Brian Silver. And one of his friends, I

guess." The brunette with him was attractive and attentive. A shadow crossed Caroline's face as she watched the man. "Brian's in charge of the lab where Justin worked. Same lab that produced the 463 trial." She shook her head. "There's something going on with that trial, but I can't quite pull the pieces together. I've been wondering . . ."

"What?"

Caroline put her fork down and looked him in the eye. "Have you already sold your shares?"

"I've told Reid to do it, yes."

"And you're committed?"

"You are much more important to me. What's on your mind? Maybe I can help."

She shook her head and lowered her voice. "What if Bethany didn't get her own cells? What if she got someone else's? It sounds so crazy to say it."

"What do you mean? Who else is there?"

"I have no—" Caroline blinked. Opened her mouth, then shut it. "Patrick. Patrick Robbins. He responded to the trial so fast. The team has been obsessed with his cells since then. What if they're using *his* engineered T cells rather than hers?"

"Wouldn't that be illegal?"

"Probably, since the trial participants were told they would receive *their* engineered T cells. It's definitely unethical." She straightened her napkin. "I wonder if other patients received the wrong cells. I haven't heard anything but wouldn't really know. The only reason I know about Bethany's challenges is because of you."

"Why would they use her?"

"I don't know." Caroline frowned as she considered the question. "Maybe because she has no family to protect her."

"How do we find out?"

She rubbed her forehead as if to push back tension. "I'm not sure my staff badge will give me access to the labs to poke around, but I can try."

"You aren't doing this alone."

"Yes, I am. Justin probably died because I asked for his help." Her chin quivered as her fists balled.

"I'm going with you, Caroline. You aren't the only one who cares about what's happening to Bethany. Maybe I should alert her caseworker."

"With what? That I think they aren't giving her the right protocol? I have no evidence. If she starts asking questions, then we'll alert whoever's involved at Praecursoria that we're suspicious." She wrapped her arms tight around her stomach.

He reached across the table and tugged on her hand. "We'll find our way through this."

She swallowed and nodded. "Thank you. I still think you're crazy to sell those shares though."

"Crazy for you."

She smiled and turned the conversation so the rest of the meal had a light feel.

If he hadn't wanted to keep the movie promise, he'd have settled in for a full four-course meal with dessert and coffee in one of those ridiculous espresso cups he could crush without a thought. Instead, he settled the bill and led Caroline back to his car. But when they reached it, he stared while Caroline groaned.

"Maybe neither of us was being paranoid after all." Her voice held a slight tremble.

One of the Porsche's tires was flat, rubber slashed. He placed a hand on her arm. "Go back inside while I call the police."

"You can do that while I'm here." She crossed her arms and looked rooted in place.

"Sure, but I need to know you're comfortable while I see if this was an accident or something more. That car I noticed behind us might have turned around and come back." Hopefully no permanent damage was done, since that would impact the price he could ask for it.

She paused and met his gaze. "I'll let Emilie know what happened. They can give us a ride back to DC if needed."

"We'll need it. If you're worried about your colleague, make the calls from the bathroom and wait there. I'll text when help arrives."

"All right." She turned and headed back to the porch.

Brandon waited until she was inside the restaurant before he approached the car. A quick inspection of the vehicle confirmed the damage was limited to the tire, but it had effectively trapped them.

In time, the blinking lights of a sheriff's vehicle pulled up, and he closed his eyes. So much for a romantic night.

CHAPTER 37

Caroline tried not to brood as she stared out the window of Reid's luxury sedan. This was not the right end to a romantic evening. They should be settled under the stars in Brandon's ridiculous sports car enjoying a movie they knew and loved. Instead, she couldn't shake the feeling that someone had followed them. A patron at the restaurant had suggested it was someone jealous of the sweet ride. Caroline had wanted to insist it was just a Porsche and far from the only one in the greater DC area, but she bit her tongue.

The slashing of a tire didn't rise to the same level as a hit-and-run, but it still unsettled her.

Emilie twisted from the front seat, her blonde hair arranged in easy beach waves around her face as she studied Caroline. "You okay?"

"No." The word was blunt but honest. Brandon reached across the seat and took her hand. "I'm kind of freaked out."

Reid watched her a moment in the rearview mirror before returning his gaze to the road. He and Brandon had stayed hypervigilant from opposite sides of the car while the sheriff made a report. "Run us through what you suspect," Emilie said.

Putting it into words would make it real in a way.

"Praecursoria is developing CAR T-cell therapies, which take a person's cells and engineer them into ninja fighters that can take out specific cancer-carrying cells like leukemia. The CAR T cells become little superheroes. This is new enough the results can be really great or really awful." She exhaled. "Right before I started this job, Sarah Hill died. She ran the latest CAR T trial in the lab that was engineering the cells. She was working with a patient named Patrick Robbins, doing pretesting for the trial. I think she found something unique in Patrick's cells." She recalled the papers Lori had dropped in the hall. *Status of Patient 1's cells as implanted in Trial CAR T 463 Phase 1 participants.* "And I think the current lab team is testing his cells in patients like Bethany. Her body seems to be in all-out rejection, which it shouldn't be. The magic of CAR T therapy is it uses the patient's own cells."

"Which Anna said should minimize the side effects and risk of rejection." Brandon rubbed his thumb over her hand, the sensation sending little waves of goose bumps up her arm.

"Last week Anna was really bothered about something, but we were still relatively new acquaintances, so while she told me some of her concerns, I didn't get all of it."

"Before the car accident," Brandon added.

"Which ended up killing her. But while she was

in intensive care, I received a package she'd sent with a flash drive. I think it was her research, but the flash drive was wiped clean when I left it at work, and then stolen with my purse Wednesday before I could get it to Dr. Ivy to recover the contents." She turned to Brandon. "Anna had to have someone inside Praecursoria getting her that data. She wouldn't have had access to all those areas without help."

"Who do you think it would be?"

"I'm not sure." She paused to consider. "Justin? It had to be someone in the lab. I've tried to talk to Lori and Tod, who worked with Justin, and they were cautious. Lori thinks Sarah's and Justin's deaths are connected but wouldn't say how or why."

Emilie nodded. "So you're thinking it's all connected."

"Yes."

"But why would that be reason to murder someone?" Reid pulled into the parking lot at Almost Home.

"Have you heard of HeLa cells?"

Emilie nodded. "They're the unique cervical cancer cells from a woman named Henrietta Lacks." Reid glanced at her and she raised a shoulder. "I read the book. They were the first, and maybe only, cells that continuously grow in a lab environment. They've become the foundation for vaccines and all kinds of medical research."

"Yes. Someone at Praecursoria thinks Patrick's cells have that same potential." She looked at Brandon. "Remember all the tests Bethany had before she was determined to be a candidate for the therapy? Patrick would have undergone similar tests. What if, in the course of reviewing his results, they determined he had a unique kind of cell or cell activity? If they thought his were like HeLas, it would have unfathomable potential for income. HeLa cells are sold for hundreds of dollars per vial."

Reid was nodding as he turned off the engine. "So it comes down to money."

"Yes. And if they could engineer his cells to work as a pseudo CAR T-cell therapy, then it would streamline the process for thousands of patients and create another income stream for Praecursoria that is essentially limitless." She sighed. "What if it really comes down to greed?"

Brandon opened the car door. "This calls for a pot of coffee."

As everyone exited the vehicle, Caroline considered what her next steps should be. "Here's the thing: I have no proof. It's all a theory."

"But it's a good one." Emilie squeezed her hand as they reached the lodge door. "Reid and I have been there. Sometimes you know something is wrong and have to chase it until you find the why."

"If I'm right, the proof is at Praecursoria.

Tomorrow, as soon as I can, I'm going to the lab."

They walked through the community space to the pass-through between the kitchen and main room, where Brandon powered up the Keurig. Caroline pulled creamer options from the large fridge.

"Who could help you?" Reid's voice was filled with concern as Brandon turned from the coffee machine.

"Samson would know what's going on but doesn't strike me as approachable. Maybe Brian Silver would be a good one to ask. He's tried to be helpful and took over the lab after Sarah's death." She had a thought, but it wouldn't rise to the surface, so she shook it off. "Maybe it's safer not to trust anyone right now. I don't know who's behind it, and the last person I asked to help died."

"Makes sense." Emilie handed Brandon a mug and coffee pod and then studied Caroline. "But you shouldn't go alone."

"It will look suspicious if I show up on a Sunday with an entourage. I need to slip in and out as unobtrusively as possible." She forced a smile.

"You need backup." There was a heft to Brandon's voice that warned he wouldn't let her go in alone.

"You can drive me and wait in the parking lot.

We can even have some kind of signal, like if I don't text you every ten minutes, you call me. If I don't answer, you call the police or come get me."

"I don't like it."

"It's the only way." As they settled in with coffee, she knew she was right. He'd come to understand that too.

SUNDAY, JUNE 6

The next morning she stood in front of her closet wondering what one wore when planning to break into their workplace early on a Sunday morning. She decided to go with a simple skirt and blouse that allowed her to argue she was headed to church. She hadn't slept well as she formed her plan.

She'd start with her office, in case anyone was watching, then head to the lab. She wasn't optimistic she'd find evidence for her theories, but she had to try.

Brandon texted when he arrived, and she grabbed her purse and a small attaché bag. She wanted it to look like she was really running in to get something so she could finish work from home before Monday morning. She would use the genetics letter as her excuse. She'd left the file behind Friday night and now had a list of questions she wanted to answer so she could finish the draft she'd circulated at Friday's meeting. What promises had the company made? And what had those utilizing the service expected?

That would give her a reason to be near a lab since the access to that sort of material was siloed. A very thin reason.

She was going to have to move fast. Especially if Brandon texted every ten minutes.

Brandon's posture was tense as he sat behind the wheel of his truck.

"You okay?"

"Not excited about you going in there alone." He rubbed a hand over his face. "Sorry. I didn't get much sleep last night."

"I get it." If he only understood how much. "I have to see what I can find. Maybe Bethany really does have her cells and the therapy isn't working for her. That's why this is a trial. But I think there's more." She blew out slowly. "What if I'm at Praecursoria in part to protect her? This company is doing so much good. It can help save lives, but that doesn't mean even one should be harmed in the process."

He pulled out of his parking slot. "I hear you, but I will text every ten minutes. If you don't respond, I'll send in the cavalry."

"Thank you. I don't love going in by myself, but I doubt I could get you past security." She nudged his arm. "You're not exactly a sneakable size."

411

That seemed to reach through his tension, because he shook his head with a small smile. "That's true. I'm hard to miss."

After twenty minutes he pulled into the Praecursoria lot and to the parking space closest to the front door. "Tell me your plan."

"I'll get through security with a quick scan, then head to my office. Build the illusion I'm grabbing a file to work on from home this afternoon. Then I'll slide over to the CAR T lab. There's a computer station in an alcove designed to let people get data without suiting up, and I'll try to log in through that."

"Using your log-in?"

"Yep."

"They'll know it's you."

"I don't have another option. That's why I'm trying this on a Sunday morning when no one should be around. It'll be a lot easier to slip in and out than to try tomorrow." She met his gaze. "You keep texting, and I'll be back as fast as I can. Bethany deserves a fast answer. So does Anna."

With those words echoing between them, she slipped out of the car and marched to the front door.

Now to find out if her ID would get her in on the weekend.

CHAPTER 38

When Caroline pushed through the door, no one sat at the security or reception desks.

She'd cleared the first hurdle.

But that meant the security officer was somewhere in the building. She'd deal with that when she ran into whoever was working and hope it was someone from the weekday cohort. Someone who wouldn't understand how unlikely it was she'd be in on the weekend.

She hurried down the hallways until she reached the executive wing. The lights were off in most of the offices. One had light, but she hurried past hoping no one was working inside. She expected to run into others, only nearer the labs, where work outside regular hours was the norm.

When she reached her office, she tested the door.

Locked.

Good. It should be. She used her key and slipped inside but kept the light off as she moved to her desk. Sunlight coming through the window was enough to find her genetics file. Then she eased back into the hallway and headed for the laboratory wing.

She hesitated at the first dim hallway. Could she turn on the lights? Would that be enough to calm the pounding in her heart? She hated darkness almost as much as she needed stealth. Her imagination latched onto it with vivid reminders of the awful things that happened in the hidden voids of the dark.

She stayed along the right wall and wondered if she should worry about cameras. If someone was back at the security desk, would they monitor her? Or would it be better to stride with purpose as if she knew where she was going and what she wanted?

Caroline hauled in oxygen and forced her right foot into the darkness.

Then she moved her left foot forward.

She would do this for Anna and Bethany. For Justin and Sarah. She repeated a name with each step, a drumbeat of courage and remembrance.

Her phone chirped from her pocket, and she squealed, clamping a hand over her mouth. Had anyone heard?

She paused to pull out and silence the phone. After reading Brandon's text, she quickly replied. In the hall leading to lab. So far so good.

He sent a thumbs-up back. Instead of sliding the phone back into her pocket or purse, she held on to it.

She forced another step forward. Each got easier as she turned down a second and then third hallway. At least this weekend it seemed no one was working, which would make the fact she *was* notable.

Her steps came quicker as she started looking for the right lab.

There. The last turn.

She froze as she noted light spilling from the small window in the lab's door.

Really? Out of all the labs, someone was in this one?

Caroline eased closer and listened for activity in the lab. Maybe the light had been left on by a careless employee. Still nothing.

The computer stood in a locked alcove on the other side of the door and beyond the wall of windows. Because of how the company siloed the computer data to minimize contamination across experiments, she had to access the lab somehow. This was the part where all her planning in the night broke down. Would her ID give her access? She wouldn't know until she swiped it, and then there would be a clear record she'd tried. She'd purposefully not told her friends about this potential problem.

The light flicked off.

She dashed across the door moments before it opened.

Hide.

She had to hide.

But where?

Brandon waited for the timer to finish its count-down so he could text Caroline again. Waiting in the car was for those who didn't mind sitting in the stands rather than fighting in the arena. He'd always been a middle-of-the-battle guy. However, no matter how he'd wrestled the problem in the dark of the night, he concluded Caroline was right. Much as he wanted to deny it, his presence would make her movements more conspicuous.

That meant he had to cool his heels and pray she would be all right.

Texting was not his idea of protecting her.

The front door opened.

A woman in a security getup walked out, glanced around the parking lot, then headed toward him, her hands braced on her belt. She motioned for him to roll down his window. "Sir, this isn't a place you can park unless you work for the company."

"I was resting my eyes." He felt the vibration of his phone as it alerted him to ten minutes gone. Without looking at the device, he tapped send on the text he had typed and ready.

"You'll have to do that somewhere else. The parking lot is private property."

"Sure. It was empty, so I didn't think it would harm anything to pull in. It was an early morning and I needed a minute before going to my next thing."

She frowned as she watched him.

Yep, he was talking too much. He turned the key in the ignition and nodded at the woman. "Have a good day."

"You too." He watched her in the rearview mirror. Surely she would leave so he could go park in a hidden corner of the lot. Caroline hadn't responded. Instead of cooperating, the rent-a-cop stood in place and watched until he had no option but to pull from the parking lot.

He needed a plan B.

Based on Caroline's lack of response, he needed it fast.

Brian Silver.

That wasn't who she'd expected.

The phone vibrated in her hand, but she couldn't do anything. She tucked it close to her body, hoping the sudden illumination wouldn't give away her location.

She was exposed.

One move and he'd see her.

Brian would know she had no reason to be in this corner of Praecursoria. Not on a Sunday morning. His red hair was disheveled in that way he liked, and he scanned the hallway as if he knew he wasn't alone. His gaze landed on her.

"Ms. Bragg. What are you doing here?"

She held up her bag. "Picking up a file."

"Did you get lost?" He pivoted from side to

side. "I'll be glad to escort you back to your car." The words sounded chivalrous and dismissive at the same time.

"No. In fact, I hoped you might be here today." The words rushed, making her sound like she was babbling. "I keep wondering what happened to the email I sent you. It's like it disappeared or was never sent. But we must have backups, right?"

"You should ask someone who knows. That's what IT is for."

"James hasn't responded to my requests about that. Maybe he couldn't find it either." She sighed. "I thought things like that had multiple copies on servers."

"Not my area of expertise."

"I sent a copy to Justin too, and I had hoped one copy survived." He stiffened but she pretended not to notice as she pushed from the wall. He certainly didn't need to know she'd received another copy via email from Anna. "He was going to meet with me the day he died. Explain what he'd found in the data. So I know it reached him." She walked past Brian but paused. "Did you know I was there? When he was hit? It was awful."

Brian took an intimidating step toward her. "I wondered how long it would take for you to poke a little too far into processes you don't understand." In the shadows it was difficult to read his face, but his voice held a hard edge.

"I'm not sure what you mean." She started walking, but he closed the distance until she was trapped with her back against the lab's exterior wall.

"What possible reason can you create to be here at"—he glanced at his watch—"7:45 on a Sunday morning?"

"I don't need a reason beyond getting the file." She tipped her chin and squared her shoulders, refusing to be threatened. She tried to stay calm as she wondered how long it would take for Brandon to respond to her lack of a text. "Since you're here, can you explain why, when I asked you about Genetics for You, you didn't tell me you were the VP?"

The man shrugged. "It didn't matter. We would have gotten rich riding the testing wave, but Quentin was sure we were wrong. Spun it off. So I cobbled together the group that bought it."

"But then you found flaws in the testing methods."

He snorted. "Something like that. The science morphed completely, exposing how wrong the early recommendations were. In an instant the sure thing was a dud."

"Why not tell me that when I asked?"

"No need to bother. It's a defunct company. Why keep a company with bad tech?"

"Did you send letters to the former clients? Those who had genetic testing done through Praecursoria?"

"Seemed like a good way to close things down. Remind Quentin what the buy-sell agreement said. He was so ready for the next thing that he trusted me to get the agreement crafted." He snorted. "Then everyone started focusing on other more lucrative advances."

Advances. The only ones people had discussed since she arrived related to Patrick's cells and CAR T 463. "Did genetics testing help Sarah find the anomaly in Patrick's cells?"

He snorted. "That was me, not Sarah. Did you know she only had a master's in biology? I'm the one with the postdoctoral education. I'm the one who figured out that his cells were multiplying and not dying. But she didn't even include me on the patent. It was my discovery, but she took all the credit, along with Samson."

"So Sarah cut you out of the patent? And out of future earnings."

"The two are connected." His teeth shone in the low light, but the smile wasn't warm. "It was all right. I found another way to monetize the cells."

Patient 1's cells are used in the other patients. The thought flashed across her mind. "You started using Patrick's cells as part of CAR T. But that's not what CAR T is. It's supposed to be the patient's own cells."

"Using his wouldn't be any more dangerous than the current mouse cells. In fact, it's probably less dangerous. A well-trained immune system

420

will detect the mouse cells and react. This was a much better solution. And it's working."

"Not for Bethany."

"She's one patient who was probably going to die anyway. There are so many lives we can save." Throughout their conversation, he never stopped watching her. He opened the lab door and gestured for her to go in.

"Since you're so desperate to see what's inside." When she didn't move, he pulled a small gun from his lab coat pocket. "I insist."

Caroline swallowed as she tried to think of a way out. As long as he didn't pull the trigger, she was okay. But how to stay that way?

Brandon parked next door and returned to Praecursoria. He wasn't sure how to get inside or where to go once he was there. But he couldn't do nothing. His phone's timer dinged again, and he wished he was friends with a police officer. Someone who could check on Caroline.

She wouldn't ignore his texts, but just to make sure, he texted again as he jogged.

you okay? you're worrying me.

After sixty seconds, he knew something was wrong. She'd have responded if she could.

He squared his shoulders, puffed out his chest, and put on his best football swagger.

With a push the doors opened, and he sauntered to the security desk.

The security officer glanced up from the book she was reading and her mouth opened. "What are you doing? I told you to leave."

"Congratulations. My friend and I were running a test to see if you'd be distracted by the fact you had a celebrity here."

She squinted at him. "I do?"

"Me." He gestured wide with his arms in a ta-da movement.

"Humph." She didn't sound the least bit impressed as she stood and placed her hands on her belt. "Sir, you have to leave, or I'm calling the police. This is private property."

"Yep, heard you the first time. Here's the thing. My friend is inside this building and isn't responding to texts. That tells me she's in trouble."

"Who's your friend?"

"Caroline Bragg. Praecursoria's attorney."

The woman didn't seem impressed. "I work nights and weekends."

Time was ticking away. "Look, Caroline is somewhere in this building. And she's not responding. We have to find her before . . ." What? It was too late? While that was exactly what he feared, he didn't know how to convince the woman in front of him.

She glanced at something on the desk. He stepped closer and took in the bank of small monitors. "Where was your friend headed?"

"Her office and then one of the labs."

She looked down and clicked a couple of buttons. "I can scan the video feeds to see if she's in that wing." She examined him. "Who did you say you are?"

"Brandon Lancaster. I was a linebacker for the . . ."

"Colts. I know. I'm a Redskins fan."

Of course she was.

"I'll take two minutes to look for your friend." The way she emphasized the last word highlighted how skeptical she was. "Then either I see her or I call the police."

"Or you see her and call the police because she's in danger."

The woman arched her eyebrows and then focused on the monitors.

CHAPTER 39

"Enough stalling." Brian aimed the gun at her head. "Move."

Caroline swallowed and tried to move but couldn't. This was her worst nightmare happening in real life. The nights she'd cowered as a child in the closet praying nothing evil occurred as her mother brought man after man into the apartment. The nights she'd tried to protect her little sister, Mel, yet knew she was too small to do it. She'd promised herself she'd never feel at someone else's mercy, and now she was at the mercy of Brian Silver and his gun.

How she hated them.

"Why?" She squeaked the word past a throat that threatened to fill with bile.

"You figured it out. Money. Did you know HeLa cells have been sold for billions of dollars, and the Lacks family never made a dime? I thought with the genetic testing I'd find something similar. I could build the testing capacity and leave the liability with Praecursoria." The man gave a hard laugh. "Quentin thought he was so smart to off-load the testing, but he's not wise about the law. Fool."

"That's why he hired me."

"Too late. After he spent years listening to

people like me advising him not to waste scant resources on bloodsucking attorneys." He pointed the gun at her head. "Into the lab now. I'll disappear before anyone even knows you're gone."

"I didn't come alone."

He sneered. "What, the football player? He won't get past the security desk. Donna's loyal. She knows not to let anyone in on the weekends that I haven't approved."

"She let me in."

"Was she at the desk?" At her silence he tilted his head. "Move."

Caroline's hope of rescue melted as she glanced around the lab. She had to keep him talking while she came up with an escape. He grabbed a pair of gloves from a box by the door.

"Do I need a set?"

"They won't help you." He slid on each glove without setting the gun down.

Normally the people who worked in the lab wore blue protective suits over their clothes plus gloves, booties, and hair masks. "Won't we contaminate the room?"

"It won't matter." His words sounded ominous, and she slid her gaze from side to side as she looked for anything that could help.

The lab was a large room with machines lining the walls and a couple of tables with sophisticated microscopes. There was nothing she could use to defend herself. A couple of spray bottles sat on one cart, but it was across the long room and there wasn't an easy way to reach it without him figuring out her intent.

"Did you know you'd kill Bethany? Was she nothing more than collateral damage to you?"

"She might have rallied. Don't forget her participation in the trial is palliative. For sure she'd die without it."

His callous disregard for the eleven-year-old made fire burn inside Caroline. "Nobody can give informed consent to treatment if you're not telling them what the treatment is."

"Which is exactly why I didn't ask. Then they can't say no." He glanced at his Rolex. "Time to move on. Head through the lab. We're going out the back."

Caroline considered refusing until he repositioned the gun at her head. Why couldn't his arms grow tired?

"Move."

The one word ended her hopes of talking her way out of the situation.

"Why did you kill Anna?"

"That was an accident."

"You hit her car into the intersection by accident?"

"I wanted to have a conversation. Bethany wasn't responding and she needed to know why. Instead of reporting the results and chalking it up to a failed idea, she kept questioning and wouldn't stop. I wasn't disappointed when she was injured."

"But she died."

"Unintended." He said it as if that cleared him of wrongdoing.

"But Justin's death was intended."

"Why would you think that?"

She stopped moving between the large vat machines. "Because I saw the vehicle pull away."

"That doesn't mean it was me." He gestured toward the door. "Keep moving."

"Who else would it be? It looked like the company security vehicle." She didn't mention she hadn't found a dent on it. "I caught a glimpse of red hair under a ball cap."

He snorted. He grabbed her arm and dragged her toward the door. "Enough of the stalling. No one is coming to save you."

His words landed as hard as his grip. He was right. Only Brandon knew for certain where she was, and he couldn't get inside.

"There." The woman pointed at the far-right screen in the bank of six. "It looks like they're leaving out the back of Lab F."

"And he's pulling her with him. Who is it?"

"Not sure. Maybe Brian Silver. He's in charge of several labs. Comes in on weekends."

Brandon wasn't sure if that mattered, but he

didn't like the way the man was tugging Caroline toward the door. At least she was dragging her feet to slow him down.

"Where does that door go?"

"There's a narrow hallway and then an outside door. The space was designed in case people need to leave quickly."

"How do I get there?"

"If I were you, I'd get outside and hustle around the building."

"Can you call the police?"

"Sure." She moved to pick up the phone. "Better hurry. They're almost to the end of the lab. There aren't cameras in the back hallway."

"Keep an eye on them as long as you can." He turned and ran toward the door. As he opened the glass door, he watched the guard set down the phone, and he frowned. There was no way she'd placed a 911 call and hung up. He tugged his phone free from his pocket and dialed 911 as he bolted around the building. The complex covered what looked like an acre or two. He sprinted around the edge without getting winded as he watched for an exit. Had the guard sent him in the right direction?

There was no way to know other than to keep running as the June heat and humidity pressed against him. It might be morning, but it was already a blazing hot day. That didn't stall his arms as he pumped his way around.

428

He heard a voice squawking at him, but he couldn't sprint and talk, so he'd have to trust they'd identify his location through the phone. And do it in enough time to help.

If they didn't, he'd do whatever it took to get Caroline to safety.

The door banged open as she struggled against Brian's grasp. The man might spend his days in a lab, but he must spend his nights at the gym because his grip didn't loosen no matter how she twisted or pulled.

She looked desperately for an escape, half blinded by the transition to bright sunlight. They were at the back of Praecursoria in an area that backed to a tree line and was hidden from the roads. Even if Brandon watched the front of the building, all Brian had to do was drag her to the trees, shoot her, and flee. By the time Brandon searched for her, it would be over.

But if she could get away . . . She could use those same trees for cover.

If that didn't work, there was a collection of trash cans and hazardous-waste containers she could run through.

She heard the sound of something pounding against the pavement.

Could it be Brandon?

Brian froze as if he heard it too, and his gaze shifted to the left.

This was her chance.

She jerked her arm with all the force she could muster and took off to the right. She dashed behind a dumpster.

"I see you." Brian's voice vibrated with anger, but she didn't stop.

She had to keep moving.

He would shoot her the moment he could, and she didn't want to learn whether he was a good shot. She pulled her phone out long enough to click the emergency button and then slid it back into her pocket. That would have to be enough to get help.

Brandon raced around a corner and into a man. In the glimpse he had, the man looked like Caroline's colleague from the restaurant. He tackled him with the best form of his life.

The man landed on the ground with an *oomph,* but he held on to the gun.

Metal glinted in the sunlight.

Brandon braced even as he rolled his weight toward the man's arm.

He had to get the gun dislodged.

Before Caroline was hurt.

He wanted to search for her but couldn't. Not while this man was free.

Sirens came closer, and the man thrust his hips. Brandon pushed back, pressing the man against the concrete.

Then he banged the man's arm against the driveway.

The gun slid free and the man howled.

"Hands up." A police officer came into view, gun clasped in his outstretched hands.

"If I get up, he'll take off. I'm the one who called 911. You can check my phone."

"Get him off of me, Officer." The man's voice vibrated with rage. "I want to press charges for assault."

"That's his gun over by the dumpster. I never touched it, so it should have his fingerprints." Then Brandon noted the latex gloves he was wearing. "Why are you wearing gloves? Trying to create deniability for the gun? What did you do to Caroline?"

The police officer's gaze bounced between the two as his radio squawked. He hit a button on it and turned to his shoulder to speak into it without shifting his gaze. "Two men in back. Backup requested." Then he returned his second hand to the gun. "Neither one of you move. My partner will be here in a moment."

"He's crushing me."

Brandon rolled his eyes but didn't move. No way he was letting this guy up until the police arrived and he could make sure Caroline was safe.

Where was she?

● ● ●

Caroline moved from one dumpster to another until she reached the trees.

There was a loud clatter, like someone throwing a body into a trash can. She wanted to look and see who it was but didn't dare. She had to keep moving.

Easing through the trees.

Looking for safety.

All alone.

She heard a voice calling her name and she collapsed.

"Caroline." The word was desperate.

"Brandon." She could barely whisper his name. What if Brian had gained the upper hand and was making Brandon say her name? She had to stay safe. She would stay safe. She was a thirty-year-old woman, no longer left to cower in a closet that she locked from the inside. She was strong and she could get to safety.

She heard sirens, but still she moved.

A voice filtered through her focus.

"Hello? Is anyone there?"

She pulled her phone free. Continued to listen.

"Police have arrived at your location. Are you safe? Can you tell me where you are so I can direct them to you?"

Caroline lifted the phone to her ear and whispered, "I'm in the trees. Behind the building. There's a man with red hair. He's wearing jeans

432

and a sports jacket and carrying a gun. There's also a large man, looks like a football player because he was one, wearing cargo shorts and a Colts T-shirt. He's with me."

"Stay on the line while I relay this information." For minutes the calm, detached female voice told her what was happening. Then she told Caroline it was safe to step from the trees.

The first thing she saw was Brandon standing with his hands on his hips, scanning the tree line, worry lines etched on his face, with two police officers nearby.

She waved and he started walking toward her. She ran to him and collapsed into his arms.

As he hugged her close and stroked her hair, she knew she was safe. The trembles eased as the adrenaline leached from her.

She had come home.

CHAPTER 40

By the time Emilie arrived at Praecursoria, the police were done taking Caroline's statement. Emilie stood next to her Mini Cooper, sunglasses on and watching, as she waited for Caroline.

Caroline couldn't give them conclusive proof that Brian had been behind the wheel of the vehicle that hit Justin, but she hoped it was enough to turn the investigation his direction. She also wasn't sure he'd said enough to connect him to Sarah's death, but it was up to the police to do that. They had him for kidnapping and attempted murder on her. Add in hitting Anna's car, and that was a start.

"You didn't need to call Emilie." Brandon studied her with concern.

"I know, but you need to get to Bethany's doctor and tell him what happened. Maybe he can give her the right CAR T cells and counteract the wrong treatment. Maybe it's not too late."

"Would you make the call? I'm not sure how to explain it all."

Caroline nodded. "Then go be present with your aunt." She placed a hand alongside his face and then reached up on tiptoe to kiss his cheek. "The funeral's tomorrow and she needs you." She stepped back and smiled at him. "I'm going home after I call the hospital to figure out what I'm going to tell Quentin."

The front door opened and the police led out the security guard. Not calling the police probably wasn't a crime, but if she'd been cooperating with Brian, then the woman was an accessory to attempted murder.

Caroline gave Brandon another hug, one she never wanted to end. "Thank you for being here." She shivered at the reality of how different it could have turned out if he'd let her come alone. "You were right that I needed backup."

He eased back and met her gaze. "I almost lost you today. Don't ever do that again."

"I don't plan to." She reached up and kissed his cheek. "I need to go." As soon as she climbed into Emilie's car, Caroline pulled out her phone. "I've got to make a call."

She needed to alert the right people that Bethany was in transplant rejection. She called Quentin and left a message before calling the hospital. It took the drive back to her apartment to get through to Dr. Hamilton.

"I was able to confirm that Bethany Anderson is receiving the wrong CAR T cells. They aren't hers, but a transplant from a donor."

The doctor inhaled. "Okay. Then the treatment for graft-versus-host disease has been the right course." He paused. "That also explains why it's helping."

"Yes, I think Bethany's body has been attacking the transplanted cells."

"I'll need more information on what she's receiving but will up the course of treatment we're on. Now we can combat it. Good news is we already used the chemotherapy to destroy her white blood cells, but if the donor cells aren't a match . . ." His words dropped off.

"Understood. I'm the attorney, not a doctor, so I'll have someone contact you." Caroline's thoughts rushed. Who should she have call the Doogie Howser back? Maybe Lori or Tod. "Can I have a direct number, and I'll have one of my colleagues in the lab call you back ASAP?"

After taking it down, she called Lori on the number in her personnel file and brought her up to speed. The woman agreed to call the physician immediately and provide whatever Bethany's medical team needed.

"Thank you." Caroline swallowed back the emotion that was rising inside. "We'll also need to start an audit to confirm whether Brian did similar things with the other patients' treatments in Phase 1. We have to know today how big the issue is."

"On it. I'll get a team in to scrub through everything in the next few hours."

"Good." Caroline sighed as she felt the reality of everything she'd dealt with collide inside her. "I can come back once I have my car."

"I'll let you know. We may be able to handle it via phone."

"Maybe." Getting this right and saving Bethany was too important to the survival of their patients and the company to play it safe at home.

Emilie pulled in front of Caroline's apartment building. "You'll be okay."

Caroline smiled at the statement as she slid the phone into her purse. "Yeah, I will." She leaned over and squeezed Emilie. "Thanks for showing up on short notice."

"Of course. That's what heart sisters are for."

"I'm grateful."

"Now go help that girl and make sure no one else is hurt. In the process you might save Praecursoria."

"I'm going to give it my all." Caroline climbed from the car and felt the weight of responsibility.

This was why she was at Praecursoria.

MONDAY, JUNE 7

Anna's funeral was a quiet affair. She was well loved, but her circle of friends and family was small. Moving so many times in her life had contributed to that. Brandon wished more people were here to support Aunt Jody. Fortunately, Uncle Clint had made it back from his training mission, so she didn't sit alone with the infant carrier next to her.

Little Jilly had been released from the hospital, seemingly no worse for her early birth. Brandon could thank God for that even as he wondered why God hadn't prevented the accident. He could have but hadn't, so Brandon had to surrender and accept the lack of answer and understanding.

The pastor did a good job trying to extend hope in a tragic situation. Anna's college roommate had them all laughing as she told how Anna collected a group to fork a friend's yard. Then Aunt Jody talked about how excited Anna had been when she learned she was a mother and how proud she'd been watching Anna persevere through the grief of losing her husband.

Through it all there was a thread of hope, gossamer thin but present.

When the service ended and the people stood and made their way down the center aisle, Brandon waited. For what, he wasn't sure.

Then he felt a small hand on his shoulder and turned.

Caroline stood in the row behind him. "You okay?"

"As okay as I can be when this feels wrong."

She nodded, then sank onto the chair next to him, lending him her presence.

Uncle Clint helped Aunt Jody to her feet, then she grabbed the baby carrier and started down the aisle. Caroline waited until they'd passed. "Are those Anna's parents?"

"Yes. Uncle Clint was whisked back by the army late last night."

Caroline gave him a pointed look. "How are things with them?"

Brandon let a slight smile cross his face. "You know, Aunt Jody and I had an interesting conversation last night. She explained how she tried to find Trevor and me, but the system blocked her. Wasn't expecting that to come up last night of all nights. I've forgiven them, though it feels prideful to say that."

"No, that's a big step. You needed help, and it's natural to want it to come from family. I'm proud of you." Her words soaked into the soil of his heart. "How can I help now?"

He wasn't sure how to answer. "Pray for them."

"Always. Praying for you too."

A man came up behind her. "Ready, Caroline? I need to get back to work."

She barely spared her boss a look. "Sure."

Brandon extended his hand to Quentin. "Thanks for coming today."

"She was a special woman and I'll miss her." The man nodded, then headed down the aisle.

Caroline stood in an elegant motion, all Audrey Hepburn grace. "Are you staying for the lunch?"

"I need to be here for them."

"Then I'll call tonight."

He stood and pulled her into a hug. Once she

was in his arms, he didn't want to let go. "Thanks for coming."

"Always."

Quentin cleared his throat, and Caroline shot him a "what are you thinking?" stare. Though Anna was a colleague, the man was blind to the grief others showed for her death. It was like he needed to thrust grief far away. Made her wonder why he'd come.

"Talk to you soon." She forced herself from the comfortable circle of Brandon's arms.

Quentin was already halfway down the aisle and toward the sanctuary doors. He stopped to murmur something in the ear of Brandon's aunt, words Caroline only got a hint of as she caught up.

"Good will come of this." Then he straightened and headed through the doors.

Caroline turned back to Brandon. "If there's anything I can do . . ." The words felt empty on her tongue. This was exactly why she hated funerals.

Caroline stepped into the sunshine that felt out of place on this day. "That was hard."

Quentin swallowed as he clicked his key fob. "We have to get back to Praecursoria. Somehow we have to salvage the disaster Silver created."

He slid into his seat and started the car while Caroline climbed in. After strapping on her seat belt, she looked out the window and spotted Brandon standing at the top of the steps, his hands shoved in the pockets of his khaki pants. He lifted his hand in a small wave, then turned and went back inside.

She shifted to glance at Quentin. "What did you mean when you said good would come from this?"

"Why?" He kept his gaze locked on the road but started tapping the steering wheel with his thumbs.

"It's an odd thing to say to a grieving mother at a funeral." Though it was probably better than her awkward silence and hug.

"There's nothing easy to say." He sighed as he pulled into the parking lot. "Look, I'm still trying to understand why Brian did this to me. We've been friends a long time—at least I thought we were. But what you say he's done? It's created bigger issues to focus on. Let's figure out how to save the company." He wiped his forehead, then parked. "Meeting in my office in ten minutes."

"All right." They separated at the door, and Caroline hurried to her office. It wouldn't be easy figuring out how to untangle the mess Brian had created, but she'd start with a call to Lori.

As she waited for Lori to pick up, she glanced around her office. She really needed to bring in something like plants or wall hangings that would make it feel like more than an institutional box.

"Lori here."

"Good morning. This is Caroline and I'm headed into a leadership meeting in ten minutes. Can you update me on what you learned about Patrick Robbins and the trial?"

"We've type tested each of the trial patients' CAR T cells. About half don't match their own. I know we engineered all their cells though. Best I can figure out, Brian mass-produced Patrick's cells and sent those to half the Phase 1 trial recipients."

Caroline inhaled sharply. "And we haven't heard about any adverse reactions from the other patients?"

"Brian was having the calls directed to him, I'm assuming so he could manipulate the data. At the time I thought it was a little odd, but we were swamped from Sarah's death. Then Justin died, and Tod and I were trying to stay above water."

"Can you get me the contact information for the other patients?"

"I can do you one better. We've already started contacting their overseeing physicians. Right now, I'm telling them there's a chance the patients have the wrong cells and couriering the right CAR T cells to them."

"Say as little as you can while getting them the right information. After this meeting I'll come help you. We've got to do all we can to help these kids."

"Understood. The good news is Brian didn't destroy the kids' engineered cells. It took a little searching, but we found them."

"Is it too late for any of these kids?"

Lori hesitated. "I don't know. I'm not a doctor and haven't seen recent labs." She sighed. "I don't know what happened to Brian. If you'd asked me a week ago, I would have denied this was possible."

Caroline closed her eyes and prayed somehow any rejections could be abated and the right CAR T cells would provide the healing each child's body desperately needed. Then she forced herself to refocus. "What do you think next steps should be?"

"I'll have Tod run a second batch of confirmatory tests this afternoon. Make sure we're convinced the engineered cells are what we think they are. Then I'm developing a protocol to make sure we have the necessary checks and balances in place to prevent this from recurring."

"That's good, but Brian was in a position to circumvent any systems we had."

"True, but we can improve to prevent a repeat."

"Let me know if you need anything or if something comes up. Otherwise, let's meet at one."

"Will do." Lori paused. "Caroline, this isn't who we are as a company. I don't know what happened to Brian, but this won't happen again."

"Thank you." She appreciated Lori's conviction, because somehow Caroline would have to convince the FDA of that fact. After her computer woke up, she pulled up the Robbinses' informed consent and compared it with Bethany's.

Informed consent was an important idea at the intersection of law and medicine. Its goal was to provide protections to patients so that doctors couldn't perform procedures or treatments on them without their full knowledge and understanding. To attain informed consent, the patient had to understand the nature of the procedure, the risks and benefits associated with that procedure, whether reasonable alternatives existed, and the risks and benefits of those alternatives. The consent had to demonstrate the patient understood both the procedure and its alternatives.

As she compared the two, she could see how Bethany's had been altered to be broader than CAR T research trials. It was signed by someone with the Virginia Department of Child Protective Services. A Tara Descane, who was probably her caseworker. In all likelihood the woman wouldn't have understood the nuances. Caroline wouldn't have before working here.

She hit Print and copied the documents before marching to Quentin's office.

The mood was somber as she strode to the table where Quentin, Samson, and Hannah waited.

Samson looked like he hadn't slept, which would be appropriate, because Brian had reported to him.

He stood and extended his hand to Caroline as she reached the table. "I owe you an apology." There was something courtly about the way he said it. "You suffered at the hands of my employee. I'm still trying to understand the extent of what he did. How do I make this right?"

"Help me save this company." She sank into the vacant chair and pulled out the papers she'd worked on before the funeral. "First, we're going to get rid of what could be a distraction. When you spun off Genetics for You, Quentin, you didn't get rid of the liability, so we'll make a generous settlement offer to the women impacted by the testing." She slid the proposed offer across the table.

Quentin sucked in air. "Brian lied to me about that too? So much for our friendship." He rubbed his forehead. "What are our options?"

She tapped the paper. "You have to resolve this so we can focus on saving what you have here now." She waited until he looked at her. "Praecursoria is doing important research. We're going to change our processes to better protect our patients, but we can't do that if we are distracted by lawsuits related to the genetic testing."

Hannah nodded. "I agree. Let's get this taken care of and focus on the new therapies."

"I'm not made of money." Quentin glanced around the table. "Where do you think this money will come from?"

"We'll have to make it a payment plan and take it from some of the research funds, but it's that or go bankrupt. Your choice."

The words seemed to shock him, but he started working with her. An hour later she had authority to call the women's attorney and make the offer. Half an hour after that, she had a promise from the man to take it to his clients.

Then they discussed systems that could be put in place to provide guardrails for future research and trials while also developing an immediate plan to work with the FDA. "This won't be an easy process," Caroline said as she made eye contact with each of the leadership team. "But it will be a critical piece to keeping this company viable. Do you believe in what we're doing?"

Quentin and Hannah nodded.

Samson cleared his throat. "With everything in me."

"Then we are going to humble ourselves and go before the FDA with a commitment to do better and cooperate fully with any restrictions they place on us. That means no running to Mexico. We have to be fully committed to the system. And I'm going to pray that Bethany and the other children don't die." She looked around the table. "This is a start, but don't think it's going to be easy. It will be a long road for the company to recover from what Brian Silver did."

She gathered her things. "Now I'm going to go check on Bethany."

CHAPTER 41

A knock at the door pulled Brandon's attention from a spreadsheet he was reviewing. Jeff stood there, looking ready for a fishing trip. He wore cargo shorts and a ratty T-shirt with a floppy hat covering his head. "You got a minute?"

Brandon paused because he really wanted to finish so he could get to the hospital for Bethany. "Sure." He swiveled from the monitor, leaving the numbers behind. "What can I do for you?"

"It's what we can do for you." A big grin cracked Jeff's face. "We're staying. Alaina and I are in this as long as you are."

Brandon's shoulders collapsed and he launched from his chair. "Really?"

"Yep."

Brandon crushed the smaller guy in a bear hug. "That is great news."

After talking through details, Brandon grabbed his keys. No way he could look at numbers with the relief coursing through him. This was really going to work. He called Caroline as he drove to the hospital, but when she didn't answer, he didn't leave a message.

He wanted to share the good news with her, not with her voicemail.

An hour later he sat in Bethany's room, the

beep of the machines feeling loud in the space. The lights were dimmed, and somewhere instrumental music played in the background, barely audible under the beeps as Brandon sat in the chair pulled next to Bethany's hospital bed. He wanted to punch something as he watched her chest barely rise and fall on each breath. The medical staff had put her on a ventilator Sunday. Bethany no longer fought the tubing, and that felt like a bad development.

It didn't help knowing why she struggled.

Her body was fighting hard against an invader.

There was a tap at the door, and Brandon looked up to see Caroline. He started to push to his feet, but she waved him back.

"How is she?" Caroline kept her voice pitched low enough it didn't disturb the resting child as she entered the room.

"No change really." He leaned back against the chair. "They're running a battery of tests. She's so weak right now, her status is doubtful. They plan to infuse her CAR T cells starting tomorrow. It really is a Hail Mary this time."

Caroline came to stand next to him, her face white as she looked at Bethany. "She looks even smaller. Paler too."

"I can hear you." The words were soft, but he caught them and stiffened.

Brandon put his hand on her head. "Hey, Bethany."

"Hey." Her voice tremored, but she smiled. "You're the first person to keep coming."

"I like doing it."

"The doctors told me I have to have another treatment."

He glanced at Caroline and she stepped forward.

"Hi, Bethany. My name is Caroline."

"I think I saw you before."

"I was here once a while ago. I work for the company that made the treatment." She sighed. "I'm very sorry, but the first one we gave you was the wrong one. But Dr. Anna knew there was a problem. With her help, I figured out how to look for the solution. Tomorrow the doctors want to give you the right one. This one will have your ninja cells."

"Do you think it will work?"

Caroline flinched slightly at the words, then sank onto the edge of the bed. "I'm not a doctor, Bethany, so I don't know. What I do know is that we're going to do everything we can to help your body win this time. There are also people praying for you. We really want you to get better and never have to come back and stay in a bed here. It's just going to take time to see if we get our wish."

A nurse entered and smiled at them. "I need to help our patient get ready for tomorrow." She looked at the monitors and then at Bethany. "It's going to be a big day for you. Your friends can come back tomorrow after the procedure."

"We'll leave in a moment. I'm going to pray for you first. You need a good night's sleep and God to strengthen you for this next step." Brandon took Bethany's hand and felt Caroline's slip into his. He cleared his throat and then prayed over her. A holy hush filled the room, and he held on tightly for a moment, then stood. "Keep fighting, kiddo."

"You too." Her smile was sweet but scared, so he touched her cheek.

"I will be back." He would as many times as she needed.

Then he followed Caroline into the hall and to the waiting room. They sat and he raked his hands through his hair, then braced his elbows on his knees. "I should do more."

"Like what?"

He shook his head. "I don't know."

"You're here and you pray for her. That's a powerful combination." Caroline placed a hand on his shoulder, the warmth pulling him toward her touch. "If Brian had given her the right treatment, it could have worked. It's been a lifeline for others. The literature is really good for 50 percent of patients."

"Bethany's in the wrong part of the 50 percent."

"Actually, we don't know." Caroline balled her hands. "It's going to take work to forgive Brian. I can't imagine getting so caught up in the science that I'd believe it's worth risking lives to see what happens."

He felt the disconnection of her touch. "Anna told me last week that it would take a miracle." The words grated his soul. "And now she's not here to help Bethany fight."

The fierce light in his eyes emphasized how much Brandon believed his words.

Caroline wished she had the answers that would save Bethany. As she had talked with the young girl in the bed, she couldn't deny that sorrow and fear weighed on her.

Bethany was one complication away from never going home.

Brandon pushed to his feet and led her to the elevator. "Bethany needs someone here that she knows. I'm not her parent and shouldn't be making these decisions."

"But you are here, and she knows you." Caroline reached up and touched his face, feeling the stubble that hadn't been shaved. It wasn't a beard, but it was more than his typical clean-shaven look. He leaned into her palm as if taking strength from her. "What do you need?"

"Wisdom." He sighed so heavily she felt it to her bones. "This is so much bigger than anything I've done before."

She smiled at the words. "Brandon, that's not

true. I've watched you wrestle with what's best for your kids since you had only a couple."

"But this is her life."

"And without you, she'd be gone." Caroline glanced back toward the hallway and her room. "Do you see what I see?"

"I don't know." His words were hesitant yet tinged with the edges of hope.

"I see a young girl who is alone day after day, hour after hour, except when you come to visit. The state hasn't found any family members who care, but you do. I've seen you show up in the ways that matter for so many kids." She turned to him and waited until he looked in her eyes. He needed to hear this, but even more it needed to seep into his soul. "And it doesn't end when the kids leave. I've seen the stacks of cards going out in the mail. You are amazing."

"I'm not." He shook his head, ending their eye contact.

She put her hands on either side of his face even though it meant she was practically on tiptoe. "Oh, but you are. To each of those kids you're a hero." She paused. "You are to me too."

He hesitated, then leaned close and put his forehead on hers. The touch was light, not a kiss that electrified her, but a moment that solidified them. They would do what they could for Bethany. It might be enough. It might not. That part was in God's hands. But they would work together.

Caroline saw the moment her words sank into his heart and soul.

His edge of constant alertness relaxed in a good way. He knew he was safe with her.

And she was safe with him.

A minute later they stepped from the elevator and he led her to a small garden off the back of the cafeteria. A couple of patients in wheelchairs were settled next to park benches, enjoying the sunshine.

Caroline followed Brandon to a vacant bench. The warmth felt good after the stale hospital air. It felt good to just be with him.

The man beside her had earned the right a long time ago to be her best friend. She trusted him with her thoughts and her hopes. He'd never let her down intentionally. Sure, there had been a time or two he'd been too casual with their friendship, but he'd always come around.

She'd watched him in good times and hard times. He'd battled through so many challenges with a focus and intensity that inspired her. Through it all he was steady and dependable. Someone who was always there.

He glanced at her. "What are you thinking?"

"Not much."

He snorted and turned to her. "I'll never believe that. You are many things, Caroline Bragg, but not someone whose mind settles into nothing."

"Sometimes it does, big guy."

"Not the woman I know." He took her hand and rubbed his thumb over her knuckles. The motion was simple but sent pulses of electricity racing up her arm. How could a simple touch from the gentle giant next to her leave her feeling so incredibly protected and leaning in for more?

He must have seen the question in her eyes, because he leaned closer and tipped her chin up. An intensity in his expression signaled that whatever he said next would be important. She leaned closer and pressed her lips to his.

They could deal with intense tomorrow.

Right now she wanted to sink into the moment.

They'd survived.

The future wasn't a clear road, but if they had each other, she'd thrive.

He broke the connection about the time she felt light-headed and leaned his forehead against hers. "Bragg, you're going to be my undoing."

"Is that a bad thing?"

"Not at all. But we're in the midst of intense times."

"Oh, I know what I want." She leaned up again and kissed him.

"I guess you do." He grinned and then deepened the kiss until she flat out could not think. When he pulled back, she moaned.

"Do you know what you want?" The words whispered between them, and she couldn't believe she'd found the courage to ask them.

"That's easy. All I want is you next to me on this journey of life." He stroked her cheek, his touch like velvet, which was surprising coming from someone who'd used his strength to batter others and protect her. "Can you imagine that?"

"I don't want anything else."

"I come with a passel of kids."

"I love them, each one."

"And I love you." His words soaked into the dry spaces of her heart, the ones that still wondered if she was worth loving. Worth protecting.

The amazing thing was that when she was with him, she believed the value he saw.

She was better with him, just as she hoped she called him to his better self too.

The road wouldn't be easy. Life hadn't worked that way for either of them. But if her best friend, the one her heart loved, was beside her, the journey would be worth every step—each hilltop vista as well as every valley.

A NOTE FROM THE AUTHOR

Each book I write has a unique background and story. Caroline's is no exception.

The genesis of Praecursoria is the story of a friend's son—in many ways his story mirrors Patrick's and Bethany's. Heather introduced me to her son's oncologist who was the inspiration for Dr. Anna Johnson. Meeting with them over coffee at Panera humanized the battle on both sides: as the parents who will do anything to help their son and the doctor who will hunt for protocols and Hail Marys. If you ever hear CAR T-cells called ninja cells, it may be because of Heather. The thread on the genetics testing was inspired by real-life stories as well. Medicine and scientific advances can be life altering for the good—or the bad.

Many of you have been waiting for Caroline's story almost as long as I have! She and Brandon have been waving their hands for a book since the beginning. The irony is that the law governing foster care group homes was literally changing as I wrote the book and still is as I write this letter. At the time of the final draft, Virginia hadn't finalized its interpretation of the federal Families First law. If you know me, you know getting it right matters deeply to me. So if you are a foster family in Virginia reading this and the law has changed, my apologies. I did the best I could with the state of the law and talking to a group home executive director in Arkansas. Adoptions are happy law, but they often come at the end of a journey that is filled with heartache. Foster care can play a key role in the in between time for children waiting for a forever home. If you are a foster parent, thank you.

I have so enjoyed writing these books about a band of women attorneys in the Washington, DC, area. Thank you for reading these books. I'm grateful for you. Thank you for joining me on this journey!

Cara Putman

ACKNOWLEDGMENTS

Many thanks to Casey Apodaca for reading this book when I wasn't sure it was ever going to come together. You gave me hope that these characters were likable.

Erin Healy, you were a joy to work with again. Thank you for catching the vision for this story and these characters. For telling me when to go deeper with the science and when I'd already told the reader more than enough. I'm so happy with Caroline's story—and Brandon's interactions with the kids make me smile.

To the HarperCollins Christian Publishing team, it's been a privilege to work with you. Thank you for helping me tell these stories and share them with the broader world. I so appreciate our partnership.

Karen Solem, thank you for believing in me and always pushing me deeper. You've been the agent that I needed.

And to Pepper Basham, Ashley Clark, and Beth Vogt, thank you for seeing the real me beneath the writer. Y'all have blessed me in so many ways. Colleen Coble, thank you for always believing in me and encouraging me. Who knew what a journey you would help launch at the book signing in 2005. Grateful for you.

My family are truly my biggest cheerleaders. Thanks for putting up with one more round of deadline haze and neurosis. I always wonder if I can write one more book, but you never do. Thank you!

And to my readers, thank you for being part of this journey.

DISCUSSION QUESTIONS

1. How far would you be willing to go to find help for your desperately sick child? Do you think the Robbinses were right to try anything they could to save Patrick, or would you have drawn the line in a different place?

2. Quentin says, " 'Every law has a gray area. Find it or this'—he gestured between them— 'may not be a good fit.' " Do you agree? If you had been in Caroline's shoes, what would you have told him?

3. Brandon has a hard time sharing his full story with Caroline even when he knows it's necessary for their relationship to deepen. Do you find it hard to share the painful part of your past? Why do you think that is?

4. Caroline has to stand toe-to-toe with her boss when they disagree about what the law is. Have you ever had to take a stand against someone in authority over you? How did you do it? What advice would you give Caroline and others in her situation?

5. Caroline is challenged by Hayden to articulate all her fears and expose them to the light. Have you ever suggested that to someone, and did it help?

6. Brandon says it takes "a special heart to

lavish a parent's care and concern on children who weren't biologically yours and were entrusted to you only for a season." What do you think would be necessary to love foster children well?

7. Brandon considers selling something precious to him so that he can help his kids. Have you done something similar? Sell an item you love in order to have more flexibility to serve others?

8. Caroline witnesses a terrible accident and is rocked by the realization she could have been in the car but for a small choice to drive separately. Are you aware of a time when a small decision changed your life's course?

9. Reid reminds Brandon that we aren't meant to do life alone. What does that mean to you, and how has that played out in your friendships?

ABOUT THE AUTHOR

Cara Putman is the author of more than thirty legal thrillers, historical romances, and romantic suspense novels. She has won or been a finalist for honors including the ACFW Book of the Year, the HOLT Medallion, and the Christian Retailing's BEST Award. Cara graduated high school at sixteen and college at twenty, completed her law degree at twenty-seven, and earned her MBA in 2015. She is a practicing attorney, teaches undergraduate and graduate law courses at a Big Ten business school, and lives with her husband and children in Indiana.

———

Visit her website at CaraPutman.com
Facebook: @Cara.Putman
Twitter: @Cara_Putman

Books are produced in the United States using U.S.-based materials

Books are printed using a revolutionary new process called THINKtech™ that lowers energy usage by 70% and increases overall quality

Books are durable and flexible because of Smyth-sewing

Paper is sourced using environmentally responsible foresting methods and the paper is acid-free

Center Point Large Print
600 Brooks Road / PO Box 1
Thorndike, ME 04986-0001 USA

(207) 568-3717

US & Canada:
1 800 929-9108
www.centerpointlargeprint.com